"Christians are losing the cultural and political battles in America because we are not defending the basic truths of our faith. *Satan's Dare* is a powerful story that will confirm the faith of Christians and challenge skeptics to search for real truth."— Dr. M. G. "Pat" Robertson, founder/chairman The Christian Broadcasting Network, Inc.

"There is more truth in this novel than just about any nonfiction book I've read. I recommend *Satan's Dare* to every person who wants to strengthen their faith in God and to every person who is searching for truth."— Josh McDowell, Josh McDowell Ministries

"The great contest being waged in America is not political. It's theological. The Far Left has made 'Secular Progressivism' their creed and are using political power as the weapon to spread their beliefs. Christians are losing the political battle because we are not defending the principles of our faith. *Satan's Dare* is a powerful story, inspiring every Christian to stand up for Truth."—LtCol Oliver L. North USMC (Ret), best-selling author of *The Rifleman* and host of the *Real American Heroes* series.

"*Satan's Dare* is different from any other Jim DeMint book, and it very well may be his most important."—Glenn Beck, Blaze Media

"If you're a skeptic, *Satan's Dare* will help answer your questions. If you're a believer, it will help equip you for the days we're living in. If you're a reader, this novel will hold you spellbound with its emotional, real-life twists and turns. Jim DeMint has created a much-needed, timely resource for all!"— Steve Berger, founding pastor, Grace Chapel, Franklin, TN

"Although the Bible tells us our true struggle is with spiritual forces, we are so surrounded with natural forces that it is hard to factor in what we don't readily see. But this compelling and entertaining novel helps us better understand what is going on around us and how we should respond. Jim DeMint is boldly challenging the theological world just as he did the political world. *Satan's Dare* answers questions most Christians are afraid to ask. Every individual should read this!"—David Barton, founder of WallBuilders (wallbuilders.com), award-winning historian, and author of numerous best-selling books

"In *Satan's Dare*, Jim DeMint crafts an all-too-familiar story in our culture these days—a misunderstanding of the sovereignty of God can diminish our love for and faith in Him when suffering eventually arrives. The good news is a rightful understanding of His sovereignty opens hearts to the good news, and DeMint shows that we definitely do have reasons for the hope that we have. The believer need not fear reason, but embrace it."—Steve Deace, The Blaze

Satan's Dare

A Novel About

Love, Freedom, Justice, and Mercy

Jim DeMint

FIDELIS
PUBLISHING

FIDELIS PUBLISHING, LLC
ISBN: 978-1-7358563-0-8
ISBN: 978-1-7358563-1-5 (ebook)

Satan's Dare
A Novel about Love, Freedom, Justice, and Mercy

Cover designed by Diana Lawrence
Interior design by Xcel Graphic

Manufactured in Canada
10 9 8 7 6 5 4 3 2 1

For information about special discounts for bulk purchases, please contact BulkBooks.com, call 1-888-959-5153 or email - cs@bulkbooks.com

Unless otherwise indicated all Scripture is taken from THE HOLY BIBLE, NEW INTERNATIONAL VERSION®, NIV® Copyright © 1973, 1978, 1984, 2011 by Biblica, Inc.® Used by permission. All rights reserved worldwide.

Sharon R. Browning, Analysis of Human Sequence Data Reveals Two Pulses of Archaic Denisovan Admixture. Taken from: https://www.cell.com/cell/fulltext/S0092-8674(18)30175-2

Fidelis Publishing, LLC
Sterling, VA • Nashville, TN
www.fidelispublishing.com

I dedicate this book to the Body of Christ
all around the world.

"Does Job fear God for nothing?" Satan replied. "Have you not put a hedge around him and his household and everything he has? You have blessed the work of his hands, so that his flocks and herds are spread throughout the land. But now stretch out your hand and strike everything he has, and he will surely curse you to your face."—Job 1:9–11

What is life if not the pursuit of truth and what is truth if not the grasp of eternity?

CONTENTS

Chapter One: Man of God Becomes an Atheist.... 1

Chapter Two: Johnny's Fall from Grace......... 13

Chapter Three: Santa Claus God................. 35

Chapter Four: Let There Be Light 49

Chapter Five: Tony's Dare to Johnny........... 63

Chapter Six: Bad News, Good News 75

Chapter Seven: New Start 93

Chapter Eight: The Love of a Woman.......... 107

Chapter Nine: Happy Valentine's Day 129

Chapter Ten: A New Heaven on a New Earth .. 147

Chapter Eleven: The Real Creation Story 157

Chapter Twelve: We Live in Satan's World 165

Chapter Thirteen: New Creation 177

Chapter Fourteen: Revelation: History, Future,
                    or Both?..................... 191

Chapter Fifteen: A New Life 209

Chapter Sixteen: Confession and Redemption 229

Chapter Seventeen: Saved by God, Ourselves, or Both? 247

Chapter Eighteen: The Only Way, Truth, and Life. 263

Chapter Nineteen: Rescued from the Power of Satan 279

Chapter Twenty: God's People Are God's Power 289

Chapter Twenty-One: Eliminating All Doubt 299

Chapter Twenty-Two: The Book of Life 325

Chapter Twenty-Three: Things Too Wonderful to Know 337

Chapter Twenty-Four: The Truth Will Set You Free 345

Epilogue 369

The Lord said to Satan, "Very well, then, everything he has is in your power, but on the man himself do not lay a finger."—Job 1:12

CHAPTER ONE

MAN OF GOD BECOMES AN ATHEIST

June 2008
(near Dallas, Texas)

The scene was too horrifying to imagine. Tony's senses collapsed. He was paralyzed, clinging to consciousness.

What Tony Guest walked into that day was so horrifying, he couldn't comprehend what he saw. His instincts told him he was viewing the end of the world. His wife and daughter lay in pools of blood. Only the husband and father could recognize what was left of the highest forms of beauty in his life.

Hours later, Tony was still sitting, semi-conscious on the floor of the little house he and Pamela loved. It was their first real house and it was where they brought their little baby Christine home from the hospital. It had been his heaven on earth. He looked at the blood on his hands, not wanting to wash it off. It was all he had left of Pamela and Christine. The police and ambulances came and went with their questions, equipment, stretchers, and sirens. Yellow tape surrounded the house and blocked the doorways. Tony just sat on the floor staring at his hands. His disbelief and sadness would soon turn to rage.

* * *

Earlier that day, Tony retrieved his latest Gospel project from a motel and dropped him off at their small farm outside Dallas. Tony was the founder and pastor of one of the largest and fastest growing churches in the world but he also loved working with his hands. His farm needed a lot of work, which was one of the reasons he chose it. Escaping the din of mega-church life to do manual labor on a remote farm was cathartic. Finding some tasks impossible for one set of hands, Tony decided to combine his need for help with the chance to throw a lifeline to ex-cons.

Coordinating with a parole officer from his church, though against some of her counsel, Tony wanted to show what a productive life could be to some hard cases. He believed the Lord would be his family's fortress as they served others.

Don Johnson was one month out of the Walker Sayle Unit in Breckenridge, Texas, east of DFW. He did four years for dealing drugs. Of the men Tony previously worked with, Don seemed to be the most receptive. They labored side by side for three weeks on a section of fence at the front of the property. Don's parole officer said he had no "priors" and was a model prisoner. But neither Tony nor the parole officer knew the sickness that had infected Don during his four years locked up with some of society's most evil men.

Through snippets of their conversation while working together, Tony came to understand Don was raised in a completely religion-free and mostly dysfunctional home. He turned to drugs in high school but managed to stay off the law's radar until his addiction pushed him to dealing. He never shook the drug demon.

For three weeks, he was treated with kindness by Pamela, Tony's wife, and Christine, their four-year-old daughter. Don thought Pamela's kindness could mean something more. Left alone with the girls for the first time, his mind fogged by cocaine and lust, Don moved on Pamela. At first, she tried to resist politely, but Don made that impossible. She screamed which brought Christine out of her room. Don's mental flash of going back to prison and his anger at being rejected erupted in a vortex of violence and murder.

Headed home from his twenty-mile round trip to the lumberyard, Tony listened to the local Christian radio station and ruminated on fodder for his next sermon. Gratitude welled up in his chest for God, his family, and his mission.

Still riding a wave of gratitude when he arrived back at his house, Tony noticed but was not concerned when he didn't see Don working on the fence. He assumed he must have stopped work for a bathroom break or something to drink. Tony drove up to his front door, breezed into the main living area, and found the remains of his world in a pool of blood.

* * *

Tony never returned to his home or church, he gave no interviews, and dropped completely out of sight after burying his life and faith in a secluded gravesite on the farm.

None of the verses, sermons, workshops or counseling Tony used to comfort others could now comfort him. He grieved in solitude for months. He refused to see any of his friends or staff. Nothing could console him. He was angry; angry at friends who appealed to his faith, angry at his congregations because they now represented the one who killed his family, and mostly, he was bitterly angry at God. The grisly sight of his dead wife and daughter was permanently burned into Tony's mind. His gratitude to God turned to loathing for everything he once believed. His anger shifted his mission from building the kingdom of God to destroying the church and Christianity.

After four months with no public comment or any discussion with the leaders and employees of his ministry, he finally released a short and dispassionate statement to his church and the media:

> *"Today, I am resigning as president and CEO of Guest Ministries Worldwide and terminating all association with the organization to which I have dedicated my life for the last ten years. I can no longer encourage people to trust in God or give their lives to God's work because I no longer believe there is a God—at least not a God I want to know."*

That was it! Tony disappeared. There were reports he left the country. Many believed he committed suicide. Within ten months, his vast ministry empire crumbled. Financial contributions to his organizations dropped to almost nothing after Tony's public statement, and the sales of his books and videos soon stopped completely. The faith and hope of millions of people around the world were dashed. His congregations lost hope and attendance as his churches dwindled to just a few hundred people who didn't know where else to go. What was the most spectacularly successful ministry in the world, quickly became the most spectacular failure in history.

Tony finally surfaced after three years in 2011 when his dissertation from the University of British Columbia in Vancouver, Canada, was published. He enrolled as a doctoral student using an alias (approved by the university) to help him escape the distraction of his celebrity. Only a few people at the university were aware the quiet, bearded man with short brownish-blonde hair was once the most widely known religious leader in the world.

Tony's second dissertation was essentially a rebuttal of his first from Covenant Seminary which was titled *The Statistical Certainty of God*. His new dissertation was backed by two years of research and peer-reviewed analyses, published as a hardback book, heavily promoted by a major publisher in America and titled *The Improbability of a Creator God and Fantasies of Biblical Truth*.

In addition to wrapping a noose around the pillars of Christianity, the book leveled even sharper blasts at the modern church and made a strong case that the loving God Tony once preached could not exist. His loss of faith was coupled with a sense of shame and guilt for his role in duping millions of people into believing God loved them. Perhaps he sought personal absolution or, in some twisted way, thought he was taking revenge on God. Whatever the drive, Tony Guest became the foremost spokesman for atheism in America and abroad.

The media loved it! University professors all around the world loved it! Liberal politicians adored it! One U.S. Senator was quoted in the *New York Times* saying, "Now we can move past all this moral nonsense tied around the necks of the American people by the religious right and get our country moving forward."

"God Fantasies," as the book was called by its cheerleaders, was the perfect permission slip the secular world needed to advance its agenda through the government, the media, academia, the church, corporations, and international organizations such as the United Nations. And there were no religious leaders in the world with the stature to refute Dr. Anthony Guest. His research and statistics seemed irrefutable. Not even the Pope spoke out against his message.

Dr. Guest (he no longer allowed people to call him "Tony") became one of the most sought after and highly paid speakers in the world. His book sold millions of copies. For four years, he traveled the world speaking to large crowds, appearing on television and radio shows, writing articles, and teaching classes at universities. His website was consistently one of the top ten worldwide sites with millions of views a month. He quickly became a multi-millionaire.

Then as suddenly as he exploded out of obscurity two years before, Dr. Guest vanished from public view once again in 2015. His website was taken down without explanation. Except for the conspiracy theories on the covers of gossip newspapers and magazines, there was little news coverage of his disappearance from the mainstream media.

Tonight, after nearly three years in seclusion, Tony had come out of hiding to debate Professor Johnny Wright on the existence of God and the veracity of the Bible. Why he chose the timing, Wright, and Palmetto Christian University to reappear held all the intrigue of a Patricia Cornwell novel and fueled the buzz that would become even more charged when the debate was over.

* * *

Tony's story was well known to everyone watching the debate. In 1998, when he was twenty-three years old, Tony Guest received his doctorate from Covenant Theological Seminary, moved to Maryland and began preaching on street corners in the rough and depressed areas of Baltimore. The tall, thin white man with long blonde hair preaching to crowds of predominately black people drew nationwide news coverage. The crowds got larger and wealthy donors from around the country sent money to help rent space for larger and larger crowds.

At first Tony rented deserted retail store fronts, then abandoned manufacturing plants. Within three years, Tony convinced the city council to donate ten acres of deserted industrial land in the middle of the city. Not being short on faith or confidence, Tony built a simple but large steel structure to hold 6,000 people. He didn't have one official member of his church because he didn't actually have a church. He had no deacon board, no choir, no assistants or management team. He just had faith.

When Tony held his first service in the new building, there was standing room only. Every politician from mayor, to City Council members, to Congressmen, to Senators, to the Vice President of the United States had to be there. Every television network, local newspaper, and dozens of radio stations from around the country demanded media privileges.

It was an incredible event with complex logistics from media pre-promotion, to transportation (150 school buses were loaned from the school district to pick up the poor and homeless from around the city), food (Tony insisted everyone have something to eat and drink), to security (the Baltimore police volunteered 300 policemen for traffic and safety), to communications (over 300 media outlets covered the service), and operations (three utility companies and two dozen local contractors volunteered their services to make sure the air conditioners and video players all worked on this hot August morning).

There were approximately 8,000 on site for that first service in August of 2002. Media experts estimated over ten million people watched the service on television or heard it on the radio. Considering the event was pre-internet, this huge audience was an unprecedented achievement. All without any paid staff. Tony pulled it off with 500 student volunteers from seven nearby colleges and universities. The event cost nothing, everything was donated, and it raised over $3 million. Nothing like this had ever happened before. Ever! Anywhere!

The service opened with about 100 student gospel singers (about half black and half white) accompanied by the Baltimore Symphony Orchestra. The sound was powerful and heavenly and when the music stopped, the room was filled with energy and expectation. Tony's message in that first service was incredible for its simplicity and power. He looked out at thousands of people—all who were there hoping for hope—and delivered a message no one would ever forget.

"We're all here tonight hoping to get something we haven't got. None of us know what that is, but we're hoping someone—maybe I—will say something or do something that will make our lives better and give us more hope for the future. We're hoping our children will get a better deal than we got and, just maybe, will not make all the mistakes we did.

We're all sitting elbow to elbow with people we don't know. Most of us are poor and powerless."

Lots of "amens" echoed throughout the building. Lots of heads were nodding with choruses of "uh huhs."

"If the poor and powerless here tonight died in their seats, the world would go on without notice. If we were lucky, our mommas would cry for us, but mine would just say 'I told that boy not to become a preacher.'"

Lots of smiles and chuckles. The crowd was loosening up and getting more comfortable.

"But there are also some rich and powerful people here tonight, too."

A few friendly boos and "yeses" reverberated around the auditorium.

"And despite what you might think, if one of you rich and powerful people were to die here tonight, the world would also go on with little notice. In fact, if you are rich and powerful, there are a lot of people who want what you've got, and many would be rejoicing if you happened to fall down the stairs on your way out tonight."

The crowd roared with laughter with much more enjoyment than the comments deserved. Everyone needed some comic relief. The media frenzy prior to this event created such exaggerated and unrealistic expectations for this sermon, no one really believed the man on stage could satisfy the hopes and dreams of the large and diverse audience. But Tony didn't expect to meet their expectations. He fully expected God to show up and touch every heart in the place. And God did show up.

"Whether we are poor or rich, whether we are powerful or powerless, we are all children of the same God. And whether we are poor or rich, powerful or powerless, whether we have expensive clothes or found them at the soup kitchen over here on 3rd Street . . ."

Everyone in the room stood up, clapped, and cheered because they knew Tony was at that soup kitchen every day hugging children and feeding the homeless. As Tony continued to speak, a stronger and stronger connection was developing between everyone in the building and those watching on television—a spiritual bond could be felt even through the television broadcast. God's spirit was taking over and Tony became a conduit to every heart.

"We are not here today looking for religion. Religion cannot help us. We are not here hoping to learn how to live better, moral lives. We are all sinners and nothing—nothing—we do or don't do will change the fact we are sinners. I can act a little better than you, but I'm still a sinner. I could stop drinking too much, but I'd still be a sinner. I could stop taking drugs, but I'd still be a sinner. If I was a politician, I could stop lying, but I'd still be a sinner."

Even the politicians had to stand up and clap at that. All around the building, the poor nobodies were hugging the nearest politicians just to let them know they were loved. It was truly amazing how Tony raised and lowered everyone to the same level. A universal bond of fellowship enveloped every heart and soul in the auditorium.

"We are here for one reason and one reason only: to find Jesus, to know Jesus, and to let Jesus love us. What does Jesus say about you and me?

'Blessed are the poor in spirit,

for theirs is the kingdom of heaven.

Blessed are those who mourn,

for they will be comforted.

Blessed are the meek,

for they will inherit the earth.

Blessed are those who hunger and thirst for righteousness,

for they will be filled.

Blessed are the merciful,

for they will be shown mercy.

Blessed are the pure in heart,

for they will see God.

Blessed are the peacemakers,

for they will be called children of God.

Blessed are those who are persecuted because of righteousness,

for theirs is the kingdom of heaven.

Blessed are you when people insult you, persecute you, and falsely say all kinds of evil against you because of me. Rejoice and be glad, because great is your reward in heaven, for in the same way they persecuted the prophets who were before you.'"

Tony paused after every stanza and the roar of the crowd grew with every pause. As the crowd got louder, so did Tony. Before he finished all the verses, the building was shaking with clapping, "amens," screams, and stomping feet.

"Some of you know these promises from Jesus written in Matthew chapter 5 in the book of truth: the Bible. Are you poor in spirit? Do you mourn? Are you meek? Do you want peace? Jesus is here today to bless you. He is here today to love you. He is here—not just in this building—but in your heart— to hug and squeeze you until you let go of all your sin, worries, and doubts, and let him take all of your burdens onto Himself. He knows you and I are miserable sinners and it doesn't bother Him a bit. That's why He came to this earth, that's why He comes to every one of us—one on one—to take our sins onto Himself and make us white as snow. I'm not talking about making your skin as white as mine . . ."

That brought the house down. Tony wasn't afraid to talk about race, and the way he talked about it made it disappear. Literally everyone in the building and likely those watching on television, were standing and hugging whoever was standing next to them.

Tony continued speaking after having to quiet the crowd by tapping on the microphone for several minutes. "Friends, we're not here today to become Catholics, Baptists, Methodists, Presbyterians, Muslims, Buddhists, or whatever flavor of religion you choose. We are here to give our minds, bodies, hearts, and souls to Jesus so He can love us, forgive and help us live joyful lives, but even more importantly, to let Jesus secure our eternity with Him. Even if no one loves us in this life and we never have a dime in a savings account, it is enough to know God has come to this earth as a brother, as a friend, as a Savior, as the Messiah—to love us, to forgive us, and to prepare a place for us to live with Him forever."

Tony kept the crowd on their feet for an hour and half, and then got them on their knees for five minutes before they left. With millions of people on their knees around the world, he prayed a sinner's prayer:

"I am speaking this prayer for anyone who will pray it with me. Dear Lord Jesus, thank You for being here today. Thank You for taking all my sins onto Yourself and for dying in my place so I can be forgiven for every sin, every mistake, every flaw, every thought, and every deed I have committed in the past and will commit in the future. Jesus, I give You all I am and all I hope to be. Please be my Savior and my Lord and send Your Spirit to live in my heart. I know I will fail You time and time again, but I trust in Your faithfulness to transform me into the person You want me to be. Amen."

* * *

Tony's fame grew and he soon added campuses in Chicago (Southside), Memphis, Atlanta, and Los Angeles. The money kept coming in from all over the world. He was a great promoter, but he was no religious huckster. He was genuine and honest. Tony never paid himself more than $99,000 a year in salary, even after his organization was raising over $50 million a year and his books and videos were bringing in many millions more. He built a large staff—paid and volunteers. Within five years, he had more than fifty pastors and associate pastors.

More than half his staff was black and almost two-thirds of his congregation was black or Hispanic.

Tony published eight books. All became best sellers. He created a business to distribute audio and video tapes of his sermons and workshops. The attendance for his stadium revivals around the world eclipsed all other evangelists, including Billy Graham.

Tony met the love of his life at a small workshop for youth leaders in Phoenix, Arizona. Pamela was a striking blonde, but even more strikingly intelligent and winsome. Together, Tony and Pamela were the storybook couple. Thousands showed up at airports just to see them get off the plane. She became the brains of the operation and took most of the management responsibilities for the huge and growing enterprise. Pamela's video seminars for women sold more than many of Tony's videos, and he couldn't have been more pleased or prouder of what she accomplished.

After two years of marriage, Tony and Pamela became the proud parents of Christine. The threesome quickly became America's family. Before Christine was born, they moved to a small farm outside Dallas where Tony enjoyed doing the maintenance and renovations himself. Working with his hands away from the crowds brought him closer to God and kept his heart closer to Pam and Christine.

Tony had never experienced deep personal loss and suffering. His faith was real, but untested. When God allowed one evil man to destroy the people he loved most, Tony was forced to ask himself the hard questions he always answered so easily for others.

*". . . Satan has asked to sift all of you as wheat.
But I have prayed for you . . . that your faith may not
fail. And when you have turned back, strengthen your
brothers."*—Luke 22:31–32

CHAPTER TWO

JOHNNY'S FALL FROM GRACE

January 2015
(Boone, NC)

The rescue team wrestled Johnny away from the gnarled car to clear the way for the "jaws of life." Patti's motionless body was trapped behind a web of twisted steel and broken glass. The frantic flashlights revealed groceries spread on the street and throughout the car—and an ashen face covered in blood. Johnny could only watch helplessly as the large iron clamps ripped one of the doors open so the medics could get to his wife.

* * *

Three years after the accident, Johnny Wright stood on a stage next to Dr. Anthony Guest. Johnny didn't have near the

13

celebrity status of Dr. Guest, but he was well known as a man of faith who had also been through the depths of despair. Their stories were very different but equally painful, and everyone knew Johnny's suffering had led him to a very different place than Dr. Guest.

* * *

December 2013
(Boone, NC)

Johnny stood in a short line at the coffee shop scanning the room for the regulars who routinely stopped by Mountain Brew on their way to work. He smiled at a few familiar faces and turned to give the young girl behind the counter his order. "Two cappuccinos with skim . . . what!" Johnny choked as he glanced down at a stack of newspapers on the counter. The front-page headline of the *High Country News* screamed, "Johnny Wright ousted!" A smaller sub-headline was even worse, "Sexual misconduct suspected."

"Add a newspaper to my tab."

Johnny sat in a small booth against the back wall starring at the newspaper. He touched the page hoping the headline would change or go away. He was embarrassed and ashamed to look up. The article was full of quotes from "unnamed sources at the church" asserting multiple allegations of sexual harassment and unacceptable behavior. This was the end for Johnny. Everything he dreamed about and worked for his entire life dissipated in less time than steam from a hot cup of coffee.

* * *

Johnny grew up in Boone, a town named after Daniel Boone in the western mountains of North Carolina near the Tennessee line. He had two older brothers, Joe Jr. and Jay, and a younger sister, Ava. His parents ran Wright's General Store on Main Street, and the whole family worked six days a week stocking shelves, sweeping floors, bagging groceries, and everything else the store and their customers required. They lived above the store until Johnny's little sister, Ava, was born. Johnny was about three and a half years old when his family moved into one side of a rented duplex about a mile outside town.

When the owner of their duplex ran into financial trouble and declared bankruptcy, the bank offered to let Mr. Wright take over the payments on the mortgage. Joe Wright took the deal and the family found themselves in the rental-property business. They rented the upstairs above their store to a professor at Appalachian State University. From there, the professor could walk to his classes. They also rented the other side of their duplex to an older couple, which worked out well since their small yard was not big enough for any more cars, trucks, bicycles, and clothes lines.

Boone grew rapidly with the help of a growing Appalachian State, along with the increasing number of skiers in the winter and constant parade of tourists in the summer and fall. Business for the Wrights was good. They expanded their general store into a connecting antique store that closed when the owners moved back to Florida. They bought a small restaurant across the street from their general store and continued to buy up as much rental property as they could afford. They started a home maintenance company to take care of their own properties, but soon expanded to include maintenance and lawn care services for other rental property owners and the general public.

Johnny learned everything about running small businesses, fixing appliances, retail merchandising, cooking, and dealing with tenants. But his love was always his church. The Wright's attended the old Blue Ridge Baptist Church near downtown Boone. Johnny's fondest memories were being in Sunday school with his friends, going to Sunday afternoon church picnics, and sleeping in tents with his dad on church campouts.

As a teenager, he was the volunteer youth pastor because his church never employed a pastor to minister to the youth in the church. That's why the church lost most of their young members when they became teenagers. The small number of kids in the youth program allowed Johnny to minister individually to the young people in his church and he took the responsibility seriously. He was always a clean-cut kid—the religious one in the family according to his brothers and sister—and he earned the nickname of "Mr. Right" with his high school friends.

All the Wright children worked in the family businesses and they were expected to continue working part-time while going to Appalachian State to study business, mechanics, or other courses of study to help make their businesses more successful. So, when Johnny started talking about going to seminary after college to become a pastor, it didn't go over well with his family. They reminded him pastors have big headaches and small salaries. Johnny was undaunted and after graduating Appalachian State in 2007 with a major in education and serving as a part-time youth pastor on campus for a Presbyterian-sponsored ministry, he received a partial scholarship to Covenant Theological Seminary in Creve Coeur near St. Louis, Missouri. Covenant is the seminary for the Presbyterian Church in America. The fact it wasn't a Baptist college did not go unnoticed by Johnny's family or his pastor.

At Covenant, Johnny excelled in his teaching and preaching courses and soon landed a part-time job as an interim pastor for a small church in nearby Chesterfield. He loved to preach and follow his sermons with a church-wide Sunday school lesson in the sanctuary. His professors often came to evaluate his performance and all who heard him agreed Johnny was extraordinarily gifted. His love for Jesus was contagious, even for the older folks in this little church. In his final year at Covenant, Johnny became the full-time youth pastor for a large church near downtown St. Louis. After his classes at Covenant, he visited local high schools and invited students to join his youth group on Wednesday and Sunday nights. Before he finished his doctorate, the church was forced to rent a nearby warehouse to accommodate over 1,500 students who came to hear Johnny preach, play the guitar, sing, and tell jokes. Johnny loved these students and knew how to make them feel the love of God.

It was in one of these Wednesday night meetings Johnny met the love of his life. A local high school student brought along his sister who was home from Clemson University on Easter break. Her family was originally from Greenville, South Carolina, and like many who grow up in Upstate South Carolina, she was a lifelong Clemson fan. Patti only applied to one college: Clemson. As a straight-A student, a leader of her championship high school volleyball team, community volunteer, and prominent Young Life leader, she had all the credentials for a scholarship to any college she chose. Patti fulfilled her dream to become a Clemson Tiger and she was proud of it. She showed up at Johnny's Wednesday night event with a bright orange vest over her white blouse glowing like a beacon among the dark winter clothes worn by most of the other students.

Johnny spotted her in the back of the room and tried to look away because he had disciplined himself to never have a romantic thought about one of his high school students. But all of his defenses broke down when he saw her big smile, long brown hair flowing down over her bright orange vest as she raised her hands in worship. He was so distracted he forgot the words to the song he wrote to celebrate the resurrection of Jesus. The song was titled "Risen Love," and it could not have been more apropos for this moment in Johnny's life.

Johnny finished the service with a quick prayer feeling ashamed of himself for becoming so distracted by someone a hundred feet away in a crowd. He shook a few hands, gave a few high fives, tapped knuckles with his volunteer leaders, and then turned to put his guitar in its case. He heard a young man behind him say, "Pastor Johnny." He turned to see one of his students with the girl in the bright orange vest. "Pastor Johnny, I'd like you to meet my sister Patti. She's a senior at Clemson University."

Johnny held the handle of his guitar case with his left hand and reached out with his right to shake her hand. But he had not latched the case and the guitar fell out, bouncing off a stool on its way to the concrete floor. Patti quickly reached out with her left hand and caught it before it hit the floor. *Obviously, an athlete*, Johnny thought. She handed him his guitar with her left hand but never let go of his right. Their arms were crossed in what looked like an awkward pose. But Johnny could almost hear the trumpets playing. He and Patti were connected with both hands looking into each other's eyes laughing nervously. They never let go.

Patti and Johnny finished school in May and were married in September. It all happened too fast for both families, but not soon enough for Patti and Johnny. They were so much in love even Patti's dad knew it would be cruel to make them wait. The wedding was held in Greenville, where most of Patti's friends and extended family lived, and only a few hour's drive from Boone for Johnny's family.

Johnny was offered a full-time job and a nice raise by the large church where he worked as youth pastor for the past year. The newlyweds decided to stay in St. Louis where they would be close to Patti's family. It seemed like the perfect plan until Johnny got a call from his oldest brother, Joe Jr., one Sunday afternoon in November telling him his dad died suddenly of a heart attack. He was only sixty-two.

Johnny struggled with how he felt about his father's death. His dad was a faithful husband, a hard worker, and always a good example as a man of God, but he rarely shared a personal thought or showed any emotion. Now that he was gone, Johnny was especially sad because he didn't feel like he ever really knew him. And he knew their lack of closeness was as much his fault as his father's. Johnny's mix of emotions and sense of guilt—combined with hearing about his father's death over the phone and being so far away from his family—gave him two sleepless nights before he and Patti made the long drive back to Boone for the funeral.

The day after the funeral, there was a family meeting in the renovated space above the old general store. The room was now rented out for banquets, receptions, and small parties. The family restaurant across the street handled all the catering. The meeting was more like an intervention. Ava was the only sibling not married and she sat on one side of the large table with her mom, Jill, and the spouses of her three brothers. Johnny noticed his mom, sister, and sisters-in-law had Patti surrounded. Johnny was surrounded on the other side of the table by his two older brothers.

Johnny's family obviously worked on their strategy for this meeting. His mother spoke first. "Patti, we are so proud to have you in our family and we are grateful to have your support during this very sad time. We know you and Johnny are very happy in St. Louis, but with Johnny's dad gone, we really need your help in the business. Johnny, you are the best customer relations person we've ever had. And Patti, with your business degree, you are desperately needed in the office to take over the management duties handled by Joe Sr."

Johnny's mother nodded across the table and Joe Jr. took his cue, "Johnny, we know your ministry is important to you and we want you to continue it. We've talked with some of our friends at the church and they've agreed to sponsor the salary for a youth pastor. Pastor Taylor has agreed it would be a good idea. Sarah Jelks has also agreed to donate her late husband's cabin to the church with the condition it be used as the home for the youth pastor. Sarah has decided to move back to Florida to be near her family."

Joe Jr. passed the baton back to his mother, "Patti, we are asking you and Johnny to consider moving back to Boone, live in the beautiful cabin by the river, and split your time working for the church and the family business. Will you consider this idea?"

Johnny was in an impossible position. He knew Patti was ecstatic about their new apartment so close to her family in St. Louis. And he was living his dream as the youth pastor of a large church. He was speechless and a long, awkward silence ensued. Fortunately, Patti came to his rescue, "Of course we will consider it! Johnny and I will talk about it and let you know. We appreciate all the work you've put into creating this opportunity. Now let's get out of this cold room and go have dinner at home by the fire." Patti wasn't a bit intimidated. She took charge of the awkward moment and everyone obeyed. The chairs slid back, everyone stood up, the girls hugged, and the men shook hands. The business meeting was over.

Johnny and Patti were staying in the guest room of the Wrights' large home on the side of the mountain overlooking Boone. It was acquired four years earlier in a bankruptcy sale. While Mrs. Wright and the girls were cooking dinner, Johnny's brothers watched football and Johnny and Patti sat in a large lounge chair under blankets on the front deck overlooking Boone and the cloud-covered mountains. As they sat, Johnny smiled nervously, rolled his eyes at Patti, and covered his head playfully with a blanket. They cuddled up and stared at the beautiful view. Not a word was said. They were savoring their lives together knowing everything was about to change. Then, with her eyes still gazing at the mountains, Patti said, "We have to do it and you have my full support."

Johnny's eyes filled with tears. He squeezed her hand and continued staring at the mountains. He had been quietly angry at his family during the meeting, then relieved when Patti helped them escape. But by the time they arrived back at the house he was ready to tell his family, "Absolutely not!" Patti's calm demeanor helped him relax and think more clearly. He knew his family needed him. Their appeal wasn't a selfish act. His dad insisted the senior management of the business always be family. Their business had over thirty rental properties, a restaurant and catering service, and a maintenance and landscape business with a total of thirty-five full-time employees and dozens of part-time student workers. It was a good business that could continue to grow for years. But he and Patti had just set up their little Camelot in St. Louis and he dreaded jumping back into the old small-town quagmire in Boone.

Patti threw off their blankets, grabbed Johnny's hand, and pulled him out of the chair. She led them back into the great room with the giant rock fireplace. The kitchen was only separated by a counter with large swivel chairs. The girls in the kitchen saw them return and stopped what they were doing. The brothers pushed the "mute" button on the remote and turned with interested but impatient expressions. The football game was close.

Johnny was not prepared to make a statement but their return from the deck created the expectation of an announcement. Patti didn't hesitate, "Johnny and I are excited to join the Wright family business." Johnny looked stunned as the family applauded and the girls from the kitchen hurried around the counter to begin the hugs and kisses. Johnny's brothers, in true brotherly style, reached back over the couch, offered him quick knuckle bumps and returned to watching the game. Johnny hadn't said a word, but though they didn't know it at the time, he and Patti had just made the most fateful decision of their lives.

Before they left Boone for St. Louis, Johnny and Patti visited the cabin soon to be their new home. It was a beautiful log home too large to be called a cabin. Hidden in the woods about two miles from Boone at the end of a long gravel driveway on the edge of a river, visitors were greeted by a large covered front deck with rocking chairs and overhead ceiling fans. The back deck was built out over the river with the piers actually in the water. From the dozen Adirondack chairs on the back deck you could see down the valley and hear the river splashing over several small falls. Johnny could fly-fish from the deck.

The downstairs of the house was one great room with an open kitchen in the back-right corner overlooking the river. A large rock fireplace covered most of the left wall. The Jelks left a baby grand piano along with most of their furniture. The room would be perfect for large gatherings of students. As they surveyed the room, Johnny and Patti looked at each other and smiled. Perhaps the move back to Boone would be more positive than they imagined.

The upstairs held a large master bedroom and two smaller bedrooms, each with their own bathrooms. Plenty of room for Patti's parents or friends to visit. The master bedroom had two large walk-in closets, two sinks in the bathroom, a shower and a large bath tub with massage jets. Double doors opened to a balcony overlooking the river. Very nice accommodations for newlyweds with no money!

Johnny and Patti returned to St. Louis, had a heart-wrenching discussion with Patti's parents, said many sad goodbyes at Johnny's church, packed up what little they had in their apartment, and were back in Boone in three weeks. Their first night back at their new log home, Johnny bought some steaks and a bottle of champagne. They celebrated on the back deck overlooking the river.

Patti went to work the next day in the main office of the Wright family business. Johnny met with Pastor Taylor to discuss how to build the youth group at the church. Pastor Taylor was not as enthusiastic about the youth ministry as Johnny was led to believe, but he did agree to let Johnny use the large fellowship hall every Sunday night. They disagreed about Johnny holding Wednesday night service for the youth group at his home. Pastor Taylor was afraid attendance at the church on Wednesday nights would be too sparse if the youth group was not there. They reached a compromise by agreeing high school students would come to the regular Wednesday night service at the church and college students would meet at Johnny's log home. The church averaged fewer than six college students on Wednesday night, so Pastor Taylor didn't think he had much to lose.

Pastor Edward Taylor was a fourth-generation pastor. His father founded Blue Ridge Baptist in 1938. Edward Taylor became associate pastor right out of seminary and took over as senior pastor when his father died in 1975. He was now seventy-three years old and continuing to lead the church hoping his son, Mike, would return to Boone to take over. Mike attended one year of seminary but dropped out and was selling real estate in Hilton Head, South Carolina. He promised his dad for years he would return to keep the church in the family, but he found it hard to give up the success and big income from selling real estate.

Johnny began working mornings in the Wright family business and spent the afternoons holding small group Bible studies at Appalachian State. These small groups helped him develop relationships and trust with the students. Once the students got to know Johnny, they were anxious to join the Wednesday night cookouts with him and Patti. It wasn't long before over 100 students were regularly attending their Wednesday night dinners and fellowships. Students packed his front porch, great room, and back deck. Two large grills on the back deck fogged the valley with continuous cooking as the students ate in shifts all night.

Patti arranged for the Wright's landscaping crew to grade and sand a volley ball court next to the deck beside the river. Except for the occasional volleyball lost to the river, it was a perfect and picturesque location for the students to play. Dozens of students would stand on the deck—hamburgers in hand—watching their friends compete on the court below. Patti, the former varsity volleyball player at Clemson, was a regular on the court challenging the boys with her powerful slam. It soon became a rite of passage for anyone who considered themselves an athlete to try to beat Patti's team.

Wednesday night became the best time of the week for Johnny, Patti, and many young students. Good food and fellowship with a bond of friendship connected by the spirit of Jesus was standard fare. After dinner, a few volleyball games, and a lot of conversation, Johnny gathered everyone into the great room, sang a few songs, and gave a short Bible lesson. He knew how to open the Scriptures to young people in a way that made them hunger for more. He never discouraged questions or even doubts expressed by those in attendance. His approach was Socratic and meant to help the college students discover God through Scripture and prayer, not rigid doctrine and pat answers. When it was all over, Johnny and Patti stood on their front porch shaking hands, high-fiving, knuckle-tapping, and hugging. No one left without a big smile and a "see ya next week."

Pastor Taylor and several of the older deacons at the church didn't like Johnny's informal style and they became increasingly critical of Johnny in the monthly deacon's meetings at the church. The large and growing crowds of students for Johnny's Wednesday night fellowship became the talk of the church and the small town of Boone. Most of the church was excited about the new burst of life in their aging congregation. Pastor Taylor seemed to take Johnny's popularity and success as a personal affront.

Things only got worse after one of Johnny's students accused him of being homophobic. The accusation came from a counseling session where the student asked Johnny's advice about being Christian and gay.

"The Bible tells us we're all sinners," Johnny began. "So being gay doesn't make you more of a sinner than me. The question from a Christian perspective is 'are you willing to give your sins to Jesus and let him help you overcome them?' All of us are born with predispositions both good and bad. The Bible says we all have a sinful human nature. Some of us are predisposed to lie or steal, or with a bad temper, or weaknesses for various kinds of addictions. But in Jesus, our human nature is not who we are. You may have a predisposition sexually, but that is not who you are in Jesus. Thousands of people have left the homosexual lifestyle. Sexual impulses of all sorts are intrinsic to the fallen nature of mankind but giving into to any sinful impulse is a choice.

"Our physical desires may be too strong for us to overcome on our own. But I believe, if we do our best to follow Jesus and

ask for support from fellow believers, God will help us overcome our human nature—nail it to the cross as the Bible says."

"If people know I'm gay, can I still come to your fellowship
dinners?" the student asked.

"Of course, you can!" Johnny replied. "You'll fit right in
with all the rest of us sinners. God doesn't expect us to be perfect and He can forgive us every day—even if we commit the
same sin over and over—because Jesus has taken all our sins
onto Himself. But I do have one request. It is one thing to be
a sinner. But is wrong to justify our sin, or to say what God
calls sin is actually good. Our fellowships are designed to help
people use the Bible to become more like Jesus. That won't
make any of us perfect, but we come together to praise God
and pray for Him to help us live our lives in ways that
please Him."

As it turned out, the gay student had no interest in following Jesus or learning biblical precepts. He was a plant from a
campus LGBT group working with the college newspaper to
expose discrimination against gays. The student recorded the
conversation with Johnny, the newspaper edited it and printed
a story accusing Johnny of hate. The front-page headline was,
"Youth pastor says being gay is sin."

Even though Johnny's church took a hardline against
homosexually, Pastor Taylor used the bad press to quietly
condemn Johnny with church leaders. Ironically, his accusation
was that Johnny was too soft on the issue of homosexuality and
should not be welcoming gays to church meetings.

Unfortunately for Johnny, the bad story in the college
newspaper was only the beginning of his undoing.

The Wednesday night front porch "goodbyes" with
Johnny, Patti, and their students became another setup by one
of Johnny's secret enemies. Mr. Richard Robertson, a senior
deacon at the church and a close friend of Pastor Taylor, didn't
like Johnny's music or teaching, but his daughter Suzie loved
Johnny. That made Mr. Robertson even angrier. He was a
strict, old-school Southern Baptist and his hardline parenting

created a strained relationship with his daughter. His insistence on Suzie living at home while going to college made things much worse. She wasn't allowed to have her own car even though she worked and saved enough money in high school to buy a car and pay all the expenses herself. She and her dad hardly spoke, even when he picked her up at Johnny's cabin on Wednesday nights.

One Thursday morning after picking Suzie up from Johnny's Wednesday night dinner, Mr. Robertson dropped by the church to meet with Pastor Taylor. They had been meeting often to discuss Johnny. Mr. Robertson regularly reported many parents were expressing concerns about Johnny's teachings. He didn't share any names of concerned parents or any specifics about Johnny's teaching, but he knew how to manipulate the pastor's ego. "This just isn't the Taylor way," he would say or "It just doesn't feel like Taylor's church anymore."

In this particular meeting, Mr. Robertson decided to go for the kill. He said, "Pastor, last night Suzie told me Johnny groped her as she left the meeting at his home. I was in my car in front of the cabin and saw it happen. He shamelessly sexually harassed my daughter. And Suzie says other girls have reported the same type of abuse. We have to do something quickly because the church is liable if any of these girls decide to report it to the police."

Mr. Robertson continued, "Pastor, we can turn this into an opportunity for the church if we act quickly. I've talked with your son and apprised him of the situation. He is ready to come back and take over as youth pastor. I know you want him to follow you as senior pastor and this is the opportunity to begin that process."

Pastor Taylor was outwardly disturbed, but inwardly over-joyed. Watching Johnny's success was painful. Not only did Johnny bring in large crowds of high school and college students, but when Johnny preached in the sanctuary on Sunday nights, the adult crowds were larger than when Pastor Taylor preached on Sunday morning. Taylor had been quietly humiliated for months. He did not want Johnny to ever become the senior pastor of "Edward Taylor's church."

Pastor Taylor called an emergency Sunday afternoon meeting of the board of deacons. Mr. Robertson met with all of the deacons separately prior to the meeting. He told them of the widespread concerns of parents and the charges of sexual harassment. None of it was true. Not one parent expressed concerns to Mr. Robertson. Suzie said nothing about being groped. Practically every member of the church was enthusiastic about the new energy and crowds of students Johnny brought to the church. But before they met on Sunday, every deacon was convinced by Mr. Robertson that Johnny was a serial pervert and a heretic to Baptist theology.

Johnny expected to preach on this particular Sunday night and Patti was co-hosting an ice cream social in the fellowship hall after the service with high school and college students. They were expecting an overflow crowd and recruited a dozen student leaders to help them set up the room and serve the ice cream. So, of course, Johnny was shocked when Pastor Taylor announced Sunday morning the evening service and ice cream social were canceled. Johnny couldn't believe Pastor Taylor would cancel the service without mentioning it to him. But when the pastor announced a special meeting of the deacons after the morning service, Johnny knew something was up.

The deacons of Blue Ridge Baptist Church agreed unanimously to terminate Johnny immediately with only two-weeks' pay, and to call Mike Taylor to serve as youth pastor. Mike and his family would live in the log home now occupied by Johnny and Patti. On Monday, December 2, 2013, almost three years to the day after he began his work with the church, Pastor Taylor and Richard Robertson met with Johnny to give him the news. Johnny couldn't believe what they were saying. He couldn't believe his fate was decided without the opportunity to defend himself in front of the deacons. He wasn't given any names of parents or students who had complained about him. He wasn't given any examples of theological problems with his teachings. All he knew was he was fired and had to be out of his home in two weeks.

Driving home from his termination meeting with Taylor and Robertson, Johnny's mind was racing in all directions. He searched his mind to find any situation where he might have touched a girl inappropriately, but he couldn't find any. Patti was always by his side when they were saying "goodnight" to the students. He was never alone with any female students. How could there have been so many complaints about his behavior? Then his mind raced to how he could continue his ministry work elsewhere. He could go to another church. No. His reputation was destroyed. Pastor Taylor would not give him a positive reference. By the time he arrived at their log home, Johnny realized his life-long dream of being a pastor was dead.

He and Patti spent the evening crying, pacing the floor, and asking questions aloud. "This is not just!" and "This is not right!" were said over and over again. They couldn't sleep. The next morning, they both got dressed, and, as usual, drove to work in separate cars because the business required them to drive in many different directions during the day. They planned to tell the family and hoped to keep Johnny's firing a quiet, private matter. As usual, Johnny stopped by Mountain Brew on his way to work to pick up coffee. That's where he found out the matter was anything but private.

The family was angry. Johnny's brothers never liked Pastor Taylor and they knew Richard Robertson was a gossip. They talked about suing the church. They talked about running an ad in the paper proclaiming Johnny's innocence, but they were too late. Mr. Robertson and several other deacons leaked their side of the story to the *High Country News*. The article claimed numerous anonymous sources reported Johnny Wright was released from Blue Ridge Baptist Church for "sexual misconduct and unsuitable" behavior. Those who wanted Johnny fired also wanted to justify their decision by destroying his reputation and humiliating him in public.

Johnny and Patti moved into the duplex where he lived with his family as a child. They both worked ten or twelve hours every day in the Wrights' business to keep their minds off the stunning setback in their lives. And they made the ten-hour drive to St. Louis every few weeks just to get away from Boone. The many hours on the road gave them a lot of time to figure out their future. Johnny was not sure whether Patti's parents believed in his innocence, but they always welcomed him with open arms. Those three- or four-day weekends in St. Louis were always a welcomed respite.

After six months of adjusting to their new lives and beginning to accept Boone as their permanent home, the young couple received some much-needed good news: Patti was pregnant. Starting a family was just what Johnny and Patti needed to refocus their lives on the future. They moved into a larger home near the best elementary school in Boone. Johnny made decorating the nursery a labor of love. But just when they thought they'd weathered the worst life could throw at them, the unthinkable happened.

Patti was driving home from the grocery store after leaving work when her car was hit broadside by another car running a red light. Johnny's brother witnessed the crash from a gas station at the intersection and immediately called Johnny. He was at the scene within minutes.

The driver who caused the accident, a freshman at Appalachian State, had too much to drink at a fraternity pledge party. Patti was in a coma for three days. Her back was broken, her hip was crushed, and she had considerable internal injuries in her pelvic area. Their baby was killed. They had just learned the week before that the baby was a girl. Patti's doctors were doubtful she would be able to have another child. Her spinal cord was damaged and Johnny was told she may never walk again.

Johnny couldn't process it all. After sleeping in the hospital for a week, his hands were shaking, and his speech was slurred. He cried out to God while Patti was in a coma, but when she finally woke up and could hardly speak, he began to mumble angrily at God. He repeated over and over again, "Just go away and leave us alone. Stop torturing us." His mumbling became louder and Patti's doctors asked Johnny's family to take him home. Joe Jr. wrestled him out of the hospital and drove him to his mother's home where she and his sister, Ava, could take care of him.

After four weeks in Watauga Medical Center in Boone, Patti was moved to a rehabilitation hospital in Asheville, North Carolina. Johnny's mother became Patti's primary caregiver in the hospital and she led the family caravan to Asheville when Patti was moved. His mom also became Johnny's primary caregiver. When the time came to move Patti, she told Johnny he would not be traveling with Patti unless he got a haircut, shaved, took a shower, and put on some nice clothes. Johnny was too beaten down to argue or fight. He complied and other than the black rings under his eyes, he almost looked like himself when they loaded Patti into one of the Wright vans for the trip to Asheville.

Patti's rehabilitation went better than anyone expected. Her strong arms and athleticism allowed her to suspend her body on the parallel bars and swing her legs until they regained feeling and strength. She was more determined than any patient the therapists ever saw. She was positive and optimistic. Within three weeks she was moving around the halls with a walker. When she wasn't working her legs in the pool or with her walker, she was in the gym rebuilding her upper body strength. She not only expected to walk again, she was determined to play volleyball again.

Johnny was quite a different story. He was negative and pessimistic about everything. Patti tried to cheer him up, but her cheerfulness just made him feel more guilty about what happened to her. She wouldn't have been hurt had they not moved to Boone or had he not been fired from the church. She wouldn't have even been on that road if they still lived in their log home. He convinced himself Patti's parents regretted her marriage to a hillbilly pervert. He hadn't gone to church or opened his Bible since he was fired from the church and never planned to have anything to do with God again. He didn't want anything to do with a God who tortured those who loved him.

But God used Patti to love Johnny back into the kingdom. When they were back in their home in Boone, Patti insisted Johnny help her get down on her knees to pray. She couldn't bend to get on the floor, so he had to hold her and let her down slowly. At first, he wouldn't pray with her, so she prayed out loud. He snorted around the room, pretending not to hear. She praised God for her nurses and doctors and for allowing her to walk again. She thanked God for Johnny and their lives together, for the good jobs they had, and the opportunity to build their lives together in Boone. Johnny found a quiet corner to cry. The next time he helped Patti to the floor to pray, he knelt with her. He didn't pray, he just cried.

Twelve weeks after the accident, Patti returned to work on her walker. She tacked on the wall behind her desk an enlarged picture of herself in full orange regalia from a college tournament, jumping two feet off the court and slamming a volleyball over the net. She printed "GOAL" with the largest font available on the printer and taped it to the bottom of the picture. The message was clear: she was going to play volleyball again. Patti brought a positive attitude and laughter back to the Wright family business. The only reference ever heard from Patti about the accident was, "My little setback." It was hard for Johnny to continue to feel sorry for himself. Patti poked and prodded him and it only took a few weeks before the office was filled again with the sound of Johnny and Patti laughing together at something silly he did. She loved and laughed him through a very dark time and now he was ready to live again.

In May, almost six months after the accident, Johnny was working late when he received a call from Dr. Howard Clark, president of Palmetto Christian University. Dr. Clark was one of Johnny's professors at Covenant and was well aware of his situation because several of his former students were pastoring churches near Boone. Dr. Clark asked Johnny to become an associate professor at the University and to teach graduate-level Bible studies. Johnny responded quickly, "Frankly Dr. Clark, I haven't opened a Bible in more than two years and only prayed because Patti has shamed me by reminding me of all I have to be thankful for." Johnny was nothing if not honest.

"That's good," responded Dr. Clark. "Now you'll have a fresh and more honest perspective of the Scriptures. God can't use people for His highest purposes until they've been broken by suffering. It sounds like you meet that criteria. And frankly Johnny, we actually need Patti more than you. We have a good job for her as assistant director of student relations. Our students need a couple to love them and to live out the love and joy of Jesus in front of them every day. This place is a little too stiff. I've reserved a nice house for you to live near the campus. Your pay will be $110,000 a year and I need you here by August 1 to handle two courses in the fall. And Johnny, this is not a request. It is a direct order from God." Then, with a little chuckle, he hung up.

Johnny never imagined life could be this complicated and confusing. He couldn't believe he now had the opportunity to return to ministry. He thought that door was closed forever. How could he teach students about the Bible when he was still angry with God? How could he ask Patti to make another major change in their lives? How could he leave the family business—again? His head was spinning. He was excited, scared, confused, and—happy!

He was anxious to tell Patti about the call from Dr. Clark, but afraid to have the conversation. He sat in his car in their driveway for twenty minutes coaching himself on what to say. He should tell her about the call, confess he doesn't want to put her through another move, and tell her he would call Dr. Clark back to decline the offer. And then hope Patti would try to talk him into taking the offer. In his heart, he was jumping for joy, but after all Patti went through, he had to defer totally to her.

Johnny walked into the kitchen slowly trying to contain his excitement. Patti was standing in front of the stove without her walker. It wasn't even in the room. This was the first time he had seen her without her walker within easy reach. On the counter was a bottle of champagne in an ice bucket and two big steaks marinating in a pan. They hadn't had champagne since moving into the log home almost five years before. He reached for her cautiously, afraid she might break. She turned and gave him a big hug and kiss. "What's the occasion?" he asked. "There's a lot to celebrate," she said.

Maybe she is just playing cheerleader again, he thought to himself. He started the gas grill, put on the steaks and poured them both a glass of champagne. He didn't want to risk ruining the celebration, but it seemed a good time to tell her about the call from Dr. Clark. "Patti, I got an interesting call today," Johnny said calmly. "Yes, I know," Patti spoke with a sly smile. "That's what we're celebrating!" As if things couldn't get more confusing. He sat there dazed, thinking to himself, "How could she know about the call I just had a few minutes ago?" Johnny didn't know what was going on, but he couldn't help but smile at the apparent conspiracy.

"Let me save you the pain of trying to tell me about your call. Dr. Clark called me last week to tell me about his idea. We agreed it was a great idea and I accepted on your behalf. I talked with your mother and she thinks it is a wonderful idea. She and your brothers have already decided the business has gotten too big to be managed entirely by the family. Everyone is working themselves to death. They are now working with a consultant to hire a professional management team and the family will be paid as the board of directors. So, we'll still get paid by the business while you're a professor at Palmetto Christian and I'm assistant director of student affairs. It's all decided and I told Dr. Clark to tell you this is a direct order from God. Because in this case, it is!" Patti saved Johnny again. They shared the whole bottle of champagne and enjoyed the two slightly over-cooked steaks he forgot were on the grill.

* * *

January 2018

Four years after sitting against the wall in the coffee shop staring at the headline, "Johnny Wright ousted," the life and career he thought were dead was now being resurrected in front of thousands of people who came to see him defend himself and his faith against the most prominent atheist in the world. The auditorium was full of friends and foes, and the cameras were ready to broadcast the spectacle all around the world. How could a disgraced small-town youth pastor have ended up on this stage?

By faith we understand that the universe was formed at God's command, so that what is seen was not made out of what was visible.—Hebrews 11:1

CHAPTER THREE

SANTA CLAUS GOD

January 2018 – the first debate
(Travelers Rest, SC)

The two men who just met backstage could not have been more different, yet they were connected by the tragic circumstances of their lives. Some of the critics of tonight's debate said the university was insensitive, if not cruel, to ask them to debate issues certain to tear open old wounds. But for most people in the auditorium and the millions who tuned in to hear their competing arguments, the awareness of Tony's and Johnny's painful faith journeys created a backdrop of anticipation far greater than anything seen in the media in decades.

The lights flickered in the auditorium as the sound system screeched to life with several seconds of ear-piercing feedback before a young man announced, "Good evening, everyone, and thank you for joining the grand opening of Frazier Auditorium at Palmetto Christian University. And now, please welcome to the stage our president, Dr. Howard Clark."

Dr. Clark bounced quickly out of his front row seat and headed for the steps on the left side of the stage. He was seventy-three years old but moved and acted like a man in his fifties. After spending his career as a professor and dean at Covenant Theological Seminary in St. Louis, he announced his retirement five years earlier. The Board of Palmetto Christian convinced him to come to Travelers Rest, South Carolina, to save the struggling university.

Palmetto was one of the few universities left in America with biblically based teachings in all subject areas, faith-based lifestyle mentorship programs, and a strong emphasis on Christian character and behavior. Dr. Clark accepted the challenge and it didn't take him long to turn things around. In five short years, enrollment doubled to over 3,000 students, professors with PhDs increased 20 percent, and the college's endowment quadrupled to over $100 million.

Dr. Clark grabbed the microphone on the podium and bent it down with the natural motion of a man completely comfortable speaking to large crowds. Tonight, all 5,000 seats in the new auditorium were occupied and numerous classrooms around the campus were packed with students, faculty, and local residents watching the debate on closed circuit TV. Three television networks had their cameras set up on the crowded media platform in the back of the auditorium with reporters from all around the country. This was a huge event for a small college in the foothills of South Carolina and the chatter from the audience rose to a roar when Dr. Clark tapped on the microphone three times with his finger. Then, almost magically, silence fell over the auditorium.

Dr. Clark was beaming with his characteristic winsome smile as he began to speak with both arms raised. "What a great crowd! What a great way to spend a Friday night! Thank you all for joining the inauguration of this wonderful new facility and for being part of this historic debate about creation and the origins of life. Palmetto Christian University is not afraid of questions or debate about what we believe. The truth is never afraid of questions! We are prepared to defend our faith and our belief in biblical truth. I am grateful for our two participants tonight. I have great respect for them and know them very well. They have both been my students."

The crowd laughed nervously and began to chatter again. Clearly, few in the audience knew the connection between Dr. Clark and the two debate participants. Perhaps that connection could explain how one of the world's most prominent atheists agreed to debate before a predominately Christian crowd in rural South Carolina.

Dr. Clark again tapped on the microphone and the crowd lapped into silence. "Let's begin with the introduction of our distinguished guest, Dr. Anthony Guest—or Tony as I knew him many years ago. Tony walked into my graduate-level Biblical Studies class twenty-one years ago in September of 1997 at Covenant Theological Seminary. He had long shaggy blonde hair, dark glasses, and a chip on his shoulder bigger than a cinder block. But he knew his stuff and he was smart. Before the end of that class, the chip on his shoulder was replaced by a passion to pursue the truth and a genuine humble spirit—at least as humble as you can be when you know everything (nervous laughter again from the audience). But I say that with the utmost respect because, of all my students, and I had plenty over more than forty years of teaching, Tony Guest knew more about the Scriptures than any student I ever taught. And he knew how to teach others in a way that brought more people to Jesus than any of my students.

"So, it didn't surprise me to see Tony graduate with honors the next year and become Dr. Anthony Guest. He then created one of the largest and fastest growing churches in the world. Within a few years, his church had twenty campuses and over 50,000 members. He wrote eight best-selling books about the Bible, creation, and how to apply faith to every area of your life. With the possible exception of Rev. Billy Graham, there was no one in my lifetime who reached more people for Jesus Christ. Unfortunately for believers worldwide, tragic circumstances in Dr. Guest's life put him on a different path."

Everyone in the audience began to squirm. No one wanted Dr. Clark to bring up the personal details that transformed one of the world's greatest evangelist into the world's most prominent atheist. It just didn't seem civil—or Southern—to invite Dr. Guest to a Christian university and then embarrass him in front of a large crowd. Everyone knew the story, but it was too painful to hear again, especially in front of the man who lived it. Mercifully, Dr. Clark didn't retrace the details of Tony's life after he left Covenant Seminary.

"Over the past several years, Dr. Guest and I have had the opportunity to meet many times and talk about a lot of things. And while we certainly don't agree on everything, I am grateful he agreed to come here tonight to challenge us with his incredible mind and sharp wit. Please welcome my friend Tony Guest."

Everyone stood clapping with enthusiasm, but heads were turned whispering questions to seatmates about what they just heard. How had Dr. Clark been meeting with Dr. Guest over the past few years when no one knew where he was? What did a Christian leader and an atheist who did untold damage to the worldwide Christian church have to talk about?

Tony Guest pulled back the curtain on the left side of the stage and proceeded to walk slowly toward the two podiums at the center of the stage. At first his head was down with a stern expression on his face. This was the demeanor the audience expected because the only pictures of him in the media since the loss of his family depicted him with stern or angry expressions. But tonight, as he walked across the stage, he lifted his head and turned toward the cheering audience, raised his hand to wave, nodded slightly and almost smiled. The people who came expecting to dislike him, were already melting with compassion for a man who often called them "idiots."

At forty-three years old, Tony seemed taller and slimmer than ever. He was wearing black cowboy boots, dress jeans with a thick belt and large brass belt buckle, a pressed and starched white dress shirt with an open collar, and a light brown suede sports coat. His beard, which had become his trademark as an atheist, was gone and his once blonde hair was still long, but sandy colored with streaks of gray. He walked past the first podium still manned by Dr. Clark and stood behind the second podium at stage right. He turned and faced the audience with his blue eyes sparkling in the spotlights. The audience stopped clapping and stared in silence. Tony was far more imposing in person than he appeared on television. He turned to Dr. Clark, "Thank you, Dr. Clark, it's great to be back on campus with you at Palmetto Christian."

Dr. Clark stepped away from his podium and welcomed Tony with a handshake and a slap on his back.

"Thank you, Dr. Guest. We are honored to have you back on campus." Dr. Clark smiled knowing the intrigue of Tony secretly visiting the campus before the debate would set off a wave of whispered questions and comments. And he was right. Everyone sat and the hum from the crowd rose like a chorus of crickets around a southern pond at dusk. Dr. Clark enjoyed watching the spectacle for about ten seconds before again tapping on his microphone. The audience obediently stopped talking and anxiously turned, hoping for another revelation.

Dr. Clark continued, "And now it is my pleasure to introduce one of our own here at Palmetto Christian, Dr. Jonathon Wright, or Johnny as I knew him when he walked into my graduate-level Biblical Studies class seven years ago."

All the students stood and clapped. Johnny, after only one full semester at the university, was already a favorite of the students at Palmetto. Cheers, friendly "boos," and catcalls of "Johnny be good" echoed around the auditorium. Johnny always had a smile to share. However, most of the audience knew he had a tragic story of his own.

Johnny was waiting alone backstage praying God would give him the right words to say. Only five months after arriving at Palmetto Christian University, Dr. Clark selected him to debate the smartest and best-known atheist in the world. Tony

Guest spent two years traveling around the world humiliating Christians in debates.

Dr. Clark finished Johnny's introduction. "Since arriving at Palmetto Christian this year, Johnny and his wife, Patti, have energized our student fellowship programs and demonstrated the love of Jesus like a spring breeze to the whole campus. I am especially proud to introduce my friend and colleague, Johnny Wright."

Johnny struggled for a few awkward seconds pushing on the curtains trying to find an opening to walk through. He finally parted the curtains and walked onto the stage to a thunderous standing ovation. Johnny knew only God could have made this moment possible. Six months before, he was a disgraced youth pastor with no possible future in any ministry. Tonight, God was loving him through the cheers of thousands of students and colleagues, and he had an incredible platform to share the love of Jesus.

Johnny walked across the stage in his old Hush Puppy shoes, baggy khaki pants, and a slightly wrinkled navy blazer. He looked, well—like a youth pastor. He was about 5′10″. The heelless Hush Puppies and baggy pants made him look much shorter than Tony who stood straight and tall on his well-heeled boots. Dr. Clark picked up a wireless microphone from his podium and stepped aside to make room for Johnny. They shook hands, Johnny smiled, pulled the microphone on the podium down to his level, and said, "Thank you, Dr. Clark, and thank you, Dr. Guest, for joining us tonight for this important discussion."

Dr. Clark began his exit toward the steps on the left side of the stage, tapped a few times on his microphone as he walked, and stopped at the top of the steps to give the audience their instructions. "Thank you all again for being here tonight. I am confident you will be courteous and respectful to both our speakers. The debate will last ninety minutes. Each man will speak for fifteen minutes at a time and then yield to the other speaker. The light on the front of the stage will turn yellow when thirty seconds are left on the clock for each session, and turn red when fifteen minutes has expired. We have no moderator or set agenda. Dr. Guest will begin."

Tony began calmly and quietly. "My friends, we are here tonight to discuss the most important questions for all of us—for all of mankind. Is there a God? Is there a purpose or reason for our lives? Is there life after death? Is the Bible true? Or—are we all just accidents of an evolutionary process with no purpose or hope for existence beyond this life? As rational beings, at least partially rational (Tony smiled a little and the audience chuckled nervously with him), it is untenable for us to believe we are accidents with no purpose.

"If reasonable people believe our brief physical lives are all we have, that our conscious existence will end when we die with no awareness we ever lived, that we will never again see any of the people we love in this life, and nothing we do or don't do in this life has any real eternal purpose—if human beings believe this is true, they will naturally be depressed, immoral, violent, and completely selfish. Why dedicate your life to one spouse? Why commit your life to raising children who have no purpose or existence beyond this life? Why help others? Why go to work every day except to get more for yourself? The fact is, unless people believe there is a god and have hope for an afterlife, this world would be in constant chaos.

"That's why human beings have always created their own gods. There has to be more than we have in this life, or life is not worth living. Since the beginning of recorded history, humans have created gods to fear, to worship, to obey and gods to protect them from their enemies. But mostly, humans have created gods to salve their fear of death. If there is no god, death is the absolute end of everything for everyone—forever. That is a frightful thought and it is why humans create gods and religions—that's why most of you here tonight believe in your God and practice your religion. And that is why I did the same thing.

"When I was a child, I believed in Santa Claus and the evidence seemed to prove he existed. My parents told me he was real and I saw all the presents he brought at Christmas.

Everything was decorated for his arrival and I actually saw Santa's helpers in department stores and ringing bells on street corners. As I got older, I began to suspect my parents were actually getting me those presents, and I calculated it was impossible for one man in a sleigh to deliver presents to billions of houses in one night. The fake beards on Santa's helpers cast further doubts on the case for Santa Claus.

"But I continued to believe in ole Santa for several more years because I wanted to believe. I needed to believe. I was afraid the presents would stop and I couldn't accept the most wonderful time of the year was based on a lie. And besides, how could the most celebrated person in the world and the most loved season of the year not be real? But there came a time in my life when the facts in my brain overcame the hope in my heart. I could no longer pretend Santa Claus existed because he didn't.

"My friends, I didn't come here tonight to insult or offend you, but to tell you the truth. You have a Santa Claus God. I had a Santa Claus God. My parents told me he was real. My church told me he was real. But as I got older, I began to see evidence indicating what I was told might not be true. Science has proved beyond any doubt this world and universe have been around for billions of years. The traditional biblical view says the earth was created in six days less than 10,000 years ago. How could that be true? And how could any god know each of us individually? How could a god communicate and care for billions of people at once, and count every hair on our heads? Do you believe the impossible!? I will talk more about biblical fantasies in my next session, but for now, let me be honest with you about myself.

"All the research I did to prove the existence of God was biased by the assumption there was a God. I looked for data to prove my point of view, to fill my need to prove there was a God. I ignored data that contradicted my beliefs. My whole ministry was based on my need to believe there was a God.

"I didn't like what I came to believe after the tragedy in my life. I never wanted to be a person who believed there was no hope beyond this life. I despaired at the thought I would never see my loved ones again. I was scared to die because I believed my conscious existence would end. That was a scary thought. But folks, we cannot continue to invent truth based on our emotional needs. We should not continue to give our children and grandchildren the false hope of a God who loves and protects them—if we can't defend that hope. We should not continue to teach children the scientific facts about life and creation in their schools, and then teach them contradictory biblical fantasies in church. If religion cannot be reconciled with what we know is true, our religion is a lie—it is false.

"As one of my mentors, Josh McDowell, once said, 'The heart cannot rejoice in what the mind does not accept.' Look around. Look all across America. Do you see Christians rejoicing? Rarely. Because the more people understand reality through science and technology, the more they question what they have been told about the Bible."

The yellow light flashed at the front of the stage, Tony paused, and smiled a little. "I hope I haven't scared you too much because there's a lot more to come."

Johnny smiled as he looked down at Patti sitting on the front row next to Dr. Clark. She rolled her eyes, smiled, and shook her head. He could see her walker hidden next to the stairs on the side of the stage. Johnny turned toward Tony. "Well, Dr. Guest, you did scare me, especially the part about there not being a Santa Claus." The audience laughed quietly enjoying the much-appreciated comic relief. Johnny's supporters were glad he had not lost his sense of humor and hoped he held his confidence.

"I'm glad you brought up our friend Josh McDowell. As you know, Josh was an atheist as a young man and set out to prove God did not exist and Jesus was a very confused psychopath. Josh looked for evidence to prove there is no God. His bias was against the existence of God. But all his finding came to the same conclusions you did when you first came to faith: there has to be a God and Jesus was the physical manifestation of God. Josh gave his life to Jesus and put all of his research into a book titled *Evidence that Demands a Verdict.* I am confident Dr. Guest knows this evidence well."

Johnny turned to the audience, "Dr. Guest has rightly questioned some of the traditional interpretations of the Bible. Science has contributed to the understanding of creation and the physical world and has actually done a lot to prove the Bible is a supernatural document. We should consider the truth of the Bible in light of scientific findings, but as we all know, science is far from infallible. I will address the evidence of biblical truth in my next session, but at this point in the debate, it is important for Dr. Guest and me to find some common ground based on scientific fact. Debating the accuracy of the Bible is a waste of time if there is no God. So, let's set aside our biases, our emotions, the Bible, and our religions for a few moments while we consider the scientific evidence of the existence of a Creator God.

"Science, through the understanding of atomic and molecular structures, and the technology to calculate the age of organic and inorganic material, has concluded the physical universe is temporal—that is, there was a time many years ago when the physical universe did not exist, and there will come a time in the future after many years of winding down, the physical world will cease to exist. We know the entire physical universe was somehow created out of non-physical substances—meta-physical matter as scientists call it, or spiritual material as some of us might call it.

"Science supports the premise physical matter and the physical universe were created suddenly billions of years ago. Scientists attempt to explain how this happened with theories such as a large explosion sometimes called the Big Bang. But the creation of physical mass and energy out of nothing violates the laws of physics.

"Okay, let's ignore the laws of physics for a moment and assume a massive explosion fueled by some unknown meta-physical substance created enough physical matter to fill an infinite universe with planets, stars, and galaxies. Did someone mention Santa Claus?"

Johnny turned to Tony with a friendly smile.

"Now if all of this physical matter were simple blobs of dirt without complex atomic structures, that would be one thing. But all of the physical matter throughout the universe is composed of trillions and trillions of atoms, each with their own internal energy supply fueling a complex orbital operation of protons, electrons, and neutrons. The splitting of just one of these atoms can set off a chain reaction capable of destroying an entire city. Where did all that energy come from and how could that much energy have been stored in a particle so small it can't be seen with a high-powered microscope?

How could an unplanned and unorganized explosion create an infinite supply of complex, well-organized atomic and molecular structures? How could all of this matter come together to form suns, planets, and moons with orbital formations held in motion for billions of years by the perfect balance of gravitational pull and centrifugal push? How could order spontaneously be created from disorder? Well, it wasn't! None of it could have happened accidently! It is physically and statistically impossible!

"Dr. Guest proved this conclusion beyond any shadow of a doubt in his first dissertation. He deftly presented all the potential variables, considered the statistical probably of the actions and reactions which had to occur in the chronological order necessary to result in the organized physical universe we have today. I can't pronounce the numerical figure he came up with to express the statistical probability of all this happening, but it had a point followed by about thirty zeroes and a one at the end. His conclusion and mine is the same. It is physically and statistically impossible for this physical world to have been created by accident. This conclusion has nothing to do with religion, the Bible, emotion, or bias. If there is such a thing as fact in this world, that is a fact.

"I said I wouldn't bring up the Bible until my next session, but after considering the science and statistics related to the origins of the physical universe, Hebrews 11:1 sounds more like common sense than religion, 'By faith we understand that the universe was formed at God's command, so that what is seen was not made out of what was visible.' This verse has much more scientific probability of being true than all the theories of accidental creation. But folks, consider this: the creation of all the incredibly complex inorganic matter in the universe is a simple feat compared to the creation of life.

"Some scientists tell us life originated when a one-cell organism was created from a chemical reaction caused by lightning or some energy source in a pool of primordial slime. It should be noted slim is organic material made up of multi-cell, algae-like plant life. The accidental first single-cell living creature could not have been born in a pool of living material, it had to be born in inorganic material. That is not possible. There is no life on earth—from single cell amoeba to human beings—able to exist without consuming protein from organic material. If a single cell amoeba was somehow created out of inorganic material—which is impossible based on all known biological science—it would have died quickly because there was nothing to eat. Life cannot continue by consuming inorganic material. But I'm spending too much time on small points."

Johnny paused and scanned the audience with a mischievous smile.

"Okay, let's assume for a moment an amoeba-like cell was somehow created out of inorganic material, was able to survive without food, figured out how to reproduce itself, and then after creating many other amoeba, came together over billions of years to begin the formation of an organism. I know I'm oversimplifying but this is essentially what the evolutionists would have us believe. And it gets even more unbelievable.

"The theories of evolution are wholly based on the assumption millions of positive mutations continuously created more complex life forms over billions of years—without any plan or guidance—eventually progressing from a single-cell organism into modern-day human beings. Yet the statistical probability of even one positive mutation is practically zero. The development of the human eyes alone, for example, with millions of carefully organized nerves, muscles, and tissues, would have required millions of carefully organized and chronologically ordered mutations. Anyone who believes this could have happened by accident, either doesn't have a brain or their brain hasn't fully evolved."

The audience responded with quiet chuckles. Johnny seemed calm and having fun.

"And there's more. How can we explain the millions of species of plants and animal life, all perfectly made to survive in many different environments around the world? I could go on and on, but the final nail in the coffin for those who argue we are all accidents of a random evolutionary process is this: for complex life such as human beings to have evolved from simple organisms, it would have required muscular, skeletal, nervous, and circulatory systems to evolve concurrently in perfect harmony. The human brain couldn't survive without a complete nervous system. The body could not survive without a complete heart. The heart could not survive without a complete circulatory system, and on and on. The statistical probability of one positive mutation is practically zero, yet some would have us believe millions of mutations occurred simultaneously to form each complex organ in the human body. And then they want us to believe all of our complex organs evolved in perfect harmony. My friends, science, biology, physics, statistics, and common sense tell us it is impossible for all matter and life to have been created by accident without design or guidance."

The yellow light flashed, Johnny paused, and turned to Dr. Guest.

"Dr. Guest, I'm sure you agree with me this universe and all life forms are incredibly complex and amazingly organized. If there are Santa Claus gods in this debate, they are the scientists who ask us to believe it all happened by accident.

"Reasonable people can disagree about the nature of God or whether the Bible was inspired by God. These are reasonable arguments. Dr. Guest and I—along with everyone who has ever lived—have good reasons to question God's motives and actions. But reasonable people must agree on this fact: an incredibly powerful and intelligent supernatural force created this physical universe and all the life in it. If Dr. Guest and I can agree on that point, we can have an informative debate about the Bible and God's reasons for creating this physical universe."

*For since the creation of the world God's invisible
qualities—his eternal power and divine nature—have been
clearly seen, being understood from what has been made, so
that people are without excuse.*—Romans 1:20

CHAPTER FOUR

LET THERE BE LIGHT

January 2018 – first debate continued
(Travelers Rest, SC)

Tony smiled as he began speaking, apparently entertained at how Johnny was trying to redirect the Santa Claus analogy.

"Let's get back to the real Santa Claus in this debate: the Bible. Friends, everything you believe about God, Jesus, and your hope for eternal life comes from the Bible. I'm aware of other scriptures such as the Koran, the Book of Mormon, and many ancient writings, but most credible religious sources are all based in part or whole on the Bible.

"Consider this important fact, Dr. Wright: the veracity and reliability of the Bible is dependent on the belief it is completely true—inerrant, or in other words perfect. This means, unless it is all true, it is not the Word of God. Unless it is all true, you don't know which parts aren't true. So, logically, if

49

we can prove any part of the Bible is untrue, it is not reliable to inform your beliefs about creation, about God—or about anything at all. It's just a book written by several dozen writers over several thousands of years.

"Let's start in the beginning. The first chapter of Genesis tells us God created the universe, all plant and animal life, and human beings in six days. And because the writers of the Bible provide the genealogy from Adam to Jesus, it is undeniable the traditional interpretation of the Bible concludes the earth is less than 10,000 years old.

"I know some of you believe God created the earth with the appearance of age and hid all those dinosaur bones underground just to fool us. But all science, archeological discoveries, and carbon dating prove beyond any shadow of a doubt this universe has been around for billions of years and life on earth originated many millions of years ago.

"On the first day, God created light. He also separated day and night on the first day. And on the third day He created all plant life. But He didn't create the sun until the fourth day. Folks, you can't have light or day and night without the sun. And no plant can live without the sun. This is pure fantasy. And then God created animals and humans and told them they could only eat plants. Do you honestly believe lions and tigers were grazing on grass?

"The Bible says God, who is a non-physical spirit, somehow used the dirt on the ground to create Adam. Dr. Wright just explained the incredible complexity of human beings and now he wants you to believe the first human being was completely formed in a few minutes out of dirt. Then God put Adam to sleep and removed one of his ribs from which he created Eve. Again, a complex human being created in a few minutes with a bone. I know you think God can do anything, but even if He could, why would He tell us He created human beings in such an unbelievable way?

"Well, perhaps you believe we can have light without the sun, day and night without the sun, and plants can grow without the sun, and humans can be created instantly from dirt by an invisible being, but tell me this, why should all of us be condemned because Adam ate some stupid, supposedly forbidden fruit? Do you really think a snake talked Eve into eating some fruit and then talked Adam into taking a bite? Why would God put Adam and Eve in a beautiful garden just to set them up for failure? And why would all of us have to take the blame? This is nonsense!

"And tell me this, after Cain was thrown out of the family for killing his brother Abel, how did he 'lay with his wife' and have a son? According to the Genesis narrative, at the time, Cain was the only person on earth except for Adam and Eve. Where did his "wife" come from? Some say he had a sister who was thrown out with him. So, he married his sister, who is not mentioned in the Bible, and you ask me to believe she—though innocent—was forced to leave her parents to be Cain's wife? And why would Cain build a city just for himself, his sister, and a son?

"And Genesis only gets less credible after Cain marries a non-existent sister and builds a city with no residents. God apparently decided to create a completely evil and violent human race. You may say it was Adam's fault but then you tell me God is all knowing and sovereign over everything that happens. If you believe in God, you must believe He created evil and allowed evil to reign on earth. But not to worry, God decided in advance after He let evil consume the whole world, He would destroy all the people with a Great Flood. Good planning, right?

"Here's where Bible fantasies get out of control. God finds one righteous man named Noah, even though the Bible tells us no one is righteous, and tells him to build a big boat to save his family and all the animals from the flood. The Bible tells us before the flood, it had never rained on earth. I don't know how all the plants and animals survived, but you have to remember we are talking about Bible fantasies. So, Noah and his sons built a large boat about the size of a football field. And somehow all the animals of the world knew when to board the ship. And somehow, all the varieties of animals in the world fit into this ship and survived for many months.

"And then it rained for the first time on earth and the flood covered the whole world. This means the flood would have been at least seven miles above sea level to cover Mt. Everest. Friends, there could not have been enough water in the sky to cover the whole earth with water seven miles deep. Not to worry. All this water dried up in a few months—we have no explanation where this much water could have gone. Noah and his sons and their wives got off the boat and started a new world. I don't know how Noah's three sons created all the different races of humanity on earth, but like I said, we are talking fiction—fantasy.

"Let's consider for a few minutes the fathers of the Jewish and Christian faiths, beginning with Abraham. God told Abraham to leave his home with his wife, Sarah, and his servants and head for an undisclosed location. Along the way, Abraham ran into some bad guys who had their eyes on Sarah. Abraham was afraid they would kill him, so he told them Sarah was his sister and gave her to them. A real profile in courage that Abraham. Fortunately, God intervened and scared off the bad guys. Well, Abe and Sarah couldn't have children, so Abe had kids with Sarah's maid, a real profile in morality and family function. Finally, when they were both over 100 years old, Abe and Sarah finally had a son named Isaac. Stay with me . . .

"Isaac had two sons named Jacob and Esau. They didn't get along. Jacob (his name means 'deceiver'), tricked his older brother Esau out of his rightful inheritance as the older son. God changed Jacob's name to Israel and he became the father—with several wives—of twelve sons who became the twelve tribes of Israel. Why do I tell you all of this? Because your religion is built on men who are cowards, deceivers, polygamists, murderers, and generally dysfunctional.

"And I know many of you believe, out of the lineage of these misfits, Jesus was born in a barn, born to a woman who had not had sex with her husband, lived for thirty years in obscurity, traveled no more than a hundred miles from his birthplace in Bethlehem, spent three years walking around with twelve mostly illiterate disciples, and then was crucified by the Romans for claiming he was God. Unfortunately for Jesus, being God put Him in competition with Caesar.

"I know why you believe all this because I did. The Bible, with all of its fantasies, is still the most credible of all religious texts. If you need to believe in God, the God of the Bible is where you should go. But it is still fantasy. There are some wise proverbs and Jesus's emphasis on love is wonderful, but there are too many fantasies in the Bible for anyone to believe it is the inerrant Word of God."

The audience was visibly relieved when the yellow light flashed. This session seemed to last forever. Tony concluded:

"I know from teaching many believers over the years, most of you have a fragile faith. Your knowledge of the Bible is shallow and it is uncomfortable for you to hear serious challenges to what you believe—because you can't defend what you believe. I'm not here to hurt you, I'm here to tell you the truth. Back to you, Dr. Wright."

Johnny surveyed the audience knowing many of them just received a severe blow to their faith. But Tony was right. Most Christians accept the Bible on faith and are not prepared to defend it as inerrant truth.

Johnny looked at Tony and began. "Dr. Guest is trying to distract us from the most important questions of this debate: is there a creator God or are we here by accident? Tonight, I have given you only a small glimpse of the mountains of scientific, physical, and statistical evidence proving the incredible order and complexity of life and physical matter. All of this did not happen by accident. Some of the most prominent and respected scientists in the world, such as Francis Collins who led the mapping of the intricate DNA structures of human genes, have forcefully stated the same conclusion. Let's build on this conclusion, even if Dr. Guest has not yet been willing to concede the obvious.

"There are many books that address Dr. Guest's criticisms of the Bible and biblical truth, and it would take hours for me to begin to respond to all of them. But I will use this short session to briefly respond to several of his criticisms and conclusions.

"First, contrary to Dr. Guest's theory, human beings naturally desire to be their own god, not create gods to serve. It is unnatural for human beings to submit to authority. It either must be forced through power or fear or persuaded by love or logic. People are naturally self-focused and tend to view themselves as the center of the universe. The 'original sin' of Adam was the desire to be like God and it is still the natural bent of all mankind.

"Human beings have always sought or created gods because there is a God-shaped void in every person. And the creation cries out there is a God, even to the most primitive and illiterate people. Romans 1:18–20 says, 'The wrath of God is being revealed from heaven against all the godlessness and wickedness of people, who suppress the truth by their wickedness, since what may be known about God is plain to them, because God has made it plain to them. For since the creation of the world God's invisible qualities—his eternal power and divine nature—have been clearly seen, being understood from what has been made, so that people are without excuse.'

"People don't need a Bible to know there is a God. Even before science proved this physical universe was too complex to have happened by accident, creation has always revealed the power and divine nature of God to every human being. Some people seek God and some run from God, but all creation knows—whether consciously or subconsciously—there is a God. There is no excuse for denying the existence of God.

"So, what about the Bible? Is this book how God has chosen to communicate and reveal Himself to mankind? Dr. Guest has concluded the Bible is fiction. Or more correctly, he has said the traditional interpretation of the Bible is fiction. He seems to be giving me an opening to suggest alternative interpretations?"

Johnny turned and smiled at Dr. Guest who very subtly returned the smile. There was a curious friendship between them, though they had not met before tonight.

"I have spent years studying science and the Bible attempting to reconcile apparent differences and searching for ways to align biblical and scientific truth. A God powerful and wise enough to create everything in this universe, could have easily created it in the blink of an eye or over billions of years. A God who lives in a timeless spiritual world, where a day is like a thousand years and a thousand years is like a day, is likely to define time and 'days' in different ways than we do. And we should all admit, when considering the mysteries of creation, our finite minds do not have the ability to understand the dynamic spiritual and physical complexities associated with the creation.

"As I look at the Bible through a scientific lens, please know I am not trying to develop a new theology, but only looking for possible explanations to the apparent contradictions between science and our traditional views of the Bible. I am not putting science at the same level as the Bible. Science has been proved wrong many times, but the Bible never has. I am only using science as one tool to assess the real meaning of Scripture.

"In all my studies, I have found nothing to suggest the Bible is not true, but I have found places where—without changing one word of Scripture—science can clarify what the words might mean. This is particularly true in Genesis where Dr. Guest has leveled his harshest criticisms. So, hold on to your seats as I speed through Genesis and attempt to address some of these criticisms.

"For decades, we have heard carbon dating and archeological discoveries have proved our earth and universe are billions of years old. Well, as it turns out, carbon dating has proved to be highly inconsistent. Items thought to be billions of years old have turned out to be thousands of years old. Skeletal fragments that were used to 'prove' evolution, have shown little genetic developmental consistency. In some cases, this so-called evidence has done more to disprove evolution and prove the necessity of creation. We have been told it takes millions of years for oil and diamonds to form, yet now we know it can happen in hundreds of years.

"My friends, there are myriad reasons to question both science and the Bible. We should question everything. Many scientific 'facts' have proved to be wrong—I just mentioned the inconsistencies of carbon dating. Science cannot prove or disprove what a powerful spiritual God could or couldn't do.

"Traditional biblical teachings say the earth and all life was created in six days and the earth is less than ten thousand years old. But the prevailing scientific view is the earth and all forms of life developed accidently and randomly over millions of years. Can these opposite points of view be reconciled? I think they can if we are willing to consider some non-traditional views of the Bible and science.

"I believe it is highly possible, in fact likely, the word 'days' in the first chapter of Genesis refers to long periods of time. And before the first 'day,' verses 1 and 2 tell us God began by creating a formless physical mass and infinite space in a dark universe. The Bible doesn't say whether this happened in an instant or over billions of years, but given what we know today, this situation probably existed a long time before God said, 'Let there be light' on the first 'day.'

"I believe the Big Bang occurred when God said, 'Let there be light.' Massive amounts of energy from the spiritual or meta-physical world exploded into the physical world as light. This was the explosion that sent matter flying throughout the universe. Millions, perhaps billions, of years passed before suns, planets, moons, and galaxies were formed. Then, if you assume the six days were six periods of time, Genesis 1 is perfectly consistent with scientific theories about creation. Day 1, God created light and separated the light from the darkness: day and night. Science tells us our sun is much younger than other suns, so it is reasonable to assume our sun was still cold and dark when the earth was first formed. The light on the earth in 'Day 1' was likely from residual fluorescent-type light emanating from particles highly charged by the energy released from the Big Bang. Scientists have found some of this residual fluorescent light still exists in the universe. And fluorescent light will grow plants.

"'Day 2' is a description of what happened as the earth cooled, again, perfectly consistent with science. Massive amounts of water vapor circled the earth. Cooling surface temperatures caused the water vapor closest to the earth to condense and fall to the ground, filling large underground caverns, while the water vapor higher in the atmosphere continued to circle. The condensation and clearing of water vapor in the lower atmosphere created a sky covered by a canopy of water miles above the surface. This resulted in a greenhouse effect with warm and humid conditions throughout the earth. On 'Day 3' vegetation appeared, thriving from the warm, humid conditions. Science concedes plant-life on earth seemed to appear suddenly, covering large sections. I can promise you amoeba didn't crawl out of slime and suddenly cover the earth with beautiful plants.

"'Day 4' is the period of time when our sun ignited and began providing more direct light and warmth. 'Day 5' is the period of time when fish and birds began to inhabit the earth, and this is exactly what science says happened. Then on 'Day 6' the animals and early humans were created. Again, this is consistent with science. I'm sure you noticed I said early humans, because it appears possible to me—even likely—the account of male and female humans being created in the first chapter of Genesis is a different account than the creation of Adam and Eve in chapter 2. We don't have time for me to provide all the evidence of why this is likely, but we have several obvious hints I'll share briefly.

"The account of the creation of Adam and Eve came after the seventh day when God rested from the work of creation. By the way, 'rest' in this context probably means He ceased creating rather than regaining strength. The whole account of the seven days of creation was given in chapter 1 and the first three verses of chapter 2. Then verse 4 of chapter 2 says, 'This is the account of the heavens and the earth when they were created, when God made the earth and the heavens.' The traditional interpretation of this verse assumes it is introducing the story of Adam and Eve as a more detailed review of the creation of humans covered in chapter 1. But I believe it is a concluding statement of all that was written before it. This seems possible because the next verse, verse 5, begins with 'Now,' suggesting we are about to be told something new.

"Verse 5 says, 'Now no shrub had yet appeared on the earth and no plant had yet sprung up.' This is a curious statement since plant life was created before humans in chapter 1. But the rest of the verse may explain the apparent contradiction, 'for . . . there was no one to work the ground . . .' Early humans were scavengers and did not cultivate the soil. Plants bearing all kinds of food were everywhere, so there was no need to plant crops.

"Adam and Eve may have been created millions of years after the creation of early humans. This theory is consistent with scientific findings that early humans were nomadic scavengers who lived off plants, fruits, nuts, and seeds. They did not eat meat or cultivate crops—'work the ground'—as we read in verse 5. Adam and Eve were the first modern humans. After the Fall, they ate meat and cultivated the soil which is evidenced by Abel bringing God a sacrifice of meat, and Cain an offering of produce from working the ground.

"Early humans may have been on earth for millions of years, but Adam and Eve were likely created less than 10,000 years ago as the genealogies in the Bible suggest. This is consistent with some scientific theories that say modern humans appeared relatively recently. Cain's unknown wife can also be explained with scientific findings suggesting modern humans bred with early humans. It is certainly possible Cain joined a nomadic tribe of early humans, took a wife, built a city, and taught his new friends how to grow crops.

"I can almost smell the fire outside where I will be burned for heresy tonight. But before you carry me out to burn me at the stake, remember I am only exploring how science and the Bible might be reconciled. God gave us science to help us discover the magnificence of His physical creation and He gave us the Bible to reveal Himself, the spiritual world, and His plan for eternity.

"Before I run out of time, I'll try to briefly address Dr. Guest's questions about the flood and the fathers of our faith. There is plenty of physical evidence of a quantum reshaping of the earth's topography about ten thousand years ago. And you can't fly over the earth's surface, particularly the western United States, without seeing mountains and valleys obviously shaped by erosion from a massive runoff of water. It's almost comical to stand at the edge of the Grand Canyon and have a tour guide tell you this incredible mile-wide ditch was formed over millions of years by the little river at the bottom. It is much easier to imagine how large amounts of water from a worldwide flood eroded the loose soil as it rushed to the sea.

"Here's how I think it happened. Remember, both science and the Bible agree large amounts of water fell to the earth as the planet cooled. As the molten rock and soil below the surface cooled, it constricted, creating an irregular, 'Swiss cheese' subterranean environment. The falling water filled the large caverns beneath the surface, creating large underground lakes, springs, and rivers. Many of these still exist today and a worldwide system of underground fresh-water springs also continue. There were no large oceans at the time, and most of the water on earth was beneath the surface. This condition existed for millions of years until further cooling on the earth and the atmosphere caused the remaining water vapors above the 'sky' to condense and fall to earth as rain.

"This deluge of water was the Great Flood. The heavy rains, lasting for forty days, collapsed the earth's surface and the 'springs from the deep' were released. The collapsing dirt and rock filled the underground caverns and forced oceans of water to the surface. As large parts of the surface collapsed under the weight, it left large mountains that are actually remnants of the earth's original surface. The flood didn't need to be seven miles deep to cover Mt. Everest; the top of Everest may have been ground level before the flood. The oceans and seas we have today are located where large sections of the earth's surface collapsed and the flood waters collected. Oh, and by the way, Dr. Guest's own research proved definitively that a pair of every species of animal life on earth could easily fit on a large floating barn with the specifications provided in the Bible."

The yellow light flashed and Johnny turned to Tony.

"Dr. Guest, may I have just a few extra minutes to address the misfits you mentioned in the Bible."

Tony was now smiling regularly at Johnny and the audience, obviously entertained by the direction of the discussion.

"Be my guest." Tony shook his head as if he was allowing Johnny to dig his own grave.

"Thank you, Dr. Guest. I'll be brief." Turning to the audience, Johnny waved his arm toward Tony. "Dr. Guest has given an accurate and, perhaps, overly generous description of the fathers of our faith. They were sinners, sometimes cowards, and even worse. But that's the whole idea. God shows His strength through our weaknesses. God became a man to save people who are sinners, not those who think they are righteous. If people wanted to create a religion, they would have not written the Bible. Even King David, the man after God's own heart, was an adulterer and a murderer. No cover-up there.

"Jesus's motley disciples were mostly illiterate. There was nothing glamorous about God's people. The dozens of people who wrote the different parts of the Bible over thousands of years wrote down what they saw and what God told them to write down. And remarkably, it is all the same story about God reclaiming His people; not making bad people good, not making life easy, but saving us from ourselves, and from evil.

"The prophecies in the Old Testament have all been accurate. They predicted where Jesus would be born and how He would die. They predicted cities would be destroyed and they were. And archeologists today are still using the Bible to locate lost cities. The statistical probability of biblical prophecies coming true as predicted is practically zero. The Bible never says the earth is flat or the sun rotates around it, all commonly held beliefs during the times the Bible was written. Other religious books have all been changed because of inaccuracies, but not the Bible. I could go on for hours, but you get the picture. The Bible could not have been written without the guidance and inspiration of God. I thank Dr. Guest for the extra time and yield to him."

CHAPTER FIVE

TONY'S DARE TO JOHNNY

January 2018 – first debate continued
(Travelers Rest, SC)

Tony reached into his coat pocket and pulled out a neatly folded but obviously well-worn piece of paper. He flattened it out on the podium, cleared his throat, grabbed the sides of the podium, and lifted his gaze to the audience. His countenance was very serious. He stared at the audience long enough to make everyone uncomfortable.

"Thank you, Dr. Wright. You make some interesting points. I will concede this world could not have been created by accidental origination and random evolution." Tony paused to give the audience a moment to contemplate what he said. The world's most famous atheist just admitted there is a God.

"Call me a deist like Thomas Jefferson who accepted the existence of a god but didn't accept the Bible as truth. He cut and pasted the verses from the Bible he agreed with and created his own Scriptures. I don't think Jefferson believed in the God of the Bible.

"My experience has made it hard for me to believe there is a wise and loving God who cares about us and has a plan for our lives—unless it is a plan to humiliate and torture us. Let's be honest with each other. Everyone in this room tonight, everyone watching this debate, will all be dead and gone in a few years. In fact, practically all of the seven billion people and just about every animal on the planet will be dead and gone in fewer than a hundred years.

"We will all live our lives, work hard, and do the best we can to get by. Some of us will die in accidents, some of us will get sick and die, some will starve, some will be killed in war, some will be killed by earthquakes or hurricanes, some will be murdered by criminals, millions will be aborted before they are born, millions more will die at birth or as small children, and a few lucky ones will just get old and die in their sleep.

"All of us will struggle and suffer in many ways, physically and emotionally. And then, once we're all gone, there will be seven billion more people to take our place, to live, to work, to suffer, and to die. What could possibly be the reason for this continuous cycle of life, suffering, pain, and death? What could possibly be God's motive for creating this mess? And make no mistake about it, this world IS a sorry mess!

"As Christians, you say God created humans to praise Him and enjoy Him forever. Are you kidding me? You have a God who is so arrogant and egotistical He created billions of pitiful subjects to praise Him."

Tony, mockingly lifted both hands and bowed several times to the audience and turned and bowed to Johnny.

"In the Old Testament, God sent a reluctant Moses to save His people. God brought terrible plagues and killed many of the Egyptians, including every living firstborn son. He killed thousands of innocent children! Then Moses led His people out of Egypt, parted the Red Sea, and God left His people in the desert for forty years. Except for a few, all of them died in the desert—perhaps millions of them! Even

Moses wasn't allowed to enter the Promised Land because of some technical violation against God. And God calls that 'saving His people.'

"God ordered His people, the Jews, to kill whole groups of other people who inhabited the land where He led them: women, children, and even all of the animals. And then He eventually allowed Israel to be destroyed and the remnant of His people to be exiled. God promised to save His people, yet He punished and destroyed them."

"But then, you tell me, everything changed when Jesus was born. God came to earth as a nice guy. He made a bunch of good wine! That's a plus. He healed the sick and was nice to the bad guys. He didn't like the religious people. He said He was God but the people turned against Him. They beat Him up, stripped Him, and nailed Him to a cross. Somehow this act is supposed to save us from all the bad stuff Adam and the Devil make us do. How is the 'shedding of the blood of Jesus' supposed to save us? A lot of people shed blood and die. Folks, you can dress all this up with stained glass windows, candles, incense, and flowery language, but it is nothing but fantasy.

"I searched through the Bible for answers after everything I loved in this world was—in cruel and brutal fashion—taken from me. I went to the book of Job because God put him through the grinder, too. The book of Job convinced me I didn't want anything to do with the God of the Bible.

"Right there in the first chapter of Job, Satan has an audience with God along with the angels. I thought God had nothing to do with evil, but here He is chumming it up with the Devil! God even starts the conversation with some niceties: 'What have you been up to, good buddy?' Satan responds he has been roaming around the earth. That's comforting to know. Then God starts to egg him on. 'How about my servant Job? He is blameless and upright, a man who fears God and shuns evil.'

"God knew how Satan would respond to His challenge. Satan says, 'Does Job fear God for nothing. Have you not put a hedge around him and his household and everything he has?

You have blessed the work of his hands, so that his flocks and herds are spread throughout the land.' And then Satan issues a dare to God, 'But now stretch out your hand and strike everything he has, and he will surely curse you to your face.' *Satan's dare*! Satan dared God to destroy Job and how did God respond?

"'Very well, then, everything he has is in your power, but on the man himself do not lay a finger.' What!!! God said 'Very well.' Satan dared God to strike Job down and God said, 'Very well.' Job loved God and obeyed Him, and God turned him over to Satan. What do you think about that? Well, you should think about it real hard because the book of Job is not just a story about how God treats one man. It is THE story about how God treats you, me, and the whole human race. Job is the story of human existence.

"Satan dares God by saying if God allows us to suffer, we will stop praising Him and, instead, curse Him. God is betting you will still praise Him even if He lets Satan humiliate you, lets Satan take everything you've worked for, destroys your health, and kills the ones you love. God is betting you will still praise Him even if He lets Satan destroy you. This is arrogance! This is cruelty!

"Well, God lost His bet when He let Satan kill my wife and daughter."

Tony's voice was starting to crack and tears began to run down his face.

"If you believe the Bible, you must believe God said to Satan, 'What do you think about My servant Tony. He has given his life to serving Me and has built a global ministry, inspiring millions to praise Me.' Satan dared God to kill my wonderful wife and daughter just to see if I would still praise God. And God said, 'Very well, very well, very well, very well, very well . . .'

Tony's voice faded and tears were dripping off his face. His hands were shaking and he gripped the podium tightly trying to steady himself. He turned to Johnny and, through his tears, he spoke haltingly with a breaking voice.

"What about my servant Johnny. He loves the Lord and loves young people. He is leading many young people to Lord. So, very well, let's have people lie about him, destroy his reputation, and ruin his ministry. Let's have a drunk kid crash into his wife's car, cripple her, and kill their unborn daughter. Let's see if he will praise Me after that."

It was painful to hear Tony speak, and even more painful to watch him suffer. His words were heart-wrenching, but he wasn't trying to be mean. He was addressing the "elephant" in the room and it was cathartic for the audience to hear Tony pour out what was on many minds and hearts.

Johnny looked down at Patti. She was trying to smile through her tears. She put her hands on her face as Dr. Clark reached around her shoulder and gave her an encouraging squeeze. Johnny felt tears rush to his face and his throat tightened. The audience sat in hushed silence. Many were crying. Then turning to the audience and trying to stand more erect, Tony spoke as he lifted both hands.

"What about all of you? How do you like living your life knowing God and Satan are cooking up some plan to take your spouse, your children or grandchildren, cause you to lose your job or reputation, take your son or daughter in Afghanistan or surprise you with cancer? Don't say God's not involved, because you believe He is sovereign over all things. What about the millions of children in third-world countries who die of starvation and dysentery every year? Is God testing their mothers to see if they will still praise Him? What could possibly be God's motive for allowing all this suffering and death?"

Mercifully, the yellow light flashed and the audience seemed to collectively inhale. But Tony wasn't finished. He looked at Johnny and lifted a finger indicating he needed a few more minutes. Johnny nodded and bit his lip trying to show a little empathy and compassion. Tony was venting at God, and it was obvious, though he was broken and frustrated, Tony was no atheist. Tony wasn't here to debate Johnny. He was here debating God.

Johnny's podium was close enough to Tony's for him to see the piece of paper Tony took from his pocket. Tony continued to press his hand across the paper trying to get it to lay flat. These were not notes for the debate, and Tony hadn't looked at the paper while speaking. But when he bowed his head to collect his thoughts or cry, he stared at the note and put his hand over it as if he was trying to hold its contents. Johnny couldn't read what it said, but he could see it was a short note with big printed letters—letters written by a child.

"I have mentioned 'God's motive' several times tonight because it is important for you to consider why your God has created this physical world and allowed such incredible suffering and death for all who pass through. Lawyers and judges know when they find the motive, they usually find the truth. If you believe the Bible, God says He wants all His children to spend eternity with Him in heaven. And if you believe the Bible, some of us are God's children and some of us are Satan's children. And we might not know which side we're on until the great harvest of the earth.

"If God wanted His children to be with Him in heaven, why didn't He just put them there? Some say this life is a test, but the Bible says there is nothing we can do in this life to earn our salvation. Even your faith is given to you, so you can't be rewarded for believing in God or Jesus. In fact, it's clear to me from the Bible all this was decided before any of us were born. I know this is a Baptist school and the subject of predestination is controversial, but there are many verses in the Bible like Ephesians 1:4–5, 'For he chose us in him before the creation of the world to be holy and blameless in his sight. In love, he predestined us for adoption to sonship through Jesus Christ in accordance with his pleasure and will.'

"Again, I ask you: if we were God's children before the creation of the world, what could possibly be God's motive for putting us all through this hell of earth. We all have some wonderful moments in this life and I've had my share. But folks, the majority of life for most people on earth is struggle, hardship, suffering, and death. No one gets out of here alive and dying is rarely painless.

"I apologize for my loss of composure tonight and I'm hopeful I have not been unfair or unkind. Let me leave you with one thought. If you choose to continue to believe in God and to believe in the truth of the Bible, I encourage you to know what you believe. Make sure what is true in your mind, is consistent with what you believe in your heart. Thank you for your kind attention and courtesy."

Tony turned to Johnny with a slight smile and swung his arm around his waist as if to wave Johnny into a room. Johnny acknowledged the gesture with a smile and a slight bow in Tony's direction. Their bond of friendship, though created from a distance through tragic circumstances, made this debate of high emotions and sharply differing opinions a civil and almost comfortable discussion. Strangely, the two didn't seem to disagree.

"Thank you, Dr. Guest. I am grateful we can agree there is a God—there has to be. Whether the Bible is true or fantasy is another issue.

"You have left us with far more questions than I can answer in the remaining five or ten minutes. For the record, Thomas Jefferson was a devout theist, believing in a benevolent creator God to whom humans owed praise. He once wrote 'The god who gave us life, gave us liberty at the same time.' That quote is carved into the Jefferson Memorial.

"Jefferson believed our freedoms come from God. But he did not accept anything without questions. I hope believers and seekers will take the advice Jefferson gave his nephew in 1787, 'Question with boldness even the existence of a god; because, if there be one, he must more approve the homage of reason, than that of blindfolded fear.'

"Dr. Guest, we've both gone overtime and the lady with the sign down front is telling me to wrap it up. I can assure you I share many of your questions about God. In fact, I'm still angry about a lot of things and fully intend to confront God with a lot of questions when I get the chance. I imagine, however, like Job, my part of that discussion will be very short.

"God will answer, 'Who are you to question Me? Where were you when I created the universe? Where were you when I wove every part of you together in your mother's womb? Where were you when I decided to bring Patti into your life? Where were you when I held out my hand to keep that drunk from killing her? Where were you when I began to heal her body? Where were you when I spoke through her to tell you to get off your rear end and get back to work? Where were you when I loved you through Patti? Where were you when I had Dr. Clark call to give you back your ministry?'"

There was not a dry eye in the auditorium. Sounds of weeping could be heard all around the room. Patti was now sobbing. Tony was bent over his podium with tears dripping on his crinkled note. The lady holding the sign telling Johnny to wrap it up, dropped the sign on the floor, and sat down.

"God is not like us, though we all hope to become more like Him. We know from His creation, He is a God of order and fixed laws—the law of gravity, the laws of physics, and the fixed program of life in DNA structures. God is not arbitrary. He holds Himself to the fixed laws of His character. This explains many of the questions expressed by Dr. Guest tonight.

"Think about just one example. God is sovereign over gravity, but He doesn't change the law of gravity if one of His children jumps off a cliff. Jesus wasn't even willing to defy gravity when Satan tempted Him to jump from the top of the temple. God doesn't change the law of gravity to save someone He loves. God might send someone to keep us from jumping or provide something to break the fall, but my point is this; there is always tension between God's sovereignty and His character. God did not even change His character to save His own Son from the cross.

"It sounds strange to say God is 'required' to do anything, but the Bible reveals His unchanging character can be described by a framework of four requirements or laws.

"First, the law of love: this compels God to love His children unconditionally. As Romans 8:39 says, 'Neither height nor depth, nor anything else in all creation, will be able to separate us from the love of God that is in Christ Jesus our Lord.' In other words, there is nothing we or anyone can do to stop God from loving us. It is as fixed to His character as the law of gravity is fixed in the physical world.

"Second, the law of freedom: this requires God to allow His children perfect freedom to obey or disobey, to love or reject Him. As Galatians 5:1 says, 'It is for freedom that Christ has set us free.' God must allow us free will and this is why Adam and the human race had to have the knowledge of good and evil. God didn't want us to have it, but His character and ultimate plan required us to have it.

"Third, the law of justice: this requires God to judge and punish all acts that separate us from Him. The law of love says nothing can separate us from God, so He cannot allow us to be separate. But God doesn't do the punishing. Our separation from God is our punishment. Like a branch separated from the tree, we die spiritually when separated from God. As it says in the first chapter of Romans, 'For although they knew God, they neither glorified him as God nor gave thanks to him . . . therefore God gave them over in the sinful desires of their hearts . . .'

"Satan is always accusing us and appealing to God's justice. God has to allow him to compete for our hearts and souls because we live in Satan's world. Satan, who is heartless and unjust, ironically demands justice from God. There is a continuous spiritual and physical war in this world. We know God is sovereign over all things, but we also know from experience God allows Satan to cause pain, suffering, and death all over the world. I don't know why, but I think God's character constrains Him.

"God doesn't make deals with Satan, but Satan has challenged God—has dared God—to allow His people to suffer. Dr. Guest referenced the first chapter of Job where Satan challenges God. And this challenge may explain why we all have to go through this physical world. Satan says if Job—and I think all God's people—are allowed to know good and evil and if we are allowed to suffer, we will not worship God, we will curse Him to His face. This is Satan's demand for God's justice. This is *Satan's dare* to God.

"God must allow people the freedom to go our own way. When we do, we step out of God's world and into Satan's. When we are separated from God, Satan owns us. Satan is the prince of the physical world. The problem for the human race is God's character requires Him to give everyone the freedom to choose good or evil. And all of us, in our own way, choose evil during our physical lives. God doesn't give us over to Satan. Our physical natures are sinful and we choose to go over to Satan. That's why God has to say, 'very well' when Satan demands to test us."

The red light on the edge of the stage was blinking annoyingly, but this was too good to stop. Dr. Clark pulled a stocking cap out of his coat draped over the back of his chair, stepped up to the front of the stage, and covered the light. The crowd laughed and clapped. Dr. Clark held up his hand and put his finger on his lips to hush the crowd as he took his seat. Johnny continued.

"Fourth, and this is the good news, the law of mercy: this is God's requirement of Himself to buy us back from Satan. If we are God's children, we belong to Him, and we will always be His because He loves us unconditionally. It is God's love that compels Him to give us the freedom to leave Him; we all chose to go our own way, and the law of justice requires we live with the consequences of being separated from Him. This means we live in Satan's kingdom and we are slaves to Satan. Unfortunately, only the blood of Jesus and the death of our physical bodies can permanently free us from Satan's hold. Romans 6:23 says, 'the wages of sin is death, but the gift of God is eternal life in Christ Jesus our Lord.'

"When the physical bodies of God's children die, we are freed from sin and Satan's power. But we don't have to wait until we die to be free because Jesus—God in the flesh—fulfilled the laws of love, freedom, justice, and mercy when He paid the wages of sin Himself. He suffers with us and died for us. This means we are free at any time in our lives to choose to accept Jesus's death as a substitute payment for our sins and to be free of Satan's control. As long as we are in our human bodies, we will not be free from temptation or the influence of sin. But the shedding of Jesus's blood paid the price for our sin and His resurrection reestablished God's ownership of His people. When we accept Jesus's sacrifice, we walk out of Satan's kingdom and back into God's."

Looking out to the audience, Johnny continued. "If you'll indulge me for a moment, to strip this down a bit, we have no more ability to understand all creation than your beloved dog has to understand quantum mechanics. Speaking of which, for all their intellect and research, the smartest folks on the planet can't even explain how light can be both wave and particle. What could possibly make us think we can judge the Creator's character and actions?

"Dr. Guest asked about God's motive for creating the physical world and all the suffering that comes with it. I don't pretend to understand it all, but I will continue to seek answers and deeper intimacy with the Father. I know this; God loves us, He wants us to be free, He will deliver perfect justice, and He will have mercy on those who seek Him."

Tony was growing impatient. He folded the note and put it back in his pocket. Then he threw up his hands and interrupted.

"Woah, Dr. Wright! We've gone way overtime and you've gone way outside the bounds of good Baptists and Presbyterian theology. I can smell the fire outside waiting for you, too! I have to admit to being very intrigued by your creative interpretation of the Bible and I wish we had a whole weekend to hear all your biblical and scientific references. But even though we are out of time, I want to issue a challenge to you before we leave. No, let's call it a dare. Consider this *Satan's dare* from me to you.

"You say you will continue to seek answers. Well, do the research. Write it down. Write it all down. Take the next year to research and document all your theories. Prove to me and everyone watching, the Bible can be reconciled with science. And give all of us a clear and understandable explanation of God's motives for life, for suffering, and for death. Publish your findings and send me a copy by next November. Then we will meet again for another debate at the same time and place next January."

Johnny smiled at Tony and turned to the audience.

"Very well, Dr. Guest. I accept your dare, and we will all look forward to seeing you again next January."

The crowd stood up, clapped, and cheered. Johnny turned to Tony and reached out his hand for a post-debate handshake. Tony walked past Johnny's outreached hand and gave him a big bear hug, practically lifting him off the ground. No one but Johnny heard Tony whisper, "Thank you, thank you, thank you!"

*"The thief comes only to steal and kill and destroy;
I have come that they may have life, and have it
to the full."*—John 10:10

CHAPTER SIX

BAD NEWS, GOOD NEWS

January 2018
(Travelers Rest, SC)

"Wake up, sleepy head." Patti kissed Johnny on the forehead as she put a hot cup of coffee on his bedside table.

"Hey, it's Saturday!" Johnny moaned. "What's with this peppy early bird stuff?" Johnny sat up and saw the coffee. "You're too sweet. I don't deserve you. Did I forget my birthday?" Johnny sat up and took a long sip of Patti's fresh ground and brewed coffee.

Patti sat on the bed next to Johnny nursing her own cup of coffee with two hands. "I thought it went well last night. I was really proud of you."

Johnny felt good about the debate, too. All the VIPs who attended the post-debate reception were effusive with their praise, although not without some teasing about his "new theology." And most importantly, Dr. Clark seemed very pleased. But Johnny could tell Patti was concerned.

"Okay, what's worrying you?" Johnny reached for Patti's hand.

"You're not going to like the news coverage. Please don't read the paper or look at the online stories today. It's all a bunch of bunk and I don't want it to ruin your day," she said knowing full well he would have to look.

"Let me have it." Johnny reached for the newspaper folded in Patti's robe pocket.

The headline on the front page of the *Greenville News* read, *"Disgraced pastor humiliated at debate."* Johnny's trials left him with considerably thickened skin, but the headline and picture for this story took his breath away. The picture caught him with his head down as if he were humiliated. The story covered all the gory details of the sexual harassment charges and Johnny's firing from the church. There was very little about the actual content of the debate. There was nothing about the most prominent atheist in the world admitting there had to be a God!

Johnny naively believed the humiliation and shaming he endured in Boone was behind him. This story tore open all the old wounds and brought back the shame and embarrassment he felt when he saw the first headline about his ouster in the *High Country News*.

Patti looked at the floor with tears in her eyes. "I told you not to look."

Patti's suffering shook Johnny out of his own pity party. This was as hard on her as it was on him. "God is good, Patti. Let's don't let the bad guys get us down. Is it too cold for a bike ride?" Johnny changed the subject and faked a smile, but his head was about to explode. His heart fell back into the abyss of despair he knew all too well after Patti's accident. But now it was Johnny's turn to be strong.

Patti discovered in the last few weeks she could ride a bike without any pain. She started on a stationary bike at the campus gym and, last weekend, she and Johnny took a short ride on their road bikes around the campus. Johnny had not seen Patti as happy since her accident.

Patti stood up. "I'll look at the weather report and you stay away from your iPad. And—I'll get you a refill." Patti grabbed the newspaper out of his hand, picked up his cup, and walked out of the room slowly—with only a slight limp. Johnny teared up as he thought about her long road back.

The temperature was still in the forties, so they decided to ride the stationary bikes at the campus gym and then drive up to Hendersonville, North Carolina, for lunch at their favorite café. It didn't have a real name. It was just called The Café. They hoped no one at The Café read the *Greenville News*.

Johnny was embarrassed and didn't want to see anyone on campus, but he was relieved when he did. Everyone they saw at the gym congratulated him for "defending the faith" and scoffed at the "stupid media." It was good to be reminded people don't automatically believe what they read in the newspaper or online.

The drive from Travelers Rest, South Carolina, to Hendersonville, North Carolina, took less than an hour. It was a beautiful drive on a crystal-clear winter's day with gorgeous mountain views and inspiring vistas of the valleys below. The Café in downtown Hendersonville was a little home built on Main Street almost a hundred years before. Several older couples sat huddled at little tables on the covered front porch sipping coffee. Hendersonville is a thriving retirement community, and seniors were out in force today enjoying the cool mountain air.

Johnny parked in the back and walked around the car to open the door for Patti. "I'm a little stiff from the bike workout. Probably shouldn't sit so long right after I exercise. Give me a pull." Johnny reached for Patti's wrists and she locked in by grabbing his wrists. She had taught him how to secure an unbreakable grip. He pulled her up and she threw her arms around his neck. "Do you want your walker?" Johnny teased. "Not on your life!" Patti fired back.

They both ordered their usual. Patti had an organic avo-cado, spinach, and kale salad. She insisted it was really good, but Johnny wasn't buying it. He ordered a toasted Reuben sandwich with a side of sweet potato fries. Except for the coin-operated box on the front porch selling the *Greenville News*, they had a wonderful time together.

They finished lunch, got a to-go bag for Patti's carrot cake dessert, and walked around the shops on Main Street for about an hour before Patti's legs gave out. She rested on a bench in front of a general store while Johnny got the car. Patti took a nap for most of the drive home and Johnny tried to think through his response to the dare he received the night before from Tony. A lot of research and writing was necessary, but he was looking forward to it. He wanted to finish his research and write about God's motives for a long time. His students could help with much of the research, and his classroom debates would flush out all the questions and possible answers for the final document. Perhaps it could be edited into a good book.

The more he tried to think about what he wanted to do in the future, the more distracted he became by the past. Dr. Clark warned him this would happen. He insisted Johnny tell his side of the story about the debacle at Blue Ridge Baptist Church. "You need to write it down and dump it out of your brain," Dr. Clark told him his first day at work. "You will relive what happened in Boone every day for the rest of your life until you organize your thoughts and tell your story."

Johnny promised Dr. Clark he would publish his story, but it had to wait for a less busy time in his life. Besides, he believed the old adage, 'you shouldn't spend too much time defending yourself because your friends don't need to hear it and your enemies won't believe it.' He began to think the whole ordeal might eventually fade from his memory. That was of course more hope than lucid thought. The morning news reminded him there would always be people who wouldn't let him forget.

Patti wanted to cook lasagna for dinner so they stopped by a local Fresh Market on their way home to pick up the necessary ingredients. When they got home, Patti headed for the kitchen and Johnny went to his study to write a Facebook post. He already knew his title and rehearsed in his mind what he wanted to write while driving home.

When Satan Steals Your Dreams

"The thief comes only to steal and kill and destroy; I have come that they may have life, and have it to the full."—John 10:10

A few years ago, I was living my dream in Boone, North Carolina: dream wife, dream home, and dream job. Actually, it was well beyond my wildest dreams. I married my dream girl while in seminary and then moved back to my hometown to become the youth pastor of the church where I grew up and to work part-time in my family's business. My wife and I lived in a beautiful log home surrounded by a river and majestic trees. Our home was perfect for holding cookouts and Bible studies for high school and college students. Within a year, our youth group grew to over 400 students. The Lord was clearly using our ministry to change lives and bring young people into His kingdom.

Then suddenly, without notice, a thief broke into my life and stole my joy, my peace, my ministry, and my reputation. One of the deacons in my church told the pastor and deacon board he saw me sexually abusing one of the girls in my youth group. The anonymous deacon also reported there were other girls who made the same claims. The claims were false and my wife knows they were false because she was always with me at our youth group meetings. There was never a time when anything inappropriate could have occurred without her knowing it. She and I worked together to ensure I was never alone with a female student.

Yet without any opportunity to defend myself, I lost my job, my home, my reputation, and all my dreams of a career as a pastor. The next year my wife was crippled in a terrible automobile accident and our unborn baby daughter was killed. It seemed God had forsaken us. But God never forsakes His people. He gave me another opportunity to minister to young people at Palmetto Christian University, and now my wife and I are once again living our dream. We have life to the full.

So why do I write this defense? A recent headline about me in a local newspaper reminded me of an old Mark Twain adage, "a lie will travel around the world two times before the truth gets on its pants." Well, a lie about me has been circling around for far too long and I have decided to put on my big boy pants and let the truth be heard. So, there you have it! Johnny Wright

Johnny hit "post" and closed his laptop hoping he was also closing a painful chapter of his life. It was not a scholarly theological defense in a prestigious religious journal. It was just a simple Facebook post, but it was done. Dr. Clark was right; it felt good to organize his thoughts and dump that poison out of his mind and into a digital cloud. He didn't care if anyone read it.

Johnny walked into the kitchen and put on the stained apron he used to cook hamburgers for his youth group in Boone. He sat down on a stool at the island in the center of the kitchen and began chopping onions and green peppers. Patti spread wide pasta strips all around the counter and was putting layers in a big pan with lots of beef, tomato sauce, cheese, and chopped vegetables between them. She was humming "Amazing Grace" and smiling like a happy kid. It had been a good day, despite the bad news for breakfast.

Johnny started a fire in the fireplace in their little den while Patti put the lasagna in the oven and loaded some sliced zucchini into a steamer. Their tradition on Saturday night was to eat dinner on trays in front of the fire and watch an old movie or television show on Netflix or Amazon. Lately they had been watching reruns of *Downton Abbey*. They enjoyed the series more the second time around because they knew what was going to happen. No emotional surprises.

Johnny and Patti watched one episode while the lasagna was cooking and another while eating. For dessert, they split the square of carrot cake from The Café in Hendersonville. Completely exhausted from the weekend, they were "lights out" before 10:00 p.m.

Sundays were Johnny's favorite time at Palmetto Christian. About two dozen professors and their spouses met for church in a little historic chapel moved to the campus from a site about ten miles away when the area was developed for a golf course. Each week, the professors took turns bringing the sermon and a Bible lesson. They called their church the C. S. Lewis Pub Church, much to the chagrin of some of the more rigid faculty who never attended. The only thing missing was Lewis's pints of ale. The goal of the Pub Church was to challenge each other with provocative perspectives from Scripture and then discuss and debate everyone's response.

Johnny was in his element when biblical scholars began to question, argue, and debate God's words, His motives, and His plan. Every service began with a prayer asking God to "show up" and give everyone His knowledge, understanding, wisdom, and love. There was always an appeal for mutual respect and civility when different opinions were expressed. The discussions were lively, sometimes heated, but always concluded with joy and laughter. There was never a dull moment and it was impossible to doze off in these services.

Johnny arranged for his graduate advanced-level Bible students to—at their option—"audit" these non-traditional church services. He didn't want to discourage their attendance at more traditional nearby churches, but he did want them to have the opportunity to hear the incredibly deep, interesting, and challenging discussions between some of the top biblical scholars in the world. Most of his advanced students intended to be pastors or to teach in schools and universities. Johnny believed they should be prepared to defend their faith. All of them came, except when they had an invitation from a potential girlfriend or boyfriend to "take them to church." College students know how to keep their priorities in proper order.

On this particular Sunday, Johnny's close friend and office mate, Dr. Alan Bunster, decided to roast Johnny and to broach the taboo subject of his past. No one on campus had been willing to openly question or discuss the accusations recounted in Saturday's newspaper. To the amazement of everyone, Alan began his "sermon" with the story about Johnny from the *Greenville News*. The women were shocked, but some of the men seemed relieved that Alan was willing to address the "elephant in the room."

"We're here today with a convicted sexual pervert. I'm sure you all saw the headline, 'Disgraced pastor humiliated in debate.' We all know the *Greenville News* is about as close to the Word of God as we will see in this life. So, we must take this story seriously."

The Pub services were provocative at times, but this "sermon" had everyone on the edge of their chairs. Johnny just had to smile and shake his head because he suspected his friend was getting ready to embarrass him, defend him, and try to clear his name. Alan was sixty-three years old and had been through just about every trial and painful experience life could throw at him. Challenges that would have discouraged, defeated, even destroyed most men, only succeeded in giving Alan a wonderful and frightening sense of humor. Johnny bit his lip, squeezed Patti's hand, and prepared himself for the deluge.

"Johnny Wright is the pervert exposed by the *Greenville News*. A worthless sinner in our midst. A predator on our youth. But wait, his only accuser is anonymous. In fact, no one accused him, even anonymously, of doing anything to them. An anonymous person said he saw Johnny do something to someone else and also heard from someone else that Johnny did something to others. But there were no complaints from any offended parties.

"We expect these kinds of accusations and this kind of gossip to go on all the time in politics, Hollywood, and the media, but when a brother or sister in Christ is destroyed by the leaders of a church, all of us should take notice.

"In Matthew 18:15–17, Jesus tells us how to deal with a fellow believer we think has sinned:

> *'If your brother or sister sins, go and point out their fault, just between the two of you. If they listen to you, you have won them over. But if they will not listen, take one or two others along, so that "every matter may be established by the testimony of two or three witnesses." If they still refuse to listen, tell it to the church; and if they refuse to listen even to the church, treat them as you would a pagan or a tax collector.'*

"Jesus describes a process that begins with a one-on-one conversation. This allows accused persons to explain, deny, or defend themselves. If the matter can be settled between two people, no public accusations will be made and no one's reputation destroyed. If the accused is not cooperative, then the concerned party can expand the circle of friends in hopes of resolving the issue before he takes it to the leaders of the church. All of this should be done humbly in the spirit of Christian love with the intent to restore a fellow believer to the fellowship. As Paul writes in Galatians 6:1–2,

> *Brothers and sisters, if someone is caught in a sin, you who live by the Spirit should restore that person gently. But watch yourselves, or you also may be tempted. Carry each other's burdens, and in this way you will fulfill the law of Christ.*

"It is certainly a serious matter if a pastor in a church is accused of molesting a young girl. All charges should be taken seriously. This can be done without embarrassing or subjecting the young girl to potential embarrassment or retribution. But Johnny's church didn't verify any of the complaints and he never had the opportunity to hear any details about the charges against him. Why is this important to us here this morning? People are falsely accused of terrible things all the time.

"The issue is important to us not only because it hurt and discredited a friend and brother in Christ, it is important because it hurt and discredited the body of Jesus, crucified Him again, and humiliated Him in front of the whole world. In the book of John, chapters 14 through 17, Jesus is speaking to and praying for all who seek to follow Him—all of His disciples then and now. He sums up all of God's commands into one: love each other. This is how we bear fruit and demonstrate our love for Jesus. In chapter 15 verses 8 through 12, Jesus says:

> *'This is to my Father's glory, that you bear much fruit, showing yourselves to be my disciples. As the Father has loved me, so have I loved you. Now remain in my love. If you keep my commands, you will remain in my love, just as I have kept my Father's commands and remain in his love. I have told you this so that my joy may be in you and that your joy may be complete. My command is this: Love each other as I have loved you.'*

"The love we show for each other as believers is our strongest and most credible testimony to the world that we love Jesus. This is how we reach others for Christ. In John 17:20–23, Jesus sums it up:

> *'My prayer is not for them alone. I pray also for those who will believe in me through their message, that all of them may be one, Father, just as you are in me and I am in you. May they also be in us so that the world may believe that you have sent me. I have given them the glory that you gave me, that they may be one as we are one—I in them and you in me—so that they may be brought to complete unity. Then*

the world will know that you sent me and have loved them
even as you have loved me.'

"Jesus's ministry depends completely on the world knowing God sent Him to save sinners. He tells us our love for each other, our obedience to Him, and our unity will prove to the world Jesus is from God. In fact, we are told in 1 John 3:14–15, just as we are in many other places in the New Testament, our love for each other as believers is the evidence of our salvation. And hating a brother or sister in Christ is confirmation we are lost.

We know that we have passed from death to life, because we
love each other. Anyone who does not love remains in death.
Anyone who hates a brother or sister is a murderer, and you
know that no murderer has eternal life residing in him.

"How do we reconcile what leaders in the body of Christ did to Johnny? I think it's fair to say Johnny was publicly hated by fellow believers, perhaps even murdered. He wasn't disciplined or admonished. How do we reconcile when we dislike fellow believers here on campus because of some imagined indiscretion? I will pause here and confess my own guilt in this matter. My point is this: we live to bear fruit for the kingdom. Our love for each other is how we bear fruit and show the world we love Jesus. So, public conflict and discord between believers is quite a serious matter to God. When we file lawsuits against believers, when we won't forgive fellow believers, when we are publicly critical of believers, when we are unfair or unkind to our brothers and sisters in Christ; we destroy our testimony and hurt the body of Christ.

"I must say Johnny handled his situation better than I would have. He didn't lash out at his accusers or try to discredit the church. Certainly, like Job, I'm sure he lodged his complaints to God. If he's human, he felt sorry for himself and for Patti. But he left vengeance to the Lord. And he may just live to see God's vengeance.

"Yesterday, Johnny finally did what Dr. Clark asked him to do when he came to Palmetto Christian last fall. Dr. Clark insisted Johnny write down his side of the story and publish it. Not to accuse anyone or denigrate his former church, just to resolve the issue in his own mind. Well, I'm not sure you can call a Facebook post 'publishing,' but that's what Johnny did yesterday."

Johnny felt a sharp elbow in his ribs from Patti, "You didn't tell me you put our story on Facebook!"

Alan continued, "I know some of you are so old you don't know what Facebook is . . ."

That brought a few boos and jeers from the Pub parishioners, all with smiles and laughter because Alan was one of the oldest ones there.

"Johnny has over 4,500 friends on Facebook, and after less than one day, he has almost 1,000 likes for his 'publication' about the events in Boone. I encourage all of you to read the comments. They are from young people who were in Johnny's youth groups in St. Louis, his youth groups in Boone, and his students here at Palmetto Christian. You usually have to go to a funeral to read so many good things said about anyone. It blessed my soul to read dozens of accounts of how Johnny and Patti changed so many lives by living out the love of Jesus."

Johnny had not opened his laptop since he posted his story, so all of this was news to him. And Patti kept whispering, "I can't believe you didn't tell me."

Alan walked around the pulpit and stood in the aisle between the rows of pews. "This is my simple message this morning. Johnny and Patti didn't just tell people about Jesus. Their love for each other and their love for everyone around them convinced people Jesus is real; Jesus is from God; His love is real. People believed God sent Jesus to save them and to love them because they saw Johnny and Patti love in His name.

"As James reminds us in chapter 1 verse 2, 'Consider it pure joy, my brothers and sisters, whenever you face trials of many kinds, because you know that the testing of your faith produces perseverance.' Pain and trials strengthen our faith. Our joy in the midst of suffering verifies our faith and purifies our love.

"But wait. What if these young people instead saw Johnny and Patti hate others—in the form of unforgiveness or resentment, gossip or harsh words, or retribution toward those who did them wrong? It would have destroyed their ministry. All the accusations against them could not destroy their ministry because people know real love when they see it. But one whiff of hate can wipe out a lot of good sermons.

"I need to wrap it up and let the rest of you speak your minds, but before I do, I mentioned that Johnny might live to see God's vengeance against those who did him wrong." Alan's face sparkled with a big smile, "Not that any of us would wish ill on anyone. The last comment I read on Johnny's Facebook post said, 'I know who lied about you and I'm going to set the record straight'"

Alan turned and spoke softly to Johnny and Patti, "It sounds like God has agreed to hear your case. Just sit back, relax, and watch Him work." Alan turned and walked back to the pulpit. "Now let's talk. You can speak from your seat or come to pulpit. Johnny, I guess I should give you the first shot if you want it?"

Johnny looked at Patti, but she shrugged her shoulders and mouthed, "I don't know?"

Johnny stood, stepped into the center aisle, and walked to the pulpit. Alan gave him a big bear hug and took a seat on the front pew.

Johnny held his head down for a few seconds, took a deep breath, and then looked up with half a smile. "I've heard a lot of sermons that seemed directed at me, but the pastors have always shown me the courtesy of not mentioning me by name." The room erupted with some much-needed laughter.

"Alan, I am grateful for your willingness to address a hard and very personal subject. You have shown great courage and love by talking about something that is surely on everyone's mind but very awkward to bring up. I must admit that despite all the love and acceptance shown to Patti and me here at Palmetto Christian, I often feel I am walking around with a scarlet letter on my old, wrinkled navy blazer. And amazingly, you were even able to turn our situation into a pretty good lesson.

"Patti will tell you there was a long period of time when I didn't count it all joy. It seemed as if God abandoned me—abandoned us—and I was very angry at Him. I didn't go to church or read my Bible for almost a year. I didn't want anything to do with God. Nothing could have convinced me He loved me—nothing except for one thing. Love. Not God's love, at least not directly, because I didn't want His love. But I could not escape Patti's love. She was hurt much more than me. She had to suffer the same emotional pain and public shame as I did, plus she endured unthinkable physical pain and suffering. And she had to deal with my long pity party when I couldn't stop feeling sorry for myself.

"She kept loving me. She was like a bright, warm light I couldn't turn off. I couldn't escape it. Even when she was flat on her back. Even when we lost our little girl and were told we could never have children. Even when they told her she would never walk again. Even when all our hopes and dreams seemed to be lost. She glowed with love like the sun unceasingly projects heat.

"I didn't know it at the time, but Patti was being Jesus for me. She was loving me for Jesus. She was showing me the love of God even when I didn't want the love of God. As I listened to Alan's lesson today, I realized the only way we can really feel the love of God in this life is through the love of other people. Our capacity to love comes from God and, as I learned the hard way, our ability to accept love also comes from God. Alan is right, our love for each other, demonstrated through words and deeds, is the only way people will know God is real and He loves them.

"It sounds simple until someone hurts you or takes something important from you. It sounds easy until God's blessings disappear and, like Job, God lets Satan run roughshod over your life. This doesn't seem right or fair. It doesn't feel like something a good God would do. But I know God is just and I think I know why He must allow suffering.

"Part of the answer can be seen through what Patti and I have been through, and what many of you have been through in equally painful ways. When Patti and I met and got married, love was easy and natural. We had it all. We were young, healthy, and beautiful." Lots of laughs and shaking heads. "Well, at least one of us was beautiful. Everything was possible. Then suddenly, everything seemed impossible. How could Patti love a known pervert with no future? How could I love someone who would be confined to a wheelchair?

"But we loved more. We loved deeper. Our pain allowed God to love us more through each other. And our love and empathy for others deepened. We were more approachable because we were vulnerable. Our love became more real to others and our ministry became more powerful. We would never choose such a path, but God can make all things work for good for those who love Him.

"Satan was trying to destroy us and turn us from God. He did break our hearts, discourage us, and crush our spirits. But God can fill an empty vessel. He can't fill a vessel that's already full with the things of this world. It's ironic that Satan actually prepared us to be renewed and filled by God."

Johnny pulled a pocket Bible out of his coat and quickly found the verse he wanted.

"Psalm 51:17 describes what God wants from us:

> *My sacrifice, O God, is a broken spirit;*
> *a broken and contrite heart you, God, will not despise.*

"The same idea is in Isaiah 57:15:

> *For this is what the high and exalted One says—*
> *he who lives forever, whose name is holy:*
> *'I live in a high and holy place,*
> *but also with the one who is contrite and lowly in spirit,*
> *to revive the spirit of the lowly*
> *and to revive the heart of the contrite.'*

"I don't believe God harms His children to break us. I believe many of us are hurt by Satan and the evil he causes in this world. But if we allow God to heal our brokenness and fill our emptiness, He can make us whole again and more importantly, He can make us His.

"Alan, today you have reminded us that nothing we do at this university has any value unless all of us who minister here love each other deeply. I'm reminded of Paul's 'clanging symbols metaphor.' Not all of us are loveable, but God's command that we love each other remains. And perhaps, the more unlovable we are, the greater the impact when someone loves us anyway. That's why loving our enemies is such a powerful witness.

"As you all know, Tony Guest has challenged me to document my theories about why I believe there is a God and why He allows suffering. The subject of love will certainly be a part of my studies. I look forward to keeping you all abreast of my progress. In the meantime, pray that Tony will know God's love through the body of Jesus. Thank you all for your love and support."

Everyone stood and clapped as Johnny returned to his seat. Several people stepped out from their seats, shook his hand, and hugged him as he walked down the center aisle. Patti was smiling through her tears and gave him a big kiss before they grabbed each other's hands and sat down. Patti never cried for herself, even during her long and painful ordeal after the car crash. But she often cried when something good or bad happened to Johnny.

Alan returned to the pulpit and motioned for everyone to sit. "Unless there is someone else who would like to pontificate about today's brilliant sermon, we have already waxed eloquent for too long. There is a lot of fresh coffee in the back, and the church lady—sorry Mary—has prepared some delicious pastries. We can continue the discussion with mugs in hand." Mary is Alan's long-suffering wife. She long ago learned to ignore his friendly jabs.

While the small contingent of believers were enjoying fresh brewed coffee and conversation in the little chapel in Travelers Rest, South Carolina, across the mountain in Boone, North Carolina, trouble was brewing for the pastors and deacons at Blue Ridge Baptist Church. Johnny's post on Facebook was read by Suzie Robertson, the daughter of Deacon Richard Robertson. Suzie knew immediately her dad was the one who lied about Johnny. And it was her comment on Facebook promising "to set the record straight."

My goal is that they may be encouraged in heart and united in love, so that they may have the full riches of complete understanding, in order that they may know the mystery of God, namely, Christ, in whom are hidden all the treasures of wisdom and knowledge.—Colossians 2:2–3

CHAPTER SEVEN

NEW START

January 2018
(Travelers Rest, SC)

Did God create the physical world as a way to escape Satan's rebellion in heaven? Are we all spiritual creatures with temporary physical bodies on a journey to a new world? How do we get to that new world? Is the unique spiritual and physical blood of Jesus the only ticket to eternity? How can we know if we have eternal life? How do we know what is really true?

There were always more questions than answers, but Johnny jumped out of bed on Monday morning believing he was on the cusp of discovering and documenting truths never before considered by scientists and biblical scholars.

Monday was the start of a new life for Patti and Johnny. Friday night's debate put Johnny in the national spotlight, for better or worse. Tony Guest's dare during the debate—broadcast around the world—established the agenda for Johnny's work over the next year and likely for the rest of his life. The encouraging comments from friends responding to Johnny's post on Facebook confirmed God's call for Patti's and Johnny's ministry together. Sunday's church service was cathartic for their souls and vindication for their hearts in front of their best friends and smartest students. And Patti's rediscovery of cycling took her recovery and athletic hopes for the future to a whole new level. For the first time in a long time, life felt sweet.

Patti and Johnny were up at six as usual on Monday morning. They drove to work together in their ten-year-old, four-wheel drive Subaru wagon—the perfect car for all the snow in Boone. They had yet to see any snow in Travelers Rest. Their brick, ranch-style home was in an older neighborhood about two miles from campus; a good distance for riding bikes to work in the spring.

Their offices on campus were in the same building. Patti, now the Director of Student Affairs, had a large private office in the executive suit with Dr. Clark. Johnny shared an office down the hall with Dr. Alan Bunster. When Johnny arrived at his desk, he found a book titled *New Earth Theories* with a barely legible sticky note from Alan, "It all happened in six real days!" Alan, in his always goodhearted style, was ready to challenge Johnny's theory that the "days" of creation in Genesis were long periods of time. And Johnny welcomed the challenge.

Alan taught classes all morning on Mondays, so Johnny had the office to himself for a few hours before lunch. His classes were all on Tuesdays and Thursdays this semester, which would give him three days each week for research and meetings with students. Today he needed to finish the syllabus for his advanced Bible studies class beginning tomorrow. His students would do much of the research for the document Johnny tentatively titled "*Satan's Dare*." Johnny knew they would need a lot of guidance, and the class syllabus was the instrument he would use to keep everyone on task.

He pulled out several files full of bits and pieces of his notes written over the last few months. He shuffled through the notes, spread them across a credenza under the window, and typed on his computer until about 11:30. He printed two copies, took the short trip down the hall for another cup of coffee, put his feet on his desk, and leaned back in his rolling swivel chair to proof his work of art.

Johnny put a sticky note on one copy of the syllabus and wrote, "Alan, I would appreciate your input." He dropped it on Alan's desk. Then he took Alan's sticky note from the book he left and wrote across the bottom, "We'll see!" He stuck it on the back of Alan's chair. There was no one Johnny respected more than Alan when it came to research, scholarship, and knowing the Bible.

Johnny grabbed his gym bag and headed out to meet Patti at the gym and for a quick lunch. Patti's rehabilitation exercise regimen resulted in Johnny developing a workout routine for the first time in his life. He lost almost twenty pounds and his old pleated khaki pants were so baggy Patti teased him about how sloppy he looked. Johnny promised for months to let Patti take him shopping, but he kept putting it off. He hated buying clothes and he still had a half dozen pairs of jeans from college that still fit. He could get away with wearing jeans and his navy sport coat, which had also seen better days.

Class Act

Tuesday couldn't come soon enough for Johnny. He anticipated and planned for this class since he first arrived at Palmetto Christian. Last Friday's debate provided a clearer focus and a heightened sense of urgency for their studies. Johnny personally selected six of the best Bible students on campus— all seniors—to participate in this graduate-level research and discussion class. He arranged for the class to meet in the fourth-floor conference room of the development office to provide a more professional setting than the standard classrooms.

The conference room was decorated and furnished for meetings with wealthy donors to the university. A large round mahogany conference table with leather swivel chairs filled most of the room. It sat eight people comfortably. The walls to the right and left as you entered the room were covered with custom bookshelves stocked with a wide array of books on faith, religion, and the Bible. The far wall on the exterior of the building was a floor-to-ceiling, wall-to-wall window with a panoramic view of the Blue Ridge Mountains—the best view from any building on campus.

Johnny wanted these students to feel special, but more importantly, he wanted them to know his expectations were very high. The class would meet Tuesdays and Thursdays from 10:00 a.m. until 11:50 a.m. Johnny arrived at 9:00 before the first class carrying a cooler full of water and soft drinks and a large bag full of donuts and sandwiches. One of the book cases had a built-in kitchenette with a mini-fridge, a microwave, a coffee machine with an automatic coffee bean grinder, and a little sink. He put the sandwiches in the fridge, the donuts on the counter, and made fresh coffee. He hoped the students would stay for lunch and informal discussions after class.

Most of the students knew each other, at least casually, but Johnny put table tent cards at every seat printed with each student's name—all with Mr. or Ms. in front of their names. He opened a cabinet in the bottom of the bookcase on the opposite wall and dragged out a heavy box full of books and notebooks he received Monday.

He spread the books along a narrow counter above the cabinets. The books were a sampling of some of the best scientific and biblical references Johnny could find at the campus library. He then put a notebook in front of every seat. The cover of each notebook had a student's name printed on the front above the title "*Satan's Dare* Research Project." The syllabus for the class was inserted in the inside pocket of the cover.

Johnny took a rolled-up neck tie out of his coat pocket and found a small mirror next to the door to tie it and make sure it was straight. He was determined his students knew he was serious. Johnny Wright wearing a tie would definitely get their attention.

The students began arriving at 9:40 and all of them were in their seats with drinks and donuts by 9:50. Neatly dressed students arriving early to class was a very positive sign for Johnny. And they were all duly impressed with their classroom. Johnny sat at the table sipping his coffee, smiling, and enjoying hearing "this is amazing" over and over again. College didn't get any better than this.

At 10 o'clock Johnny called the class to order, "Good morning and welcome to the most important class you will ever take." He paused and looked around the table before continuing, "Over the next four months we will be considering and researching some of the most important questions for mankind: How did we get here? Why are we here? Is there a God? Is there a devil? Is there a heaven? Is there a hell? Is the Bible true? Is Jesus really God and why does it matter? Does science disprove God and the Bible? Why does a good God allow suffering and death? Is there life after death? What are the criteria for eternal life and entering heaven?

"These are just a few of the questions we will ask and answer. We are not here to parrot the traditional talking points of Christianity or of any particular denomination. We are here to question everything we know—or think we know—and to find answers. We hope to find certainty wherever it is possible. Hebrews tells us, 'Faith is being sure of what we hope for and certain of what we cannot see.' Faith is certainty, but where we can't find certainty, we will at least identify the possibilities supported by the Bible and credible science.

"I will introduce some of my own theories and hypotheses in a few minutes—we talked about a lot of these ideas at our meetings last fall—but first I'd like for each of you to introduce yourself and tell us a little about yourselves. Most of you know each other, but I doubt if you really know what each other believes or the deep dark questions lurking in your hearts."

Johnny smiled and hesitated a few seconds just to be sure everyone knew he was only prodding them. Everyone seemed to be
comfortable and smiling so far.

"Let's start with Lydia on my right. Just tell us your full
name, where you're from, your denomination, briefly how you
came to follow Jesus, and a few observations or questions from
the debate last Friday. Nothing real long, but don't hold back.
Be honest. You can't offend me. Lydia—"

Lydia Johnson, Tennessee

"Thank you, Dr. Wright. Thank you for including me in this
class and for this awesome classroom. I'm Lydia Johnson from
Johnson City, Tennessee—near your hometown Dr. Wright.
I like to say Johnson City was named after me. My father is the
pastor of an African Methodists Episcopal Church. I grew up
in the church and always considered myself a Christian, but
never made a personal decision to follow Jesus until I got
involved with a Young Life group in high school.

"I consider myself a fundamentalist when it comes to the
traditional interpretation of the Bible, but must admit my time
at Palmetto Christian has caused me to question many things—
not my faith, which has grown stronger and more real, but
questions like you and Dr. Guest discussed at the debate. The
most disturbing question for me from the debate relates to
God's motives and the verses in Job where God had a discussion with Satan. I was crying the whole time Dr. Guest talked
about what happened to him, you, and others. And I was thinking about things that happened in my life, too. I hope this class
will give me some answers."

Lydia was tearing up but smiling as she motioned for
Johnny to move on to the student beside her. "Thank you,
Lydia. I'm sure all of us have some deep hurts we want to ask
God about. That's why we're here. Okay, Henry, you're next.

Henry Harrison, North Carolina

"Thank you, Dr. Wright. I'm Henry Harrison from Greens-
boro, North Carolina. My family is Southern Baptist, but I'll

be honest. I didn't want to come to Palmetto Christian and I'm not sure I'm a real Christian. I'm surprised I was allowed in this class. I was not a good boy in high school and my parents gave me the choice of working in the family machining business while going to tech school at night, attending Bob Jones University, or coming to Palmetto. This was the least worse choice."

Everyone enjoyed a laugh with Henry. He was popular on campus even though he sometimes mercilessly mocked others for believing traditional Bible teaching. He was genuine and honest, a straight-A student, and laughed more at himself than others.

"But I have challenged myself to know the Bible better than anyone here and to decide for myself what is true. I have been pleasantly surprised by how many professors have encouraged me to ask my crazy questions and challenged me to find answers. And the other students have been remarkably patient with me. I loved the debate Friday night. Dr. Guest asked many of my questions. Dr. Wright, your responses were good, but they didn't go far enough and I've never heard some of the ideas you mentioned. I'm hoping this class will continue the debate and help me find answers."

Henry was certainly an enigma. He had unusually deep knowledge and discernment of the Scriptures for someone who did not profess a personal faith in Jesus. But Johnny believed Henry's brutal honesty and tireless persistence would be beneficial to the class. "Julie, you're up."

Julie Black, California

"Thank you, Dr. Wright. You make a good cup of coffee. I'm Julie Black from San Diego, California. I grew up in an independent Bible church and wanted to leave the Left Coast for college. Not many of my friends are Christians and I didn't want to end up with them at Berkley or Stanford. I'm also a conservative and a political junky, so I didn't fit in well in California.

"I have been reading Christian apologetics since middle school and books like Josh McDowell's *Evidence That Demands a Verdict* had a big impact on me. I have also studied many of the books related to intelligent design and scientific evidence of biblical truth. I'm not sure when I became a Christian. I just found the more I studied the Bible and searched for answers, the more real my relationship with Jesus became.

"The debate was amazing! Dr. Guest tore my heart out, so I was very sympathetic to his arguments. And, Dr. Wright, some of your ideas piqued my curiosity, so I'm excited to find out more."

Julie was a serious student and she was also an ardent political activist. She was president of the William Buckley Society on campus and a perennial volunteer for conservative candidates representing the upstate of South Carolina. Unlike California, conservatives usually won in South Carolina. She interned in a congressional office in DC the summer after her junior year and hoped to return as a full-time staffer after graduation.

Johnny jumped out of his seat and headed for the coffee machine. "Anyone who wants a refill, help yourself. Matt, you're up."

Matt Hobson, Pennsylvania

"Hey, I'm Matt Hobson from Erie, Pennsylvania. I was raised in the Catholic Church, but when I was fifteen, my mother took me, my younger brother and sister to a Methodist church after she and my dad were divorced. She also took us out of the Catholic school and sent us to a public school near our home. We usually went to church, but there were never any discussions about God in our home.

"A few friends from my Catholic school days got me involved with a 'gifts' ministry back at the Catholic Church when I was in the 10th grade. It was a charismatic and evangelical movement in the church supported by the youth pastor and scorned by the senior priest. There was some weird stuff like speaking in tongues, but it got me reading the Bible for the first time in my life. And we had some great discussions about having a personal relationship with Jesus.

"When I was in the 11th grade, I fell in love with a girl who wouldn't go out with me until I 'prayed to receive Christ'—her words. I went with her to a Presbyterian church a few times—it was one of those PCA conservative-type Presbyterian churches—and, dog-gone-it if I didn't pray to receive Jesus. I still don't know if I was moved by the Spirit or the girl, but it worked. God was faithful. He opened my eyes and ears to the gospel and I've been trying to follow Jesus ever since. I've had a few hits and misses, if you know what I mean, but Jesus has changed my life. Oh, and I'm still following the girl, too. You all know Maggie. That's how I ended up here at Palmetto. My dad thinks I'm nuts.

"The debate was incredible. I still can't believe Christians are actually willing to ask questions and entertain critics who threaten traditional orthodoxy. It was almost scary to hear Dr. Guest destroy his former beliefs, but it was evident he believed in God. He is really angry with God and doesn't know what to do with his anger except to try to discredit God. Sorry, I've gone too long."

Matt was usually quiet and shy, so everyone enjoyed hearing him open up. He and his girlfriend, Maggie, were like an old married couple. He did whatever she told him to do, and one of the things she told him was to wait until marriage to have sex. They openly shared their commitment of celibacy with other students and always had extra copies of Josh McDowell's *Why Wait?* to share with anyone who was interested. But Matt was his own man when it came to the knowing what he believed. He was a serious student of the Bible and science and though he was usually quiet, he was always ready to defend his faith like a bulldog.

"Thanks, Matt. Rachel, let's keep it moving."

Rachel Levin, New York

"Thank you, Dr. Wright. I'm Rachel Levin from Long Island, New York, and I'm Jewish. My parents were non-practicing Jews and they divorced when I was ten. My dad married a wonderful Christian lady who treated me and my brother as her own children. We prayed together and I became very interested in her Jesus. She taught me all about the history of Jews and all their laws and traditions. Instead of trying to turn me against my Jewish heritage, she helped me embrace it by showing me the Jews were chosen to bring the Word of God to the world and the Savior for all mankind.

"My stepmother brought the Old Testament to life for me and helped me see Jesus on every page. I prayed to receive Jesus when I was fourteen at a Jews for Jesus rally I attended with several of my Christian friends. I've been studying the Scriptures ever since and I'm very interested in many of the ideas and questions that came out of the debate. I'm anxious to research some of Dr. Wright's hypotheses about Genesis, Job, and Revelation. That's enough from me."

"Thank you, Rachel. I want to meet your stepmother!" Johnny was taking notes with every introduction. He was a master at knowing his students. "Okay, Ed, you're our cleanup batter."

Ed Hart, South Carolina

"Hey, I'm Ed Hart from Greenville. Unlike the rest of you, I'm a good Southern Baptist. Raised in the church, walked the aisle at a Billy Graham crusade, baptized by getting dunked under water like you're supposed to, and now at a Southern Baptist college. I want to know who let the rest of you guys in this Baptist school?"

Ed was the class clown, but he was also a serious student. He was a by-the-book traditional Baptist, but he was also the first to question anyone who presented "biblical rules" that weren't really in the Bible. He knew his Bible and was always quick to separate traditions from biblical truth. Ed was well known for his trademark question, "Where do you find that in the Bible?"

"The debate was fun. I wanted to jump up and answer some of Dr. Guest's questions or should I say, accusations. Dr. Wright you did a good job, but with a little work, I think we can do a lot better the second time around. Science has done so much to open different possibilities about creation theories and what God is actually doing here on earth. I can't wait to get started with our research."

HYPOTHETICALLY SPEAKING

"Thanks everyone. Before I give my opening monologue—you might call it a filibuster when I'm finished—let's take five minutes to refresh our drinks and grab another donut. Bathrooms are down the hall. And, by the way, if any of you want to stay after class for more discussion, I've got some sandwiches in the fridge. It's optional, so if you need to be somewhere else, you can take off at noon."

All six students immediately began talking to the person beside them. Their brief introductions piqued their interest in each other and it seemed everyone had a follow-up question about something they had in common. This was the personal chemistry Johnny loved to create in his classes and youth groups. It was especially important in this small class. One bad relationship could ruin the class. Fortunately, this class was off to a good start. Johnny gave them a few minutes to talk and refill their drinks.

"I hate to break up the conversations, but we need to get this class underway. Please sit, open your notebooks, and pull out the syllabus. This is our work order. We don't need to follow the chronology, but the outline is a logical sequence of questions and theories. I'd like for each of you to consider which areas you would like to work on first and send me an email tomorrow. If you have interests not listed in the syllabus, let me know what you'd like to add. We will work in teams of two most of the time, but this doesn't mean you won't be doing a lot of work on your own. I will rotate team members every few weeks so you will all have an opportunity to learn from each other.

"Since we will be using the Bible as one of our primary resources, we must prove it is a credible source and, maybe even a supernatural document. The statistical probability that all the prophesies in Bible actually happened as predicted is near zero, yet they happened as written. This suggests the Bible is very different from any other book ever written.

"The Bible proves itself to be true by predicting historical events hundreds of years before they happened. We need to research and document the prophecies in the Old Testament and when the predicted events actually happened. The Bible is a compilation of books written by dozens of different authors over thousands of years, yet its message is consistent as if it was written by the same person. I believe it was written by the same person—God—but we need to prove that hypothesis beyond a reasonable doubt.

"We also need to dig into the origins and credibility of science. Very few people know the Bible was one of the main catalysts for the Age of Reason and many of the advances of science. Before Christ, the pagan religions of the world had many gods who the people believed arbitrarily ruled the world and controlled the destinies of mankind. There was no presumption of design, order, or spiritual and physical laws, except with the Jews. Without a belief in fixed laws, there can be no systematic discovery of scientific truth or development of political and economic freedom.

"The advent of Christ and the focus on the individual indwelling of God's Spirit began to change the self-image of mankind. But after the first century of exponential spontaneous growth, the Christian church increasingly became a centrally controlled theocracy that discouraged individuality and individual thought.

"Then, in the early sixteenth century, a monk named Martin Luther refocused the church on the central focus of the gospel of Jesus—which is God loving and indwelling every individual. Luther sparked the Protestant Reformation and revolutionized science. We need to document the connection between the explosion of the Christian religion with the expansion of scientific discovery. What you find will be exciting—I guarantee it!

"Science has done much to enlighten and improve the conditions of mankind, but it is a big mistake to assume science is infallible or even in agreement with itself. Many scientific 'facts' have been found to be wrong. We need to help people learn to use current scientific theories as resources, but to always question scientific conclusions and understand the research methodologies that led to those conclusions.

"We will spend the next few weeks researching the credibility of the Bible and science and discovering where the Bible and science agree. This will include traditional as well as non-traditional interpretations of the Bible. I will spend the last hour of this first class sharing some of my own hypotheses about different interpretations of the Bible related to creation, the relationship between the spiritual and physical worlds, and the reasons God created us and the physical universe.

"But before we move on, I'd like to hear your thoughts on the syllabus and anything else on your minds." Every hand went up and the next twenty minutes was filled with questions and comments from every student. Most wanted to make sure their particular questions would be included in the research. Everyone seemed to like the flow of work outlined in the syllabus and they were anxious to get started with the research and discussions.

May the Lord make your love increase and overflow for
each other and for everyone else, just as ours does for you.
—1 Thessalonians 3:12

CHAPTER EIGHT

THE LOVE OF A WOMAN

February 2018 – one month after the first debate
(Middleburg, VA)

"Dad, would you like to hold your daughter?" Nurse Angie rubbed the newborn with wipes on a little table beside the delivery bed and wrapped her in a big pink towel. Tony, covered in his blue surgical gown, shoes and mask, cautiously reached for the little bundle. Nurse Angie pushed the baby into Tony's chest and bent his arms tight around her. "Hold her tight, she won't break. What's her name?"

"Her name is Mary Elizabeth Guest," Tony whispered. "She's named after her mother, Elizabeth, because she did all the work. We will call her Liz." Tony walked to the side of the bed where Elizabeth was beaming with a big, but twitching smile. She was completely exhausted after a long labor and difficult delivery, but she was very relieved and happy. Carrying and delivering a baby at thirty-nine years old has a lot of challenges. Tony sat on the edge of the bed holding his daughter tight. His emotions were difficult to control. He tried not to think of Pamela and Christine, but this scene brought back many sad and wonderful memories.

Tony laughed and cried as he looked at Elizabeth and Liz. It was hard for him to believe he was being given a second chance at love, fatherhood, and family. Gratitude overwhelmed him as he realized he was actually hopeful and happy. For the first time in a long time, he wanted to live. And for the first time in a very long time, he was grateful to God. Well, maybe not the first time. That happened when he met Elizabeth.

* * *

June 2016 – a year and a half before the first debate
(Chicago, IL)

It was Friday in late June. Tony was in Chicago speaking to a large luncheon event sponsored by George Soros. Soros is considered one of the top villains in the world by Christians and political conservatives, but it was just another speech and book signing for Tony. He traveled the globe speaking and signing the same book for four years. *God Fantasies* was one of the top-selling books in the world for four straight years. Over 100 million copies of *God Fantasies* were sold in ten languages. He netted about five dollars a book. His book was one of the best sellers in history, and Tony was one of the richest authors in the world.

Tony became wealthy from the sale of his books and he was now earning up to $100,000 per speech. He was giving twenty to thirty speeches a year. He traveled on a private jet. No one knew where he lived. The media loved him and gave him his privacy.

Tony was signing books after his luncheon speech in Chicago in a large meeting room overlooking Lake Michigan. The long line of fans guided by red velvet ropes snaked around the room. Tony contracted with a local bookstore to order his books and manage the sales on site. The sales would be counted toward the "Best Sellers" lists if they were sold through a bookstore.

One of the people from the bookstore was a beautiful woman with "Elizabeth" on her name tag. She was responsible for replenishing the stacks of books on the signing desk. Every fan bought a voucher at the door when they entered the room. They handed the voucher to Tony when they arrived at his desk so he would know they paid for the book.

Elizabeth was also walking the line of fans in front of the desk carrying a pad of yellow sticky notes. She handed each fan a sheet and told them to write down their first name and give it to Dr. Guest so he could spell their name correctly when he signed their book. It was a well-organized system allowing Tony to sign nearly 300 books an hour. On this windy day in June, Tony sat for over three hours after his speech and signed nearly 1,000 books. By the time the last book was signed, Tony was completely infatuated with Elizabeth.

Tony was not looking for a girl and avoided even making friends since he lost his family and denounced his faith. Today he just wanted to get back to his plane and go home. The bookstore crew was packing up when Tony stood up to get his sport coat off the back of the chair. He threw his coat over his shoulder and turned to leave, but Elizabeth was standing in his path with a big smile.

"Thank you, Dr. Guest, for allowing our store to sell your books today. I hope you'll call us again when you have your next event in Chicago."

Tony managed to work up a smile. "I sure will. You guys did a great job. Please thank the owners for me."

"I am the owner," Elizabeth replied with a playful roll of her eyes.

Tony noticed a silver cross on Elizabeth's necklace and her joyful spirit embraced his soul like a warm blanket. She had "Jesus" written all over her face. He didn't want it, he didn't like it, but he couldn't resist it.

"I guess you don't think much of me." Tony seemed embarrassed as he looked at the cross again and back at Elizabeth's face. He just spoke to 3,000 people and signed 1,000 books denouncing God and religion. Elizabeth looked into his eyes and her face turned serious.

"Tony, Tony, why do you persecute Him? It is hard for you to kick against the goads." The "Dr. Guest" was gone. The subservient bookseller was gone. The challenge to Tony's authenticity was powerful and completely unexpected. The message was infuriating and unwelcomed, but the messenger was sweet and irresistible. Elizabeth was using a Bible verse Tony knew well. It was from chapter 26 of Acts where Paul was describing his "Damascus Road" experience.

In that passage, Paul, who was called Saul at the time, testifies he was traveling from town to town persecuting people who were followers of Jesus. On one of these journeys to Damascus, Paul was blinded by a bright light and God spoke to him.

"Saul, Saul, why do you persecute me? It is hard for you to kick against the goads."

A goad is a long pole with a sharp point on the end used to guide sheep and oxen. Kicking the sharp point on the end of a pole was rather stupid. That was God's point to Paul and Elizabeth's point to Tony. Tony could have taken it as an insult, but he knew it was spoken with love.

"Would you join me for dinner?" Tony surprised himself, but the words were out of his mouth before he could bite his tongue. He was embarrassed at his weakness and braced himself for a quick rebuke. He felt small and dirty in front of Elizabeth.

"I know a nice place on the way to the airport. Do you need a ride?" Elizabeth seemed unsurprised by his invitation.

Tony smiled. "I've got a car and driver. Why don't you ride with me and show me this nice place?"

"Sounds good. I'll tell my team to head back to the store without me." Elizabeth walked over to talk to her two staffers who were packing boxes with posters, notepads, markers, and a few extra books. Tony was intimidated and disoriented by her calmness and confidence. No one had stood up to him in years.

They dined at a small Italian restaurant with red tablecloths and candles. Nothing fancy. Old fashioned with good wine and food. Before they left, they knew everything about each other. Elizabeth and her husband, Charles, were high school sweethearts and married the week after graduation. They both worked at a Christian bookstore while attending a local community college and had two children before they were twenty-one.

After graduating college, they continued working at the bookstore and, when they were twenty-five, they bought the store. They doubled the size of the business with innovative ideas, including adding a section for atheists to attract them to the store. They also encouraged their Christian shoppers to read the anti-God books so they would "know what the other side was up to."

Elizabeth's husband died of prostate cancer when he was thirty-four, three years earlier. Elizabeth managed the business and took care of her children alone. Her son and daughter both graduated high school a year early and were freshman and sophomore at Liberty University, a Christian college in Virginia. Her business was doing well, but she was looking for a buyer so she could get out of Chicago. She fell in love with Virginia and was dreaming of a place where she could have horses.

Unlike many of her Christian bookstore peers, Elizabeth was able to maintain a loyal and growing clientele working closely with local churches and doing special events. She was however, growing weary of Illinois's ever more socialist political leanings. Another reason she yearned to relocate.

Tony finally got around to asking the question haunting him, "Aren't you angry with God for taking your husband, for leaving your children without a father, and for leaving you alone to fight for yourself?"

Elizabeth reached across the table and took Tony's hand. "I'm grateful for the time God gave Charles and me, and I know the next time I see him he will have a big smile and a strong healthy body. Tony, we are all spiritual beings living a short physical experience. There is a reason we are all going through this difficult earthly existence and I enjoy trying to figure out why. I have some theories I'll share with you sometime. And, by the way, God didn't leave me alone. I'm not alone tonight, am I?" Tony put his other hand on top of hers. "No you're not, and neither am I."

Tony was tired and, after a few glasses of wine, his defenses were down. "Why did you confront me?" Elizabeth wasn't surprised by the question. "I really don't know. I've never done anything like that in my life. I'm usually shy with people I don't know. I spoke before I knew what I was doing. I hadn't thought of that verse in years. Why didn't you just tell me to mind my own business?"

"Because I needed to hear it and I needed to hear it from you." They stared into each other's eyes. Neither wanted a relationship, but both recognized all the signs. It seemed God had brought them together.

Elizabeth rode with Tony to the private airport on the outskirts of Chicago. They drove through an open gate and onto the tarmac. Elizabeth and Tony stood and talked beside the car for another thirty minutes.

"Can I see you again?" Tony asked before boarding his plane.

"Tony, as much as I'd like that, you know it will never work."

Tony was stunned. He knew about "love at first sight," and he was now experiencing it firsthand—yet the door just closed in his face.

"Can I call?"

"Tony, I know it sounds corny and naïve, but Jesus is my first love. You have made Jesus and His people your enemy. That means, regardless how wonderful it feels tonight, you will come to see me as your enemy, too."

"You could never be my enemy." Tony squeezed her hand, dropped his gaze to the ground, and mumbled to the driver. "Please give this sweet lady a ride home."

Tony boarded his plane and within a few minutes he was looking down on the lights of the Windy City. They sparkled like diamonds. He had never felt so empty and alone.

The next few weeks were tortuous for Tony. His anger against God was rekindled. How could God set him up with Elizabeth and then crush him again? What kind of God is this?

"I don't know why I'm angry with something that probably doesn't even exist!" he shouted to himself in the mirror.

But he couldn't get Elizabeth off of his mind. He canceled two speeches and asked his editor to write his syndicated articles for him—he could not bring himself to "kick against the goads" any longer.

Then, three weeks after he met Elizabeth, Tony surrendered. He didn't want anything to do with God, but he desperately wanted Elizabeth. And he knew he couldn't have Elizabeth without reconciling with God.

Sunday was usually Tony's day to read and watch sports on television. But on this Sunday, Tony knew—despite his poor motives and the incredible awkwardness of it all—he had to do business with God. He didn't know where to start, so he did what he always did when he needed to think. He took a cup of coffee to the back porch, sat in his rocking chair, and stared at the mountains. Only this time, Tony took his old Bible. He put it on the little table next to his chair usually reserved for his coffee and iPad.

Tony began his conversation with God by being thankful for all the beauty around him. That was something they could agree on. He wasn't ready to address his real need: repentance. He still needed to believe God was wrong. It was painful to admit he was the one who cut and run when evil—the evil he had often preached about—invaded his life. He knew he needed to ask God's forgiveness.

Tony's heart began to soften as he thanked God for meeting Elizabeth. He prayed for her health, her children, and her business. He prayed she would achieve her dream of selling her business and finding a place in Virginia where she could have horses. He prayed his place would be that place.

He asked God to extricate him from his life as an atheist and show him purpose in a new life. He asked Jesus to take his anger and nail it to His cross. He asked God to hold Pamela and Christine tight in His arms. He prayed earnestly for God to restore his faith. And he asked God to show him how to repent for all the harm he did to His kingdom.

A sense of peace surrounded Tony and begin to pour into his heart. He had never experienced anything supernatural, but he was certain he felt the hands of angels on his shoulders. A cool breeze—unusual for July—caressed his face. Tony knew it was God caressing his face.

"My God, please take me back. Let me be a servant in your household. Forgive me for all the harm I've done. Restore my heart and my faith."

"It is done!" Tony didn't hear God's voice, but the thought in his head was louder and more certain than any voice he ever heard. Tony visualized himself as the prodigal son returning home with his father wrapping him in his finest robe. He knew his life as an atheist was over. He didn't know if Elizabeth would ever want to be with him, but he knew the brief encounter with her saved him. He had to let her know.

Tony didn't have her number, but he had all the contact information for her bookstore. He emailed Elizabeth with a simple message, "Please call me, Elizabeth. I've stopped kicking against the goads. Tony."

The email went straight to Elizabeth. As the bookstore owner, she had to be available for shipping and promotion information seven days a week.

Despite her rejection of Tony, she had been praying every day for God to move in Tony's life.

When Tony's phone rang ten minutes after he sent the email, he could hardly speak. He sobbed for several minutes before Elizabeth finally said, "Tony, why don't we get together and talk about it."

Tony was certain he was going to have a heart attack because his chest felt like it would explode. They talked for nearly an hour before Tony worked up the courage to ask Elizabeth to visit him in Virginia.

"Elizabeth, I'm happy to visit you in Chicago, but may I propose you visit me in Virginia?"

"Virginia?" Elizabeth was puzzled. "You know I love Virginia."

Tony spent the next ten minutes describing his estate.

"I've never been in my barn and there are no horses there, but we can inspect it all together."

They agreed on a plan. Tony would meet Elizabeth at noon on Friday at the airport where he last saw her. He couldn't believe she agreed to see him—at his home.

"Tony, do you have someone to talk to about all the decisions you will have to make?"

"Yes, I do, Elizabeth, and I will call him tomorrow." Tony had already decided who he needed to call.

Tony was up early Monday morning for a meeting with Ben, his groundskeeper. He texted Ben Sunday night after speaking to Elizabeth and asked him to meet at his barn at 8:00 a.m. Tony wanted the barn to look like it was ready for horses by next Friday. All the junk—old tractor parts and rusty barrels—had to be taken to the dump. Ben suggested ordering a truckload of straw to spread in the stalls and around the corral outside. He also promised to bring in a crew to clear the riding path that circled the entire 150-acre ranch. It was nearly two miles long. Tony had one last request as he got in his golf cart. "Let's make this place look like the home of a Kentucky Derby champion. Whatever you need, get it. This is important.

"And Ben, if any of your other clients have two horses with some saddles and tack I could rent for the weekend, that would be wonderful."

When Tony got back to his house, he went to his office and started searching through some old files. He found a letter from Dr. Howard Clark offering condolences and prayers after the deaths of Pamela and Christine. Dr. Clark encouraged

Tony to come spend a week in South Carolina at his home. Dr. Clark also offered to come wherever Tony was to be with him during his sad and dark time. He pleaded with Tony not to deal with it alone. He warned that Satan would take advantage of his weakened conditioned if he was alone.

Dr. Clark had just become president of Palmetto Christian College when he wrote the letter, but he was ready to take a leave of absence to do whatever he could to help Tony. On the bottom of the letter he wrote his cell, office, and home phone numbers with a note to "call any time 24/7." The letter was smeared with Tony's tears. He never responded to Dr. Clark letter. Unfortunately, Dr. Clark's warning came true.

Tony sat on his back porch in a rocking chair with a cup of coffee and dialed the cell phone number on Dr. Clark's letter. "Hello, Tony, I've been praying you would call." Dr. Clark still had Tony's cell number in his phone contacts after more than fifteen years.

"Dr. Clark, I need your help. Would you meet me on Wednesday or Thursday this week if I fly into Greenville?"

"You've met a girl." Dr. Clark was matter-of-fact.

"Doggoneit! Are you spying on me? How did you know?" Tony expected a deadly serious response, maybe even a lecture from Dr. Clark, but instead they were both laughing.

"The love of woman can heal an angry heart. And I didn't have to read that one in a book. Sure, I'm free Wednesday afternoon. Where would you like to meet?" Dr. Clark was making this much easier than Tony expected.

"I'll land at the downtown Greenville airport at noon. I will reserve a meeting room at the Phoenix Hotel right next to the airport. Do you mind driving into Greenville from the college?"

"No, that's fine. I know the hotel and will meet you there at 12:30."

"Sounds good. I'll bring some box lunches. Can't thank you enough—didn't know who else to call."

Tony walked back into his kitchen to pour another cup of coffee. He got his briefcase out of his office and returned to his rocking chair on the back porch. For the next hour, he just stared at the distant mountains. Then he began listing everything he had to do to close down his business. The first step would be sending out a press release explaining why he was no longer an atheist. He had no idea what he would say. There would be countless painful and humiliating interviews.

He would take down his website and discontinue his regular blog. He needed to close all his social media sites and accounts. He had to cancel all his appearances and speeches scheduled around the world for the next twelve months. He needed to break the contract with his publisher to write a new book. There was a documentary scheduled with CBS that had to be canceled. This would also be the demise of his weekly syndicated radio show. Closing his office in DC and dismissing some of his staff would be the most painful part of the process.

He would keep his business manager, Betsy, to help him with his schedule and financial affairs. His public relations firm would not know how to write a press release or manage the stories about Tony returning to his faith. His lawyer would be busy for months trying to cancel dozens of contracts. Lawsuits were certain to be filed against him. He wouldn't need to keep his website manager or the writers for his blog, Facebook page, and Twitter account. And he would no longer need his three junior administrative staff. He hated that people who'd come to depend on him would lose their jobs. There was too much to do and Tony didn't know where to start.

He picked up his cell phone to tell Betsy the news, but he paused before dialing her number. Perhaps he should talk to Dr. Clark before he launched this personal and public relations nightmare. He was once an international celebrity for his Christian ministry and then made a fortune by renouncing his faith. No one would believe he genuinely returned to God. Everyone would have good reasons to think he was either crazy or a con man. Tony didn't see any way out: Christians and atheists all over the world would hate him.

Tony began to doubt if Elizabeth would want to share her life with such a controversial and despised man. He didn't know what to do. He didn't need to work for money, but he didn't want to spend the rest of his life hiding out in Virginia. Decisions that seemed clear and easy when he was with Elizabeth, now seemed confusing with hopelessly negative outcomes. He wasn't sure he could make it until Friday without seeing her again.

Monday afternoon Tony went jogging on the riding path around his property. There was already a team of workers with several tractors clearing the path overgrown by years of neglect. One of the tractors was following the others along the path pulling a large trailer full of mulch. Two men stood on a small ledge on the back of the trailer using shovels to spread the mulch on the cleared path. Tony was impressed his groundskeeper had assembled this team so quickly. He finished his jog, took a swim in his indoor pool, and then texted Betsy to cancel his Wednesday speech in New York. He didn't give a reason.

Tony was up early Tuesday morning reading some old devotionals. It had been a long time since he had a morning quiet time with the Lord—and it was still more than a little awkward. He finished his pot of coffee and continued to read until noon. Then he took a walk to his barn. He had to kill some time until Elizabeth was home from work. They agreed Tony would call at 6:00 p.m. her time, 7:00 p.m. in Virginia. The barn already looked totally different. All the trash, debris, and junk were gone from inside the barn and around the yard. There was a large stack of straw bales in front of the barn. Tony began to think it might be fun to have horses.

He took another jog, had a frozen dinner, and was back in his rocking chair at 7:00 with his cell phone 100 percent charged. But he was afraid to call. He was sure Elizabeth had changed her mind about spending the weekend at his home. He tried to prepare himself for the letdown.

"Hello, Elizabeth. Is this still a good time for you to talk?" Tony held his breath.

"Tony, this is a perfect time. I'm glad to hear your voice. I've been worried about you and afraid you might have changed your mind about kicking the goads."

Tony laughed. He was so worried Elizabeth might change her mind he didn't even consider the possibility she might be worried about him.

"No, Elizabeth, I can't change my mind because you made it clear you weren't going to hang around with anyone who was stupid enough to kick against the goads. And I'm counting on you hanging around with me this weekend. Are we still on for this Friday?" Tony held his breath again.

"I'm counting on it. I'll meet you at the airport as we agreed on Friday at noon. I don't have to be back in Chicago until Tuesday afternoon, so we'll have plenty of time to look around Middleburg and your barn. I'd also like to take a side trip to see my kids in Lynchburg. Could you arrange for me to have a rental car to drive over on Sunday morning to attend church with my kids. I'll need to leave early because it's a three-hour drive."

The relief he felt rendered him speechless for a long moment.

"Tony, what's—"

"You won't need a car. My plane can get you to Lynchburg in less than thirty minutes. I'll arrange for a car to pick you up at the Lynchburg airport and take you to the Liberty campus. What time do you need to be there?"

"That's way too expensive. I should drive. The church service begins at 11:00 so I need to meet my children about 10:30. We'll have lunch and visit a while. I'll probably leave to come back to Middleburg around 2:00."

"Elizabeth, I have to pay for the jet and pilots whether I use them or not. The airport here is only fifteen minutes from my house. I'll put you on the plane about 9:30 and you'll be at the Lynchburg airport by 10:00. It's only about a five-minute drive to the Liberty campus."

"Well, if you insist. I'm not going to kick against the goads. It sounds like fun. Okay, tell me: have you talked to the person you mentioned about your situation?"

"Yes. I called my old seminary professor, Dr. Howard Clark. We're getting together tomorrow in Greenville, South

Carolina, near the university where he is now president. Elizabeth, you won't believe this, but he seemed to be expecting my call. And when I asked him if we could meet, the first thing he said was, 'you met a girl.' This whole thing seems to be choreographed from above."

"I've had the same feeling."

"Elizabeth, I've been worried about bringing you into the fire that will result from my changing my mind again about God. People will hate me, say all kinds of bad things about me, and they will have every right to think I'm crazy. I don't want you to suffer because of me."

"Tony, let's not get ahead of ourselves. Let's just have a nice weekend together. God will make it all work out for good if we trust Him. It won't be easy and we don't know where our paths will lead, but like they say, nothing good is ever easy. We'll get through it and who knows—we might just go through it together."

Tony again found himself laughing with tears in his eyes. He was so relieved and grateful he was silently screaming "Thank You, God" the whole time he and Elizabeth talked on the phone. He told her about the list of things he needed to do to prepare for the change in his life and she told him all the things she needed to do to get the bookstore ready to sell. They talked until the sun set over the mountains and Tony's cell phone was flashing "low battery."

"Elizabeth, we better hang up before my phone goes dead. I'll call you tomorrow night after I talk to Dr. Clark. Thank you for being my strength."

Elizabeth thought of Tony as a man of steel, so it seemed odd for him to need her strength. But it felt good to be needed. "Call me when you get back from Greenville. Be safe and goodnight."

Tony found his phone charger and returned to his rocker to send some texts. The first text went to his groundskeeper. "Ben, the barn and riding path are looking great. Thanks for making it happen. Have you had any luck finding horses?"

"The horses with tack will be in the barn Friday morning."
Ben was always efficient.

The next text was to his housekeeper. "Molly, I will have a
house guest this weekend. She will stay in the guest house.
Please make a special effort to be sure it is clean and well sup-
plied, especially the kitchen with coffee, orange juice, and
Chardonnay. Thank you, Dr. Tony." Molly was all Southern
and she insisted on calling him Dr. Tony.

A third text went to his pilot. "Berny, I'll be at the airport
at 10:30 tomorrow morning. As we discussed, we'll land at the
downtown Greenville airport. Please bring two box lunches
with the usual sandwiches and fruit. Also, arrange for someone
at the airport to drive me to the Phoenix Hotel. It's only a few
blocks, but I'll be carrying the lunches. Thanks, Tony."

Tony put down his phone, walked to the bathroom, and
began shaving his trademark Fu Manchu. He grew it when he
published his book because he wanted to look stern, dark, and
evil. He often used a black rinse on his hair and beard to add
to the effect. Tony hoped, without the beard and with his
naturally brownish blonde and slightly gray hair, he might not
be as recognizable in public.

Wednesday morning, Tony was up early for a swim and
some reading on his back porch. There was a mist hanging over
the pasture in his backyard and the clouds made it hard to see
the mountains. He opened his Bible to Psalm 8:3–9.

When I consider your heavens,
the work of your fingers,
the moon and the stars,
which you have set in place,
what is mankind that you are mindful of them,
human beings that you care for them?
You have made them a little lower than the angels
and crowned them with glory and honor.
You made them rulers over the works of your hands;
you put everything under their feet:

all flocks and herds,
and the animals of the wild,
the birds in the sky,
and the fish in the sea,
all that swim the paths of the seas.
Lord, our Lord,
how majestic is your name in all the earth!

Tony didn't know what to pray. "Holy Spirit, please pray for me. Pray the words I need to pray. I need forgiveness, but I don't even know where to begin. I have done immeasurable harm to the kingdom of God. Redeem me. Buy me back, dear Lord."

The flight to Greenville took about an hour. The clouds cleared and most of the flight was over the beautiful Blue Ridge Mountain range. It was a good day and Tony was looking forward to seeing Dr. Clark.

Dr. Clark burst into the meeting room and gave Tony a big bear hug. "I hardly recognize you without that ugly beard. You look young again. I hope you feel half as good as you look. Let's eat!" Dr. Clark was doing his best to relieve the tension and make Tony feel comfortable. They both took out their sandwiches, but before Tony took his first bite, he had a serious question on his mind.

"Dr. Clark, I'd like to read you a verse from Hebrews and ask your opinion.

'It is impossible for those who have once been enlightened, who have tasted the heavenly gift, who have shared in the Holy Spirit, who have tasted the goodness of the word of God and the powers of the coming age and who have fallen away, to be brought back to repentance. To their loss they are crucifying the Son of God all over again and subjecting him to public disgrace.'

"Dr. Clark, I have crucified my Lord all over again and subjected him to public disgrace. This verse says it is impossible for me to be brought back to repentance."

Dr. Clark lowered his sandwich and took a sip of water. "Tony, you're not the first pastor to fall. Tell me this: have you been brought back to repentance?"

"Yes."

"What does that tell you?"

"Either I didn't really fall away or I never really knew Jesus in the first place. Or maybe, I have asked for forgiveness and it has not been given because it is impossible for a believer to leave and then come back."

"Tony, you have definitely been a lost sheep, but let me assure you; you are His sheep. Nothing in this world, including you, can pry you out of God's hands. I'm guessing you knew a lot about Jesus but never allowed Him to reach you at a personal level. That happened to me when I was a young preacher. I knew the Scriptures, I prayed and studied, and I obeyed God. But there is something about being a teacher and a preacher that makes it harder to be a hearer, a listener, and a receiver. I was always transmitting the Word. That made it harder for me to be receiver of the Word—and harder for me to know God's love in a personal way. I was always trying to be a good example, when I needed to be broken—to be real. I was always trying to give love to others, but too perfect to need or receive love. So, when my crisis came and my perfect world crashed in on top of me, I responded just as you did.

"Before my life fell apart, I preached for ten years and then became a professor at Covenant Seminary. I was at Covenant for twenty years when my son, Howie, was killed in Afghanistan. He had a wife and two children."

Tony interrupted, "Dr. Clark, I never knew. I am so sorry."

"Thank you, Tony. I was very angry. My wife, Donna, and I received several letters from Howie complaining about the rules of engagement endangering our troops. Several of his friends were needlessly killed. Our soldiers couldn't use their weapons in civilian areas without authorization. The enemy knew our rules and often attacked our troops in urban areas because they knew we couldn't shoot back.

"One day on the outskirts of Kabul, Howie and four other soldiers were pinned down near a public market. They could have taken out the small number of enemy combatants when they were attacked, but they had to wait for radio authorization to return fire. While they waited, enemy reinforcements surrounded them and killed all five of them. Our political leaders killed my son. The rules were stupid and dangerous and they all knew it.

"Well, I couldn't forgive our country and I couldn't forgive God. I took a leave-of-absence from Covenant and contemplated another career. It was hard for me to imagine ever teaching anyone about the love of God. Any of this sound familiar?

"My Donna was equally distraught. Howie was always her baby even though he was over thirty years old. But Donna immediately shifted gears from grief to love. She loved our daughter-in-law and our two grandchildren. And she loved me and coaxed me until I finally gave up feeling sorry for myself. It took me a whole year before I finally got down on my knees and pleaded for God's help.

"I couldn't accept God's love until I was broken, and I finally realized I could only feel God's love through others. God loved me through Donna and my grandchildren. He loved me through some friends at Covenant. All this love was available before Howie was killed, but I didn't know how to let it in. Which means I never really knew the love of God until tragedy tore down all my defenses.

"Tony, I want to be clear. I don't believe God killed Howie to break me. I believe God used a terrible tragedy in my life to show me how to receive His love through the love of others. I don't like the way this world works, but I don't blame God for what happens in the physical world. God is sovereign over all things, but He has obviously limited Himself in this physical world for reasons we may not understand. Otherwise, He would not have allowed His own Son, Jesus, to be killed in such an excruciating way. We have been told Satan is the Prince of this physical world. Why? That's a question I intend to answer before I leave this world.

"The tragedies in my life did not end with the death of Howie. A few years later, just before I met you, Donna contracted a rare form of cancer and died within a few months. She used those few months to convince me of God's love. She made me promise not to feel sorry for myself or blame God. She teased that God would demote her to a smaller mansion if I complained about her arriving in heaven a little early. And she told me not to join her in heaven until our grandchildren graduated college. Then, and only then, would she allow me into her mansion. Donna still loves me and I have learned to let her love me from eternity.

"Tony, what happened to me does not lessen the pain and betrayal you feel from the loss of Pamela and Christine. But it does help me understand a little better of what you're going through. I know God loves you and has a wonderful plan for your eternity, including being with Pamela and Christine. But He also has a plan for the rest of your life here on earth. Discovering His plan must now be your goal."

Tony leaned back in his chair and stared out the window of their little meeting room. "Dr. Clark, for a long time I selfishly assumed I was the only one who has endured great tragedy. But I've come to realize everyone has tragedies, and many much worse than mine. If God will allow me to work in His kingdom again, I would like to spend the rest of my life helping people who experience suffering and tragedy—and helping us all understand God's motives for creating this physical world. But first, I need to figure out God's motives for myself. I need to know why God would create a physical world so full of pain, suffering, and death."

Dr. Clark picked up the second half of his sandwich, "That's what I want to talk about today, but first, tell me about the girl!" He smiled, took a big bite of his sandwich, and leaned back in his chair.

"Okay, okay! Her name is Elizabeth." Tony recounted everything about how they met, how he instantly fell in love, how she spurned him at first, how his feelings for her forced him to reconcile with God and their planned weekend together. He tried to explain how Elizabeth, with only a few words, destroyed his pretense of atheism and opened his heart again to receive God's love. Then he began to talk about the disaster he was getting ready to bring onto himself and Elizabeth when he announced his return to Christianity.

Dr. Clark lifted both his hands to form a "time out" signal. "Tony, I've been thinking a lot about your next moves since we talked on Saturday. I think it would be a mistake to announce anything. You should go dark—just disappear. If you announce you're no longer an atheist, and have returned to Christianity, both the secular and Christian worlds will hate you. You will be ridiculed as a fraud by both sides. The noise will be so loud it will be impossible for you to do anything. My recommendation is to cancel all speaking engagements, interviews, and meetings. No explanation. Take down your website and social media accounts. Don't explain anything. There will be a lot of internet gossip for a while, but by the time the talking heads in the media figure out you're gone, most people will have lost interest.

"I'd like to propose a partnership. Work with me to study the reasons God created the physical world. There has to be more than we've been teaching in seminary. Let's look at science and biblical evidence of how this world was created and the reasons it was created. Let's take a non-traditional look at the whole Bible and try to discover more about God's motives and why a sovereign God allows such terrible things to happen. This could be the most important contribution we make to God's kingdom. When we're ready to publish something, that's when you can announce the evidence that changed your mind. What do you think?"

"Dr. Clark, it makes a lot of sense to me. That approach will at least delay a worldwide backlash against me. And you're probably right; after a year or two, most people won't even care what I'm doing. I also like the idea of working with you on a serious research project. We can trade notes via email and get together every month or so to talk in person. I like it!"

"Tony, I'll email you my notes on our proposed project. Would you edit them and help me develop a scope of work? I can use some of my research assistants to help collect information. Could I give you a ride back up the street to the airport?"

"I could use a ride and I can't thank you enough for meeting with me. Your wisdom today saved me a lot of pain and heartache."

"I'll expect a call with a full report after your weekend with Elizabeth."

"You'll be the first one I call." Tony was so buoyant, he wondered if he needed the airplane to get home.

Love does not delight in evil but rejoices with the truth.
It always protects, always trusts, always hopes, always
perseveres.—1 Corinthians 13:6

CHAPTER NINE

HAPPY VALENTINE'S DAY

August 2016 – before the first debate
(Middleburg, VA)

Queen Elizabeth would not have received as much preparation for the weekend at Tony's. The pastures were mowed, the barn and corral were covered in fresh straw, the riding path was packed with bark chips, and the meticulously manicured flower beds around the entrance gate made the entire estate look like a resort. Inside the house, everything was clean and organized. Two chefs were working in Tony's expansive kitchen preparing a private dinner for his guest. The whole house smelled of spices and fresh baked bread.

Tony's plane landed in Chicago at 11:30. He arranged for a car to pick up Elizabeth so she wouldn't have to leave her car at the airport. She arrived at 11:50. Her driver pulled onto the tarmac and stopped at the red carpet leading to the steps of the jet. Tony stood on the carpet as if he were greeting the Queen.

"This is just too much," Elizabeth complained as the driver opened her door. "You're really putting on a show!" She got out of the car and gave Tony a kiss on his cheek as if they'd known each other for a lifetime. "I like the clean face. You look like a new man!" The pilots put her luggage in the cargo compartment under the plane and within a few minutes, they were looking down on Lake Michigan.

"Could I talk you into a glass of champagne?" Tony reached for a bottle in an ice bucket across the aisle.

"I think you could. I feel like celebrating." Elizabeth and Tony were both relieved. Neither changed their minds or had second thoughts about their potential relationship. Now they only worried it might all be too good to be true. Tony filled two glasses and handed one across the little table to Elizabeth. She lifted her glass.

"Tony, I have good news—I think. A potential buyer for my bookstore has made an offer contingent on reviewing our financial statements. The offer is within the range I could accept, so the sale of my store might be happening sooner than I expected."

"That is good news. Will it be hard to walk away from something you and Charlie built together?" Elizabeth was grateful Tony was comfortable talking about her late husband. Charlie would always be a part of her life and she didn't want Tony to avoid talking about him.

"Yes, it will, but Charlie and I often talked about selling the store after the kids went to college. We wanted a new adventure. It will be hard to walk away, but I'm ready to try something new."

Tony reached his glass across the table and tapped hers. "Well, let's toast to a new adventure for both of us." He took a sip and leaned back in his seat.

"I think I have some good news, too. I told you my meeting with Dr. Clark went well, but I didn't tell you much about what he said—except he somehow knew I met a girl. He had some good advice, but I want your opinion as well. After I went over the list of all the things I needed to do to get out of the atheism business, beginning with a press release about my restored faith, Dr. Clark didn't like my plan.

"He said there would be an international backlash from both the secular and faith worlds. Both sides would consider me a con man. He suggested I go dark, just 'disappear' to use his word. He also invited me to partner with him on an extensive study to better understand God's motives for creating the physical universe. I am very excited about the prospect of working with him—and with you—to explore why God put us in an evil world where we all experience suffering and death. You said you were interested in the subject yourself."

"Tony, I am interested and that sounds like good advice from Dr. Clark. I agree you shouldn't announce or explain anything now. There will come a time when the reasons for your change of heart will make more sense to everyone. Your research with Dr. Clark will hopefully provide the foundation for your new life. I've got a lot of books I could give you for your research." They shared a laugh and Elizabeth asked for a refill of her champagne.

The short drive through the country from the small airport to Tony's house was filled with superlatives from Elizabeth. The large estates, rolling hills, and open pastures with cows and horses were like being in a Gainsborough painting. When Tony turned his Jeep into his own estate, Elizabeth was speechless. She was overwhelmed.

Tony drove up the long driveway lined with trees and pulled into a little courtyard separating the guest house from the main house. He carried Elizabeth's luggage into the guest house. She followed slowly, continuing to gaze at the house, the fields, and the mountains in the distance. The guest house was one large room but for the bathroom, with a kitchen on one side, a rock fireplace with gas logs on another wall, a king bed in one corner with a sitting area in the middle of the room.

"I wanted to make sure you had your privacy while you were here. The fridge is full of good stuff. There's coffee and a little private deck so you can sip your coffee while looking at the mountains. Would you like to take a walk before dinner?"

"I'd love to. Give me a few minutes to put on my jeans and walking shoes."

"Just come across the courtyard to the house when you're ready. I'll be waiting in the den. And Elizabeth—thanks for coming."

"Tony, I'm grateful you wanted me to come. And I am overwhelmed at all you've done to make me feel welcome."

"You haven't seen anything yet!" Tony flashed a big smile and closed the door as he left the guest house.

Elizabeth wanted to see the barn, so they walked down a path to a grove of trees hiding the big, red, six-stall barn. As they walked together, she took Tony's hand and began swinging their arms. Tony felt like a stupid teenager—and he loved it. As they crested a little hill, the barn came into view. Elizabeth exclaimed, "This looks like a scene from one of those old western movies with Jimmy Stewart or John Wayne."

The fresh straw spread neatly all around the barn and corral made the whole area look new. Tony opened the doors at the front of the barn and Elizabeth saw two horses looking at them from their stalls.

"You're kidding me! Horses! Where did you get horses? You said you'd never been in this barn." Elizabeth walked to the first horse and began stroking its neck.

"This is the first time I've ever walked into this barn. Until this week, it was a junk yard. I borrowed the horses along with two saddles and riding gear. And I hope you remember how to put them on the horses. I haven't ridden a horse since I was eighteen."

"Where is the tack? I'd like a rope to lead this one around the corral." They found a room where Ben put the saddles, bridles, halters, and several ropes with clips to hook on the halters. It didn't take Elizabeth more than a few minutes to put a halter on one of the horses and attach a rope. She led the horse around the corral beside the barn. After one lap, she used a lower board on the fence to climb aboard and ride around the corral several times bareback. Tony stood on the other side of the corral fence watching with his arms folded on the top slate. Watching Elizabeth having so much fun filled him with joy.

"Tony, can we go for a ride tomorrow morning?"

"Anything you want to do."

Dinner was like a scene out of a romantic movie. Tony set up a small table on his back porch with a red tablecloth and candles. He wanted to recreate the atmosphere of the Italian restaurant where they ate several weeks before in Chicago. It was cool outside, but they would eat next to his gas fire table. The two chefs prepared a five course Italian-style meal with a different wine for every course. The sun was setting as they toasted their new friendship. The clouds put on a display of pastel colors until the first stars appeared in the crystal-clear evening sky.

Tony opened their dinner with prayer.

"Father, I do not deserve to come before You, yet in spite of all I've done, You still invite me to sit on Your lap as Your child and call You Daddy. I did not think I could ever love again and do not deserve a second chance at love, yet You have given me the gift of Elizabeth. I did not think I would ever know Your love again, yet You have allowed me to know Your irresistible love through Elizabeth. Thank You for this food tonight and the beauty of Your creation all around us, especially the beautiful lady sitting in front of me tonight. Amen." Tony opened his eyes and looked at Elizabeth sheepishly. "I hope I wasn't too presumptuous in my prayer."

"It was my prayer, too." Tears were running down Elizabeth's cheeks, but her smile was beaming brighter than ever.

After dinner and an extended conversation running more courses than dinner, it became apparent to both of them their thoughts about life and the future assumed they would be together for the rest of their lives. They knew it was happening too fast, but neither had any interest in slowing it down. After dinner, Tony walked Elizabeth across the courtyard to the guest house.

"Did you find everything you needed?"

"Oh yes. I could live here a month and never go out for supplies."

"I hope you feel safe. The whole area is fenced and no one could get near the house without alarms going off."

"Tony, I live in Chicago where I sometimes hear gunshots at night. This feels like Mayberry." Elizabeth took a few steps into the guest house, but Tony stood holding the open door.

"Good. How about breakfast at eight and then we'll go riding. I'd like to drive you around to see the area tomorrow afternoon and I've made early dinner reservations at the Red Fox Inn in downtown Middleburg tomorrow at five thirty. It is an old historic inn and I doubt anyone will recognize me with my new look."

"Tony, I'm not worried about anyone recognizing you. I'll see you at eight." Tony wanted to hold and kiss her but, since Elizabeth was a guest in his house, he was being careful not to be too forward. He stood at the door like a lost school boy. Elizabeth turned and walked back to the door. She put her arms around him and kissed him. This was a real kiss that sent chills all the way down to Tony's toes. She stepped back and Tony balanced himself by holding the door.

"Was that my tip for the meal?" Tony was shaking his head half-pretending to shake off the intoxicating impact of Elizabeth's kiss.

"I'll see you at eight." Elizabeth smiled and turned to walk away. Tony, still shaking his head, turned the lock on the inside knob and closed the door as he left. As he walked across the courtyard he whispered aloud, "What a day, what a night, what a woman, what a great God I have!"

Tony was up at 6:00 having coffee in his rocking chair on the back porch. After his first cup, he walked to the side of the porch where he could see part of the guest house. Elizabeth was on the little deck with a cup of coffee in her hand, her feet propped up on a table and a Bible in her lap. She didn't see Tony. She was looking the opposite direction at the sunrise breaking through the mist above the tree line on the far side of the east pasture.

Elizabeth was her own person. She wasn't needy. Her love had power because it came from the fullness of her heart. Tony was grateful her love was directed at him. He prayed his empty and confused heart could somehow return that wonderful love.

Tony's cooking skills were rusty, but he was the head chef for a lot of meals at his church. The thoughts of his former life sent waves of images and emotions over him and he had to brace himself on the counter until they faded, just in time to keep the oatmeal from turning to concrete. When Elizabeth arrived in the kitchen at 8:00, Tony had a spread of fruit, yogurt, oatmeal, and eggs still in the carton on the kitchen bar.

"What would you like for breakfast. I could use an assistant chef."

"Okay, I get it. This is a test. You want to make sure I can cook."

"Can't be too careful. I'll need someone to mush my green beans when I lose my teeth."

"If you've got some bacon and cheese, let's cook some omelets."

Elizabeth quickly took charge of the kitchen and Tony enjoyed being her assistant. They prepared a breakfast feast with omelets and cappuccino complementing the oatmeal. They ate and chatted at the same little table on the porch where they had dinner the night before.

"I can't ever remember eating this much in a twenty-four-hour period. I'll need to take a little jog after we ride the horses—if I can still walk." Elizabeth, no longer a guest, was completely comfortable as the lady of the house. It was not hard to take the leadership role from Tony. He had lived in the house for almost three years, but his constant travel almost made his home feel like another hotel room. Until this week, he had never been in the guest house, the barn, and hardly used the kitchen.

Ben was at the barn feeding and brushing the horses when Tony and Elizabeth arrived in the golf cart. He assisted Tony in saddling his horse, but Elizabeth knew exactly what she was doing.

"Ben, call an ambulance if my horse comes back without me."

"Will do. I hope you included me in your will."

"Don't count on it. Thanks again for getting us these horses."

"They are for sale if you decide to keep them." Ben laughed and held Tony's horse while he climbed aboard. Elizabeth was already on the riding trail.

They walked the horses along the trail until they reached the far side of Tony's property. The trail opened to a large pasture. Elizabeth turned her horse into the pasture.

"Let's see if these horses can run."

She was off and Tony's horse was inclined to follow. Both horses were in a full gallop. After a few seconds feeling off balance, Tony began to feel as natural as he did when he rode horses every summer at his grandfather's farm. Just like riding a bicycle.

They rode the horses down to a pond at the other end of the pasture and stopped at a gazebo with a little dock. There was a post next to the gazebo to tie the horses. This must have been a riding destination for the previous owners. Tony and Elizabeth dismounted and walked through the gazebo to the dock. A canoe was upside down on the dock with two paddles inside. Tony had only seen this pond from a distance in a realtor's golf cart when he was considering buying the property.

"Let's see if this thing floats." Tony flipped the canoe over and knocked off a few spider webs with one of the paddles. They spent the next hour paddling around the pond and sitting on the swinging bench in the gazebo. Then they circled the property again on their horses, put the horses back in the barn, and took the golf cart back to the house for lunch.

Tony put the top down on his Jeep for the afternoon ride. Their first stop was downtown Middleburg, a small picturesque town virtually unchanged in the last fifty years. They walked around downtown, visited an equestrian store and an art gallery, and then drove for a couple of hours around the country side. The fall colors transcended any painter's palette.

They returned to Middleburg and stopped at the National Sporting Library and Museum, one of the largest buildings in town. It is dedicated to preserving, promoting, and sharing literature and art related to equestrian, angling, and field sports. Tony was interested in trout fishing, and Elizabeth couldn't get enough of everything related to horses. They browsed around the 15,000-square foot museum until it was time for dinner downtown at the old Red Fox Inn.

After dinner, they were having coffee at their table in a dark corner of the Inn. Tony planned a little speech.

"Elizabeth, I did a lot of counseling with young couples in my church. I always told them the first phase of love, what I called infatuation, was a form of mental illness. They were blind to each other's faults and idiosyncrasies—things that might really annoy the other when they settled into the routine of life. I warned them, before they married, to work through that phase until they could see each other as real people—warts and all.

"I'm older and hope a little wiser than those young kids, but I am fully in love and completely infatuated with you. If this is a mental illness, I want to keep it the rest of my life. I know we should take this slow and give ourselves some time, but I want you to know I love you with all my heart and soul. I want to be with you every minute and no amount of time will ever change my mind. I would like your advice, maybe a little therapy."

Elizabeth was listening intently and hesitated to speak. Tony's heart was in his throat.

"Tony, I'm suffering from the same mental illness and not sure how to handle it either. This all seems too good to be true. My experience in life tells me if something seems too good to be true, it usually is. I've tested my feelings with 'worst case' scenarios. I've imagined hundreds of reporters and protestors at the gates in front of your house with us hiding for the rest of our lives. I've imagined my children refusing to speak to you. I've considered the possibility that if things go very badly, your anger with God will be inflamed again.

"But here's the bottom line for me. Even if all that happens, I want to be here for you. I love you more than I ever thought I could love anyone after Charlie, and I want to be with you every minute. I know this infatuation phase will cool for both of us, but I also know real love when I feel it. Tony, what we have is real love and I'm convinced God brought us together to show us how much He loves us. And I'm also convinced He has an important purpose for our lives together."

The sun was setting over Middleburg when they got back into the Jeep. It was still light, but much colder than when they arrived. Tony put the top up and grabbed a blanket folded on the back seat. He spread the blanket over Elizabeth's lap. "This will keep you warm until we get home."

Tony flew to Lynchburg with Elizabeth on Sunday morning. While Elizabeth visited her children, Tony met with an old friend from his ministry days who was now teaching at Liberty University.

Elizabeth's meeting with her children didn't go well. The threesome were having lunch after church at a small restaurant when Mary finally pried out of Elizabeth where she was staying. Elizabeth told them everything about how she met Tony and how she ended up spending the weekend at his house.

Her son, Chuck, was livid. "Are you kidding me? Seriously, Mom, you've got to be kidding! Are you really spending the weekend with the world's most notorious atheist?"

There was no greater villain in the world for students at Liberty University than Dr. Anthony Guest. He was the subject of scorn and fierce animosity to all the students and professors at the Christian college.

Chuck became uncontrollable and finally walked out of the restaurant. Elizabeth followed him out to the sidewalk, imploring him to come back inside. But Chuck began to run and didn't stop until he was back at his dorm. Elizabeth cried with Mary, but not much was said after Chuck left.

The plane ride back to Middleburg was painful.

"I guess this is my first taste of my welcome back to the faith." Tony was somber, knowing this was probably the end of his relationship with Elizabeth.

"Elizabeth, I can't and I won't force you to decide between me and your children. I knew it wasn't fair to bring you into my life and this confirms my worst fears. I'm so sorry."

"Tony, I love my children, but this is my life. And I love you. I don't know how this will end, but I'm not ready to give up on you or my children." Elizabeth forced a smile through her tears as she stared at the mountains far below.

* * *

Tony and Elizabeth met every week at the Chicago airport for the next two months. She spent weekends in the guest house and, even though the weather was getting colder, she rode her horse every day. It was now "her" horse because Tony bought both and she knew the moment she first walked into the barn which she preferred.

Elizabeth called Mary several times a week, and Chuck finally agreed to speak with her over the phone. He was much calmer, but no less convinced his mother should have nothing to do with Dr. Guest.

"Chuck, I understand how you feel and I respect your feelings. But please do me one favor—at least meet Tony. Please do that for me."

"Okay, Mom. I'll do that for you, but it won't change my mind." Chuck wasn't ready to give an inch. But he agreed to spend the next weekend with Mary and his mom at Tony's home.

Tony sent Elizabeth in his jet to pick up her children at Lynchburg, but he didn't go with her. He wanted her to have some space and time to help her kids adjust to the situation. They were impressed by the limo and driver that picked them up at their dorm and especially taken by the red carpet leading to Tony's jet. They enjoyed seeing their mother treated like a queen. Ben picked them up at the airport in Middleburg and drove them to Tony's house. Elizabeth showed them her guest house first to make sure they knew she and Tony had separate quarters.

They walked across the courtyard and met Tony in the den.

"Tony, this is my son, Chuck, and my daughter, Mary. Guys, this is Dr. Anthony Guest."

"Hold on, Elizabeth. That's my former name. I'm a new creation. Hello, Chuck and Mary. My name is Tony and I'm glad to have you as my guests. Could I show you to your rooms?"

They followed Tony down a long hall to a two-bedroom suite with views of the pond at the far side of a pasture.

"There's sandwich makings in the kitchen fridge if you want a snack before dinner. I left the golf cart in the courtyard if you'd like to look around the place. The path goes to the barn and you can follow the riding trail around the whole property and down to the pond. Help yourselves to the canoe if you'd like to paddle around. I appreciate you two joining us for the weekend. I'm sure you have a lot of questions for me and I'll try to answer them at dinner."

Tony was not the devil Chuck and Mary expected. He was soft spoken and his smile was disarming. He didn't look anything like the picture on the cover of his book. He looked like a normal guy in jeans and sweatshirt.

Chuck and Mary sensed their mother was comfortable and happy. That made them happy. They found her in the kitchen fixing a cup a tea and she made some sandwiches for them to take on their golf cart adventure.

"Stop by the barn and introduce yourselves to Black Beauty, my new horse. His name is written on a piece of tape on his stall. I call him Beau."

Chuck and Mary were gone all afternoon. Their tour included a picnic in the gazebo and a paddle in the canoe around the pond. They found an old cabin in the woods Tony didn't even know existed. They waded in a very cold stream and reported it was full of trout. Both had fly fishing lessons at camp and when they saw the literature about trout fishing Tony collected from the museum, they offered to teach him.

Chuck and Mary were unexpectedly at ease. They dominated the dinner conversation. They talked about their limo ride from campus and laughed about their friends' expressions when they saw them get into the big black car. They described every aspect of the jet ride, including the soft drinks, snacks, and views of the mountains. They saw a fox from their golf cart and a large bass while padding around the pond. They thought they saw an eagle, but maybe it was a hawk. And they imagined how an old hermit once lived in the secret cabin for years. Elizabeth and Tony just listened and, somehow, their listening told Chuck and Mary everything they needed to know. They couldn't help but like this guy, and they could see he loved their mother.

Tony and Elizabeth were in the kitchen cooking when Chuck and Mary awoke Saturday morning. They all ate on the large swivel stools around the granite island in the center of the kitchen.

"Well, kids, the sale of the bookstore was completed this week. I'm free!" Elizabeth toasted the air with her cup of tea.

"What are you going to do now?" Mary smiled slyly and looked at Tony. But Chuck didn't smile.

"I could move into the old cabin you found in the woods." Elizabeth laughed and reached for a plate of biscuits. "Would anyone like another biscuit?"

"Okay, Mom, you're changing the subject." Chuck was more serious than Mary.

"I've been thinking about selling our house in Chicago and finding a place in Virginia. What do you think about that idea?"

"You've talked about that for a while and if that's what you want to do . . ." Mary didn't want to push too hard. She could tell this conversation was getting awkward for Tony—and Chuck.

"How 'bout your mom and I saddling the horses so you two can take a ride? You better bundle up. It's cool outside." Tony smiled and stood up. Chuck and Mary laughed at his diversion, but their expressions told Tony they were warming to him a little. Elizabeth could hardly suppress her joy. Tony, with very few words, had begun to win the hearts of her kids. It now seemed possible her imagined "worse-case scenarios" might drop off of her list of future disasters.

Chuck and Mary retraced their route and stops from the day before, only this time on horseback. They rode the horses back to the house for lunch and tied them to a hitching post in the courtyard. After lunch, they rode back to the barn, put the riding gear back in the tack room, and brushed the horses while talking about their mom and Tony.

"Chuck, I think they are serious."

"Mary, I still don't like it but I'm just a guy—you know, not too smart about these things—and I haven't been able to imagine Mom with anyone but our dad, but it makes me happy to see Mom happy with Dr. Guest—or Tony—whatever."

"I think Mom may be looking for our approval." Mary was looking for a little guidance from Chuck.

"Okay, let's just say they get married and she moves into this place. He's been the most famous atheist in the world. Even if he has really returned to faith, he will always be controversial. I'm thinking it could be a hard life for Mom."

"Chuck, I'm sure Mom has thought about all that and she wouldn't marry Tony unless she was sure he was a believer. And I don't think she will marry him if she thinks we're against it."

"I don't know any more. I'm not sure if I'm against it. I want her to be happy. And this wouldn't be a bad place to visit on the weekends. Hey, besides, we're probably jumping to conclusions. He might become an atheist again after meeting her bratty children."

"Chuck, this is serious!"

"Yes, it is and I'm still very conflicted about the whole thing. But it's her decision and she needs to know we support whatever she decides to do—even if I have to fake it."

"Come on, Chuck. We need to be honest with her and with ourselves. Let's keep praying about it. I have to admit; I'm kind of excited about it."

Saturday afternoon the foursome drove into Middleburg and walked around the shops. Tony bought Mary a pair of riding boots and Chuck a cowboy hat. They stopped by the National Sporting Library and Museum on their way home. Saturday night they cooked hamburgers with Chuck managing the grill and Mary cooking French fries and vegetables in the kitchen. Tony dragged a second rocking chair across the porch and positioned it next to his. He and Elizabeth sat under blankets close to the fire table while the kids prepared the meal. It felt like family. It felt like home.

Sunday morning they attended a small church where Tony and Elizabeth visited the last two weeks. No one recognized Tony and he introduced himself using only his first name. He enjoyed being back in church as an anonymous member of the congregation. Dr. Clark was right. He felt a lot closer to God when he was listening instead of preaching.

Chuck and Mary flew back to Liberty University alone on Sunday, but two weeks later, they were back for another visit. This time, after the weekend together, Elizabeth stayed at Tony's house and Tony accompanied Mary and Chuck on the flight back to Lynchburg. Tony wanted to talk with them alone and give them the opportunity to talk to him. Once the plane was in the air, Tony had a captive audience.

"Chuck, Mary, I have enjoyed getting to know you and it was gratifying to see your mother having so much fun being with you."

Mary interrupted with a big smile. "I think she was having fun being with you."

Mary was doing everything she could to make this easy for Tony, taking charge just like her mother.

"I enjoy being with her too. In fact, we're having trouble being apart. This has all happened very fast for us and, I'm sure, it seems even faster for you. But I want you to know I love your mother more than life itself. She took control of my life the moment I met her."

"Sounds like Mom." Chuck seemed to be trying to help Tony, too.

"She helped me know the love of God for the first time in my life. She helped restore my faith and made it impossible for me to continue to pretend God didn't exist." Tony paused for a few seconds and shifted his gaze back and forth to meet their eyes.

"I cannot replace your dad, and he will always be a part of your mom's life. But I want to commit the rest of my life to taking care of her and doing everything I can to make her happy. You two are her family and the loves of her life. I wouldn't do anything to hurt your relationship with her. So—I am asking for your support before I ask your mother to marry me."

Tony knew he was taking a terrible risk. If one of them said "no," he could not ask Elizabeth to go against her children. Chuck and Mary looked at each other with somber expressions. Then Mary smiled. Chuck smiled. They toasted with the cans of Coke. Chuck reached across the aisle and touched knuckles with Tony. Mary pulled off her seat belt, jumped up, and grabbed Tony around the neck. She was crying and laughing. Tony tried to stand up with Mary still hanging on his neck. He managed to stand up enough to return her hug and to share a few happy tears.

Chuck was now rolling his eyes thinking this was a little too much. "Are you sure she is going to say 'yes'?"

* * *

Tony texted Ben from the Lynchburg airport to ask if he would saddle the horses and leave them tied to the post in the courtyard. Ben quickly responded he would have them there by 4:00 p.m.

Tony then texted Elizabeth telling her he would be back at the house about 4:30 and asked if she would take a short ride with him before dark. She replied within seconds, "I've got my spurs on."

Through the weeks since they first met, Tony put together his plan for this day. Elizabeth assumed Tony wanted to talk to her children about their potential marriage, but she wasn't prepared for anything this soon. They rode their horses to the pond, tied up, and walked into the gazebo. With the sun setting over the trees, geese honking above their heads, and Elizabeth's hand in his, Tony got on one knee, pushed a big diamond ring onto her finger, and asked—

"My dear Elizabeth, the love of my life, the essence of all my hopes and dreams—will you grant me the honor of walking with you for the rest of our lives?" Elizabeth got down on both knees and threw her arms around his neck.

"Forever, forever, and forever more!" Elizabeth held his face in her hands and looked into his eyes. "It must have gone well with the children." They both sat on the floor and laughed.

"Yes, it did. In fact, that's the second big hug I've had around my neck today."

"And I know the other one didn't come from Chuck."

"You're right. He wasn't sure you would say 'yes.'"

"That's my Chuck. Apparently, Mary was a little more animated."

"Yes, she was. Definitely her mother's girl."

They walked back to the barn, leading the horses and holding hands. Tony cooked a pasta dinner and opened his best bottle of champagne. It was hard to sleep separately, but they were committed to doing this the right way. And they wouldn't have to wait long. They decided that night to set the wedding day for Valentine's Day, just over two months away.

* * *

They were married in front of the gazebo by the pond. Dr. Clark performed the ceremony. Tony chartered a plane to fly Elizabeth's parents, her sister and family, along with about twenty of Elizabeth's friends and coworkers from the bookstore. There was no white dress or tuxedo. Tony led Beau with Elizabeth aboard down the aisle between the folding chairs and tied him next to the gazebo. For Tony and Elizabeth, it was the happiest Valentine's Day ever.

Tony assumed Elizabeth would have no interest in having more children and never even mentioned the idea. She was thirty-eight when they married and he was forty-two. He tried not to think about having children of his own, but Elizabeth decided to see what the Lord had in mind. It didn't take long for her to find out. Four months after they were married, she found out she was pregnant.

Then I saw "a new heaven and a new earth,"
for the first heaven and the first earth
had passed away.—Revelation 21:1

CHAPTER TEN

A NEW HEAVEN
ON A NEW EARTH

January 2018–immediately after the first debate
(Travelers Rest, SC)

"I've never thought about it like that before," Lydia exclaimed. "It makes so much sense. Why don't we discuss things like this in church?"

Johnny's first class was going exactly as he hoped. His six students were engaged and comfortable with him and each other. They were politely listening, but not afraid to interrupt with questions and comments. The chemistry was good, but the real test was next. Could these students think outside the strictures of their current thinking? Could they consider different interpretations of the Scriptures without losing confidence in their faith?

"This is a research and discussion class where you are all equal partners. I will not monopolize the conversation, except for the next hour. I want to expand the framework of your thinking by presenting some alternative hypotheses about how we interpret the Bible, particularly regarding creation, God's motives, and the end times. Please keep in mind, I am presenting alternative interpretations that appear to be possibilities supported by Scripture. I am not asking you to accept any of these ideas as final truth. I'm not even suggesting I have accepted them myself. My goal is to challenge your thinking and to encourage you to search for more alignment between credible science and the Scriptures.

"Today, I will focus on the beginning and the end, using the first few chapters in Genesis and several sections from Revelation. I will also reference Job, which was a focus for Dr. Guest in the debate. I will be jumping around in the Bible, throwing verses up on the screen, and it may be a little confusing. But you all know your Bible well, so it will make more sense to you than most. My hope is, working together, we can translate these complicated ideas into more understandable concepts for the average person."

Johnny stood, picked up a remote control, pointed it at the flat screen TV on the wall, and a title appeared.

Heaven comes to us

"Let's start at the end. Revelation is the last book of the Bible. On the screen is Revelation 21:1–4. Lydia, will you read this for us?" Lydia looked surprised, but quickly began to read.

> "'Then I saw "a new heaven and a new earth," for the first heaven and the first earth had passed away, and there was no longer any sea. I saw the Holy City, the new Jerusalem, coming down out of heaven from God, prepared as a bride beautifully dressed for her husband. And I heard a loud voice from the throne saying, "Look! God's dwelling place is now among the people, and he will dwell with them. They will be his people, and God himself will be with them and be their God. 'He will wipe every tear from their eyes. There will be no more death' or mourning or crying or pain, for the old order of things has passed away."'"

"Thanks, Lydia. We've all been told we will go to heaven when we die. That's not the complete picture of what the Bible says. These verses say heaven and earth will pass away and God will come live with us on a new earth."

Johnny put the remote down on the table. "Think about what this means. It means someday the current spiritual and physical worlds will end and be replaced by a new heaven on a new earth—a unified heaven and earth. The current order will pass away. 'God will dwell among his people.'

"We won't be floating on a cloud in a spiritual world for eternity. We will live on a new earth in physical bodies and God will live with us. It seems clear to me, once the current spiritual and physical worlds end, there will be a new world that combines spiritual and physical characteristics. We know the resurrected Jesus had a physical body capable of eating and being touched just like us. He had a real physical body, but He could walk through solid walls and transport Himself instantly over great distances. Jesus has a perfect physical body with all the capabilities of a spiritual body. And the Bible says His children, those who have His blood and have their names written in the book of life, will be like him for eternity. Julie, please read these verses." Johnny touched the remote again a new title and verses appeared.

Two sides of eternity

"*Revelation 21:27. 'Nothing impure will ever enter it, nor will anyone who does what is shameful or deceitful, but only those whose names are written in the Lamb's book of life.'*

And Revelation 22:14–15. 'Blessed are those who wash their robes, that they may have the right to the tree of life and may go through the gates into the city. Outside are the dogs, those who practice magic arts, the sexually immoral, the murderers, the idolaters and everyone who loves and practices falsehood.'"

"Thanks, Julie. These verses make it clear there will be two kinds of people in eternity: those who are inside God's kingdom and those who are outside. In other verses in Revelation the 'outside' is called the 'Abyss' and the 'lake of fire.' We usually call it hell. You should note, everyone lives eternally. No one can escape eternity. The Bible refers to both eternal life and eternal death. 'Death' is anything outside the gates of God's kingdom. So, the question is, 'How do we qualify to live inside God's kingdom?'" Johnny aimed the remote again at the screen.

The unique blood of Jesus

"The default destination for everyone appears to be the 'outside.' We know we are all sinners, effectively we are the sexually immoral, the murderers, and the idolaters these verses are referencing. Without some kind of redirection or intervention, none of us qualify to enter this city with streets paved with gold. No one can say this is not fair, because everyone will get what we deserve—unless we ask God to cover our sin with the righteousness of Jesus.

"These verses say we must 'wash our robes' and have our names 'written in the Lamb's book of life.' We know 'washing our robes' refers to being cleansed by the blood of Jesus. The whole of Scripture tells us without the blood of Jesus, there is no forgiveness of sins. Why is the blood of Jesus so important?

"Here's where we need to read between the lines in the Bible. By that I mean we must allow the whole of Scripture to inform what we're currently reading. Think about this: Jesus is the only person who ever lived with spiritual and physical blood. He was conceived by the Holy Spirit—He did not have a physical father—but His mother was a physical human being. So Jesus's blood is unique—no one who has ever lived has His blood type.

"Why is this important? Because the new heaven and earth will be a unified spiritual and physical world. Only people with spiritual and physical bodies can live there. Try to follow me here because this is a little complicated, but important.

"Remember the spiritual world is passing away. Nothing can stay in the spiritual world because it is disappearing. Even God left heaven and passed through the physical world on His way to the new heaven on earth. I believe everything in the spiritual world must pass through the physical world before it can enter the new heaven on earth. Why? I'll try to explain as simply as I can.

"Science and the Bible say the current physical world will also disappear. The Bible tells us this will happen after everything in the spiritual world has passed through the physical world—'after all have come in' as the Bible says. So, everything that currently exists in the spiritual and physical worlds will have no place to go except the new heaven on earth where Jesus is King, or outside in Satan's lake of fire, the place we usually call hell. Modern science, backed up by many studies, believes the cosmos or universe is 'winding down,' and will succumb to entropy just like all life. The timing of biblical and scientific projections for the 'end' may be different, but the outcome is the same.

"I believe we are spiritual beings passing through this physical world, just like Jesus did, except we are not God. We didn't begin our existence on this earth. We're told this in many places in the Bible, but Ephesians 1:3–10 is one of the clearest statements. It's almost too much to fit on the screen. Matt, will you read it for us?"

"*'Praise be to the God and Father of our Lord Jesus Christ, who has blessed us in the heavenly realms with every spiritual blessing in Christ. For he chose us in him before the creation of the world to be holy and blameless in his sight. In love, he predestined us for adoption to sonship through Jesus Christ, in accordance with his pleasure and will—to the praise of his glorious grace, which he has freely given us in the One he loves. In him we have redemption through his blood, the forgiveness of sins, in accordance with the riches of God's grace that he lavished on us. With all wisdom and understanding, he made known to us the mystery of his will according to his good pleasure, which he purposed in Christ, to be put into effect when the times reach their fulfillment—to bring unity to all things in heaven and on earth under Christ.'"*

"God chose us to be His children before the creation of the world. We are pilgrims. This world is not our home. We are redeemed by the blood of Jesus. Redeemed means to buy back. That means we left God's spiritual world, perhaps because it is disappearing for reasons we'll discuss later, and went to Satan's physical world which will also disappear. God purchased us back from Satan by giving His own physical life and by unleashing His unique blood into the world. We must have the physical and spiritual blood of Jesus to live in the new heaven on earth because only those with His blood can enter and live in a physical and spiritual world.

"Some people may ask, 'Why can't I live in this new heaven on earth without Jesus?' That's like asking 'Why can't I live underwater?' Because we are physically incapable of living under water, just as we are physically incapable of living in a spiritual heaven. Only the unique blood of Jesus makes it possible for spiritual or physical beings to live eternally in the new world.

How are we saved?

"Okay, one question remains; who has the blood of Jesus and who doesn't? How do we get this blood? And I'm not talking about putting physical blood in your veins. How do we become a part of the body of Jesus with His blood giving us eternal life?

"Most Christians will say we are saved when we pray to receive Jesus. That may be true, but it seems to conflict with many ideas in Scripture, including the verse on the screen that says God chose us before the creation of the world. It also conflicts with the idea that nothing we do in this world, none of our good works, will save us.

"There are plenty of verses in the New Testament suggesting the willful act of believing in Jesus will save us. 'Praying to receive Jesus' is an act that has defined the Christian since Jesus lived on the earth. Nothing I'm going to say should be construed to mean this act is not essential to becoming a Christian.

"But I would like you to consider the possibility that the act of believing and giving your life to Jesus is not the cause of your eternal salvation, but the evidence you have been God's child from the beginning of time. Consider the possibility that your ability to hear the gospel, understand it, and believe it is the confirmation you have always belonged to Him.

"Please don't misunderstand what I'm saying. I do not believe you can know God in this life and be spiritually alive unless you have willfully given your life to Jesus. That is the only way you can 'wash your robes' as the Bible says and acquire the unique, invisible blood of Jesus. But consider the possibility the act of praying to receive Jesus is the evidence your name was written in the Book of Life before you were born.

"This question is important because it allows for the possibility that many of God's children may not be consciously saved in this life, but are nevertheless redeemed for eternity by the blood of Jesus. Millions of people have lived on this earth without ever hearing the name of Jesus. It is hard to believe they are all condemned to hell.

"I want you to think about and research this question of cause and effect related to salvation. We'll discuss it more later. But in our search to understand God's motives for the creation of this physical universe, we need to make sure we understand when and how we become God's children, why we ended up in a world so heavily influenced by Satan, and when we are redeemed—bought back—by the blood of Jesus.

Is Revelation about the end times or all time?

"Before we jump back to Genesis, I'd like to point out a few alternative perspectives in Revelation. Most people avoid Revelation because it seems really weird. Revelation is complicated because it is hard to tell if it is describing the past, present, or the future. I have come to believe it is describing the whole history of human existence. Rachel, please read the verses on the screen."

> *"Revelation 12:7–9. 'Then war broke out in heaven. Michael and his angels fought against the dragon, and the dragon and his angels fought back. But he was not strong enough, and they lost their place in heaven. The great dragon was hurled down—that ancient serpent called the devil, or Satan, who leads the whole world astray. He was hurled to the earth, and his angels with him.'"*

"Thanks, Rachel. There are many interesting things about this passage. We have all been told Revelation is about the end times, maybe the last seven years before the Lord returns. But we know Satan was in the world before Adam and Eve, and this verse in Revelation is about Satan and his angels being thrown out of heaven to earth. These verses suggest Revelation could be about the entire history of the physical world.

Sin originated in heaven

"These verses also seem to confirm sin did not begin on earth with Adam. Evil apparently existed in heaven until Satan and his angels were thrown out. We should consider the possibility God created the physical world as a way to separate evil from heaven. There is no death in the spiritual world. Satan will live for eternity. God may have used the physical world as a type of prison for Satan.

"God used the physical world to separate evil from good, and it may be that our faithfulness in this world is being used to defeat Satan. I don't know about you, but it never occurred to me until recently that I might be part of God's army in heaven fighting Satan. What we do in this physical world may be directly connected to what happens in the spiritual world.

I'm convinced our prayers and praise during our physical lives are how God defeats Satan.

Our prayers and praise defeat Satan

"I want you to research the possibility this great battle in heaven is somehow related to the spiritual battle we are constantly fighting in this physical world. Could our actions as humans be related to the outcome of this great battle in heaven? We should remember the concept of time as we know it in this physical world may not exist in the spiritual world. It is certainly possible this battle we read about in Revelation is happening right now. Ed, please read the verse on the screen."

> *"Ephesians 6:12. 'For our struggle is not against flesh and blood, but against the rulers, against the authorities, against the powers of this dark world and against the spiritual forces of evil in the heavenly realms.'"*

"This verse, like many others in the Bible, says we are currently in a spiritual battle, not only against dark spiritual forces in this physical world, but we are also involved in a spiritual battle in heaven right now. Have you ever considered the possibility your actions here on earth might influence or impact the outcome of the battle between God and Satan in the spiritual world? It's an important question, because the answer will help us discover why God created the physical world and why we must endure suffering and death."

This is the account of the heavens and the earth when
they were created, when the Lord God made the earth
and the heavens.—Genesis 2:4

CHAPTER ELEVEN

THE REAL CREATION STORY

January 2018—continuation of Johnny's first class
(Travelers Rest, SC)

"Okay! I know this is too long and in the deep weeds. But stay with me a few more minutes. Remember, there are sandwiches and drinks waiting for you in the fridge." Johnny could tell he was pressing everyone's attention span.

"There is a whole lot more in Revelation, but we need to turn back to Genesis to begin connecting the pieces of this puzzle. All of you have your tablets, so call up the first chapter of Genesis. Before we consider alternative interpretations to the Bible's creation story, let's try to find all the evidence we can to substantiate the traditional teaching that this physical universe was created in six days, and also try to make the case Adam and Eve were the humans created in chapter 1.

"I've got some books here by theologians who credibly present the traditional interpretation. Let's look for any

157

scientific support for six-day creation we can find, but it will be hard to find much scientific evidence supporting anything paranormal or metaphysical. That's why they call it 'physical science.' Just remember, there are a lot of things science cannot measure or prove. And besides, science is often wrong. Which is why intellectually honest scientists avoid making definitive statements about anything spiritual—although many have theorized about the apparent connection between the physical and metaphysical worlds. As we know, certain things like gravity cannot be denied, but it also cannot be touched or seen and scientists continue to develop new theories about how it works.

"As we consider creation, there are two alternatives to the traditional creation account in Genesis that can put the Bible and science in perfect alignment. If we interpret the 'days' in the first chapter of Genesis to be long periods of time, we can reconcile the Bible with scientific evidence that the world is millions of years old. And, if the account of Adam and Eve in chapter 2 occurred many years after the creation of the first humans in chapter 1, the Bible is perfectly consistent with scientific theories about the advent of modern mankind.

"I've got the first verse of the Bible on the screen. Lydia, will you do the honors again?"

> *"In the beginning God created the heavens and the earth. Now the earth was formless and empty, darkness was over the surface of the deep, and the Spirit of God was hovering over the waters."*

"As you research six-day creation, consider this verse describing the situation before the first day. It could easily represent millions of years. It allows for the possibility there was a long period of time before 'Day One' when everything in the universe was formless—gases floating around in empty darkness. Science actually supports this scene before the Big Bang, as they call it. The 'surface of the deep' is likely a description of the endless universe, because it says the earth was formless. So, it's unlikely the 'deep' is describing the oceans on earth. I suspect God's Spirit was hovering over massive clouds of water vapors, which is also consistent with some scientific theories before the Big Bang.

"I mention this first verse because, even if we accept the traditional Genesis six-day creation theory, the Scriptures still allow for the universe to have been hundreds of millions of years old before God said, 'Let there be light.'

"Science supports the theory that this solar system—our earth, planets, and sun—are younger than other parts of the universe, so the formation of planets and suns in other parts of the universe could have been going on for millions of years while the earth was still formless.

The physical world allows for separation
of good and evil

"As you look at Genesis, consider a few other pieces of the puzzle. You'll find the whole first chapter is consumed with the word and the idea of separation. You see the word 'separated' used for light and darkness, water above and below the earth, and day and night. God also separates water from dry land on earth. He separates plants and creatures 'according to their own kind.'

"I think this idea may be important because the concept of separation, as we know it, may not exist in the spiritual world. But, like we see with the rich man in the book of Luke, there will be a separation between heaven and hell in eternity.

"The physical world allows for separations and distinctions that might not be possible in the spiritual world, such as the separation of good and evil or life and death. If this is true, it may provide one reason for the creation of the physical world.

"As I mentioned before in Revelation, Satan and his angels rebelled against God in heaven. Evil was comingled with good. The physical world created a way for God to restore heaven by separating good from evil. And importantly, the coming of the new heaven on a new earth will provide a permanent separation of good and evil because only those who have the sinless blood of Jesus can enter. It's just a theory, so check it out yourselves.

"The creation account in the first chapter of Genesis generally follows the chronology theorized by many scientists—light and water, plant life, fish, birds, mammals, and then mankind. Science says it happened over billions of years. The traditional view of the Bible says it happened in six days. My view is simple. If there is an eternal God powerful enough to create this universe, He is not limited by time and could have easily done it all in six seconds or six billion years.

"There's one other thing we need to explain in the first chapter. We have light announced on the first day and plant life created on the third day, but the sun wasn't created until the fourth day. Dr. Guest mentioned this apparent contradiction.

"The verse we read earlier in Revelation could provide one explanation. In the new heaven on earth we will not need a sun because God will provide the light. That may have been the case when He first created the physical world. God is light and He is the beginning and the end. In the beginning, God filled the whole universe with His light. Just a theory, and you should all consider other explanations.

Adam and Eve: the creation of modern mankind

"After we gather the evidence to substantiate the six-day and the six-period creation theories, I'd like for you to consider another possibility. Let's look at chapter 2, verse 4. Henry, read this for us."

Henry was frantically writing on his notepad. "I'm having trouble keeping up. This is great stuff. Okay,

> *Genesis 2:4. 'This is the account of the heavens and the earth when they were created, when the LORD God made the earth and the heavens.'"*

"This is a pivotal verse in the Bible. Traditionally, it is thought to be the preamble to the creation account of Adam and Eve. And traditionally, we have been taught the account of Adam and Eve is a more detailed review of the creation of mankind from the first chapter. This is important for several reasons. First, the biblical clock on the age of the earth begins with Adam. If the creation happened in six days and if Adam was the 'mankind' created in the first chapter, then the earth is less than 10,000 years old. Archeological discoveries and carbon dating of these discoveries appear to prove this to be impossible.

"There are many inconsistencies with archeological finds, and carbon dating methodologies have proved to be inaccurate on many occasions. But when all evidence is considered, it seems highly improbable, at least for human understanding, for this earth and universe to be less than 10,000 years old. I'm certainly not ruling it out and we need to do the research, but there is a plausible scriptural alternative you should consider.

"I believe the verse on the screen is a summary of all that came before it. It is a concluding statement of the account of when heaven and earth were created. It cannot be an introduction to the next section about Adam and Eve because that next section is not about the creation of heaven and earth. It's just about Adam and Eve.

"So, what if verse 4 of chapter 2 is actually the last verse of chapter 1? Remember, God didn't denote the chapters in the Bible. Using my assumption, the first verse of chapter 2 would begin with 'Now.' This tells me we are getting ready to hear about something different—a new subject. Ed, please read the next verse on the screen."

"Yes, Sir. Genesis 2:5 or maybe now it's Genesis 2:1 since we are reorganizing the Bible. Just kidding!

'Now no shrub had yet appeared on the earth and no plant had yet sprung up, for the LORD God had not sent rain on the earth and there was no one to work the ground, but streams came up from the earth and watered the whole surface of the ground.'"

"Thanks, Ed. Don't let the chapter and verse designations get in your way. They are not the inspired part of the Scriptures. This is a very curious verse. We know from chapter 1 that plants and vegetation were created on the third day before human beings, yet this verse says 'no plant had yet sprung up' and 'there was no one to work the ground.'

"This is our first hint that the account of Adam and Eve which follows this verse is not the same account of the creation of male and female humans described in the first chapter. I'll just lay out my whole theory and then we can circle back around to discuss different parts of it. Hold on to your seats because this will sound crazy until you think about it.

Satan thrown to earth after the creation of humans, but before Adam and Eve

"First, the chronology related to Satan being thrown down to earth changes our traditional understanding of Genesis and Revelation—everything we think about the beginning and the end. We know Satan was thrown down to earth after the seven 'days' of creation because God said it was all good after the creation was complete. There was no evil in the world, so Satan could not have been here. And there could not have been a tree with the knowledge of good and evil described in chapter 2.

"But we know Satan was in the world before Adam and Eve because he tempted them with the knowledge of good and evil. That means the creation of Adam and Eve came later, perhaps much later than the creation of mankind in chapter 1.

"Also, Revelation includes the account of Satan being thrown down to earth. This means Revelation is not just about the end times. It may be about all time. Once you consider that possibility, the book of Revelation is a completely different story, especially when you understand the story is describing happenings in both the spiritual and physical worlds. Revelation is still confusing, but it makes a lot more sense when you know it is describing the beginning and end of the physical and spiritual worlds, as well as the advent of a new and unified physical and spiritual world.

"Let's consider the possibility that after the six periods of creation and a long period of rest and peace on earth, Satan and his demons were thrown down to earth. Revelation tells us a little about what happened. The fire and smoke likely devastated the earth for thousands of years. The verses I just put on the screen are the ones describing a scene just before Satan was thrown out of heaven and down to earth. Matt, please read it for us."

"Alright, Dr. Wright, but good Catholics don't get into this crazy stuff.

Revelation 12:1–6. 'A great sign appeared in heaven: a woman clothed with the sun, with the moon under her feet and a crown of twelve stars on her head. She was pregnant and cried out in pain as she was about to give birth. Then another sign appeared in heaven: an enormous red dragon with seven heads and ten horns and seven crowns on its heads. Its tail swept a third of the stars out of the sky and flung them to the earth. The dragon stood in front of the woman who was about to give birth, so that it might devour her child the moment he was born. She gave birth to a son, a male child, who "will rule all the nations with an iron scepter. And her child was snatched up to God and to his throne. The woman fled into the wilderness to a place prepared for her by God, where she might be taken care of for 1,260 days."'"

Johnny looked out the window and began to speak. "I think the woman in these verses is the image of the physical world. The sun, the moon, and the twelve stars are physical symbols. The woman is getting ready to give birth to a son who will rule all the nations. This could be Jesus—the Alpha—the firstborn of modern mankind. He was taken up to God and protected until His physical birth thousands of years later.

"The woman, perhaps the symbol of the lineage of Jesus, may have been taken to the Garden of Eden where God created Adam out of dirt from the ground. Adam began the lineage of Jesus. Adam was 'born' in a place prepared by God as described in Revelation. This was the Garden of Eden.

"Okay—that's enough for today. I know I've covered a tremendous amount of ground. I know I'm introducing perspectives on Scripture you may never have heard or seriously considered before. There are certainly propositions I'm making here some might even consider heresy. From my heart, please hear that I am not wavering to any degree from the essence of the gospel or who God says He is. In fact, it's my love for Him and His plan for us that drives me.

"My guess is about now, you're as tired of sitting as I am of standing. Let's take a break."

*"Woe! Woe! Woe to the inhabitants
of the earth . . ."*—Revelation 8:13

CHAPTER TWELVE

WE LIVE IN SATAN'S WORLD

January 2018–continuation of Johnny's first class
(Travelers Rest, SC)

After their break, when everyone was reassembled in the conference room, Johnny returned to his position next to the video monitor and tapped the remote control.

> Satan has been pursuing the sons and daughters
> of Adam ever since he was thrown down to earth.

"Let's consider what might have happened in the physical world when Satan and his demons were thrown to earth. This would have been after the seven days of creation and God's 'rest,' and before the creation of Adam and Eve. The world was beautiful, full of lush vegetation, humans, and animals. And there was no sin in the world.

165

"But after Satan was thrown down, everything changed. Remember we read this verse in Revelation, 'But woe to the earth and the sea, because the devil has gone down to you! He is filled with fury, because he knows that his time is short.' The verse we read before the break talks about the wings of an eagle saving the woman who may symbolize the physical world.

"I'm fairly sure the book of Revelation does not follow a physical chronology because sections from the timeless spiritual world are interspersed throughout the book. It appears to me the verses I will now put on the screen, which come before the other verses we just read about Satan being thrown down, are describing the situation on earth after Satan and his demons exploded into a peaceful and sinless physical world.

"I will put several excerpts taken from Revelation 8:13–9:21. I'll read the verses as I put them on the monitor.

'As I watched, I heard an eagle that was flying in midair call out in a loud voice: "Woe! Woe! Woe to the inhabitants of the earth, because of the trumpet blasts about to be sounded by the other three angels!" The fifth angel sounded his trumpet, and I saw a star that had fallen from the sky to the earth. The star was given the key to the shaft of the Abyss. When he opened the Abyss, smoke rose from it like the smoke from a gigantic furnace. The sun and sky were darkened by the smoke from the Abyss.'

"Satan is the star falling from the sky to earth and he has the keys to the Abyss. The smoke from the Abyss created darkness around the world.

"The next verse indicates Satan infected mankind with his wickedness, again, likely long before Adam and Eve were created.

'The rest of mankind who were not killed by these plagues still did not repent of the work of their hands; they did not stop worshiping demons, and idols of gold, silver, bronze,

stone and wood—idols that cannot see or hear or walk. Nor
did they repent of their murders, their magic arts, their
sexual immorality or their thefts.'

"Chapter 6 of Revelation seems to be a summary of the creation
of the physical world order, Satan's domain. We have the stars
falling from the sky which suggests this is when Satan and his
angels are thrown down to earth. Again, this does not follow our
concept of chronology, and we will talk more about it later, but
the 'hiding in caves' in these next verses caught my attention.

> *Revelation 6:12–17. 'I watched as he opened the sixth seal.*
> *There was a great earthquake. The sun turned black like*
> *sackcloth made of goat hair, the whole moon turned blood*
> *red, and the stars in the sky fell to earth, as figs drop from*
> *a fig tree when shaken by a strong wind. The heavens*
> *receded like a scroll being rolled up, and every mountain*
> *and island was removed from its place. Then the kings of*
> *the earth, the princes, the generals, the rich, the mighty,*
> *and everyone else, both slave and free, hid in caves and*
> *among the rocks of the mountains. They called to the moun-*
> *tains and the rocks, "Fall on us and hide us from the face of*
> *him who sits on the throne and from the wrath of the Lamb!*
> *For the great day of their wrath has come, and who can*
> *withstand it?"'*

"Why does all this crazy stuff matter? Because if Satan's entry
into a perfect physical world created these conditions before
Adam and Eve, there would have been an ice age with many of
the people and animals on earth killed. This may have been
when the dinosaurs and other prehistoric animals were wiped
out. This may have been when early humans who were made
in the image of God, hid in caves and devolved into savages
over many years. Their physical stature would have deteriorated over generations because the vegetation—the nutrients
from fruits, nuts and berries—would have died without

adequate sunlight. Many of the scientific theories about the ages could be explained by this one occurrence.

Adam and Eve were created in Satan's world

"Let's jump back to Genesis. Write down your questions and we'll get back to them. I'll put verse 5 of chapter 2 back on the screen.

> *'Now no shrub had yet appeared on the earth and no plant had yet sprung up, for the LORD God had not sent rain on the earth and there was no one to work the ground, but streams came up from the earth and watered the whole surface of the ground.'*

"Let's assume, just for discussion purposes, when Adam and Eve were created the conditions on earth were like those we just read from Revelation after Satan took dominion over the earth. Nomadic tribes of savages scoured the earth for food and lived in caves for generations. Perhaps the smoke, after hundreds or thousands of years, cleared and the sun was once again shining on earth.

"The verse makes perfect sense if you assume the humans on earth at the time were scavengers and didn't cultivate the soil. This is consistent with scientific theories that the cultivation of crops began with modern man. I'm suggesting this verse is referring to the cultivation of crops because it says there was no one to work the ground. Plants were growing before humans were created in chapter 1, but cultivated crops began with Adam and Eve.

"I'm jumping around a lot, but I'll help you connect all of this as we go along. You should note another interesting connection between the first chapter of Genesis and Revelation 4:7–8. The four groups of living creatures created in Genesis are represented as the four living creatures worshiping Jesus in Revelation.

'The first living creature was like a lion, the second was like an ox, the third had a face like a man, the fourth was like a flying eagle. Each of the four living creatures had six wings and was covered with eyes all around, even under its wings.'

"I believe the lion represents the wild animals in Genesis, the ox represents the livestock, the living creature with the face of man represents early humans, and the eagle represents the birds and the fish. Scientists put birds and fish in the same evolutionary category. If everything in the spiritual world must pass through the physical world, the four living creatures could represent different types of spirits passing through this physical world on their way to the new heaven. That's good news for those of us who love dogs!

"Later in chapter 7 of Revelation we see a different group of humans. Revelation 7:9 says,

'After this I looked, and there before me was a great multitude that no one could count, from every nation, tribe, people and language, standing before the throne and before the Lamb. They were wearing white robes and were holding palm branches in their hands.'

"These are the people who come out of the Great Tribulation. We've all been taught this will occur in the future, in the end times. But I think it is very possible the Great Tribulation refers to the time here on earth for all of God's people. The journey through this physical world is a 'great tribulation' for everyone, and every human being experiences sin, separation, suffering, and death. I mention this because it will help us discover God's motives for creating the physical world.

"Back to Genesis. If Adam and Eve were the humans created in the perfect world described in chapter 1, then the Garden of Eden would not have been necessary. The entire earth described in chapter 1 was filled with plants and trees producing fruits, nuts, and berries. Everything was good, so as I said before, there could not have been a tree of 'good and evil.'

"But if Adam and Eve came after the seven days or periods of creation, and after Satan was thrown down to earth, the earth would have still been suffering from the devastation caused when Satan and his demons entered the physical world. Humans on the earth at that time were likely savage and violent. If that were the situation before Adam and Eve were created, then the Garden of Eden would have been essential because it created a protected oasis in the middle of a dangerous world.

Savages outside the Garden of Eden

"I keep getting sidetracked, but remember, we are demonstrating the credibility of the Scriptures by showing biblical creation is consistent with what appears to be credible science. We know the Bible is true and we don't need science—which is often wrong—to prove it is. But I think we have an incredible opportunity to hit the critics of the Bible square in their jaws with real facts.

"Here are a few more things that suggests the creation of mankind and the creation of Adam and Eve are not the same event.

"After the fall, Adam and Eve worked the land, cultivated crops, kept herds of cattle, ate meat, and offered animal sacrifices to God. But apparently, Adam's son Cain refused to offer an animal sacrifice. He brought an offering of fruits and vegetables. This event reveals how serious God is about the need for a blood sacrifice to be offered as a substitute for our sins. God showed his displeasure to Cain when he refused to obey.

"Cain became angry and took his anger out on his brother Abel. Cain killed his brother, and much like Satan being thrown out of heaven, God banished Cain from 'the land' and forced him to become a 'restless wanderer on the earth.' Cain was afraid 'whoever found him would kill him.' But, according to the traditional teachings of the Bible, Cain was the only person on earth except for his mother and father.

"I think Cain was afraid because he knew evil and violent savages lived around them. So God gave him a mark that frightened other humans and warned them not to hurt Cain. My theory about roaming nomadic tribes outside the Garden of Eden also answers another question mentioned by Dr. Guest. Cain left his parents and slept with his wife. Where did this 'wife' come from? I once heard a Sunday school teacher say Cain married his sister. No sister is mentioned in the Bible and that wouldn't be a good situation anyway.

"Here's another question: why would Cain build a city if there were no other people? He might if he joined a nomadic tribe. If you follow the history of Cain, you will see a lot of things that suggest he was mixing with a different race of people. And that fits with recent scientific findings that report modern men mated with primitive women.

"Most scientists still think this cross breeding between modern men and Neanderthals happened hundreds of thousands of years ago, but I've seen enough research to conclude it was certainly possible for Cain to have mated with women from a primitive tribe of humans less than ten thousand years ago.

"We're running out of time, so I'll wrap up quickly with a few verses from Job."

Ed put his hand up but didn't wait to be called on. "Sorry to interrupt, Dr. Wright, but I've been in church and reading the Bible since I was a baby. I can't believe I've never seen the obvious contradictions to the traditional interpretations of Genesis or even considered the connection between Satan being thrown down in Revelation and the fact he was in the Garden of Eden before Adam and Eve. Why have I never heard these questions in church or even here at this Christian university?"

"Ed, I never noticed any of this either until I began to question my faith after I experienced a lot of tragedy and injustice

in my life. I wanted to know why God created a world so full
of sorrow, suffering, and death. It didn't make sense and none
of the traditional answers worked for me. As I looked for
answers, I began to see things I never noticed before. Probably
because I had not wanted to consider anything that might
discredit the Scriptures. But the more I dig and have an open
mind about considering non-traditional interpretation of
Scriptures, the more credible the Scriptures have become. Let
me wrap up our time today with this.

Satan's conversation with God

"I know my presentation today has been disjointed. These ideas
will make more sense as we dig deeper and connect the dots
throughout the Bible. I think we can create a credible logic path
for people who have some knowledge of the Bible, but we're
going to have to work very hard to write our conclusions in a
way that can be understood by unbelievers and believers who
don't know the Bible. That may be impossible, but I want to
do all we can to help everyone see the Bible is the ultimate
source of truth.

"Before we break for lunch, let's consider one of Dr. Guest's
primary complaints to God. Dr. Guest talked a lot about
Satan's conversation with God in the book of Job. This conversation could explain a lot about the suffering and death in
this physical world. Rachel, will you read this for us."

"Dr. Wright, I have a lot of questions about your presentation today, but all this new stuff is really fun to think about.

> *Job 1:8–11. 'Then the LORD said to Satan, "Have you
> considered my servant Job? There is no one on earth like
> him; he is blameless and upright, a man who fears God and
> shuns evil."*
>
> *"Does Job fear God for nothing?" Satan replied. "Have
> you not put a hedge around him and his household and
> everything he has? You have blessed the work of his hands,*

so that his flocks and herds are spread throughout the land.
But now stretch out your hand and strike everything he has,
and he will surely curse you to your face."'"

Johnny stood and pointed to the verses on the screen. "Satan is accusing God of bribing Job and buying his love and obedience. And he is accusing Job of being bought—of being a puppet of God. Satan is demanding justice from God. We read in Revelation earlier about Satan accusing the brothers and sisters in heaven. Then we read how the testimonies of the brothers and sisters, along with the blood of Jesus, defeated Satan and resulted in him being thrown to earth.

"It sounds to me like God must allow Satan to cause suffering and death because Satan has accused us of being spoiled children and demanded we have the freedom to know good and evil. Satan has dared God to let us suffer and predicted we will curse God to His face if He doesn't surround us with blessings. This is *Satan's dare* to God and it may be the reason we all have to pass through the physical world and endure suffering and death.

"And it may be why the Bible tells us to be thankful in all things and praise God—because our praise proves Satan wrong. When we praise God and thank Him despite all the pain and suffering in this world, we prove Satan wrong and defeat Him. I believe the collective praise of believers in this world creates the power that throws Satan and his demons out of heaven— and satisfies the justice demanded by Satan.

In Summary

"I'll sum up my hypothesis and then all of you can develop your own. God is all-powerful and sovereign over all things, but He governs Himself by four immutable characteristics or laws. I mentioned these during the debate. He gives His people perfect love, perfect freedom, perfect justice, and perfect mercy. Just like He created an ordered physical universe governed with unchanging laws, God holds Himself to laws He won't change. He is sovereign over all things, but He is never arbitrary.

"God's plan has always been for the spiritual and physical worlds to unite into a new physical/spiritual heaven. Perfect physical bodies with spiritual powers will give His creatures the highest possible quality of life for all eternity.

"God's plan includes giving all His creation complete independence and freedom. But God knew Satan would use this freedom to lead a rebellion against Him. Satan chose to be god in his own kingdom rather than be a part of God's kingdom—just like many people choose to be the god of their own lives rather than a part of God's kingdom.

"The first phase of God's plan was to create a physical world that would provide the transition—the bridge—to a new heaven. Heavenly spirits had to journey through the physical world and inhabit physical bodies to gain the characteristics—water and blood—necessary to live in the new heaven.

"There was no evil in the physical world when it was first created and all the living creatures freely obeyed and praised God. There was no violence and neither animals nor mankind ate meat. It is possible there was no physical death in the world until Satan was thrown down. I'm not sure. Or it may have been that, even in this perfect world, physical bodies died in order to free their spirits to return to a special area of heaven described in Revelation—a waiting room—until all the spirits from the spiritual world passed through the physical world.

"It's also possible when Satan realized God's plan required all the angels—and even God Himself—to take on physical bodies and pass through the physical world, he led a rebellion against God. Satan accused God of not giving His creatures the freedom to choose evil and for bribing them with blessings to obey and praise Him. Satan challenged God to allow His creatures to have the knowledge of good and evil, claiming they would choose evil and follow Satan rather than God.

"Just like in the book of Job, which I believe is an allegory about all mankind as well as God's children in heaven, God's plan from the beginning was to answer *Satan's dare* and respond with perfect justice. He chose to give His people freedom to choose good or evil, to follow God or Satan. He allowed His people to suffer and be tempted with evil.

"Our response to all the difficulties in this physical world may decide the ultimate outcome of the battle between good and evil. God's people in this fallen physical world may collectively decide whether God or Satan prevail in the great battle in heaven. We know the people of God will ultimately prevail, and we know the battle has already been won in the spiritual world. But it's still scary to think the outcome of the battle in heaven may depend on us—the physical body of Christ in this world.

"I've probably left you all confused today, but hopefully you now have enough questions and theories to help us develop a broad array of hypotheses to guide our research. How many of you can stay for lunch?"

Every hand went up.

Therefore, if anyone is in Christ,
the new creation has come: The old has gone,
the new is here!—2 Corinthians 5:17

CHAPTER THIRTEEN

NEW CREATION

January 2018—after the first debate
(Travelers Rest, SC)

Dr. Wright, this is Suzie Robertson. You'll remember me (I hope)
from your youth group in Boone. Can we talk in person? I work in
Charlotte now and can drive to Palmetto Christian any time. It's
important. Please let me know. Suzie.

Johnny was not completely surprised by Suzie's email. He
thought of Suzie when Alan Bunster mentioned the mysterious
Facebook post in his "sermon" during last Sunday's service.
When Alan highlighted a response from someone claiming to
know the truth about Johnny's firing from the church in
Boone—and promising to do something about it—he immediately suspected the post might be from Suzie. Johnny had
long believed Suzie's father, Richard Robertson, was involved
with the lies that led to his firing. And now he was guessing his

own Facebook post about what really happened at the church helped Suzie connect the dots.

It was Wednesday morning. Johnny forwarded Suzie's email to Patti with a note.

Patti, could we ask Suzie to drive over Friday afternoon and spend the night at our house? I'm guessing this is about my firing from the church.

Johnny had a lot of work to do before his Thursday class. His mailbox was already full of emails from his students about their areas of interest. Henry and Matt apparently stayed up most of Tuesday night diagraming Revelation. They wanted to make a presentation to the class on Thursday. Patti's response popped up on Johnny's screen.

Johnny, that sounds good. We've got lasagna in the freezer, so dinner will be easy—if you don't mind eating it again.

Johnny immediately pulled Suzie's email back up and hit "reply."

Suzie, could you drive over this Friday afternoon? Patti and I would love for you to have dinner and stay at our house for the night. It will be good to catch up.

It took Suzie only a few seconds to respond.

I'll leave work a little early Friday afternoon and be there about 5:00. I can get a hotel or drive back to Charlotte Friday night—don't want to put you and Patti out.

Suzie, we love to have friends stay at the house. We'll have a nice dinner, lots of conversation, and send you on your way with a good cup of coffee Saturday morning. I'll email you detailed directions to our home in a few minutes. We're looking forward to seeing you. Dr. J.

Johnny found the well-used computer file with directions to his home and forwarded it to Suzie. He hadn't come to fully trusting GPS after being misled a few times. He was extremely curious about what Suzie wanted to tell him. Why did she need to drive all the way from Charlotte to tell him in person? He tried to put his questions aside and refocus on the preparations for his Thursday class.

* * *

January, 2018 – Johnny's second class
(Travelers Rest, SC)

Johnny's students were focused and busy. Lydia created a group email address file including Johnny and all six students. Johnny watched the emails flying back and forth all morning. His students were doing the work for him. They were pairing up and agreeing to work on different topics.

Ed and Rachel wanted to research and write the section on the credibility of the Bible. Both had written several papers their freshmen and sophomore years about how the Bible was put together, the accuracy of the Bible, and other evidence the Bible was supernaturally inspired.

Matt and Henry, the class skeptics, wanted to research the history and credibility of science as it relates to the Bible, but decided first to research the possibility Revelation could be about the history of the physical and spiritual worlds. They asked Johnny to reserve thirty minutes during Thursday's class for their presentation about alternative theories of Revelation.

Lydia and Julie wanted to research the first two chapters of Genesis and consider Johnny's theoretical possibilities that the six days of creation could be six long periods of time and Adam and Eve were created long after the creation of the first human beings. They also planned to research scientific evidence related to the Great Flood.

Johnny arrived thirty minutes early for his Thursday class with donuts, sandwiches, and drinks. Henry and Matt were already there making sure the memory stick with their Power-Point presentation worked with the conference room computer and would connect with the big monitor on the wall. The technology seemed to be working well. By 9:45, all the students were in their seats with coffee or soft drinks. It was clear from their conversations the three teams met separately for breakfast.

"Thanks again for organizing yourselves and getting started so quickly. Let's begin by confirming our three initial teams. Ed and Rachel will be researching and compiling information establishing the credibility of the Bible. Matt and Henry will research the credibility of science in general and as it relates to the Bible and creation. They also jumped ahead into Revelation and will make a presentation today.

"Lydia and Julie will dig into the first two chapters of Genesis and consider six days or six periods of creation, whether Adam and Eve were the humans created in the first chapter, and the hypothesis that Satan didn't arrive in the physical world until after the seven days or periods of time in chapter 1. They will also research scientific evidence of the Flood and look for biblical explanations of why a flood was necessary.

"Ed and Rachel, will you start the discussion today with your ideas about the credibility of the Bible?" Rachel stood up and took a memory stick out of her purse.

PROVING THE BIBLE IS TRUE

"If Matt and Henry don't mind me temporarily disconnecting their setup, I'll show you the outline we've developed to prove the Bible is true." Rachel replaced the memory stick in the laptop on the counter with her own. She carefully reviewed several pages of excerpts from scholars who documented the evidence of biblical consistency and truth. "Ed and I will provide all the detail and a summary for our final report."

Rachel pulled her memory stick and replaced Matt and Henry's. "This is critically important to our work because—as Dr. Guest said in the debate—everything we believe as Christians is based on the Bible. I am very anxious to prove Dr. Guest wrong." Rachel's tone toward Dr. Guest was surprisingly harsh.

"We must have confidence in the veracity—the truth—of the Bible and be able to defend it to skeptics. The Bible provides many internal proofs, which means the Bible, by its very nature, proves itself to be a supernatural document. There is nothing like it in the world today.

"The Bible is a remarkably consistent book in terms of its message, yet it was written over many years by numerous different writers from different lands and languages. It is filled with geographic designations still being used by archeologists today to find lost cities and civilizations. And, unlike every other religious book, the Bible has never had to be changed because of error or false teachings. It never says things like 'the earth is flat' which was the common belief until several hundred years ago.

"Perhaps the most compelling evidence is what we call external evidence. For example, there is much scientific evidence supporting the fact there really was a Great Flood and many other writings verify it as well. And Ed has a few teasers about the statistical probability of Bible prophesies. I'll turn it over to him."

Ed was feverishly working his tablet. "Let me see if I can get the mirroring app to work with this antique screen."

Johnny was refilling his coffee cup. "Ed, that screen is only three years old."

"That is an antique Dr. J." A large title—Statistical Improbability of Bible Prophecies—appeared on the screen.

"Okay, my tablet was able to connect with the distant past. Now I'm ready. By way of full disclosure: Rachel and I didn't do all this yesterday. We've been working on this stuff since we got to Palmetto. It's really important because everything we believe about life, salvation, and eternal life comes from the Bible. It's stupid for anyone to assume the Bible is true without proof. As it says in Hebrews 11, 'Faith is being *sure* of what we hope for and *certain* of what we cannot see.'

"But most of the world believes science has disproved the Bible. That's what they teach in schools. Many Christian churches don't teach the Bible is true. If we can't defend the accuracy of the Bible, I don't know how we can in good conscience tell people to follow Jesus.

"Our research will focus on five areas of proof of biblical accuracy. They're on the screen and I will read them.

1. *Archeology*
2. *Dead Sea Scrolls*
3. *Secular History*

4. *Fulfilment of Biblical Prophecy*
5. *Consistency of the Bible's Internal Evidence*

"Rachel mentioned a few of these already. We'll discuss why archeology and old scrolls are important, but biblical prophecy is, at least for me, the most convincing proof of the supernatural inspiration of the Bible. On the screen is a good opening statement about prophecy.

> *What is prophecy? 'the foretelling of future events, by inspiration from God. . . . A true prophecy can come only from God; and is the highest proof of the divine origin of the message of which it is a part' (American Tract Society Bible Dictionary).*

"Real prophecy can only come from God because only God could know what is going to happen in the future. So, if many statistically improbable prophecies in the Bible have come true, this provides objective evidence of the existence of God as well as evidence God wrote the Bible. It means the Bible is true. Here's a quick example of one prophecy from a math expert.

> *The Messiah will be born in Bethlehem (Micah 5:2). The average population of Bethlehem from the time of Micah to the present (1958) divided by the average population of the earth during the same period = 7,150/ 2,000,000,000 or 2.8 × 10⁵*

"So, the probability of this one prophecy coming true is about one in two hundred and eighty thousand. The same expert then did the calculation on eight different prophecies that all came true. He calculated the probability of all of them coming true was one in one hundred quadrillion—that is the number one followed by seventeen zeros!

"None of us are math majors, but I believe these numbers tell us it was statistically improbable, if not impossible, for

Micah to have guessed from all the places in the world and over an unknown period of time the Messiah would be born in a small and relatively obscure village in Israel. Yet Jesus was born in Bethlehem even though his mother lived in Jerusalem.

"If the likelihood of just one biblical prophecy happening as predicted is virtually impossible, what is the likelihood many biblical prophecies would happen as predicted? Zero! Nada! These events could not have all been accurately predicted unless the writer already knew the future. And only God can know the future because He's already there.

"Rachel and I will compile substantial research in the five categories of proof we had on the screen. I can guarantee you it will confirm this Bible app on my tablet was written by people who were guided by the hand of God. Well—maybe not the app itself, though it's good, but certainly the original books of the Bible."

Johnny started the applause and the other four students joined him. "Bravo, Rachel and Ed. This will be a powerful introduction to our document. Be sure to include a section about the Bible canon—the explanation of how the books of the Bible were selected and put together—and why some manuscripts were left out. Also, in everything we do, we need to include the best counter arguments from atheists, critics, and skeptics. Let's refute all the claims against the accuracy of the Bible."

WAS THE UNIVERSE CREATED IN SIX DAYS?

"Okay, Lydia and Julie. Tell us what you're going to do with Genesis."

Lydia and Julie were sitting next to each other pointing at the other's iPads. Lydia spoke first.

"The debate between those who believe creation occurred in six twenty-four-hour days and those who believe the 'days' in Genesis represent ages—long periods of time—has been going on for more than a century. Neither of these theories questions the inspiration or accuracy of the Bible, they are just honest differences of opinion about how to interpret the text.

"The day-age theory originated in the nineteenth century as an attempt to reconcile the Bible's creation account with new scientific theories which appeared to confirm the earth was millions of years old. Both sides of this debate make good arguments and we will document the pros and cons of each.

"Dr. J's theory, or 'possibility,' as he likes to call it, that the creation of Adam and Eve is a different account than the creation of human beings in chapter 1 of Genesis is an interesting theory some of us discussed last year during our dinners at Dr. J's house. His theory seems to have some merit because God pronounced everything good after the six days of creation. That means there was no evil. There couldn't have been a fruit tree that imparted the knowledge of good and evil. Satan couldn't have been thrown down to earth at that point. But Satan was in the Garden of Eden with Adam and Eve. Dr. J also asks some interesting questions about Cain's wife, his building a city, and other anomalies to the traditional interpretation of Genesis. We're going to look into all of this and document what we find.

"We shouldn't change or twist the Scriptures to fit scientific theories, but we should be open, as Dr. J has talked about, to consider different interpretations of Scripture based on credible science. We will study the Hebrew text and other uses of the word 'day' in the Bible to provide the evidence for both sides of the argument.

"However, if Adam and Eve were created on the sixth day in chapter 1, whether it is a twenty-four-hour day or a long period of time, the genealogical clock starts. If the genealogies in the Bible are correct, the time from Adam until Jesus is just over 4,000 years. If we add the 2,000 plus years from the time of Jesus to the present, the Young Earth theorists conclude the earth is less than 7,000 years old. Some Bible scholars suggest that genealogical records in the Bible sometimes skip many generations which would expand the years since Adam, but even those scholars usually say the earth is less than 10,000 years old.

"Anything is possible in the context of an all-powerful and all-knowing God. But as Dr. J said in the debate last Friday, God gave us science to reveal His glory and to confirm the Scriptures. We shouldn't be afraid to use science to better understand the Bible, but we should always begin our research with the knowledge the Bible is true. If credible science suggests alternative interpretations of the Scripture, we should consider those alternatives. That's what we intend to do. Lydia, you have some ideas about Dr. J's theory."

"Thanks, Julie. We obviously haven't had a lot of time since Tuesday to consider the idea that the creation of Adam and Eve in chapter 2 of Genesis happened many years after the creation of mankind in chapter 1. But it didn't take us long to find this theory consistent with scientific theories and even consistent with the Bible text.

"If you keep reading the next several chapters in Genesis, it is clear there are different races of humans, including giants. This doesn't seem likely if Cain left the garden and married an unnamed sister. And who were "the sons of God"? Perhaps they were the humans made in the image of God in the first chapter. Maybe "the sons of man" were those made from the ground like Adam and his offspring. Very interesting.

"There's a lot to think about and study with this theory that God created a race of human beings long before He created modern men in the form of Adam and Eve. But it does fit with science. Julie and I will gather more information and we are also going to research the scientific evidence of the Great Flood and Noah's Ark. But first Julie wants to share a few thoughts about creation."

DID GOD DOWNLOAD THE PHYSICAL WORLD?

Julie stood and walked toward the screen. "Technology opens new possibilities for different theories about creation. Dr. J talked about this briefly in the debate and some of us discussed it in his class last fall. Think about digital technology. Keep in mind humans didn't create the digital world. God did. It has existed since the beginning of time, and maybe before. People just recently figured out how to use it. The digital world could be a bridge between the spiritual and physical worlds. This is just a thought and I'm using rather limited human terms to describe transcendent spiritual principles."

Julie held up her cell phone. "I can take this phone out to the middle of nowhere and download thousands of apps and digital files from distant servers in unknown places. Right here in this room an invisible digital system exists connecting us with servers holding billions of bits of information and files. It's invisible. We can't hold it in our hands unless we have compatible hardware, but it's all here. I can download an invisible digital file I stored five years ago. It will look new on my phone or tablet, but it's been around for a long time. Then I could change that file, save it, and it would be new—yet still created a long time ago.

"Okay, think about the creation of the world in terms of downloading a file. We all know this verse on the screen.

Hebrews 11:3. 'By faith we understand that the universe was formed at God's command, so that what is seen was not made out of what was visible.'

"The Bible never tells us God created this world out of nothing. It tells us the world was made out of materials that were not visible. Now think about this in the context of the spiritual world transitioning into the physical world. The invisible becomes visible. The spiritual world is downloaded into the physical world. The spiritual file still exists, but we can now see it on a physical screen.

"This is consistent with mankind being made in the 'image' of God. It is consistent with the accounts in the Bible of angels appearing as men. They were downloaded into the physical world. It is consistent with the idea that each of us as God's children exist in the spiritual world like a digital file while we are booted up in the physical world. And it is consistent with the idea the physical world is continuously connected to a spiritual app while we are operating as human beings. What we do in the physical world changes the digital files in the spiritual world. Our battle is not against flesh and blood. We are vitally connected to a great spiritual battle and what we do in this physical world will shape the outcome of that battle.

"I don't know about you, but this changes the way I think about creation. If the creation of the physical world was, in effect, the downloading of pre-existing spiritual files, that means all the physical matter in the universe is the visible image of something that exists in the spiritual world. The six days of creation were the chronological downloading of the spiritual into the physical. This includes the living creatures and first humans which are likely the physical images of different types of spiritual beings. Everything in the spiritual world is being downloaded into the physical world and then the spiritual world will be erased—trashed. Why? That discussion will be fun and we will spend a lot of time on it later.

"So, to summarize, the twenty-four-hour, six-day creation becomes much more plausible if we consider the possibility the physical world is a projection, download or translation of pre-existing matter and living beings. It certainly doesn't rule out this download was accomplished over millions of years, but the length of time for creation doesn't seem nearly as important as how the creation actually happened.

"There is a lot of scientific evidence this world is connected to what scientists call a metaphysical dimension—what we call the spiritual world. We'll get back to you with research on that topic, but before we run out of time, let's consider another part of biblical history. Lydia, give them a little teaser about the Flood."

"Thanks, Julie. Julie and I toured the life-sized replica of Noah's Ark in Kentucky last year. It was built using the specs

God gave Noah in the Bible. It's amazing and we recommend it to all of you. The account of the Great Flood in the Bible is critically important because if there was no flood, the Bible is not true. We believe the Flood offers a great opportunity for us to merge science and the Bible.

"There are a lot of angles to consider about the Flood. First, why was it necessary? Here's part of the explanation in Genesis 6:1–4.

> '*When human beings began to increase in number on the earth and daughters were born to them, the sons of God saw that the daughters of humans were beautiful, and they married any of them they chose. Then the Lord said, "My Spirit will not contend with humans forever, for they are mortal; their days will be a hundred and twenty years." The Nephilim were on the earth in those days—and also afterward—when the sons of God went to the daughters of humans and had children by them. They were the heroes of old, men of renown.*'

"God clearly didn't like the sons of God marrying the daughters of humans. But why? Were the sons of God the early humans who were made in the image of God, but now possessed by Satan? Were the daughters of humans descendants of Cain who were breeding with the deteriorated race of early humans? Or, could the sons of God be the angels of Satan in human form? One-third of all the angels in heaven—sons of God—were thrown to earth with Satan. Did they possess all the humans on earth? Look at the next few verses. I'll read them.

> *Genesis 6:5–8. 'The Lord saw how great the wickedness of the human race had become on the earth, and that every inclination of the thoughts of the human heart was only evil all the time. The Lord regretted that he had made human beings on the earth, and his heart was deeply troubled. So*

the LORD said, "I will wipe from the face of the earth the human race I have created—and with them the animals, the birds and the creatures that move along the ground—for I regret that I have made them." But Noah found favor in the eyes of the LORD.'

"We know from Revelation that one-third of all the angels were thrown to earth where they serve as Satan's demons. There were likely millions, if not billions, of demons seeking physical hosts. They covered the earth like locusts possessing humans and animals. The whole earth became evil.

"Demons could move from one physical host to another—from humans to animals and back to humans. If one host died, they would possess another. But the Flood deprived these demons of physical hosts and they were trapped in the Abyss somewhere between the spiritual and physical worlds. They couldn't return to heaven because they were thrown down to the physical world, and they could not live in the physical world because the Flood killed all physical hosts except for Noah's family and the animals who were protected by the ark.

"If the Flood imprisoned all or most of Satan's demons, the world would have been a totally different place for Noah, his family, and all living creatures to live. Human beings still had a sin nature and Satan was still prince of this world, but God filled the world with many of His people after the Flood.

"I know some of this sounds a little weird, but this is just a teaser. It will get even weirder. We will pull together a lot of scientific evidence of the Flood, but today we wanted to get everyone thinking about why. Thanks Dr. J."

Johnny again led the class in a round of applause. "Lydia and Julie, you have opened lots of cans of worms, but they are all cans we need to sort through. It's going to be fun and it will challenge our thinking. We've got about fifty minutes left. Let's take a ten-minute break before I turn it over to Matt and Henry."

*"Here I am! I stand at the door and knock. If anyone hears
my voice and opens the door, I will come in and eat with
that person, and they with me."*—Revelation 3:20

CHAPTER FOURTEEN

REVELATION: HISTORY, FUTURE, OR BOTH?

January 2018–Johnny's second class continued
(Travelers Rest, SC)

"Normal people don't even read Revelation," Rachel mumbled. "I'm afraid it will confuse and alienate people if we include it in our report."

"Rachel, you're right!" Johnny smiled. "We should probably add a warning in our final document explaining it is only for those who want to dig as deep as they can go. It is certainly not necessary for salvation. Revelation is like a 'black diamond' run on a ski slope. Only experts should attempt it. But for the brave at heart, it is thrilling to discover what God is really doing. I don't think you can ever see the whole picture of God's plan without understanding Revelation."

Johnny continued, "Revelation seems complicated and weird because John is writing it while 'in the spirit.' God is showing him things in the spiritual world, the physical world, and in the new heaven. It doesn't translate easily into words or physical understanding. But God knew when we approached the end times, events around the world would shed more light on the real meaning of Revelation. I think we may be near the end times now.

"I only recommend Revelation to people who are serious about trying to understand the mysteries of this life and the next. But my hope is we can make it more understandable and our work will help people grow in their confidence in the truth of the Bible."

Johnny was thrilled his students were willing to question traditional orthodoxy but concerned the discussions might create more confusion than confirmation of biblical truth. When everyone was back in their seats, he offered some reassurance.

"I'm sure you're all discovering as you dig below the surface in the Bible—the Bible you've read and accepted for years—there is a lot you've never considered. It's easier to accept the Bible as true and skip over the hard parts until we are forced to defend it to those who say it is not true. The secular world today has firmly established, at least in their own minds, the Bible is nothing more than a bunch of mythical tales. And most Christians don't know the Bible well enough to defend their own beliefs. We have to do better. We owe it to the world to do better. Truth is more than a feeling in our hearts.

"When I became skeptical of God, I began to question everything in the Bible for the first time in my life. I realized I never really studied it. And when I did, it seemed disjointed and confusing. But the more I studied the Bible as a skeptic, the more I began to see a clear pattern of God's purpose, plans, and motives.

"So I can promise you, if you're willing to question everything and deal with a lot of initial confusion, your confidence in the Bible will increase dramatically. Set aside all your preconceived notions and look at what the Bible really says. It will all make a lot more sense if you always keep God's ultimate purpose foremost in your mind: to unify all things in heaven and earth into a perfect physical and spiritual world with no suffering or evil where God will live eternally with those who choose to be His people.

"Matt and Henry have asked to present a different look at Revelation. It doesn't get much weirder than Revelation—much of this book will likely remain a mystery—but we need to try to understand what God is telling us in Revelation because it describes the finality of this world and the beginning of the next. If we look at Revelation as a history of the physical world, it helps explain the different possibilities we are considering for the creation account in Genesis.

"Once we pull all of these possibilities together, we will see much more alignment between the Bible and science. Then we will have a clearer picture of how and why God created this physical world. So be patient and please remember, we are just exploring possibilities, not teaching a new theology.

"Okay, Matt—Henry—let's have it." Matt jumped out of his seat and walked to the screen.

"Henry and I will outline our plan to research the relationship between the Bible and science in our next class. Today, we will open Pandora's box by trying to organize Revelation into something that might make more sense.

"As you all know, some of us have been exploring a completely different take on Revelation since last fall and, after Dr. J mentioned it again on Tuesday, Henry and I spent a lot of time attempting to outline Revelation using the assumption it is the entire history and future of the physical world, not just the end times. With the help of a few pots of coffee, several Cokes and candy bars, we worked all Tuesday night. And believe me, Revelation gets even weirder in the middle of the night.

"Henry will give us a quick tour through Revelation." Henry stood up with his iPad as Matt took his seat.

"Everyone, go to Revelation on your tablets and I'll give a quick walk-through. We can't get into a lot of detail today, and

Dr. Johnny has already talked a lot about Revelation in our first class, but Matt and I hope to help create a new framework of understanding about the Bible.

"Chapter 1, verse 1 says,

> *'The revelation from Jesus Christ, which God gave him to show his servants what must soon take place.'*

"The word 'soon' in the first verse in Revelation has led most of us to conclude it is about the future. But Revelation was written 2,000 years ago, so it obviously wasn't 'soon' as we understand it.

"We're not ruling out the possibility Revelation is only about the future, we're just saying the first verse in Revelation allows for the possibility that it includes all history, because—since God and Jesus are one—God almost certainly gave this revelation to Jesus before the creation of the physical world.

"Also, as we have discussed, the spiritual world very likely has no past and future—no beginning or end. It may be a continuing present where everything from a physical perspective is happening at the same time. So, when Revelation gives an account of what's happening in heaven along with an account of what's happening on earth—both sides of the scroll—it can get confusing.

"I won't go through the details of all seven letters to the churches in the first part of Revelation. But assume for a moment these letters to the seven churches are messages to all the children of God before, during, and after they pass through the physical world. The letters are all addressed to an angel, which can be translated 'messenger.' The church is the body of Christ and these letters are warnings and encouragements for those who are traveling through the physical world. The verses on the screen are from the first letter to the angel of the church of Ephesus.

> *'Do not be afraid of what you are about to suffer. I tell you, the devil will put some of you in prison to test you, and you*

will suffer persecution for ten days. Be faithful, even to the point of death, and I will give you life as your victor's crown.'

"All the letters have an ending similar to this one to the church of Ephesus.

'Whoever has ears, let them hear what the Spirit says to the churches. To the one who is victorious, I will give the right to eat from the tree of life, which is in the paradise of God.'

"Only the children of God have spiritual ears to hear Him. The letters are warnings to all His children. We all have the weaknesses and failings mentioned in every letter. The letters reference actual physical places and specific people from the time Revelation was written, but much about these letters suggest they are written for the whole body of Christ to help us through this physical experience on earth.

"Okay, let's assume these letters are messages given to God's children before they became physical beings. It's a reasonable assumption because these same admonitions and warnings are given many times in the Old and New Testaments. After John receives these letters to the body of Christ, he is called up to heaven in the spirit. I'll begin at the first verse of chapter 4.

THE "DOOR" IN HEAVEN IS THE ENTRANCE TO A "WAITING ROOM"

'After this I looked, and there before me was a door standing open in heaven. And the voice I had first heard speaking to me like a trumpet said, "Come up here, and I will show you what must take place after this." At once I was in the Spirit, and there before me was a throne in heaven with someone sitting on it. And the one who sat there had the appearance of jasper and ruby. A rainbow that shone like an emerald encircled the throne. Surrounding the throne were

twenty-four other thrones, and seated on them were twenty-four elders. They were dressed in white and had crowns of gold on their heads.'

"There is a door in heaven that leads to an area where human and animal spirits are waiting until all the heavenly spirits pass through the physical world. We might call this a holding room with the spiritual digital files of physical beings that have been downloaded into the physical world. This scene is in the time-less spiritual world so they are all called 'living creatures' even though they are continuously living and dying in the physical world. The verse now on the screen is Revelation 4:6–8.

'In the center, around the throne, were four living crea-tures, and they were covered with eyes, in front and in back. The first living creature was like a lion, the second was like an ox, the third had a face like a man, the fourth was like a flying eagle. Each of the four living creatures had six wings and was covered with eyes all around, even under its wings. Day and night they never stop saying:

"'Holy, holy, holy is the Lord God Almighty,' who was, and is, and is to come."'

"As we discussed before, these four living creatures represent the four categories of animals and early humans in the first chapter of Genesis. They have six wings—and six is symbolic of the physical world—which tells us they are traveling or have traveled through the physical world. All the eyes in these living creatures represent the multitude of spirits that have passed through or are living in the physical world. This is good news for those of us who hope our dogs will be in heaven. I'm guess-ing my dog is part of the living creature that is like an ox since it represents domesticated animals. I'm kidding, but not really.

"Seriously, we know all living creatures suffer and die in the physical world. That's why our praise of God is so impor-tant. When living creatures praise God in the physical world—as we see in this verse—they defeat Satan in the spiritual world.

They prove him wrong. When physical beings praise God while facing suffering and death, they prove Jesus worthy to save His people and justify God's love and mercy for His people. When God's people in the physical world praise Him, they are victorious over Satan.

"This door in heaven shows us the place where the spirits of physical beings who belong to God praise Him when they are alive and where they wait under the altar after they die. The four living creatures praise God because they are spiritual counterparts to physical beings who are alive—they are doing what their counterparts are doing on earth. And, as we've said, their praise is the power that continually throws Satan out of heaven and keeps him trapped in the physical world.

THE TWO-SIDED SCROLL REPRESENTS THE PHYSICAL AND SPIRITUAL WORLDS

"Okay, I can see some of you rolling your eyes about animals in heaven, but remember our first assumption. Everything in the spiritual world must pass through or be downloaded into the physical world. Everything in this physical world is a representation of something that already exists in the spiritual world. That includes dirt, plants—everything. Hold your questions and we'll have plenty of time for discussion in later classes.

"Chapter 5 describes God giving the Lamb a scroll with writing on both sides. We are theorizing this scroll is the history and future of the spiritual and physical worlds—spiritual events on one side and physical events on the other. Only Jesus can open this scroll because He is the only being who is both physical and spiritual, and only His body and His blood can enter the new heaven. We are all spiritual beings in physical bodies, but we have physical fathers and mothers. Only Jesus has God as His Father. Keep in mind God's children are now the physical body of Jesus and only they have His blood.

"The rest of Revelation is taken from this two-sided scroll. The accounts of several events are repeated because some represent actions initiated in the spiritual world, and then retold later with similar descriptions of what happened in the physical world. These are not separate accounts. They are the same accounts from different perspectives. What happens in the spiritual world is being continuously downloaded into the physical world. And what happens in the physical world is uploaded and impacts what happens in the spiritual world. It's confusing because the spiritual world doesn't follow a logical chronology.

SATAN ESTABLISHES THE WORLD ORDER

"Chapter 6 describes the characteristics of the physical world after Satan establishes his dominion. All of this happened after the first six days of creation. These events are not in the future, they have already happened. The horses in these next verses represent the power of the world order. On the screen, I have excerpts from the first four seals of the two-sided scroll being opened.

First Seal: Ambition and Pride

'I looked, and there before me was a white horse! Its rider held a bow, and he was given a crown, and he rode out as a conqueror bent on conquest.'

Second Seal: Power and War

'Then another horse came out, a fiery red one. Its rider was given power to take peace from the earth and to make people kill each other. To him was given a large sword.'

Third Seal: Money and Commerce

'I looked, and there before me was a black horse! Its rider was holding a pair of scales in his hand. Then I heard what sounded like a voice among the four living creatures, saying, "Two pounds of wheat for a day's wages, and six pounds of

barley for a day's wages, and do not damage the oil and the wine!"'

Fourth Seal: Suffering and Death

'I looked, and there before me was a pale horse! Its rider was named Death, and Hades was following close behind him. They were given power over a fourth of the earth to kill by sword, famine and plague, and by the wild beasts of the earth.'

"The world order we are now a part of was established by Satan. Our world is still Satan's dominion, but he has been defeated by the body of Christ and he knows his time is short. More on that later. Let's open the fifth seal.

Fifth Seal: Departed Souls Waiting for New Heaven

'When he opened the fifth seal, I saw under the altar the souls of those who had been slain because of the word of God and the testimony they had maintained. . . . Then each of them was given a white robe, and they were told to wait a little longer, until the full number of their fellow servants, their brothers and sisters, were killed just as they had been.'

"We don't think these verses on the screen are referencing only the people who are killed in this world because of their faith. All of God's children will be 'killed' as physical beings in one way or another because we are part of God's family and have to experience physical death to escape these sinful bodies. That's just a guess, but it fits a pattern that will become clearer as we dig deeper.

"The sixth seal is one of several descriptions in Revelation of what happens on earth when Satan is thrown down. Remember, the opening of the seals does not represent the chronological order of events. It is collectively the story of what happened on earth when Satan was thrown down.

Sixth Seal: Satan Is Thrown to Earth

'I watched as he opened the sixth seal. There was a great earthquake. The sun turned black like sackcloth made of goat hair, the whole moon turned blood red, and the stars in the sky fell to earth. . . .

Then the kings of the earth, the princes, the generals, the rich, the mighty, and everyone else, both slave and free, hid in caves and among the rocks of the mountains.'

"We are told early humans lived in caves. Well, this is why.

"The first six seals are about Satan's impact on the physical world order. But the sixth seal also includes the beginning of God's response. Chapter 7 continues with events from the sixth seal and seems to be the description of the lineage from Adam who were designated to transmit the Word of God and provide the savior of God's people.

"The last part of chapter 7 shows people in white robes waiting in the holding room in heaven after their deaths. We are told they came out of the Great Tribulation. Christians have been taught the Great Tribulation is a short period during the end times. But we are theorizing along with Dr. J, the Great Tribulation is the time we all spend on earth in the physical world—we are all pilgrims passing through a period of suffering and tribulation in this world.

SATAN'S FALL FROM HEAVEN CREATES DESTRUCTION ON EARTH

"Chapter 8 is a review of what happened on earth when Satan was thrown down. Dr. Johnny has described the destruction that occurred when Satan was cast from heaven.

"Chapters 8 and 9 continue with Satan's destruction of earth and the earth being consumed with sin. This is the same condition on earth described in Noah's time. We can see what happened if we jump forward to chapter 12 which provides an overview of the reason for the great battle in heaven. Take a look at the first two verses of chapter 12 on the screen.

'A great sign appeared in heaven: a woman clothed with the sun, with the moon under her feet and a crown of twelve stars on her head. She was pregnant and cried out in pain as she was about to give birth.'

"We believe the woman in these verses could represent the physical creation or the creation of the line of modern humans that will eventually lead to Jesus. The woman is clothed with the sun, standing on the moon with twelve stars on her head— all physical descriptors.

"She is ready to give birth to the savior of God's children. The first step of this plan is for God to become human, but Satan—a mighty angel in heaven—rebels against God's plan and threatens to kill God when He is born as a physical being. Satan is the 'enormous red dragon' in verses 3–5. The stars are the angels who rebelled with him and were thrown to earth.

'Then another sign appeared in heaven: an enormous red dragon with seven heads and ten horns and seven crowns on its heads. Its tail swept a third of the stars out of the sky and flung them to the earth. The dragon stood in front of the woman who was about to give birth, so that it might devour her child the moment he was born.'

"We know Jesus is 'the first and the last,' and these next verses give us an idea of how He might have been first, yet not born until many years later. God entered the physical world as a person before Adam, but was 'snatched' back to the spiritual world for protection.

'She gave birth to a son, a male child, who "will rule all the nations with an iron scepter." And her child was snatched up to God and to his throne. The woman fled into the wilderness to a place prepared for her by God, where she might be taken care of for 1,260 days.'

"This scene in the spiritual was played out in the physical world when Jesus was born. King Herod sent his soldiers to

Bethlehem to kill him, but Mary and Joseph escaped with Jesus to Egypt where they lived until Herod died. Satan is always pursuing God's children.

"The place in the wilderness prepared by God to protect the woman might have been the Garden of Eden where Adam began the lineage for the eventual birth of Jesus. Satan pursued the 'woman' to Eden and caused the fall of Adam and the corruption of the human race. The human race became sinful and wicked and God destroyed most of them in the Flood. The only evidence of a possible flood in Revelation are verses 15–17 in chapter 12.

> 'Then from his mouth the serpent spewed water like a river, to overtake the woman and sweep her away with the torrent. But the earth helped the woman by opening its mouth and swallowing the river that the dragon had spewed out of his mouth. Then the dragon was enraged at the woman and went off to wage war against the rest of her offspring—those who keep God's commands and hold fast their testimony about Jesus.'

"The water from the Flood drained into large canyons under the earth's surface and left Noah and his family on dry land (the earth opened its mouth and swallowed the river). Satan was greatly weakened by the Flood's mass destruction of evil and most of his demons, but he continues to this day to wage war against all of God's children. Of course, all of this is just our theory.

"Chapters 15 and 16 describe seven terrible plagues that will be 'poured out' onto mankind before the final great battle. Our generation doesn't have any idea of what can happen during a plague—or pandemic as plagues are called today—but we may soon find out.

IS AMERICA THE BABYLON IN REVELATION?

"Chapters 17 and 18 describe the fall of Babylon which could represent a world government, powerful country, or great city.

We don't like to consider this possibility, but there is only one country in the world today that fits the description of Babylon in Revelation: the United States of America. We like to think of ourselves as a righteous nation, but the sad fact is the United States is the largest exporter of immorality to the rest of the world: pornography, prostitution, abortion, homosexuality, same-sex marriage, other forms of sexual immorality, gluttony, slothfulness, materialism, and many forms of idolatry. And we are the largest consumers of immoral substances and activities produced by the rest of the world, such as drugs and human trafficking.

"We need to devote a whole class to Babylon because it has huge implications about how we should live in America and the world.

"The final chapters of Revelation cover the return of Christ and the establishment of His kingdom on earth, the final great battle between Satan and God, the judgment of all people, the salvation of God's people, the eternal punishment of Satan and all his children, and the beginning of a new heaven on a new earth.

"There is a lot of research needed here. We've only scratched the surface today, but hopefully we've whetted your appetite enough to dig much deeper into this amazing book of the Bible."

Matt turned off the screen and sat down. The class sat silent with everyone looking around to see how others were responding. Johnny stood up and began to clap, but it took a few awkward seconds for the rest of the class to join in. Johnny was anxious to close the class and have a lighter conversation at lunch.

"Matt and Henry have done an amazing amount of work in the last two days and we've all got a lot more work to do in Revelation. Listening to their presentation reminded me how descriptions of events are repeated throughout the book. Matt and Henry, I think it would be a good idea for you to diagram Revelation with graphs and charts to help us visually simplify the interaction between the physical and spiritual worlds.

"Revelation might be summarized into several broad concepts: God warning His children as they travel through the physical world, the war in heaven resulting in Satan being thrown to earth, Satan setting up his world order in the physical world, God sending His children to earth, Satan pursuing God's children, the terrible plagues on earth, the great battle between Satan and God's armies, the judgment of the world, and the establishment of God's kingdom on a new earth.

"The big question about Revelation: is it only about the end times or is it a history of the physical world? The description of Satan being thrown down to earth in Revelation—and we know that happened before the creation of Adam and Eve in Genesis—suggests Revelation is about much more than the end times. For now, everyone, keep digging and post your thoughts on our shared website. Next Tuesday we'll talk more about the credibility of the Bible and science. How many of you can stay for lunch?"

Everyone raised a hand. Johnny was happy all his students wanted to stay for lunch, but his hopes for a less intense discussion were quickly dashed. Everyone was talking about Revelation as they grabbed a sandwich and a drink. And that's all they talked about until lunch was over.

A STORM IN PARADISE

After lunch, Johnny returned to his office to catch his breath, collect his thoughts, and summarize his notes from the class. He was ecstatic about the dynamic discussions by his students. He was amazed at how quickly these college-age kids crashed through centuries of theological dogma to search for answers on their own. What if all young Americans were challenged to search for answers and think for themselves about immutable truth? Johnny was deep in thought when he heard a knock on his office door.

"Come in, Bob!" It was Dr. Robert Andrews, a thirty-year professor at the university. "Have a seat in Alan's chair. He has classes this afternoon, so we have the place to ourselves." Johnny closed the door, sat down in his swivel chair, and turned to face Bob.

"Dr. Wright," Johnny knew immediately this wasn't a social call. "I come to you in the spirit of love as directed by Matthew 18. As brothers in Christ, it is my obligation to tell you personally of an offense against me and God." A sense of dread poured over Johnny. He knew what was coming next.

"Dr. Wright, this is a traditional Baptist university. We believe the Bible is the preeminent truth. You are making science equal to the Bible and you are using science to change biblical truths accepted by the church for hundreds of years. The Bible is our truth. It needs no defense. Our students must be taught the Bible is true and this university should not be used to teach students to question the truth of the Bible.

"Your students are sharing this nonsense from that silly debate and your class with other students at the university. Parents are complaining and members of our board have been notified. It is hard for many of us to believe you are actually teaching there is no need to accept Jesus as Lord to be saved! This cannot stand!"

Johnny knew Dr. Andrews was offended when Dr. Clark chose him—a newcomer with a soiled reputation and questionable Baptist credentials—to represent the university in the debate.

"Dr. Andrews," Johnny was trying to remain calm, "I am grateful you have come to me in love as a brother. I assure you my goal is to encourage students to ask questions and to seek answers to confirm their faith and the truth of the Bible. Everything I'm doing is designed to prove the Bible is true."

Dr. Andrews was shaking with anger. "There is no need to prove the Bible is true. It is true. It is our truth!"

"Dr. Andrews—" Johnny tried to speak but Dr. Andrews interrupted.

"Dr. Wright, if you are not willing to admit you are in the wrong, the next step in Matthew 18 is for me to ask two or three other brothers to confront you. Are you willing to issue an apology to the university and stop these discussions in your class?"

"Dr. Andrews, I would love to discuss your concerns with others—including Dr. Clark—but it seems premature to issue any statements related to the various theories I have offered in the debate or my classes."

Dr. Andrews stood. "In that case, I have no other choice." He quickly left the room and slammed the door behind him.

That didn't feel like love, Johnny thought to himself.

Johnny immediately picked up the phone to call Dr. Clark who assured him he should continue his work. "We'll handle this together. I'll talk to Dr. Andrews. Don't worry. And don't tell Patti."

But Johnny couldn't help but worry. This felt eerily like a replay of his ordeal with Blue Ridge Baptist Church.

The next week, Dr. Andrews was back with two board members of the university. The conversation was even more intense and the board members threatened board action against him if he didn't recant and apologize.

Two weeks later, a special board meeting was called. Johnny and Dr. Clark were "invited" to make presentations. Dr. Clark was an ex-officio member of the board, so he knew all the directors. After several board members presented a long list of accusations, Johnny was asked to speak.

"Thank you for the opportunity to defend my approach for teaching here at the university. All of the students here have grown up in a secular culture where the Bible is irrelevant. In fact, for most young people in America today, all real truth is irrelevant. Like many other college students all around the country, many of our own students have worldviews built with indefensible lies. Yet when asked to defend their views, they deflect all questions with the statement, 'that's my truth.'

"The church must offer the world something more credible. The Bible is the truth—the only truth. And it can stand up to tough scrutiny. Universities are not seminaries. It is not our goal to indoctrinate students, but to teach them to think, to research, to ask questions, and find answers for themselves. When it comes to the Bible, this is the only way students will leave here with confidence in what they believe—and the ability to defend what they believe."

Johnny gave the board answers to all of their questions but their expressions told him most of them weren't really listening. When he finished, he was told to leave the room and Dr. Clark asked for the opportunity to speak.

"Before you speak, Dr. Clark," the board chairman stood at the end of the table, "you should know we already have the votes to terminate Dr. Wright."

"Take a seat, Mr. Chairman," Dr. Clark had fire in his eyes. No one on the board had ever seen Dr. Clark angry or heard him raise his voice and everyone was stunned.

"Before I speak, you should know there is only one vote that matters when it comes to Dr. Wright or any other staff member of Palmetto Christian. That's my vote. My contract is clear: I serve at the pleasure of the board and everyone else serves at my pleasure. So, if you want to get rid of Dr. Wright or anyone else at this university, you will have to get rid of me first.

"The reason this university was failing and essentially bankrupt before I arrived was this board." Dr. Clark paused as he glared at the well-known trouble makers on the board. "We are not here to teach Baptist or Presbyterian philosophy or any religion. We are here to teach students how to succeed in life in the context of biblical truth and a Judeo-Christian worldview.

"The only truth you need to think about today is this: your approach has failed and mine has succeeded. I am well aware no progress is made in this world without stepping on the toes of those who are holding tight to the status quo, so I'm always prepared to take the grief thrown my way. But if any of you ever attack one of my staff again, I'm out of here. And you can be darn sure all of the best staff at this university will be right behind me. And this place will close down within a year.

"Now, before I leave and since we are giving ultimatums today, you will have my resignation by five o'clock today unless I am told you want me to continue as president and unless I am also told that at least half of this board will be replaced within a year with more thoughtful and constructive members."

"But Dr. Clark," the chairman's voice bounced off the door closing behind Dr. Clark.

Later that day the chairman called Dr. Clark. "The board has agreed with your requests and I want you to know, I was with you all the way."

"Thank you, Mr. Chairman. I have always appreciated your loyal support. And by the way, I want to be one of those new board members."

Johnny's phone rang a few minutes later. "Johnny, Dr. Clark here. Good job today with the board. I just wanted you to know the board came around to your point of view. So, 'as you were,' my friend. Stay the course." Dr. Clark thought it best to spare Johnny all the drama.

*We were therefore buried with him through baptism
into death in order that, just as Christ was raised
from the dead through the glory of the Father,
we too may live a new life.*—Romans 6:4

CHAPTER FIFTEEN

A NEW LIFE

August 2017 – before the first debate
(Middleburg, VA)

"You're whaaaat!!!" Tony couldn't believe the news. "How long have you known?"

"About two months," Elizabeth responded sheepishly. "I didn't want to tell you until I was sure it was really going to happen. But now I'm two and a half months pregnant, so I'm pretty sure we're going to have a baby." Elizabeth clapped her hands and Tony joined her in applause before throwing his arms around her for a big bear hug.

"That's why I've taken a break from riding and why I stopped drinking wine. I didn't really hurt my back and I'm not on a diet. Those were just fibs to keep you from asking questions."

"Elizabeth, I am overjoyed! I was afraid to even mention the idea of children, but this is the best news I've heard in a long, long time. We've got to start planning. This changes everything."

"Relax, Tony. We've got plenty of time and I've already done a little planning. Would you like to see where the nursery will be?" Elizabeth flashed a beaming smile, grabbed Tony's hand, and led him down the hall to a room next to their master bedroom.

The six months since their wedding was a mixture of chaos and Camelot. Tony and Elizabeth became regular equestrians and often took their horses to nearby ranches and parks to ride with a fun group of new friends. They explored trails in the afternoons and then enjoyed receptions and dinners at alternating incredible estates in the Virginia countryside. When Elizabeth "twisted her back," she and Tony just skipped the afternoon rides and joined the group for the dinners.

Elizabeth made several trips back to Chicago to close the sales on her bookstore and home. The transactions went smoother and were more profitable than she expected, allowing her to put aside a sizable nest egg for Chuck and Mary. Tony gave her an unlimited expense account, but Elizabeth didn't want to ask him to pay for her children's tuition, weddings, or other expenses. Tony insisted she should feel good about using his money to help her children because his money "came from atheists who bought his books." Elizabeth chided him for his bizarre sense of humor.

Tony had regular meetings at their house with his lawyer, his accountant, his broker, and his business manager. There were a few threats of lawsuits from his publishers, organizations that had already produced material promoting Tony as their keynote speaker at upcoming events, and several media syndicates where he had contracts to write regular articles and host radio shows, but Tony's lawyers were able to settle these at very little expense. The threats of negative tweets and Facebook posts from Tony provided enough leverage to make all the lawsuits go away. That simplified Tony's life considerably.

There were numerous news articles and many online conspiracy theories when Tony disappeared and took down his website, but just as Dr. Clark predicted, political controversies, Hollywood scandals, and global crises soon pushed Tony out of the news. Ironically, the flurry of news articles about his mysterious disappearance created a rush for Tony's books and CDs. He made more money after he disappeared than when he was still in the limelight.

His good fortunes constantly reminded him of Romans 8:28, even though he still felt guilty about how poorly he had shown his love to God.

And we know that for those who love God all things work together for good, for those who are called according to his purpose.

But he fell more in love with God than he ever knew was possible, which also reminded him of another verse, 1 John 4:19. He knew he could only love God because Jesus first loved him—through Elizabeth.

We love because he first loved us.

Tony was careful in his mind and heart not to ever diminish the love he shared with Pamela. Her love was deep and genuine, but Tony had not understood her wonderful love was God's way of showing him how personal and intimate His love was for Tony. Somehow he missed the point and separated the joy of Pamela's love from God's unconditional love for him. He never knew the warmth of God's love until he accepted His love through Elizabeth.

Tony retained his business manager to work with his accountant and broker to oversee his investments and business affairs. Since royalties and re-publications would continue for years, he also needed help managing the operation, staff, and expenses of his home and properties. He would keep his jet and pilots to allow him to travel with anonymity anywhere in the world. Tony, Elizabeth, Chuck, and Mary often flew to secluded islands in the Caribbean for weekend vacations.

Elizabeth loved to ride horses on the beach and Tony enjoyed sailing catamarans around the islands. Chuck and Mary just loved to fly anywhere.

It was on one of their trips to the Caribbean when Elizabeth told Chuck and Mary they would soon have a baby sister. The three were sitting in a cabana on the beach eating ice cream and looking out at the crystal-clear water.

"Mom, that's going to be weird," responded Chuck. "I'll have a sister the same age as my children."

"Are you expecting too!" Elizabeth teased. "You should be worried about finding a wife who will put up with you."

"I think it's wonderful." Mary was the ever-optimistic encourager. "When is she due?"

"In February next year, I'm about three months along. I thought I'd better tell you now before you started thinking I was getting fat." Elizabeth patted her stomach and smiled. Mary and Elizabeth stood and hugged. Chucked joined with a one-handed hug, still holding his ice cream.

"Mom, I really do think it's exciting. Weird, but exciting."

"Thanks, Chuck. That means a lot—coming from you." The three had a good laugh. They stood together looking out over the ocean and watching Tony land his catamaran on the beach.

"Mom, are you as happy as you look?" Chuck was serious for a moment.

"More than you'll ever know, Chuck. I didn't think I could ever be this happy again."

"That's what I thought and that makes me really happy." Elizabeth couldn't remember Chuck ever being this sweet. "Now Chuck, I'm going to cry if you start being sweet to me."

"When I think of how good God has been to the three of us, it almost makes me cry, too." Chuck dropped his empty cup in a trash can and gave Elizabeth a real hug. "I said almost. I haven't seen a tear yet, but I've been close."

* * *

September 2017 – Labor Day weekend before the first debate
(Middleburg, VA)

Back home in Virginia, Tony was emailing regularly with Dr. Clark about their joint research project. They were trading biblical and scientific references along with various hypotheses about why and how God created a physical universe. All of this was in preparation for a visit from Dr. Clark to Tony's home in Virginia over the Labor Day weekend.

Tony's pilots flew Dr. Clark from Greenville to Middleburg's Hickory Tree Airport on Friday morning. Tony met him at the airport in his Jeep and drove him back home for lunch with Elizabeth. It had been six months since Dr. Clark first met Elizabeth at their wedding. Their reunion was a joyous celebration. So much had happened—Tony's "disappearance," the sale of Elizabeth's bookstore and Chicago home, the news of the baby, and their adventures to the Caribbean.

Lunch lasted for nearly three hours. Most of the discussion was about Tony and Elizabeth, but Elizabeth was intent on getting Dr. Clark to talk about his life. Dr. Clark finally opened up and shared a little about himself. His daughter, Jennifer, finally married at thirty-five and had two children. Dr. Clark laughed at himself for saying "finally married" because he and his wife, Donna, weren't married until he was thirty-five. Jennifer, their first child was born when Dr. Clark was thirty-eight.

Dr. Clark's daughter-in-law, Howie's widow Kati, along with her daughter and son lived with him for two years after Donna's death and before she was remarried to Ken, a professor at Palmetto Christian. Ken had been a good friend of Dr. Clark's for years, so he was thrilled to have him in the family.

As for Dr. Clark, he said he was still married to Donna and Jesus. His four grandchildren lived nearby, so he was never lonely. That's all he needed. He loved his solitude and he set aside long hours for study and prayer. He was grateful for his life at Palmetto Christian but hoped to retire as president within the next five years. His plan was to continue as a professor and do more writing.

The three put away the lunch dishes and moved to a small conference table in Tony's study. Dr. Clark unloaded a large briefcase full of notes, and Tony moved a stack of papers from his desk to the conference table. Elizabeth disappeared for a few minutes and returned with several well-worn spiral notebooks full of color-coded page markers and sticky notes. She wasn't going to miss this.

Dr. Clark began the discussion by introducing a new perspective of God and the Bible. "Tony, you and I have been emailing articles and theories back and forth for the last few months, and Elizabeth, I know you have been working with Tony on a lot of these ideas. We have all day tomorrow to expand the scope of our work, but for the few hours we have this afternoon, I'd like to focus and simplify our discussion.

"Smarter people than us have been sifting through the Scriptures for centuries, so it won't be easy to identify new ideas and perspectives. However, I do believe that discovering God's motives for creating the physical universe and all living creatures could help God's people overcome the apparent contradictions between physical and spiritual truths that have weakened the church, and along with it, the fabric of our nation.

"We teach in our churches and seminaries that the chief purpose of mankind is to worship God and enjoy Him forever. I believe this is true—but—it doesn't mean God's purpose for creating mankind was for us to worship Him. We worship Him because He is 'worthy' of our worship and, as we have discussed, our worship of God may make us participants in the great battle between God and Satan, between good and evil.

"There are several issues we can easily dispense with. The first is the question of whether there is a God. We know the intricacies and complexities of physical matter and higher forms of life make it statistically and physiologically impossible for this universe to have been created through accidental origin and random evolution. For any objective researcher, science has proven beyond any doubt there had to be a designer and creator. There is no need for us to argue with people who say there is no God because they are ignoring obvious truth. But we should be prepared to give them the facts—beginning with all the scientific evidence to disprove Darwin's theory of evolution.

"We can also say with much confidence the Bible is a supernatural document. There are dozens of specific biblical prophecies, written centuries before the actual events occurred, that happened exactly as predicted. This is statistically improbable if not impossible. The dietary laws God gave the Jews have been scientifically proven to be perfect prescriptions for health at a time when it was not humanly possible for anyone to have this knowledge. The historical accounts chronicled in the Bible have proven to be correct and the geographical descriptions of locations in the Bible are still being used by archeologists to find lost cities.

"But 'supernatural' and 'inerrant' are two very different things. And our claim of the Bible being written by God is a high bar to prove. Tony, your work in *God Fantasies* will be helpful in addressing the many points of controversy in the Bible. We will need to spend some time proving the Bible is true and we must be open to alternative interpretations to what the Bible is really saying. Science has brought many traditional interpretations of the Bible into question. Even though science is often wrong, we cannot run from these questions. We must consider honest questions objectively without fear of offending some ecclesiastic order.

"We must prove the Bible to be a credible resource because it is our only reliable source of information about God and His true motives. There are other religious books but none of them can even approach the internal and external proofs of accuracy we have for the Bible.

"Let's consider, using the whole context of the Bible, some of the possible motives God might have had for creating the physical universe. God makes His ultimate purpose clear and simple in the Bible. In Ephesians 1:8–10, Paul writes:

> 'With all wisdom and understanding, he made known to us the mystery of his will according to his good pleasure, which he purposed in Christ, to be put into effect when the times reach their fulfillment—to bring unity to all things in heaven and on earth under Christ.'

"Then we see how God will unify all things at the end of Revelation." Dr. Clark turned to a marked page in his Bible. "This from Revelation 21:1–6:

> 'Then I saw "a new heaven and a new earth," for the first heaven and the first earth had passed away, and there was no longer any sea. I saw the Holy City, the new Jerusalem, coming down out of heaven from God, prepared as a bride beautifully dressed for her husband. And I heard a loud voice from the throne saying, "Look! God's dwelling place is now among the people, and he will dwell with them. They will be his people, and God himself will be with them and be their God. He will wipe every tear from their eyes. There will be no more death or mourning or crying or pain, for the old order of things has passed away."
>
> He who was seated on the throne said, "I am making everything new!" Then he said, "Write this down, for these words are trustworthy and true."
>
> He said to me: "It is done. I am the Alpha and the Omega, the Beginning and the End."'

"The Bible tells us the current physical and spiritual worlds will pass away. God will make everything new. The new world and universe will 'unify' the characteristics of the spiritual and physical worlds. We know this because God is the prototype. God the spirit became a physical being, died, and was resurrected in a new body with physical and spiritual capabilities. We also know humans, and likely all living creatures, are spiritual beings passing through this physical world. We are pilgrims.

Again, God is our prototype. He exists as a spirit, He lived and died as a human being while still existing as a spiritual being, and then He was resurrected with a spiritual and physical body. And because the final reality will be spiritual and physical, only the unique blood of Jesus will allow living creatures to enter into the new heaven and new earth.

"This is a clarifying point. Our salvation requires the blood of Jesus because nothing can enter this final, eternal destination without spiritual and physical blood. Jesus is the only one who has this unique blood because only He had a spiritual father and a physical mother. This is not an elusive spiritual mystery. It is a physiological requirement.

"If God is the prototype and He fills the entirety of the spiritual world, we can assume everything in the spiritual world will pass through the physical world before the spiritual and physical worlds end—disappear. Then, all physical matter and living creatures who are part of the body of Jesus will fill the entirety of the new heaven on a new earth.

"The question we have to resolve is why God would force a sinless, harmonious, and eternal spiritual world, including Himself, to go through this convoluted and painful process to get to a new world? I have concluded, at least for the purpose of our initial discussions, that God had two primary motives.

"First, I believe physical matter and human senses offer a superior existence when combined with spiritual characteristics. We are not destined to be amorphous spirits floating around on clouds. God wants all of us who are part of His body to have the freedom of individual existence and the physical experience of touch, sight, hearing, and smell. He wants us to enjoy human emotions as well as spiritual perfection.

"God wants us to touch, see, and hear Him and enjoy relationships with each other as physical beings. And He wants to touch, see, and hear us. He wants us to enjoy the reality of physical space as well as the miracle of moving instantly across infinite space. He wants Elizabeth to ride horses or some other magnificent creatures. He wants Tony to sail across infinite waters. He wants us to have perfect physical bodies that can never suffer or die. God wants all of this for us because He loves us more than we can ever imagine.

"The second motive for this creation—and this is something the church has totally missed—there was and is a war in heaven. The spiritual world is not sinless and harmonious. Satan leads a continuous battle in both the spiritual and physical worlds, constantly accusing God of fraud and His children of loving God only because He bribes them with His blessings. This is straight out of the first chapter of Job. Satan accuses God of fraudulently bribing His people with blessings and denying them the freedom to know evil as well as good. Satan claims if living creatures suffer and know evil, they will not worship God.

"The physical world allows this war to play out, just as we see in Job. There is no death in the spiritual world. All God's children are part of His spiritual body, they know Him intimately and freely worship Him. But Satan led a rebellion against God and sought to separate from Him. The problem is: there is no separation from God in the spiritual world. And, because there is no death, Satan and his angels will live forever constantly 'accusing the brothers.'

"I believe God created the physical universe as a way to permanently separate good from evil, as a place where God's children—separated from Him and His love—would prove Satan wrong, and as a place where God's children could acquire the physical 'DNA' necessary to live in a new heaven.

"In this context of allowing justice to play out in the physical world, God can't shield us from suffering or death, although I am convinced our praise and prayers justify His intervention in our lives. We are warriors in the continuous battle between God's people and Satan. But ultimately, the only way we can get into eternity is to shed our physical bodies and acquire new bodies with the blood of Jesus in our veins.

"Many questions remain but I hope we can agree these two hypotheses are worthy of consideration. Then we need to discuss when and how salvation occurs. The Scriptures seem to suggest our status as God's children was determined before we were born. Scriptures are clear that none of us can do anything on earth to earn our salvation.

"But our decision to follow Jesus in this physical world has very real implications. When God's children make a willful decision to accept His forgiveness and follow Jesus while we are still on this earth, the Spirit of God enters our physical bodies and awakens our souls. The Spirit reconnects us with our spiritual counterparts and makes us part of the body of Jesus.

"This possibility challenges us to consider a new perspective of salvation.

"I'm not sure if the act of 'praying to receive Christ' actually saves us for eternity. That issue was likely settled before we were born into the physical world. But I am thoroughly convinced that giving our lives to Jesus is the only way we will know the peace and love of God in this life.

"Perhaps the act of accepting Christ proves we were already saved—that we have always been God's children. If the act of receiving Christ saved us, we could take credit for it. Rather, the Scriptures indicate all God's children are justified and saved only by the blood of Christ—and we need to consider if Jesus' sacrifice might redeem people who don't accept Him during their lives on earth.

"God's Spirit pursues us and stirs us to seek Him so we will know His love in this life. When we accept His love and forgiveness, we also join the battle against Satan. And, if our actions in these physical bodies are actually connected to the outcomes in the spiritual world, the prayers and worship of God's people in the physical world may ultimately decide the outcome of the battle between God and Satan. Why else would God tell us to put on the full armor of God and join the battle in the spiritual world? That's straight from Ephesians six.

"This is why evangelism and preaching the gospel is so important. We are recruiting people to help defeat Satan by 'worshiping God and enjoying Him forever.' God's children waste their physical lives—and enter heaven with the 'smell of smoke' as the Bible says—if they live their entire lives on earth without knowing the joy and peace that comes from being part of the body of Christ. We preach the gospel so people will know they have eternal life and not fear death.

"I believe many of God's children through the ages have lived and died without ever knowing Him or calling on the name of Jesus, but they will still be saved by the blood of Christ because He has redeemed—bought back—all His children. After Jesus was crucified and before He was resurrected, He preached the gospel to the dead. The traditional church teaches there are no second chances after this life, but Peter seems to be telling us something quite different." Dr. Clark opened his Bible.

"*1 Peter 3:19. 'After being made alive, he [Jesus] went and made proclamation to the imprisoned spirits.'*

1 Peter 4:6. 'For this is the reason the gospel was preached even to those who are now dead, so that they might be judged according to human standards in regard to the body, but live according to God in regard to the spirit.'

"I think we should be open to the possibility that many of God's chosen people—the elect—may never know His salvation in this life, but are, nevertheless, redeemed for eternity by the blood of Jesus.

"All this begs the question of when and how it was determined who are God's children and who belongs to Satan. If this was determined before we were born, it might have something to do with the great war in heaven. One-third of the angels chose to fight with Satan and the rest were loyal to God. These angels apparently made a free will decision to be with or against

God. Are God's children on earth the physical counterparts of those angels who are loyal to God in the spiritual world?

"Are we God's children by our free will choice in the spiritual world or did God arbitrarily create some people who would belong to Satan and spend eternity in hell through no fault of their own. That's a hard idea for me to accept, although as Job learned, who are we to question God?

"I'm anxious to hear your opinions about all this, so I'll take a break, sip my tea, and enjoy listening to you two for a while."

Tony and Elizabeth were fascinated by Dr. Clark's perspective and his concise summary of centuries of theological complexity. Little did they know Johnny Wright and his students were independently reaching essentially the same conclusions.

WHAT IS THE ROLE OF "THE CHURCH"?

Tony stood up and reached for a bottle of water before introducing a new perspective on the role of the church. "Dr. Clark, your theories make a lot of sense, but as you know, they go against the traditional understanding of the Bible. I look forward to discussing them in more detail tomorrow. Today, perhaps my best role in this process is to share some thoughts about how these new ideas might change the role of the church. As you know, I've had an opportunity to see the good and the bad of the modern church around the world.

"In the Bible, the 'Church' is described as 'the body of Christ.' It is not a building, denomination, or an organization. The 'Church' is a spiritual and physical composite of all the followers of Jesus from around the world throughout history. We do not know who these believers are and it is difficult for us to know who is a child of God and who belongs to Satan. God's children are likely part of every religion around the world, and many are certainly not part of any religion.

"It may sound odd, but we really can't know for sure who is a child of God. There have been some really bad people who have come to faith, and there have been some very religious people who disavowed their faith and became atheists." Dr. Clark and Elizabeth shared an empathetic laugh with Tony.

"The Bible tells us there will be people who say they believe in Jesus and do many good things in His name, but will not be saved. Jesus says in Matthew 7:21–23:

> *"'Not everyone who says to me, 'Lord, Lord,' will enter the kingdom of heaven, but only the one who does the will of my Father who is in heaven. Many will say to me on that day, 'Lord, Lord, did we not prophesy in your name and in your name drive out demons and in your name perform many miracles?' Then I will tell them plainly, 'I never knew you. Away from me, you evildoers!'"*

"Jesus is talking about people who do good things and claim to be Christians. They believe in Jesus. So apparently, a sincere belief that Jesus exists does not save us. As we are told in Scriptures, even the demons believe in Jesus and tremble.

"The Bible also seems to tell us people can be saved without praying to receive Christ or doing good works. The thief dying on the cross next to Jesus acknowledged his own sin and asked Jesus to remember him. Perhaps that was enough, but as far as we know, he didn't receive Jesus as Lord and agree to follow Him.

"Jesus told the thief he would be in paradise with Him that day. The thief was obviously saved, but did his words save him? Did those few words change the eternal destiny of the thief? Or did they simply confirm the thief was being redeemed by Jesus because he was always one of God's children? I'm guessing we will discuss that question more tomorrow.

"As we consider the role of the 'organized' Christian church—which is a different concept than the body of Christ—I think we should make a distinction between the followers of Jesus and the children of God—people the Bible calls 'the elect.' I define followers of Jesus as those who have made a conscious decision to accept Jesus as their Savior and Lord and are indwelt with the Holy Spirit. True believers seek to follow and obey His Word.

The children of God are a larger group that includes true believers as well as many others who are chosen by God but have not yet acknowledged Jesus as their Savior.

"In this context, a principle role of the organized Christian church is to call all the children of God to faith in Jesus by appealing to everyone to accept Him as Savior and Lord. This is how people receive the blood of Jesus, reconnect with God, and join the battle against Satan. And, as we have discussed, this is the only way people can experience the joy and peace of knowing God during our physical lives.

"Since we don't know who are the children of God, we must proclaim and preach the gospel of Christ to everyone. Those who have 'ears to hear' will respond because they are the children of God and they know, at least subconsciously, the voice of Jesus, which is the gospel message. It must always be a priority of the church to invite all God's lost sheep to come home.

"The other principle role of the organized Christian church is to disciple believers and help them grow in their faith. This involves teaching believers how to follow Jesus and encouraging them to share the good news of salvation with others. And it means helping believers become confident in their faith, which is only possible if people are confident in what they believe.

"This brings us to the crux of the issue for the modern Christian church: is the Bible true? There is only one Savior—Jesus—and He can only be known through the Bible. There is only one gospel and it is the good news described in the Bible. And there is only one way to follow Jesus and it is the way described in the Bible. If churches are not teaching the Bible as God's inerrant Word, they are teaching a man-made religion—a religion with no power to save.

"I'm afraid this is what's happening with the organized Christian church all around the world. Fewer and fewer pastors and priests are willing to teach the Bible as the inerrant Word of God for many reasons, but primarily because of scientific conflicts with the creation story, doubts about the virgin birth and the miracles of Jesus, and the growing chasm between biblical morality and our secular culture.

"We will have a lot of research ammunition to prove the truth of the Bible and show how the Bible can align with science on the creation story, the Flood, and other historical accounts. We can also prove Jesus is a real historical figure and make a strong case that He actually did rise from the dead. There were many witnesses to His miracles and His resurrection. In sum, I think we can make a good case for the Bible being historically true, scientifically consistent, and very likely inspired words from God.

"Perhaps the more difficult challenge is how we make the case that people who accept and seek to follow Jesus must also try to conform to the moral teachings in the Bible. Jesus said this in the book of John.

> *"Whoever has my commands and keeps them is the one who loves me. The one who loves me will be loved by my Father, and I too will love them and show myself to them."* (John 14:21)

"People who really love Jesus and seek to follow Him will obey His commands. He tells us one of the most important commands is to love others.

> *"A new command I give you: Love one another. As I have loved you, so you must love one another. By this everyone will know that you are my disciples, if you love one another."* (John 13:34–35)

"'Love' is the safe teaching for most churches. But it's much harder to talk about other verses like this one from Galatians:

> *The acts of the flesh are obvious: sexual immorality, impurity and debauchery; idolatry and witchcraft; hatred,*

discord, jealousy, fits of rage, selfish ambition, dissensions, factions and envy; drunkenness, orgies, and the like. I warn you, as I did before, that those who live like this will not inherit the kingdom of God.' (Galatians 5:19–21)

"Adultery, premarital sex, homosexuality, and many other forms of 'sexual immorality' are so prevalent today many pastors are afraid to say these behaviors are wrong. Calling anything a sin is tantamount to hate. Any comment about morality can be attacked as racist or hateful. This is one of the main reasons so many churches are moving away from the Bible as the only source of truth. It offends people.

"The whole culture around us is shamelessly endorsing these 'acts of the flesh' listed in Galatians. Encouraging 'factions' has become a political tool, and many politicians use 'jealousy' and 'envy' to get votes. I could go on and on, but you get the picture. The 'acts of the flesh' are no longer considered wrong or sinful in America and many other cultures around the world.

"It's important because Christians who continue in willful sin will harden their hearts and live defeated lives. Christians who are living in sin can't grow in their faith because they don't even like to be around believers who are genuinely trying to follow Jesus. And they sure don't want to go to a church that teaches biblical morality.

"We've got to show believers how they can love others, but still admonish each other when they do something the Bible says is wrong. We need to show God's love and still speak the truth about sin—always keeping in mind we are all sinners."

Elizabeth interrupted, "But we have to be clearer that we are not judging or condemning people—especially people who are not trying to follow Jesus. It's none of our business how non-believers live. The secular world can live any way they want, whether or not they consider or even care about the consequences."

Dr. Clark rejoined the discussion, "But the secular world not only wants to deny biblical morality for themselves, they are trying to take away the rights of believers to live out our faith in every area of our lives." Dr. Clark put down his tea, stood, and walked to the window. "We have to work on our message here. Christians shouldn't try to impose their beliefs and values on others. But Christians should have the right to practice and espouse biblical morality in their own lives. This includes having the choice to send our children to schools that teach our values and not being forced to honor behavior in the workplace we believe is immoral."

"We're starting to sound like politicians." Tony put his hands on his head and rolled his eyes.

"I know, I know!" Dr. Clark laughed at himself. "We've got to figure out how to teach followers of Jesus to honor God and still be good neighbors, friends, and citizens in a secular culture."

Elizabeth jumped in, "Which means we have to make it clear we don't want to impose our values on non-believers and make sure we don't push them away from God by telling them they have to be perfectly righteous before they can give their lives to Jesus. And we can't discourage new believers by expecting them to immediately stop sinning. Christians are still sinners and God still loves us."

"You're right, Elizabeth." Tony leaned forward in his chair. "Our discussion is demonstrating why it is so hard to talk about biblical morality. We need to remind believers who choose to follow Jesus that they are new creation. As Paul said in Galatians 2:20,

> 'I have been crucified with Christ and I no longer live, but Christ lives in me. The life I now live in the body, I live by faith in the Son of God, who loved me and gave himself for me.'

"The point is not to condemn or judge people, but to help followers of Jesus grow closer to God and be happier in their lives. We should always put more emphasis on the goal, which is described in the next few verses in Galatians 5.

'But the fruit of the Spirit is love, joy, peace, forbearance, kindness, goodness, faithfulness, gentleness and self-control. Against such things there is no law. Those who belong to Christ Jesus have crucified the flesh with its passions and desires. Since we live by the Spirit, let us keep in step with the Spirit. Let us not become conceited, provoking and envying each other.' (Galatians 5:22–26)

"That's a good reminder, Tony." Dr. Clark was still looking out the window. "The church should use verses like these as diagnostic tools to help believers know how they are doing. Biblical morality shouldn't discourage or condemn believers. Jesus covers all our sins, no matter how many times we fall. As long as we live in these physical bodies, we will all continue the 'acts of the flesh.' But if we seek God and fellowship with others who aspire to honor God, we will begin to see more of the 'fruit of the Spirit' emerge in our lives."

Tony continued, "Too many churches are afraid to teach biblical morality because it might discourage attendance and membership, but I think we are getting close to developing some ideas that will help the modern church teach the truth of the Bible without alienating and discouraging people who are trying to follow Jesus.

"Biblical morality is important not only to help individual believers grow closer to God and to live more joyful lives. If our theories of the war in heaven are correct, obedience to God's commands is how the body of Christ defeats Satan and ushers in the kingdom of God. If *Satan's dare* to God in Job is why we must go through this physical world, then obedience to God in the midst of powerful pressure from our culture is how we prove God right.

Tony leaned back and sighed, "We've got a difficult task in front of us, but we've made a good start with our discussion today. Tomorrow, I'd like to talk more about the role of the church, how people can be sure they are saved, and how every life serves an eternal purpose."

Dr. Clark closed his notebook. "And tomorrow, I will cover the parallels between the stories of physical events in the Bible—like the story of the nation of Israel—and discuss how these stories reveal God's purpose and motives—and confirm the Bible is true."

Tony held up a copy of *God Fantasies*. "And I will also begin to refute my case for atheism."

"Sounds like fun." Elizabeth was teasing with a little sarcasm. "I'd like to share some thoughts about when we are saved, some different meanings of the word 'salvation,' and I'd also like to pick up on Tony's thoughts about how we can teach right and wrong while still showing love for each other. It's shouldn't be that hard. Sometimes the best way to show love is to tell people the truth.

"Let's try for a little lighter conversation during dinner. How about a walk down to the pond before we eat again? We all need a little exercise." Elizabeth walked to the door of Tony's study. "Come on guys, let's get some air!"

If we claim to be without sin, we deceive ourselves and the truth is not in us. If we confess our sins, he is faithful and just and will forgive us our sins and purify us from all unrighteousness.—1 John 1:8–9

CHAPTER SIXTEEN

CONFESSION AND REDEMPTION

February 2018 – after the first debate
(Travelers Rest, SC)

Suzie Robertson rang Johnny and Patti's doorbell with suitcase in hand at 5:30 on Friday afternoon.

"Your directions were perfect. Am I too early?"

"You're right on time. Come in. Come in."

Patti gave her a welcome hug and Johnny took her suitcase.

Patti put her hands on Suzie's shoulders and gave her a good look. "Suzie, it's been too long. You look great. We can't wait to hear about your life in Charlotte."

Suzie looked at Patti with amazement and then burst into tears.

"Patti, they told me you couldn't walk! You look wonderful! I was expecting to see you . . . I mean . . ."

"Suzie, it's fine. I'm getting stronger every day. God is good. Let's get you settled in your room. Then we can talk."

Patti had a pitcher of lemonade and some snacks on the kitchen table. The lasagna and garlic bread were heating in the oven. The house smelled like an Italian restaurant. The warm and casual atmosphere put Suzie at ease and she was ready to talk.

"Pastor Johnny—or is it Professor Johnny now? I read your post on Facebook."

Patti interrupted, "Suzie, I know you've got a lot to tell us, but first, tell us what you're doing in Charlotte."

"Okay, I should have known. You two always cared more about others than yourselves. I took the first job I could find that got me out of Boone. My relationship with my father only got worse after you left. I am a community relations officer for Bank America in Charlotte. It's a fun job. I speak at Rotary Clubs, go to groundbreaking ceremonies, visit lots of organizations, and deliver checks to charities. I live in a little apartment in downtown Charlotte near the Panthers' stadium."

Patti kept prompting, "Well, is there anyone special? Have you made some good friends?"

"I stay very busy and keep to myself, so making friends has been a little slow. I went to a couple of Panthers' football games with a group from work. It's a fun group and we sometimes meet for drinks after work. I've been visiting different churches but haven't joined one yet. So, no church friends yet, but a couple of the girls at work are believers and we've become close. I had dinner twice with a guy who lives in my apartment building. He's nice and I kind of like him, but I'm hesitant to jump into anything."

"I don't want to pry, but why?" Patti wasn't going to let her off the hook.

"Patti, I don't know. I think it's just the bad feelings I have about my father and all the bad things that happened in Boone. I feel like damaged goods. That's why I need to do something to make things right. The whole thing is stealing my peace."

Johnny jumped in, "That's a good way to put it, Suzie. There are always things in this world stealing our peace. We've certainly been through it ourselves. The best thing to do is leave judgment to God and move on, but as I found out, sometimes you can't move on until you let others know the truth."

"That's why I'm here. I need to tell the truth so I can move on." Suzie teared up and Patti handed her a tissue. "Is it okay to talk about the issue now?"

They all laughed and Johnny said, "Yes, it is. Lay it on us."

Suzie took a small notepad out of her purse, opened it, and sat it on the table.

"I've made some notes so I won't ramble. Here's my story. Pastor Johnny, when you were fired from the church, none of us were told anything about what happened. We read in the paper about sexual abuses, but I knew that wasn't true. They canceled all youth meetings for a while, so we couldn't meet with our friends to find out what others knew.

"We all assumed there was something bad we didn't know about. But gradually over the next few months, most of the girls who attended the meetings at your home and the youth group at church got together on Facebook. We created an exclusive chat room only for those who actually attended the meetings. We were the eyewitnesses, so to speak.

"None of us ever experienced or saw anything improper from you or anyone else. Those meetings at your home were the best thing that ever happened to us. We all grew in faith and hunger for the Word. And we developed lasting friendships. After your firing, we knew something wasn't right, but we didn't know what to do. We've all left the church but we've stayed in touch. I've heard the youth program at the church is gone and Pastor Taylor's son, Mike, is preaching most of the Sunday sermons to very small crowds.

"When I read your Facebook post last Saturday, I immediately knew what happened. I got in my car the next day and drove to Boone. I knew my mom and dad would be having lunch alone at home after church, so I timed my arrival to catch them at the table together.

"I walked in without a greeting and sat down at the table. I looked at my surprised dad and said, 'Why did you do it?' Then I shut up and waited. He acted like he didn't know what

I was talking about, but I could tell my mother knew exactly
what I was talking about. Then I really went after him.

"'You lied about Johnny Wright! You told the church he
sexually abused ME! You used ME to destroy his ministry and
try to destroy his life. Why? Why? Why did you lie?'

"My dad mumbled like he didn't know what to say, but he
must have believed someone from the church told me what
really happened. I was mostly bluffing, but he thought I knew
the truth. Then he confessed.

"He said, 'Suzie, I did it for you and the church. Johnny
was not right for our church. His teachings were more Presbyterian than Baptist and his music was that new age stuff that
leads people astray. It's just not worshipful.'

"That really set me off and I pounced. I stood up and threw
a copy of the infamous, post-debate Saturday front page from
the *Greenville News* on the table. It had the headline about you
as a disgraced pastor. 'Dad! You lied about a good man and
tried to destroy him because you didn't like his music? He and
Patti have to live with what you did every day. Look at this
headline! How could you? And how could you use me as your
victim? Johnny was bringing hundreds of young people to the
Lord. He was teaching about Jesus, not some stupid denomination. How could you be so blindly self-righteous? I am so
ashamed to be your daughter!'

"Then I gave him an ultimatum, 'Dad, you must confess to
the church. And I'm sure Pastor Taylor is in on this too. You
better confess soon because me and the girls who were in Johnny's youth group are going to tell the whole town, in fact, we're
going to tell the whole country the truth.'

"I looked at my mother and said, 'I feel sorry for you. It's
time you stood up to this beast.' She just looked at the floor.
Then I walked out without another word and drove back to
Charlotte.

"Suzie . . ." Johnny tried to jump in.

"I'm almost finished, but you need to hear the plan. All of
the girls from the youth group have signed an editorial telling

the whole story. We have arranged for it to run in the *High Country News* in Boone on Sunday—a week from this Sunday. I hope it will be as much a surprise for my dad and Pastor Taylor as the news story about your firing was to you.

"We will post the story on Facebook and YouTube and we have arranged with almost 200 former members of your youth group to tweet it out to their lists. I am hopeful the story will go viral and be picked up by newspapers and online news services all over the country. Okay, now I'm finished."

"Wow!" Johnny sat back in his chair and closed his eyes. "Suzie, is it too late to think about this?"

"Yes, it is. I didn't come here to ask permission. I came here to apologize for my dad and the church, and to ask your forgiveness for being the stooge in all this mess."

"Okay, I get it. But you had nothing to do with anything that happened, so get that part out of your mind. I'm sorry your dad has hurt you and caused so much pain for so many people. Unfortunately, he has been a stooge of Satan. Satan used him to divide and destroy a church, and he has pushed many people away from the Lord.

"But before we judge your dad too harshly, let's remember how God has forgiven you and me. It's hard to accept and I know you don't want hear it right now, but we're all as sinful as your dad. He has caused unimaginable pain to you, me, Patti, and many others, but no more pain than each of us caused Jesus on the cross.

"It's a spiritual battle and I hope your dad will take your advice and confess. But regardless what he does, you must forgive him. Jesus knew the pain of betrayal and lies but He still looked down on those who nailed Him to that cross and asked God to forgive them. We are the body of Jesus and we can do no less."

"You're right about one thing, Pastor Johnny." Suzie sighed and smiled, "I don't want to hear it."

Patti squeezed Suzie's hand, "Suzie, I don't like to hear it either and I have to confess it's still hard for me to forgive those who took my baby, my health, my hopes, and dreams. But I pray almost every day God will forgive them, even when I don't mean it. The more I fake it, the closer I come to actually meaning it. That may sound hypocritical, but it's actually practicing obedience. And obedience is how we conform to the teachings of Jesus.

"And I keep reminding myself that forgiving those who hurt me doesn't benefit them, it saves me from bitterness. I cannot know the love of Jesus while I'm hating others. It doesn't matter if your dad ever confesses or asks forgiveness. What matters is for you to try as hard as you can to do what Jesus does for you; forgive him, love him, and move on."

Johnny felt a deep sense of sadness. This was the first time he heard Patti express any sense of loss or hurt. He knew why. She was afraid sharing her pain would only make it harder on him. He should have been her strength. Instead, he was the weaker vessel through their whole ordeal.

But tonight, Patti was willing to be honest with Suzie, perhaps believing Johnny was ready to handle it. And he was able. God used Patti to overcome his weakness and lack of faith, but now his confidence in God's love and strength was stronger than he ever imagined it could be. He was ready to be strong for Patti, for Suzie, and for whoever else God gave him to encourage.

Patti and Suzie continued to talk while Johnny just listened. As he watched them share their hurts and encourage each other, he could sense Jesus sitting at the table with them. Jesus was telling him his and Patti's journey through "the valley of the shadow of death" was complete. *It is finished*, he thought to himself. He knew there would be many more valleys to travel, but God strengthened their faith and deepened their love by demonstrating He would never leave or forsake them, even in the deepest, darkest valley imaginable.

The timer on the oven interrupted Patti and Suzie's discussion. Johnny jumped up to get the lasagna out of the oven and serve the plates. The conversation over dinner turned to memories of Wednesday night cookouts at the cabin by the river.

Suzie confessed she was always in awe of Patti—her hair, her physical conditioning, her volleyball serve, her voice, and her laugh.

"You were an inspiration to all us girls because you were so selfless, humble, and caring, yet you seemed so perfect."

"Johnny will tell you I'm far from perfect," Patti demurred.

"No, I won't! You are perfect." Johnny was quick to say. "And this is a perfect meal for old friends to enjoy together."

Before they adjourned from the table, Suzie had something else on her mind.

"When we contacted all of the kids who were part of our youth group, many asked about having a reunion in Boone. After the story breaks next weekend, it would be a big encouragement to all of us if the two of you would host a cookout for old time's sake. Everyone wants to know you're okay. We could do it any time in the next few months. Would you consider it?"

Johnny and Patti looked at each other. Both smiled and nodded. "That would be fun." Patti was delighted by the idea.

"Do you have any plans to come to Boone in the spring?" Suzie wanted to set a date.

Johnny got up and found his iPhone on the counter. "Yes, we do." He was scrolling through his calendar. We have to be in Boone for several meetings and a court appearance the week of March 15. Is that too soon to plan something?"

"No, that would work. What are you doing in court?"

"The lawyers and insurance companies have been trying to sort out the charges and settlement from the accident that injured Patti. The poor soul who hit her is charged with felony DUI and manslaughter for killing our child. He is facing a long jail sentence. The insurance company is trying to reach a settlement with our lawyer for all the medical costs, pain, and suffering—lots of legal mumbo jumbo.

"We've been working with the prosecutors to try to keep the young driver from going to jail. He was a model student who made a very stupid and costly mistake. We don't want that mistake to cost him his whole life. Nothing can bring back our daughter or completely restore Patti's health but it will be even more tragic if this young man's life is ruined."

"You're back trying to forgive the unforgiveable." Suzie rolled her eyes and shook her head, then held up her finger at Johnny, "I know, I know. You don't need to tell me again that I'm a sinner, too." The three had one last laugh before bed.

* * *

The story in the Boone newspaper played out just as Suzie and her friends planned, but with one powerful and unexpected addition. Without knowing about the editorial in the paper on the same Sunday morning, Suzie's dad gave a tearful confession in front of the entire congregation of Blue Ridge Baptist Church. And he arranged for it all to be videotaped by a young staffer from his business.

Richard Robertson detailed every aspect of his false accusations and lies. He confessed he was a miserable father and abusive husband. He revealed the conspiracy between Pastor Taylor and his son, Mike, to replace Johnny and destroy his reputation. He explained how he turned the entire deacon board against Johnny without any evidence against him. And before he finished, he turned to the camera in the back of the room and pleaded with Suzie to find it in her heart to forgive him. Then he collapsed behind the pulpit and was taken to the hospital.

It was one of the most powerful and extraordinary demonstrations of conviction of sin by the Holy Spirit Johnny ever witnessed—and Johnny along with millions of others saw it all because the young staffer who taped Mr. Robertson's confession posted it on Facebook and YouTube.

Suzie's editorial and the video confession by her dad became online viral sensations. Suzie watched the video of her dad's confession a dozen times. She went from hating him to being sorry for his anguish. She spent two days next to his bed in the hospital crying with him and her mother. She must have told him a hundred times he was forgiven.

* * *

After all the revelations from Richard Robertson, the deacon board of Blue Ridge Baptist Church resigned. Two weeks later, with strong pressure from the congregation, Pastor Taylor also submitted his resignation. Mike Taylor took the title of Senior Pastor but was soon relieved of his duties and his job when a representative from the Southern Baptist Convention came to Boone to take control of the church. The congregation, once nearly 1,000 strong, dwindled to fewer than 100 people for Sunday services led by a rotation of visiting pastors. All of this happened before Johnny and Patti came to Boone in March.

They took a week off from their work at Palmetto Christian in March and scheduled a busy week in Boone with his family and many old friends. While he was gone, Johnny arranged for his students to meet for class on their own. He was confident they would have more interesting discussions without him as the referee. All he asked was that someone take good notes so he would know how "to repair the damage" when he returned. He often teased them about their unorthodox theories, but they didn't hesitate to remind him he was usually the instigator.

Johnny and Patti drove to Boone after their Pub Church meeting on Sunday. They stayed with his mother in her large home on the mountainside overlooking the town. She lived there alone because Ava, her daughter, married the superintendent at their family business. Ava and her husband were the only remaining family members still working in the business.

Knowing Johnny and Patti would be in town, the Wrights called a special board meeting and dinner for their family business on Monday. Their board meetings were usually conference calls, except at Christmas, because both of Johnny's brothers moved to Charlotte to start an investment company.

The family business continued to grow and it provided a good income for all of them. They regularly received offers to sell the business, but Ava and her husband always objected— until now. A large national property rental and management company out of Dallas made an extraordinary offer to buy the Wright family business. The offer included a five-year employment contract for Ava and her husband. Ava was pushing the family to sell.

The board meeting and dinner were held at Johnny's mother's home. The gathering was a joyous reunion even though they all saw each other at Christmas a few months earlier. Johnny's public vindication was a cause for celebration, and the prospect of selling their business had everyone excited.

The family was uncharacteristically relaxed for this board meeting because they didn't plan to spend hours discussing all the problems with their business. The potential sale of the business was the entire focus of Monday's board meeting. And it was an easy decision for all of them. They would each become millionaires and no longer be burdened by the constant decisions, problems, and liabilities of a business with over 100 employees.

Joe Jr. presented the details of the offer and made a strong case they should accept it. There were a few questions about various properties owned by separate LLCs, but Joe Jr. explained the base corporation along with all the LLCs that were part of the business operations would be included in the sale. All properties and equipment would be sold, except for their mother's home which was also owned by a family LLC. Ava called for a vote and it was unanimous. The Wright family business would be sold on June 30.

Everyone was ready to celebrate. Johnny's mother and Ava pulled several trays of hors d'oeuvres out of the refrigerator. Joe Jr. rolled a catering cooler in from the deck filled with their best champagne. Johnny opened two bottles and Patti began filling glasses. When everyone had a glass, Johnny called for a toast to celebrate their father and the business he started. Everyone lifted a glass and cheered, but Johnny noticed Patti was toasting with her ice tea.

"You okay?" Johnny whispered.

"I'm good, just a little queasy in the stomach. Too much excitement and too many snacks, I guess. Congratulations to us! I guess we're rich. Now, maybe I can buy you some new clothes." They hugged and walked out on the deck where, six years before, they made the decision to leave St. Louis and come back to Boone. A great many things happened since that cool, starry night.

Tuesday morning, Johnny and Patti met with a reporter from the *High Country News*. Suzie Robertson's editorial about her dad and the conspiracy against Johnny at the Blue Ridge Baptist Church was intensely critical of the paper's "shoddy reporting." The publisher wanted to make things right.

The interview lasted more than an hour. Suzie had already given the reporter all the sordid details about what really happened at the church. She also told him about the reunion of Johnny's youth group on Saturday and the surprise announcement that Johnny and Patti would be speaking and preaching on Sunday morning at Blue Ridge Baptist Church.

Johnny and Patti talked to the reporter mostly about their lives after he was fired from the church. Very few people in Boone knew he was teaching at a university or that Patti was walking again—even riding a bike. The reporter was also interested in the origin and purpose of the debate with Tony Guest and Johnny's plans for the second debate. Johnny was happy to share how he and his class were planning to prove the existence of God and the truth of the Bible.

Tuesday afternoon, they met with their attorney about a proposed settlement offered by the insurance company for the young man who crashed into Patti's car. Their attorney gave them two choices: take the case to a jury trial which would likely result in at least at $10 million settlement, or accept a $2.5 million lump sum settlement plus medical expenses for life.

He explained a court case would take more than two years and could go much longer with appeals. He estimated after attorney's fees and taxes they would net from $3 to $5 million, but nothing was guaranteed. He recommended the second option. They would net about $1.5 million after taxes, attorney fees would be paid separately by the insurance company, and all of Patti's medical costs would be covered for the rest of her life—even doctors' visits for the cold and flu. She would essentially have free healthcare for life.

It was an easy decision for Patti and Johnny. The money was not their priority. They just wanted the whole thing to be over. They instructed their attorney to take the settlement if it could be completed quickly. Johnny finished with an unusually stern voice, "Let them know our acceptance of the settlement is based on everything being wrapped up—checks in the bank, medical guarantees in writing, and attorney's fees paid—before June 30. Is that a realistic request?" The attorney assured him it was realistic and more than fair.

Tuesday night, Johnny's mother had a reception at her home with a group of old friends and some of Johnny and Patti's favorite employees from the business. It was a fun time and, as it turned out, therapeutic. They both had a lot of bad memories from their time in Boone and the reception with friends lifted a dark cloud and reminded them of the many good times they had.

Wednesday morning, they met with the defense attorney's and parents of the young man who caused the accident with Patti. It was unusual for the victim and plaintiff in a felony case to be meeting with the defense. But Patti had been working for months to help convince the judge not to put the young man, who plead guilty, in jail.

The judge was known for his toughness and, so far, was unwilling to budge. He was insisting there were mandatory sentences required in this case, but the defense attorney presented numerous cases where judges in North Carolina suspended the required jail time. Unfortunately, this judge seemed intent on handing down a maximum sentence. The family asked Patti to make a personal appeal for mercy in the hearing the next day with the judge. Since the boy pled guilty, the judge had the authority to make any sentencing decision he wanted.

The hearing was scheduled for 10:00 Thursday morning at the Watauga County Courthouse in downtown Boone. Johnny and his mother attended with Patti. Until this day, Patti had never met the boy who changed her life forever. His name was Dan Godfrey. He was pale, thin, and couldn't look her in the eye. She was quite certain the last three years were much worse for him than it was for her.

The hearing was held in the judge's personal chambers. The chairs were arranged in a circle for nine people: Patti, Johnny and his mother, the young man and his parents, a federal prosecutor, the defense attorney, and the judge. A stenographer sat quietly off to the side.

The prosecutor presented the government's case in less than five minutes. The judge asked if the victim—Patti—would like to make a statement. The prosecutor sheepishly responded that the victim would be speaking on behalf of the defense. The judge sat back in his chair, stared at Patti, and spoke sternly:

"Most people who have been injured in an accident like yours show up in my court with neck braces and walkers demanding justice. Yet you walk in here like nothing happened ready to defend the person who ruined your life."

Patti looked at the defense attorney. "Is it okay to speak?" The judge didn't wait to hear from the defense attorney.

"I appreciate your compassion for this young boy, but his crime is not just against you. He broke the law and carelessly caused great personal harm, property damage, and millions of dollars of expenses. I'm afraid there is nothing you can say, Mrs. Wright, that will make me change my mind."

"I've waited a long time and come a long way. May I speak?" Patti wasn't giving up. The judge nodded.

"Your Honor, I am grateful for your service to our country and your adherence to the law. But—may I speak openly?" The judge nodded. "If the law was always black and white, these cases could be decided by a computer. We have good judges like you to use their wisdom—their good human judgment.

"The accident killed my baby and injured me, impairing me for life. But God has been good. My husband and I have built a new life and have much to look forward to. I am walking again and even riding a bike. We both have good jobs and many good friends. I am happier than I've ever been in my life.

"The accident caused no expense to the citizens and taxpayers you are sworn to protect. The insurance companies have covered all the material and medical expenses. And we don't have to worry about their profits." The judge was forced to share a smile with Patti.

"Other than our personal loss as a family, which is mostly irrecoverable, the greatest personal loss is this young man. Nothing you can do will change what happened to me and my family, but this young man's life is now in your hands. If he goes to jail, there is little hope he will ever have a happy and productive life. He will not be recoverable. Another life will be lost.

"Even if you suspend his sentence and give him the opportunity to start over, justice will be done. This young man will pay a heavy price for what he did. He will carry the burden from his actions for the rest of his life.

"I want him to know I have forgiven him and God wants to forgive him and give him a new life. It is not your job to forgive him, but my hope and plea is you will give him a second chance at life—and take this burden from my heart, too."

The judge continued to look sternly at Patti. "But it's not all recoverable for you, Mrs. Wright. You will never have children. I have a daughter who cannot have children and it has diminished her life and broken our family."

Everyone suddenly knew why the judge couldn't let this young man go. He experienced what infertility could do to a loved one and it apparently wreaked havoc with his family.

Patti looked at Johnny and then at the judge. "But Judge, I will have children."

Every eye was on Patti. The judge smiled sympathetically. "I admire your optimism, young lady, but I have read the medical report from the accident. I'm afraid you may have an impossible dream." The judge's words seemed mean, yet he was hurting for Patti. But Patti wasn't hurting and she knew there was only one way to save the young man.

"Your Honor, nothing is impossible with God. I'm not just hoping to have children, my doctor told me last week that I am nine weeks pregnant—right now." Johnny looked at Patti with a stunned expression and quivering lips. He couldn't move, but his mother jumped up and screamed, "I knew it! I knew it! You are glowing like a light from heaven." She kneeled in front of Patti and threw her arms around Patti's neck. They wept. They were wailing and laughing. Johnny clasped Patti's wrist as she wrapped her arms around his mother. He closed his eyes and bowed his head.

The scene created an extremely awkward situation for the judge. He could see Patti had not told anyone about her good news. And he was profoundly moved by the realization she only revealed her pregnancy today to save a young man who she didn't even know. He allowed the cries and laughs to continue for several minutes before trying to restore order.

"Mrs. Wright, the best lawyer in America could not have changed my mind about this case. But you have. It is against my best legal judgment, but as you suggested, perhaps this is a good time to use my best human judgment. I am required to sentence Mr. Godfrey to five years in prison, but I will suspend the sentence in lieu of a five-year probation, including 500 hours of community service that will be determined by Mrs. Wright. This case is closed."

The judge stood and walked over to Patti. She stood and reached out her hand. "Thank you, Your Honor." He smiled. "No, thank you, Mrs. Wright, and congratulations."

Young Dan Godfrey sat in his chair crying until Patti walked over and put her hand on his head. She kneeled in front of him and he finally looked up into her eyes. "Dan, you are forgiven. God loves you. I love you. Now go thank God, follow Jesus, and start your life over. Will you do that for me? Promise me you will forgive yourself today and put all this behind you."

Dan was a trembling wreck. "I will try. I promise to do my best."

"You better do your best because you are going to be working for me—500 hours' worth." That brought a slight smile to

Dan's face. His parents could only cry and repeat "thank you, thank you" over and over again.

"Patti, let's get out of here and head home. There are a few things we need to talk about." Johnny was beaming. He tried to take Patti's hand, but his mother grabbed her first. "She's walking with me."

Friday morning, Johnny and Patti were treated to a front page, full-color photo of themselves in the *High Country News*. It was their "glamour shot" from the newsletter announcement of their arrival at Palmetto Christian. The story was all positive. It treated them like returning hometown heroes, and in a way, they were. It was the type of story great novels are made of—good people are done wrong by bad people, but then justice prevails and the good people are lifted to a higher place than they were before. Or maybe it was just the story of Job being played out again with new actors.

The newspaper story also included details of the coming Saturday reunion, and Sunday morning service at Blue Ridge Baptist Church, so both events were packed. The reunion was held at a park just outside Boone and was catered by the Wrights' business. Johnny served as the main chef, but he required several assistants to manage five large grills. Patti served as the honorary referee for the volleyball games held in her honor. Instead of the 200 expected for the event, there were nearly 1,000 crowding the grounds. Many of the parents, family members, and friends of former youth group members wanted to welcome Patti and Johnny home.

The Sunday service at Blue Ridge Baptist Church was more like a giant celebration than a church service. All the pews were full for the first time since Johnny left. The walls were lined with folding chairs and there were several television cameras in the back of the room. Johnny brought his guitar and opened the service with one of the favorite songs of his Wednesday night youth group—"Risen Love."

Suzie Robertson introduced Johnny and Patti on behalf of all the young people whose lives they impacted. She also introduced her dad who was crying on the front row.

"I want to thank my father who forgave me for hating him. He showed me God can do all things and forgive all things." The entire room erupted in applause. It was the most incredible display of redemption and restoration anyone ever witnessed.

Johnny and Patti told their story, start to finish. Johnny detailed his loss of faith and how God brought him back with Patti's love. Patti surprised Johnny by telling the congregation how, despite his "argument with God," Johnny was her strength and inspiration. "I've never seen anyone wrestle so vigorously with God, argue so vociferously with God, and yet never let go of his grip on God. Johnny is a man after God's own heart, and my heart will always be his." Johnny brought a good sermon, but Patti's words were the most memorable—especially the last few words of her talk: "Oh, and by the way, Johnny and I are expecting."

The applause could have brought down the Walls of Jericho.

Therefore since it still remains for some to enter that rest,
and since those who formerly had the good news proclaimed
to them did not go in because of their disobedience, God
again set a certain day, calling it "Today." This he did
when a long time later he spoke through David, as in the
passage already quoted:

"Today, if you hear his voice,
do not harden your hearts."—Hebrews 4:6–7

CHAPTER SEVENTEEN

SAVED BY GOD, OURSELVES, OR BOTH?

September 2017 – Labor Day weekend continued
(Middleburg, VA)

Dr. Clark bounded into the great room where Tony and Elizabeth were pouring cups of coffee at the kitchen counter.

"Good morning, Tony and Elizabeth, I've been watching the sun rise over the lake. Your guest house is something else. I'd love to spend a few weeks hiding out over there working on my next book. And this view of the Virginia mountains from here in your kitchen is almost as beautiful as my view of the South Carolina mountains from my back porch. What a beautiful place you have here! I'm so happy you two can share it together."

Dr. Clark was full of energy as he poured his own cup of coffee and led the way to the porch. Tony enjoyed listening to

Elizabeth and Dr. Clark talk for a few minutes before he went
back to the kitchen to begin setting up for breakfast. He and
Elizabeth were making their "famous" cheese omelets for their
guest.

At breakfast, Elizabeth prodded Dr. Clark to talk about his
work at Palmetto Christian. Her bookstore did business with
many universities and she was curious about what Dr. Clark
thought about the state of America's youth.

Dr. Clark surprised her with his optimism. "I have been
extremely encouraged by the minds and spirits of the young
people who come to Palmetto Christian. Even though most of
them were educated in public schools where the culture is
antagonistic toward Christian beliefs, they come to Palmetto
anxious to grow in their faith and their knowledge of the Bible.
And, of course, they are also very serious about obtaining the
knowledge and skills to succeed in the business world."

Tony joined the questioning. "Dr. Clark, how many of
your students can defend their faith against the increasing
number of opponents of their beliefs—atheists and critics like
me—and pastors who don't believe the Bible?"

"I'm afraid most of our students are willing, but few are
well-prepared. We have debate teams that travel to churches
and hold mock debates, but the fact is, there is not a lot of good,
concise research and relevant publications to equip these young
people to defend their faith in the context of modern science
and progressive religion. Tony and Elizabeth, this is the reason
for the project I hope you will help me complete before I leave
Palmetto."

After breakfast, they set up to work in the large den adjoining the kitchen. It was more comfortable than Tony's study
with more light through the large windows, more room to walk
around, and refreshments could easily be moved from the
refrigerator to the large counter surrounding the kitchen.
Dr. Clark set the parameters of their discussion.

"Yesterday, we teed up three broad areas for discussion
today. I will talk about some patterns in the Bible that seem to

confirm the theory we are all on a pilgrimage from heaven. Elizabeth will follow with more discussion about what 'salvation' means, when it occurs, and why obedience is important. Tony will talk more about the role of the church and—using his research from *God Fantasies*—cover the main criticisms of biblical truth. Our goal today is to identify areas for follow-up research over the next few months.

"Let's begin today with Abraham. The nation of Israel is clearly a physical representation of God's spiritual chosen people. The Jews are not, as a whole, the physical counterparts of God's spiritual children because we know some physical Jews, like individuals from all the different groups of people in the world—belong to Satan. That may sound shocking, but in John 8, Jesus is arguing with some Pharisees, the top echelon of the Jewish nation, about who are the real children of Abraham. Jesus makes a distinction between the physical children of Abraham and his spiritual children, and in verses 42–44 he is painfully blunt with the Pharisees."

Dr. Clark picked up his well-worn and dog-eared Bible.

"'If God were your Father, you would love me, for I have come here from God. I have not come on my own; God sent me. Why is my language not clear to you? Because you are unable to hear what I say. You belong to your father, the devil, and you want to carry out your father's desires. He was a murderer from the beginning, not holding to the truth, for there is no truth in him. When he lies, he speaks his native language, for he is a liar and the father of lies.'"

Dr. Clark put his Bible on a coffee table and paced around like he was in front of a class.

"Of course, we also know many physical Jews are spiritual children of Abraham. Jesus, His disciples, the prophets, and most of the early Christians were Jews. We know these were all children of God. And we know believers—followers of Jesus—have since come not only from the Jews, but from all nations, religions, and ethnic backgrounds. I'm convinced there are also many people—including Jews—who have not accepted Jesus as their Savior, but are children of God. We can talk more about that later.

"Clearly, one's heritage or physical characteristics have no relationship to whether we are children of God. It is all about this word 'faith.' In Hebrews 11 beginning with verse 8—and we all know these verses—we find what qualified Abraham to be the physical representation of God's spiritual children on earth."

Dr. Clark returned to his Bible on the table next to his seat and quickly turned to a marked page.

> "'By faith Abraham, when called to go to a place he would later receive as his inheritance, obeyed and went, even though he did not know where he was going. By faith he made his home in the promised land like a stranger in a foreign country; he lived in tents, as did Isaac and Jacob, who were heirs with him of the same promise. For he was looking forward to the city with foundations, whose architect and builder is God. And by faith even Sarah, who was past childbearing age, was enabled to bear children because she considered him faithful who had made the promise. And so from this one man, and he as good as dead, came descendants as numerous as the stars in the sky and as countless as the sand on the seashore.'

"I will draw several theories from these few verses. Abraham is representative of God—the father of all of His children. Before we were born into this world, we were all at home in heaven, a part of God's spiritual body. But God—for reasons we will continue to explore—told us to go to the physical world, a place we didn't know and where we would be 'strangers in a foreign land.'

"Why did God send Abraham to a foreign land and why did He send us into this physical world? The Bible tells us it was to create 'descendants as numerous as the stars in the sky and as countless as the sand on the seashore.' These physical descendants carry the souls of God's children through their earthly pilgrimage.

"Why couldn't Abraham create descendants where he lived and why did God want us to leave heaven to become physical? Because Abraham's descendants would be spiritual heirs to a promise and they were destined for 'a city with foundations built by God.' Abraham and his spiritual descendants—that includes us—were not just destined for the physical land of Israel; they were destined for the new heaven on a new earth we read about in Revelation—just as God's children are destined for a new physical and spiritual heaven.

"My main point is Abraham couldn't accomplish God's purposes without leaving home and neither could we. But what qualified Abraham for this central role in creating the heirs to this city built by God? And what qualified each of us as God's children to be selected as pilgrims on earth and heirs to the new heaven? Could it be as simple as we read in Romans 4:3?"

Dr. Clark didn't need his Bible for his next verse: "'Abraham believed God, and it was credited to him as righteousness.'

"What if God told all spiritual beings to leave heaven and go to earth? What if some of us obeyed and God credited that one act to us as righteousness? What if Satan and his angels refused to go? And what if that one act made it impossible for them to be adopted into physical sonship and to enter the new heaven?

"Apparently, Satan's refusal to leave heaven started the war that resulted in Satan and all his angels being thrown down to earth. I am theorizing all of God's children and all of Satan's children have to eventually take physical bodies on earth. Everything has to pass through the physical world. All of God's children are part of the physical body of Jesus and are redeemed by His blood. They have the physical and spiritual characteristics necessary to live in the new heaven.

"All of Satan's children are part of his body and do not have the blood of Jesus because they didn't want to be part of God's family. Without the blood of Jesus, Satan and his children cannot enter or exist in the final spiritual and physical world. They are blocked from the new heaven. Okay, now I'm getting to the hard part."

Dr. Clark walked over to the kitchen counter and poured another cup of coffee.

"What if our eternal destiny was decided in heaven when we willingly obeyed God and left heaven? Could this act of faith have saved us for eternity? Was this decision to obey God—as with Abraham—credited to us as righteousness?

"And what if the opposite was true for those who decided they did not want to be part of the physical and spiritual body of God? Think about it. In heaven, everyone had complete knowledge of God. There were no 'poor children in Africa' who would go to hell because they never heard of Jesus or good people anywhere in the world who are lost for eternity because they didn't go through the motions of 'receiving Christ.' Everyone in heaven knows everything about God—at least everything a created being can know.

"So, one of my theories is this: all of God's spiritual body may have determined their own eternal destiny before being born on earth. We all made free-will, fully informed decisions about whether we wanted to be a part of God's body or Satan's. Those who chose to be part of God's body were physically separated from Him while on earth with no conscious memory of our lives in the spiritual world. This separation from God is what we call sin. Sin—separation from God—is the dominion of Satan. We are slaves to Satan when we are separated from God. He owns us—until Jesus resurrects our spirits and restores our relationship with God.

"Our state of sin is not defined by what we do, it is defined by where we are—on earth in physical bodies separated from God. We commit acts of sin because we are separated from God. We are all sinners because we are separated from God when we are born in physical bodies. This is why human nature is naturally sinful. As human beings, we are separated from God and—at least temporarily—owned by Satan.

"Only the physical and spiritual blood of God can pay the price to buy us back from Satan and restore us as part of God's body. This all makes perfect sense; we must have God's blood to be part of His body. As we are told in Leviticus, 'The life of the creature is in the blood.'

"Abraham, Isaac, and Jacob are figuratively the Father, Son, and Holy Spirit. Isaac, a depiction of Jesus, was figuratively sacrificed and brought back from the dead. Jacob, whose name was changed to Israel, is a physical representation of the Holy Spirit who builds the whole spiritual body of Jesus in the physical world. The history of the nation of Israel tells us a lot about the path of God's children in this physical world, especially the nature of salvation. This will be a good lead into Elizabeth's discussion.

"Think of the nation of Israel as a physical representation of God's spiritual children. The Jews were called 'God's chosen people' because they were chosen to show and tell the world about God and His plans. Like Israel, God's spiritual children began in the Promised Land—the spiritual heaven. They left home for Egypt to survive a famine. Egypt is representative of the physical world. God's people became slaves, in our case to Satan, in a foreign land—earth.

"The Jews left home and went to Egypt because of a famine. They left home to save themselves. But their 'savior,' Israel's son Joseph, was sent as a slave before them to prepare for their salvation. The same is true for us. God's children left heaven because the war with Satan created the 'famine' necessitating the destruction of heaven and the spiritual world. But God became a human—essentially a slave—to provide the way of escape for His children.

"Here's the fun part. When did the Jews become God's chosen people? Tony—Elizabeth—?"

Elizabeth smiled. "They were God's physical children when they were born because they were physical descendants of Abraham. The Jews had nothing to do with deciding if they were God's children."

"Right!" Dr. Clark was pacing again. "So, continuing with my analogy, when do human beings become God's children?"

Tony joined in. "It was decided before we arrived on earth, or in your example, before we arrived in Egypt."

"Right again!" Dr. Clark was in a rhythm. "When were the Jews saved?"

Elizabeth was enjoying the ride. "Was it before they left Egypt when the angel of death passed over them and saved their firstborn sons because they painted a cross with blood on their doors, or when Moses led them out of Egypt, or when they entered the Promised Land?"

"You got it, Elizabeth. There are several aspects of salvation depicted by the Jews. They represented God's children, at least in a physical sense, until Jesus was resurrected and the Holy Spirit began to build the church with God's spiritual children. The parallel here is the Jews were God's physical children before, during, and after they went into slavery in Egypt, just as God's spiritual children are His before, during, and after they come to earth. Nothing can happen while we are on earth that changes our eternal destiny with God.

"The battle between Moses and the Egyptian pharaoh is a depiction of, or perhaps, even a physical representation of the ongoing battle between God and Satan. God demands Satan let His people go but Satan always resists. Satan will literally put all people through hell—the plagues, pain, and suffering of the physical world—to keep God's children in slavery. But when God allows the angel of death to kill Satan's children while passing over His own as He did in Egypt and with the Great Flood, Satan has to release God's children.

"So, what happened when the angel of death killed the firstborn sons of the Egyptians, but 'passed over' the firstborn sons of the Jews because of the cross painted with blood on their doors? This was a picture of how the blood of Jesus saves God's children from spiritual death when they are in slavery to sin on earth. And those who are not covered by the blood of Jesus—the lineage of Satan—have no escape from death.

"Did the Jews have to do anything to save themselves from physical death? Yes, they did! They had to put the blood of a sacrifice on their doors and hide behind the blood in their homes. The blood covered their sin and saved all God's people. This covering was not based on individual decisions of faith by the Jewish people—although the head of every household must have believed Moses when he warned them about the coming angel of death. The blood on the doors was a blanket covering of sin for all God's children on earth—in this case in Egypt. This reminds us of the verses from Romans 5:6–8." Dr. Clark turned to another marked page in his Bible.

> "'You see, at just the right time, when we were still power-less, Christ died for the ungodly. Very rarely will anyone die for a righteous person, though for a good person someone might possibly dare to die. But God demonstrates his own love for us in this: While we were still sinners, Christ died for us.'

"While the Jews were still in Egypt, trapped in slavery, and powerless against the Pharaoh, the blood of a sacrifice saved them. While God's children are on earth, separated from God, slaves to Satan, the blood of Jesus saves all of us. This blood is painted as a cross on the door of all God's kingdom. The next two verses in Romans reminds us while we were still enemies of God, the blood of Jesus justified God's claim on us and reconciled us to Him. We did nothing to deserve justification and reconciliation. God did it all and we did nothing. But the last part of this next verse suggests 'eternal salvation' is something different that will happen in the future.

"This is Romans 5:9–10:

> 'Since we have now been justified by his blood, how much more shall we be saved from God's wrath through him! For if, while we were God's enemies, we were reconciled to him through the death of his Son, how much more, having been reconciled, shall we be saved through his life!'

"The next step for the nation of Israel was to cross through the Red Sea and spend forty years in the wilderness. God did everything for them. The Jews followed a pillar of fire out of Egypt, God parted the Red Sea, killed the Egyptians who were trying to reclaim them, He fed them, and gave them water—yet they rebelled against Him, complained, and worshiped idols.

"I believe the Jews in the wilderness represent God's children on earth who have not received Jesus—they have not entered God's Sabbath rest as we read in Hebrews. God has justified and reconciled all His children with His blood, but many don't know about Jesus or are too busy enjoying their sinful existence to want to know Him. God calls all His people, by faith, to cross over into the 'Promised Land' and to be born again into spiritual life, restored to God's family, and to live in God's presence while still living in physical bodies.

"Forty years in the wilderness is representative of a lifetime, and it is clear many of God's children live and die—'die in the desert'—without ever entering His rest by coming to a saving knowledge of Jesus. Do they lose their eternal salvation? I don't think so.

"In the wilderness, God uses Moses to deliver the law and to make an everlasting covenant with His people. The law, written on stone tablets, is the physical version of a spiritual truth. God writes His laws on the hearts of all of His children to convict us of sin and to drive us to Him. All creation provides evidence of a creator God and His laws are written on our hearts. We know right from wrong, even before we know Jesus, but the only way for us to know God's salvation in this life is to confess our sins and to willfully rejoin God's spiritual family. This is the idea of being born again into God's kingdom.

"When the nation of Israel finally believed God, crossed the Jordan, and entered the Promised Land, they were showing us what happens when we accept Jesus as Savior and Lord. Satan is still our enemy just as the Jews had many enemies in the Promised Land. God told the Jews to conquer and expel all their enemies, just as He tells us to conquer sin and to stay away from temptation.

"I've gone on too long, as usual. Let's take a short break and then hear from Elizabeth."

Tony took a vegetable tray out of the refrigerator and put it on the counter. He added a few soft drinks to the ice bucket and opened a bottle of sparkling water.

"Could I bring anything?"

"I'll take a cup of that sparkling water." Elizabeth was shuffling through her papers and making some notes. Dr. Clark returned from the guest house with another briefcase full of papers. Elizabeth waited for her two colleagues to sit down.

Elizabeth looked up from her stack of papers. "I'll try to pick up where Dr. Clark left off. When I really dig into the Scriptures, I often find a physical event that seems to be playing out a spiritual truth. In Dr. Clark's example, Joseph was the first son of Jacob with his wife Rachel. He was sold into slavery by his brothers. Joseph was taken to Egypt where he was a slave, a prisoner, and then became like a king—a savior of his people. Was Joseph representative of Jesus being sold into slavery in heaven by His own family and sent to earth as a slave, only to become the Savior of all God's people? It's fascinating, but I'm off subject. Let's talk about salvation.

"When it comes to the issue of salvation, the Christian church runs the gambit. The more liberal, large denominations teach all humans are God's children and He shows His love through the teachings and sacrifice of Jesus. Some teach that Jesus is God and others don't. Most teach, or at least imply, Jesus gave His life for everyone and it is not necessary for people to confess their sins and accept Jesus as Savior and Lord to have eternal life.

"The more reformed, Bible-believing churches teach that everyone is a sinner and destined for hell. But God calls all of His children to Himself, and those who are His respond with an individual confession of sin and the acceptance of Jesus Christ as their Savior and Lord. To be saved, one must name the name of Jesus. This seems to be what the Bible is saying.

"First, what is the name of Jesus? He has many names. His name is actually Immanuel, which means 'God with us.' If people believe God is with us, are they saved? Isaiah tells us the Savior will be called Wonderful Counselor, Mighty God,

Everlasting Father, Prince of Peace. If someone calls on a Mighty God, will they be saved?

"Many of us as evangelicals insist only the name Jesus can save. But think about this for a minute. The whole creation confirms the existence of God and He has written His laws on our hearts. Many people all over the world—literate and illiterate—worship a Mighty God and hope their God will save them. Do we believe they won't be saved because they don't know the specifics of the God in the Bible or the gospel of Jesus?

"We know the thief on the cross next to Jesus and the people who were saved at Pentecost never saw a Bible because it didn't exist. So, will people be condemned to hell because they do not pray the sinner's prayer in a biblically correct way? Will God send us to hell on a technicality? That can't be true. But what is true?"

Elizabeth spent the next thirty minutes talking about the different theories of salvation and then summarized the first part of her presentation with one word. Faith.

"One last word about faith. We are told we are saved by faith. As I've postulated, I don't think what we believe makes us a child of God or gives us eternal life. I believe faith saves us from the grip of Satan in this life and saves us from the fear of death. And consider this: faith is not what we believe, it is our confidence in the One we believe in. As we've read in Hebrews 11:1:

'Now faith is confidence in what we hope for and assurance about what we do not see. This is what the ancients were commended for.'

"Faith is not about believing in God or Jesus. Satan and his demons do that. Faith is not only about praying to receive Christ. Faith is being certain God will fulfill His promises— certain enough to obey and follow Him our whole lives. Hebrews defines faith clearly. It is being certain of what we hope for. What do we hope for? That God will give us eternal life with Him in a paradise more wonderful than anything we can imagine. We hope to be reunited with our loved ones. And we also hope and pray God will protect us and our loved ones in this life.

"The New Testament is full of references of how believers can know they are God's children and have eternal life. The fruit of the Spirit listed in Galatians is a key indicator of whether we have the Spirit. Do we love other believers? Do we obey God's Word? Do we help the poor? Do we love our enemies? So much of the gospel is about showing God's children how they can be assured they belong to Him. Praying to receive Jesus as Lord and Savior is certainly a key indicator of salvation, but that act alone is no assurance of eternal life if it is not followed by obedience to God's Word.

"In 1 John 5:13–15, we see a good example of why we preach the gospel. God wants us to 'know' and have 'confidence' we are His.

> *'I write these things to you who believe in the name of the Son of God so that you may know that you have eternal life. This is the confidence we have in approaching God: that if we ask anything according to his will, he hears us. And if we know that he hears us—whatever we ask—we know that we have what we asked of him.'*

"What we're saying, I think, is the act of repenting and giving our lives to Jesus does two things: it confirms we are God's children—saved unto eternal life—and it reconnects us to God, allowing His Spirit to enter our hearts and resurrect our spirits—saving us from Satan's control and slavery to sin while we are still in our physical bodies. This gives us the ability to resist sin and work out our salvation during our physical lives. We are still sinners, but we are saved from slavery to the law and to sin.

"The free-will act of 'declaring' and 'believing' is what saves us from Satan's grip in these physical bodies, but we cannot believe unless we are already God's elect—His children. This is an important and controversial distinction. We are suggesting the possibility God determines our eternal destination based on our decision to follow Him before we are born, but His children on this earth have the option whether to obey Him and follow Jesus while we are alive.

"Those who are reconnected with God in this life can experience the joy and peace of His presence and have all of the spiritual blessings from heaven in advance of eternity. But God's children who do not respond to His call in this life—like the Jews who died in the wilderness—will live defeated lives, and yet, because the blood of Jesus justifies all of God's children, they will 'suffer loss' as the Bible says, but still have eternal life with God's family.

"The Scripture says those who receive Jesus have the confidence of their salvation. It also speaks of those who hear the gospel yet reject Jesus. This rejection of the gospel by those who hear it is a sign they may not be God's children. Romans 2:8 is one of many times the Scripture uses the word 'reject.'

'But for those who are self-seeking and who reject the truth and follow evil, there will be wrath and anger.'

"Again, my guess here is the acts of receiving or rejecting do not determine your eternal destiny, they determine if you will know God in this life and they are strong indications whether you are a child of God or Satan.

"It's getting late. Just one last thought about salvation before lunch.

"Noah and the Great Flood provide a picture of what God does for us. Like Noah, we are all living in a sinful world, separated from God. In the Bible, water is the symbol of the physical world. The waters of the flood destroyed all living beings, except for those who were saved by the ark. Ironically, it is the water that destroys and the water that saves. Without the water, there would be no escape from evil and no new world for Noah's family. I think that is why believers are baptized with water.

"The ark and the Flood provide a picture of how the physical world provides a bridge to the new heaven and new earth. The physical world will ultimately destroy Satan and his demons, but because Jesus—our ark—saves us and delivers us to the new heaven, the physical world is actually our salvation.

"This helps me see why God had to create the physical world and send everyone through it. The physical world separates us temporarily from God and causes us to suffer under Satan's control, but it is necessary to destroy evil. God—the physical Jesus—provides safe passage for all His children and takes us to the new heaven and new earth where Satan cannot follow—just like the Egyptians couldn't follow the Jews across the Red Sea. The 'Red Sea' just might depict the blood of Jesus.

"Let's break for lunch and then we can give the whole afternoon to Tony."

Jesus answered, "I am the way and the truth and the life.
No one comes to the Father except through me. If you really
know me, you will know my Father as well. From now on,
you do know him and have seen him."—John 14:6–7

CHAPTER EIGHTEEN

THE ONLY WAY, TRUTH, AND LIFE

September 2017 – Labor Day weekend continued
(Middleburg, VA)

"I couldn't think straight for a long time. My mind was a jumbled mess." Tony still found it hard to contemplate everything he'd been through. "But reading back through *God Fantasies* has actually been helpful in many ways—both painful and therapeutic."

Tony was speaking with his hand tapping on a copy of his book—one of the best-selling books in history—a book now being used all around the world to disprove the existence of God, discredit the Bible, and denounce Christianity.

"Reading through these pages again rekindled my anger, but bringing my anger out in the open helped me let it go. It also forced me to deal with my sadness instead of continuing to bury it in anger. And this project with you two has been helpful as well. The research and discussions we've had over the last few months have been difficult but liberating.

"Elizabeth, thank you for your strength, love, and wisdom, and Dr. Clark, thank you again for spending this weekend with us plumbing the depths of the great mysteries of life. Yes, I am making fun of us. We have to be seriously nerdy and a little bit crazy to spend Labor Day weekend trying to understand the Beauty and the Beasts in Revelation. But so far, it's been a lot of fun!

"In the next hour or two, I'd like to focus our attention on the most credible criticisms of the Bible. But first, I'll share a few of my thoughts on the topic of salvation and some reflections of my state of mind when I first decided to write *God Fantasies*. Then I'll talk a little about the atheists, deists, and others I've met around the world who seem to revel in the idea of a Godless existence. We need to understand how to deal with people who insist there is no God and those who laugh at the Bible as a source of truth. All of this will, hopefully, give us fresh insights into a more effective role for the church.

SATAN USES SUFFERING TO PUSH PEOPLE AWAY FROM GOD

"When I lost Pamela and Christine, my mind wouldn't function. My thought pattern was circular. I couldn't plan the sequencing of simple activities for one day, let alone for a week or a month. Every thought bounced around the empty canyons of my mind. It was disorienting—like speaking into a microphone with loud, screeching feedback. Solitude became too noisy to bear, but I avoided being with anyone. It was a grave mistake for me to be alone because my cold, dark existence created a witches' brew of anger, resentment, and a drive for retribution. I cut myself off from God and, without knowing it, gave myself completely to Satan.

"I was so ashamed when I considered all the hurting people I counseled who described the same dark feelings and paralysis of their minds. These people were dying of cancer or lost a spouse of fifty years or a young couple who lost a child. I pretended to understand and gave them the standard verses about how God loved them and would protect them. But after going through my own trauma, I know their minds couldn't even process what I was saying. They just needed to be around people so God could love them through others.

"I mention this today because, in retrospect, I can see how Satan uses suffering to separate people from God and take control of their lives. God, for reasons we have discussed, allows the battle between good and evil to play out on this earth. He has to let Satan take his best shot at each of us, just like He did with Jesus during His forty days of testing in the desert. He had to give me the freedom to choose good or evil, and for a time, I chose evil.

"But I also learned how God is always calling His lost sheep to return home and how He makes all things work for good if we trust Him. He usually doesn't do it with the kind of direct intervention He did with Paul on the road to Damascus. For most of us, we hear His quiet call through the voices of people who love us. Dr. Clark did it with his letter offering to take a leave of absence to be with me. God spoke to me through Elizabeth at the book signing in Chicago. And I'm sure thousands of people around the world joined the battle for my soul with their prayers. Jesus tells us in the book of John the world will know we love Him by the way we love each other. I have learned we can only know God's love through the love of others.

"We have begun to uncover the reasons why we all have to go through this painful mess here on earth. We are the body of Jesus—God's children—and we have seen what God allowed to happen to His own body on the cross. As the Bible says, 'I have been crucified with Christ.' I didn't understand what that meant until I found myself repeating the words Jesus spoke on the cross, 'My God, my God, why have you forsaken me?'

WE ARE RESTORED TO GOD THROUGH THE BLOOD OF JESUS

"But, thankfully, the resurrection is more real than the crucifixion because the resurrection is permanent—it is for eternity.

And just as we are crucified with Jesus as part of His body, we are resurrected with Him with new bodies for eternity.

"Now I know God did not forsake me. In the name of freedom and justice, He allowed me to be separated from Him, just as He did with Jesus. But unlike Jesus, who was sinless and could not be held captive by Satan and death, I need a savior. I was born into Satan's dominion as a sinner and lived as a sinner. Satan owned my soul and my physical body and because the wages of sin is death, a sinless sacrifice was required to save me from eternal death and restore me to the family of God.

"Physical death without the blood of Jesus means eternal separation from God and eternity in Satan's kingdom. Death is Satan's domain and everyone who has ever lived will spend eternity in his kingdom unless there is an acceptable payment made for their sin. If anyone thinks he or she can pay for their sin with their own deaths, they are dead wrong. Our human blood is sinful and binds us to Satan's kingdom.

"This is why we need Jesus to be a substitute sacrifice. As part of His body, we have a claim to His physical and spiritual blood—His resurrection—which saves us from eternal death, separates us from evil, and allows us to live in the new heaven where there will be no evil or death.

"We know, as Jesus told us, only His sheep will recognize His voice. Only those who are part of the body of Jesus—the 'elect'—can hear the call of God. I think the 'elect' are spread all over the world and are part of every race, religion, and nation. And I'm guessing God's 'elect' hear His voice in different languages and worship in ways we might consider biblically unsound. And some of God's people may not even acknowledge God at all during their physical lives.

TWO KINGDOMS—ONLY TWO FINAL DESTINATIONS FOR EVERYONE

"I'll leave this subject with one simple thought—we've mentioned this several times. The Bible makes it clear there are two kingdoms in eternity: one is God's and the other is Satan's.

God's kingdom is holy, sinless, and full of light, love, and life. Only those who are holy and sinless can live there and only one person who has ever lived on this earth is holy and sinless: Jesus.

"I am constantly amazed by how few people seriously consider the implications of this biblical fact. There is nothing more inevitable than physical death and it is foolish for anyone to assume they will end up in God's kingdom without an extraordinary event that cleanses them, separates them from their sin, and makes them a part of the resurrected body of Jesus.

"Satan's kingdom is permanently separated from God, dark and consumed with death. Every person ever born with a physical father has a sinful human nature and is separated from God's kingdom. So, we are all born as citizens of Satan's kingdom and cannot enter God's kingdom because of our sin.

"There is only one way sinful humans can enter God's kingdom—as part of the body of Jesus with His blood. I don't know if God applies this invisible blood of Jesus to all of His children automatically or if we have to consciously ask for it, but why would anyone want to risk their eternity by leaving that question to chance? We must continue to plead with everyone who has ears to hear; give your life to Jesus and let Jesus give His life to you!

The Bible must be our source of truth

"Okay, I need to shift gears back to my journey in the wilderness. When I first decided to write a book to refute all the evidence from my first book about the existence of God and the accuracy of the Bible, I knew I could not disprove the existence of a creator God. Every year there are more scientific and medical discoveries of the intricacies and organized complexities of life and matter. It is impossible for all of this to have happened without a planner, designer, and creator.

"Many scientists have concluded the energy sustaining everything in this world must come from a continuous source in a meta-physical dimension we can't see or understand.

Science and deductive reasoning strongly suggest a spiritual world is connected to this physical world.

"I confess my *God Fantasies* project was written much like a negative political campaign. I created a 'straw man' to be my opponent. I fabricated my own definition of the 'traditional interpretation' of the Bible and then used science to discredit my own interpretation. By selecting a few major events in the Bible and defining them in scientifically implausible terms, I made the whole Bible suspect. If the Bible is suspect, it is easy to make people question whether there is a God. And if there is no God, there is no sin, no judgment, no heaven or hell, no need for Jesus—all the tenets of our faith collapse if the Bible is not completely true.

"As I mentioned yesterday, there are three key biblical accounts I attacked in *God Fantasies*: the six-day creation, the genealogies indicating the earth is less than 10,000 years old, and the Great Flood. I also challenged the sovereignty of God in light of all the evil in the world. Where did evil come from if God didn't create it?

"You've both read my book. It makes the biblical accounts look contradictory and silly. But I plan to make my own silliness look even sillier by proving I was wrong. I've already collected and compiled most of the research I need, it's just a matter of organizing it into a coherent and simple narrative.

ALTERNATIVE BIBLICAL VIEW OF CREATION

"I plan to show how the traditional, literal interpretation of the creation story is scientifically possible, but I will also explain why I don't believe creation was completed in six twenty-four-hour days. I'll take a few minutes today to summarize my alternative theory.

"First, if we accept the premise, or at least the possibility, all spiritual life must pass through physical bodies, then long periods of time are necessary for the physical reproduction necessary to create the living vessels that will transport spiritual creatures through this physical world. When God created animals and humans, He told them to be fruitful and multiply. Multiplication was clearly a priority for God's creation.

"After years of study, contemplation, and consternation, I have concluded the 'days' in Genesis represent six long periods of time. Not because I believe God couldn't do it all in six days. God could have spent an eternity creating this universe in a timeless spiritual dimension and then flashed it all into physical existence in an instant—just like a movie projector creates an image on a screen by shining light through film. The interplay between two dimensions makes it foolish for us to limit God to our physical understanding.

"I believe the creation story covers six long periods of time because it is logical, it is consistent with what the Bible says, and it is consistent with science. We know the word 'day' is used to denote long periods of time in many Bible prophesies. And we know, without the creation of the sun until the fourth day, it would have been difficult to measure twenty-four-hour days—even though day and night were separated on the first day.

"If we assume the first chapter of Genesis is describing six long periods of time, I have collected a lot of research to prove the descriptions and chronological order of creation in the Bible are perfectly consistent with the most credible scientific explanations. I'll document all this for our final report.

"I'll also document my theory that God pre-programmed the physical world to grow and develop over time like a seed—like DNA guides the development of babies from one cell at conception to billions when the child is born. What appears to scientists to be random evolution over billions of years, was likely programmed development that occurred over much shorter periods of time.

"In addition, I will provide evidence the creation of Adam in chapter 2 of Genesis occurred thousands—maybe millions—of years after the creation of mankind in chapter 1. I don't think the males and females created in chapter 1 of Genesis were Adam and Eve. The account of Adam and Eve in the second chapter of Genesis contains very different descriptions than the creation account in chapter 1.

"In chapter 1, the whole earth was covered with all kinds of seed-bearing plants, fruits, nuts—plenty to eat everywhere. God created 'mankind' in His own image. The context suggests He created many males and females and I suspect they were direct translations of living creatures in the spiritual world. They were made in God's image because they were part of God's body. God said 'let us make mankind in our image.' I think He was speaking to living creatures in His spiritual family. And after they became physical beings, God told them to multiply.

"The humans and animals in chapter 1 were created without a sin nature. God couldn't have said His creation was all good if there was any evil in the world. There was not a tree with the knowledge of good and evil mentioned in chapter 1. I'm theorizing these first physical creatures were counterparts of spiritual creatures in God's household in heaven, but probably not angels. They remained seamlessly connected to God and had both a physical and spiritual consciousness. They were not separated from God while in physical bodies and there was no sin in the world.

"I suspect there may have been physical death because of the need to continuously transport large numbers of spiritual beings through the physical world. If there was physical death, it was likely a very different experience than we know today because, with their direct connection to the spiritual world, physical death for sinless creatures would have been like taking off a worn-out coat and putting on a new one. There would have been no fear or dread.

"All of this is just my theorizing and it's not relevant to the bigger issues of salvation and eternal life, but it's still important to think about how the physical world could be seamlessly connected to God and the spiritual world.

"Based on the accounts in Revelation, early humans were not the savages depicted in textbooks today. They built civilizations and the whole earth was like a Garden of Eden—until Satan was thrown down. My theory of early humans later interbreeding with modern humans is consistent with recent scientific discoveries.

"Revelation describes a global apocalypse when Satan and his angels are thrown to earth. This had to occur after the six periods of creation and before the creation of Adam and Eve. Satan was in the Garden of Eden, but he was not on earth when God rested and declared everything 'good.'

"Satan's entry into the physical world—as described in Revelation—darkened the sky and polluted much of the water around the world. This likely precipitated the Ice Age described by scientists and resulted in the destruction of much of the vegetation, animal, and human life around the world. This is probably when the dinosaurs disappeared and when many humans became cave dwellers. Mankind experienced hundreds of years of cold, limited sunshine, malnutrition, and physical degradation.

"Satan's demons covered the earth like locusts, possessing animals and humans. The physical world was separated from the spiritual world and death became a fearful and constant reality. Animals and humans killed and ate each other. Satan established his kingdom on earth and evil consumed all living beings. All life on earth—once vitally connected to the spiritual world—was separated from God.

"Into this situation God created the Garden of Eden. Perhaps the skies had cleared around the world. Nomadic tribes of early humans were roaming around scavenging for food. God needed a safe place—like we read about in Revelation—to begin the race of people to carry the spirits of His children through the physical world and to eventually provide the vessel for God Himself to become human and offer His blood to save all of His chosen family.

"Adam was created from dirt in the second chapter of Genesis. Adam means 'the man,' but the name was derived from the word 'soil' or 'dirt.' The humans described in the first chapter were created in God's image—no dirt was mentioned. We don't know exactly what 'image' means, but I doubt it is saying they looked like God—more likely they came from heaven and carried part of God's spirit. They were called the sons of God later in Genesis.

"Adam was made from the physical world and was the first in the lineage of sons of man. He was the first modern human. Jesus called Himself the Son of Man. Adam and Eve had a direct and personal relationship with God before they acquired the knowledge of good and evil. Sin was in the world, but not in the garden—until Adam and Eve acquiesced to Satan's temptation.

"Justice required Adam and Eve to be subjected to temptation by Satan. Unlike the first humans, they had the freedom to choose between good and evil. There was a tree in the garden with the knowledge of good and evil. This tree had to be there because of *Satan's dare* to God. When Adam and Eve listened to Satan and ate the fruit of this tree, they experienced spiritual death and were separated from God. God cannot associate with evil. Adam, Eve, and all of their descendants became the property of Satan and could no longer live in God's presence or have access to the Tree of Life—that is until the blood of Jesus redeemed them and freed them from the control of sin.

"Once we understand, or at least consider the possibility the creation of the physical world happened over six long periods of time and Adam was created after the seventh day of God's rest, the biblical age of the earth becomes consistent with scientific theories. And the interbreeding of modern and primitive humans can be explained by Cain joining a tribe of early humans. I've gathered a lot of scientific research to explain and support these theories and I'm working on summaries to include in our final report.

"I need to jump ahead to the Flood. When I wrote *God Fantasies,* I had to ignore a lot of scientific facts to discredit the biblical account of the Flood. I'll share some of the facts on my list." Tony reached for a notepad next to his Bible.

"Here are some quick bullet points:

- God's descriptions of the separations of the waters in the first chapter of Genesis creates the perfect conditions for floodwaters to come from both the sky and the springs from deep below the ground.
- A large layer of water vapor in the upper atmosphere is consistent with scientific theories of the early stages of the earth's development before cooling caused the vapor to become liquid and fall to the earth.
- A covering of water vapor around the earth would have created a consistent warm and humid climate in every part of the world. This is why scientists have found vegetation and dinosaur bones in the ice at the North Pole.
- Massive accumulations of water in springs and rivers under the earth's surface explains how plants could be watered by 'mist' from the surface without rain. The moist soil, along with the warm and humid climate, were ideal for plush vegetation to grow all around the world.
- The massive amounts of rain that fell on the earth's surface during the early stages of the Flood came from the condensation of the water vapors in the upper atmosphere. The weight of these flood waters probably collapsed the crust of the earth. This would explain how the huge underground reservoirs of water were forced to the surface. The combined weight of all the waters caused large parts of the earth's surface to collapse even further and continental plates to shift. Some parts of the earth were pushed up and others collapsed miles below sea level. This resulted in high mountains and deep canyons where floodwaters drained and became our oceans.

- The geological layers and sediment beneath the earth's surface can only be explained by a massive flood.
- The huge reservoirs of fossil fuels—coal, oil, and gas—formed by decaying dead animals and plants over thousands of years, can only be explained by a calamitous flood that swept massive amounts of plant and animal life into large cracks deep below the earth's surface.

"That's just a few of the scientifically provable data points I will include with references in our report. I believe the Great Flood is a geological fact and it is the only way to explain many observable physical phenomena. The Flood also accomplished many spiritual objectives by eliminating the physical hosts of millions—maybe billions—of Satan's demons. They are now bound in the Abyss until the end times.

ATHEISTS ARE BLIND TO OBVIOUS TRUTH

"I should finish up, but I'll leave you with a few thoughts about those who say they're atheists. I've met a lot of people who claim there is no God. But most of these people know there is a God, they just don't like what they know about Him. Many don't like the idea of their behavior being judged by biblical standards, and they cling to the notion that science has discredited the Bible. Others can't accept the thought that anyone will go to hell. I have concluded most of the people who call themselves atheists have misguided ideas about the Bible and want to be free of any rules, standards, or judgment.

"Being an atheist is exciting and liberating at first. Most of the people who came to hear me speak about *God Fantasies* were giddy—as if I was sticking it to the 'Man.' Being around hundreds of other atheists gave them comfort. But I talked to a lot of them in private who lived as atheists for many years. Almost all of them described their journey as something like turning onto a dead-end street. At first, it seemed like an enlightened shortcut from the heavy traffic of religion, morality, and tradition. But eventually they came to the inevitable end of the road where they realized without God their whole life was a dead-end. There was no hope, only a fear of death and the end of consciousness—or worse, hell."

Tony stood and made a "time out" sign with his hands.

"That's enough from me. Let's take a short break and then come back for about an hour to discuss and summarize all the points we've covered today. Then we need to get ready for dinner in the big city at the Red Fox Inn."

"I'm going to leave the summaries to you men," Elizabeth stood and grabbed her notebooks. "This baby is stealing all of my energy. I'm going to take a nap. You guys can figure it all out and explain it to me later. I'll be ready to go at six." Elizabeth gave Tony a kiss on his cheek and headed down the hall.

CRAFTING A MESSAGE OF HOPE

An afternoon summer thunderstorm rolled over the Virginia mountains bringing clouds, rain, and wind across Tony's estate—cooling the temperatures down into the seventies. Tony and Dr. Clark took their notepads outside to the little table on the covered porch. The clouds were putting on a show of colors and shapes over the top of the mountains as the two men resumed their discussion. They spent the next hour trying to simplify all their theories and "possibilities."

Dr. Clark was intent on publishing a document—or maybe even a book—that made the gospel message simple, credible, and persuasive. Later that night at dinner, he presented Tony and Elizabeth with an idea he thought would help focus national attention on their work and, perhaps, set the stage for a launch of a fundamentally new approach to sharing the gospel.

"Tony and Elizabeth, I have an idea I'd like you to consider. It goes against my recommendation for Tony to disappear but I never meant for him to disappear forever. In fact, my idea may be the most credible way for Tony to transition back into the Christian world. Here's the plan:

"We will stage a debate between you and one of my professors at the university. Your appearance will attract national media attention. You will present your case for atheism and criticism of the Bible, but your attacks on the Bible will be based on the 'straw man' of traditional interpretations you mentioned earlier today. That will leave an opening for your opponent to show how different perspectives of the Bible create possibilities completely consistent with credible science.

"The goal of the first debate is to set up a second debate that will allow you to present the findings from our research and your justification for renouncing atheism. The second debate will be coordinated with your opponent. In other words, he will be in on the ruse in the second debate, but not the first."

Tony was shaking his head with suspicion about Dr. Clark's idea. "I suppose you have already identified my opponent or should I say your victim?"

"In fact, I have." Dr. Clark smiled slyly. "You have probably heard his story. His name is Johnny Wright. He was a student of mine about ten years after you. Many of the alternative interpretations of Scripture we've been discussing actually originated with Johnny. He and I have corresponded for years about his ideas, I shared them in my classes. You will recall some of my letters to you included alternative interpretations of Scriptures. Those ideas came from Johnny. They must have stirred your interest because you included some of them in your early books.

"Johnny has literally been through hell the last few years but he joined our staff as a professor this semester. He will be a perfect opponent because his mission in life is to show how science is confirming the accuracy of the Bible. I'm sure he will agree to join you in a debate. I will feel a little guilty for not telling him I set him up, but I'm afraid it would be awkward for him if he knew you were no longer selling atheism. He will naturally shoot down your straw men and offer his ideas about how science can reveal possible alternatives to traditional interpretations of the Bible.

"You can challenge him to document his ideas and join you for a second debate in a year. Then, after the first debate, we can invite him to join our work in preparation for the second debate. The second debate will be your 'coming out' party. What do you think?"

Tony and Elizabeth looked at each other and smiled. Elizabeth spoke first. "It's devious, but I like it. It creates a glide path for Tony to come out of obscurity and it might focus a lot of attention on some important ideas for the church around the world."

Tony was still shaking his head but smiling. "It might work, but I need to think about it for a few days. It will be difficult for me to debate as an atheist."

Dr. Clark clenched his fists. "Sounds like we almost have a deal. How about this—Tony, you fly with me back to Greenville tomorrow and let me take you for a tour of the university. Students are coming back to school this weekend and it will be chaos. I show visitors around the campus all the time, so no one will pay much attention to me giving you a tour. I can show you the new auditorium where we will hold the debate and that will help you visualize the setting. Then maybe I could get Elizabeth to join you for a second trip later in the fall for us to spend our next working weekend at my house."

Tony looked at Elizabeth and back at Dr. Clark. "Sounds like a plan. We'll leave the airport about ten tomorrow. That will give us plenty of time to drive to Palmetto, take a tour, and get me back home before dark."

Tony's first tour of Palmetto University went as planned. No one recognized him without his beard and with his sunglasses and straw hat. Six weeks later, Tony returned with Elizabeth to spend the weekend with Dr. Clark. Elizabeth loved the campus and the setting in the Carolina mountains. They set the date for the debate in January at the beginning of winter semester. Dr. Clark confirmed Johnny Wright would participate.

*"I will rescue you from your own people
and from the Gentiles. I am sending you to them
to open their eyes and turn them from darkness to light,
and from the power of Satan to God, so that they may
receive forgiveness of sins and a place among those
who are sanctified by faith in me."*—Acts 26:17–18

CHAPTER NINETEEN

RESCUED FROM THE POWER OF SATAN

March 2018
(Travelers Rest, SC)

"Dr. Johnny, you've got a lot of news to share." Ed lifted a copy of the *High Country News* with Patti and Johnny pictured on the front page.

Johnny was quick to respond with a big laugh.

"Where did you get that, Ed? Okay—okay—I promise to tell you all about what happened last week in Boone. You probably know most of it already from Twitter and Facebook, and obviously in the newspaper, but I'll answer all your questions at lunch."

Johnny's students were full of questions, but before they were distracted by his personal news, he was anxious to hear what happened in the two classes he missed. "For now, I want to hear what you folks did while I was gone."

Tuesday's class was a review of the discussions from the previous week. Johnny was pleased to find his students reviewed the original class syllabus to make sure they were following a logical sequence for their research. They spent almost an entire class discussing the apparent "credibility gaps" between science and biblical teachings. And they identified numerous theological and scientific publications to fill those gaps.

Lydia, last week's designated secretary, had ten pages of notes along with a list of dozens of books the class wanted to borrow from nearby libraries or buy from online book sites. Most of the books could be borrowed from libraries, but Johnny approved their budget of $250 for books only available from online sources.

The class discussions the previous week revealed a growing consensus among the students supporting several concepts developed the first few weeks of class. Lydia flashed the class's summary points on the screen and read them point by point. "Dr. Johnny, these are brief summaries of theories where we are finding some agreement."

Lydia and the other students spent the next hour presenting and discussing their points of agreement. They all agreed much more work was needed to support their hypothetical concepts.

As Lydia finished her presentation, Johnny thanked the class for their hard work and cued Julie for her presentation.

"Julie has asked for a few minutes to go deep on a subject that has challenged Christian theologians for thousands of years. It may be naïve for us to think we can find answers never before found but that shouldn't keep us—with genuine humility—from searching the Scriptures to find answers for ourselves. Julie, the floor is yours."

JULIE'S THEORY ON THE SOURCE OF GOD'S POWER ON EARTH

"Thank you, Dr. J. It's really exciting to see the class come together on a lot of these new ideas. Once we understand our physical world was created and exists within a spiritual world, it provides a whole new perspective of science and the Bible.

"Today, I'd like to talk about a very heavy subject—the apparent contradiction between a sovereign God and the operation of Satan. We often say God is in control of all things, but Satan seems to operate with impunity all around us. If God is sovereign, He controls all things. Does this mean God allows Satan to roam freely all over the world wreaking havoc, misery, and death? If God has the ability to stop Satan, but doesn't, He is complicit in all kinds of evil. That's a heavy thought.

"Here's my theory. God created the physical world to accomplish two goals: first, to create a bridge for His body—His family—to cross over to the new heaven; and second, to separate Satan, his followers, and all evil from God's future kingdom—kind of like the Red Sea blocking the Egyptian army from following God's people into the wilderness.

"Here's my main point: when God's children choose good, we give God more power over evil in the physical world. On the other hand, when we choose evil, we empower Satan to cause suffering and death to God's people on earth. I am suggesting God may have limited His power in the physical world to the collective obedience of His people.

"This is consistent with *Satan's dare* to God in the book of Job. Satan appeals to God's justice, and justice requires a fair fight between good and evil. The outcome may depend on the actions of God's people in the spiritual and physical worlds. More on that in a minute, but first let's step back and review the big picture again.

"We have been theorizing that all God's creatures—including modern humans and the four categories of living creatures we see in Genesis, Revelations, and other places in the Old Testament—must travel through the physical world to become part of the physical body of God through the blood of Jesus. The rebellion by Satan and subsequent war in heaven, precipitated the need to use the physical world as a way to separate good from evil.

"The physical world is a bridge we must cross and Satan is like the troll under the bridge. But why doesn't God protect us from this troll Satan? God is sovereign over all things, right? Well, think of the first chapter of Job. Remember in the debate, Dr. Guest talked a lot about the interchange between God and Satan. Job represents all God's children. When God calls attention to the righteousness of Job, Satan mocks him. 'Does Job worship God for nothing?' Satan challenges God—as Dr. Guest said; Satan dares God to allow Job to suffer. Satan is demanding justice. He is demanding God's children experience separation from God. He is demanding God give His children the freedom to choose Satan, evil, and death.

"God's nature requires Him to be perfectly just and give His creation perfect freedom. Satan knows God's nature. Yet the passages in Job suggest Satan must ask permission from God before he brings harm to Job and, I'm guessing by implication, to any of us who belong to Him. God restrains Satan to a degree, but not completely. Why not completely?

"God is in control and Satan operates under God's sovereignty. Perhaps that's why God takes responsibility for what Satan does. In Job 2:3, after Satan brought great harm to Job and his family, God says to Satan, '. . . you incited ME against him to ruin him without any reason.' But God didn't hurt Job—at least not directly.

"Does God take responsibility for Satan and all the evil in this world? If He is truly sovereign, and we believe He is, then He is ultimately responsible for everything that happens. Could this be why He became a physical man to suffer and die to pay Satan's price for sin Himself. Satan demands this price of death be paid by every living thing. Satan is the angel of death. We must all suffer and die to pay Satan's price for sin, but we can only rise from the dead as part of the body of Jesus.

"The last chapters in Job help us make more sense of all this. A mystery man, Elihu, appears at the end of the book of Job. He is not mentioned when Job's three friends come to visit him. Job does not respond to him and God does not mention him when criticizing Job's friends. In fact, the text never mentions a fourth person, but after the three friends finished their debate with Job, Elihu spoke.

"I'll put some verses on the screen and make a few comments. First, this guy Elihu, though young, thinks a lot of himself. Job 36:3–4 are just a couple of verses that suggest Elihu is speaking for God.

> *"'I get my knowledge from afar;*
> *I will ascribe justice to my Maker.*
> *Be assured that my words are not false;*
> *one who has perfect knowledge is with you.'"*

"Elihu is introduced in Job 32:2–3:

> *'But Elihu son of Barakel the Buzite, of the family of*
> *Ram, became very angry with Job for justifying himself*
> *rather than God. He was also angry with the three*
> *friends, because they had found no way to refute Job,*
> *and yet had condemned him.'*

"Elihu tells Job and his three friends that all have sinned, but God will deliver us from the 'pit.' This doesn't mean He will deliver us from physical death. It means we will be saved from hell and have eternal life. Job 33:27–28 says,

> *'"And they will go to others and say,*
> *'I have sinned, I have perverted what is right,*
> *but I did not get what I deserved.*
> *God has delivered me from going down to the pit,*
> *and I shall live to enjoy the light of life.'"'*

"These next verses provide some clues about the dynamic relationship between God's sovereignty and Satan's evil intentions. In Job 34:14–15, we see that unless God holds Satan back, everything would be destroyed.

'"If it were his intention
and he withdrew his spirit and breath,
all humanity would perish together
and mankind would return to the dust."'

"Satan is the destroyer. He roams the earth like a lion seeking those he can destroy. The earth is Satan's dominion and without God constantly intervening and holding him back, Satan would destroy everything. But why doesn't God stop Satan completely?

"I believe the war in heaven and the continuing war in the spiritual world explains most of this. And God's nature of perfect freedom and justice explains the rest. God's hand is holding Satan back from completely destroying the world and as long as God's hand is raised, Satan is limited. But what if we as His children determine the strength of God's hand in this physical world? What if we are His physical body? What if we really are part of the war in the spiritual world? Remember when Israel was fighting the Amalekites. Look at Exodus 17:11–13:

'As long as Moses held up his hands, the Israelites were winning, but whenever he lowered his hands, the Amalekites were winning. When Moses' hands grew tired, they took a stone and put it under him and he sat on it. Aaron and Hur held his hands up—one on one side, one on the other—so that his hands remained steady till sunset. So Joshua overcame the Amalekite army with the sword.'

"Is God limited in this physical world by the love, prayers, worship, and action of His body? If we are the hands, feet, eyes, and ears of Jesus, then we must have a role. God could have destroyed the Amalekites, but He told His people to do it. Could it be God works through His body to bring about His will in this world?

"And, perhaps, His people can only succeed if we all hold up the hands of God. Moses needed help from the spiritual leaders of his people to keep his hands up. This story suggests God is empowered to act on behalf of His people by the obedience, praise, prayers, and worship of His people. God tells us if we resist Satan, he will flee. As the body of Jesus, we have great power— underutilized power. When we complain about God not acting, perhaps we should look to ourselves and others who call on the name of Jesus.

"Job 34:29–30 tells us God is over the nations to protect His people, but we know there are many nations persecuting His people.

> *"'Yet he is over individual and nation alike,*
> *to keep the godless from ruling,*
> *from laying snares for the people.'"*

"Job 35:6–8 helps us to begin to understand our sin doesn't affect God. The collective wickedness of humanity causes suffering and death, and the collective righteousness of God's people restrains Satan from completely destroying God's people.

> *"'If you sin, how does that affect him?*
> *If your sins are many, what does that do to him?*
> *If you are righteous, what do you give to him,*
> *or what does he receive from your hand?*
> *Your wickedness only affects humans like yourself,*
> *and your righteousness only other people.'"*

"Job 36:16–17 explains God is constantly coaxing us to act,

> *"'He is wooing you from the jaws of distress*
> *to a spacious place free from restriction,*
> *to the comfort of your table laden with choice food.*
> *But now you are laden with the judgment due the wicked;*
> *judgment and justice have taken hold of you.'"*

"Those verses tell us we are burdened by 'the judgment due the wicked.' We suffer for our own sins and the sins of others.

But it is not God who causes the suffering. It is Satan empowered by the wickedness of this world.

"Job 37:23 is clear. God does not oppress.

> "*The Almighty is beyond our reach and exalted in power;*
> *in his justice and great righteousness, he does not oppress.*"'

"When Job speaks to God in chapter 42:1–6, he reminds us—
as we try to figure out what God is doing in this world—we are
not capable of understanding the plans of God. After everything Job suffered, he says it was all too wonderful for him to
understand. And importantly, he repents.

> '*Then Job replied to the LORD:*
> *"I know that you can do all things;*
> *no purpose of yours can be thwarted.*
> *You asked, 'Who is this that obscures my plans*
> *without knowledge?'*
> *Surely I spoke of things I did not understand,*
> *things too wonderful for me to know.*
> *"You said, 'Listen now, and I will speak;*
> *I will question you,*
> *and you shall answer me.'*
> *My ears had heard of you*
> *but now my eyes have seen you.*
> *Therefore I despise myself*
> *and repent in dust and ashes.*"'

"God then commended Job for speaking rightly about Him
and condemned Job's three friends for insisting Job was being
punished for his sins. Many of us suffer for our own stupidity
and disobedience but God does not punish His children for
their sin. He punishes Himself. He pays the price for our sin
Himself. But as part of His physical body, we suffer with Him.

"Job's repentance empowers God to restore and bless him
and Job's prayers for his friends allows God to forgive them. If

we step back and look at the whole picture of the book of Job and the entire Bible, we see our God calling on His people to fight Satan and restrain evil in the world. Satan and his demons are roaming the world destroying everything in their path. It is only God's people empowering God's Holy Spirit that keeps Satan from destroying the whole physical world—at least for now. We know, after all God's people have passed through this physical world, God will withdraw His hand of restraint and allow Satan to destroy everything."

Julie sat down, looked up, and smiled. "I meant to make that simple, but it didn't come out that way. I hope it wasn't a confusing mess."

Johnny quickly came to Julie's defense, "Julie, I think you explained it better than anyone I've ever heard who tried to explain why God allows evil in the world." Johnny led another round of applause.

"First, Julie, you are dealing with the most difficult issue of the Christian faith. How can we have a sovereign God who lets Satan run roughshod over His people? We see God in the Old Testament saving His people when they are obedient, but apparently, He has to let their enemies destroy them when they are disobedient.

"God's actions appear to be governed—at least in part—by the actions of His people in this physical world. But we can access God's power when we serve Him. He tells us in Ephesians 6:10, 'be strong in the Lord and in his mighty power.' So, while God may limit His power in the physical world based on the collective power of His people, He will channel His power through those who follow Jesus. We have the full armor of God available to us when we come together as believers.

"So, when we ask 'why does God allow suffering?', we must consider the possibility God's people might be the ones who allow suffering and pain. And we should remember we have all of God's power available to us.

"Are we the ones who are fighting and determining the outcome of the war in heaven and on earth? The evil in the world doesn't mean we are losing; it just means the battle is still waging. And maybe we need to fight harder. We know we will win in the end, but we must keep fighting."

Johnny stood and suggested a ten-minute break before discussing the notes from the previous week and Julie's presentation. They spent the rest of class debating, arguing, laughing. Tuesday's lunch discussion was a thorough interrogation of Johnny about his week in Boone. From the sale of his family business, to the editorial and news article in the newspaper, to Richard Robertson's confession, and finally the news about Patti expecting a baby. Everyone enjoyed taking a "time out" from theology and talking about Dr. Johnny.

Finally, be strong in the Lord and in his mighty power.
Put on the full armor of God, so that you can take your
stand against the devil's schemes. For our struggle is not
against flesh and blood, but against the rulers, against
the authorities, against the powers of this dark world and
against the spiritual forces of evil in the heavenly realms.
—Ephesians 6:10–12

CHAPTER TWENTY

GOD'S PEOPLE
ARE GOD'S POWER

March 2018
(Travelers Rest, SC)

Johnny knocked on Dr. Clark's open office door. "Dr. Clark, may I come in? Thanks again for your help with the board. Is everything really okay with those guys?"

Johnny was Dr. Clark's first appointment on Friday at 9:00 a.m. Dr. Clark was grinning like a Cheshire cat.

"I've been expecting your visit." Dr. Clark stood. "Let's sit at the table." They both moved to the little conference table in Dr. Clark's office.

"The board is fine, in fact, they have asked me to become an official member."

"That's good to hear, but today I have something else on my mind."

"I expect you do." Dr. Clark flashed another smile.

"Okay, Dr. Clark, let's have it! That debate was rigged, and I know you were the ringleader."

Johnny knew something was going on between Dr. Clark and Tony Guest before the debate ended. It was obvious to Johnny, if not the audience, Tony was no atheist. And Tony was too experienced a debater to give Johnny such wide openings to counter his "traditional" interpretations of the Bible. Why did Tony visit the Palmetto Christian campus before the debate? And why did Tony whisper "thank you" several times to Johnny after the debate?

Despite Johnny's many questions about the debate, he had been too busy starting his new class, dealing with Dr. Andrews and the board, settling his family business, dealing with lawyers and insurance companies, and spending a week in Boone to follow up with Dr. Clark. But after returning from Boone, his first call was to Dr. Clark's secretary to schedule a Friday appointment. He wanted to get through his classes on Tuesday and Thursday before meeting with Dr. Clark.

"You're right. The debate was rigged. Sit back and let me explain." Dr. Clark told Johnny everything. He described how Tony met Elizabeth and how her love vanquished Tony's anger, atheism, and restored his faith. He reviewed all the previous year's events, including Tony's wedding, Elizabeth's pregnancy, and new daughter, their Labor Day weekend at Tony's home, Tony and Elizabeth's visit to the campus of Palmetto Christian, and the strategy for the first and second debates.

"Johnny, you were not a pawn in the debate, you were the leader. I couldn't tell you because you wouldn't have been willing to fake it. And I wasn't worried about the outcome. I knew you could refute every point Tony presented. And you did. Tony didn't want to argue for atheism and he didn't. You pushed him into a corner and he had to admit what he knew was true; there has to be a God." Dr. Clark leaned back in his chair. "Can you forgive me?"

Johnny looked somber. "That depends on how we work this out. We have to come clean in the second debate and make sure people don't feel like they've been bamboozled. And I want to integrate the work you're doing with Tony and Elizabeth with the work we're doing in my class."

"That's the plan." Dr. Clark reached into his oversized briefcase and pulled out a large three-ring binder full of notes. "This is a summary of our work to-date. If you have notes from your class when you finish this semester, make me a copy so I can send them to Tony. We would like you and Patti to join us for a few days at Tony's home after classes end in May. We can discuss the format of our final document and the plan for the next debate. Does that work for you?"

Johnny continued to look serious. "Dr. Clark, I feel like I'm involved in a conspiracy, but I have to admit, it sounds like a good plan to refute the critics of Christianity and to call attention to our work. I'm in, unless Patti doesn't like the plan. I don't suppose you've already talked to her?"

Dr. Clark smiled slyly. "No Johnny, I thought I'd let you handle this one. But don't mess it up."

"I'll try not to." Johnny turned to leave and then looked back at Dr. Clark. "Wow! That's really great news about Tony. God never ceases to amaze me!"

Patti was not surprised by Johnny's conversation with Dr. Clark. She knew something was odd about the debate. All her instincts told her Tony was a broken man who wanted to come home. As it turned out, he already had. She didn't like the deception but was happy Johnny was completely innocent in the whole affair. And she was excited about the chance to meet Elizabeth—and her new baby.

Mary Elizabeth Guest was born in February a few weeks after the first debate, two days before Tony and Elizabeth's first anniversary. Patti's baby would be born in September, a little more than four months away, and she was anxious to see Elizabeth's baby and hear all about her experiences.

* * *

WEEKEND AT TONY'S

Johnny's classes wrapped up the third week of May. He and Patti left on Friday with Dr. Clark in Tony's jet carrying a suitcase full of notes from the first semester of Johnny's class. The class was a tremendous success and all the students left school for the summer with long reading lists to prepare for the fall semester.

Johnny and Patti arrived at Tony's home like two children entering the gates at Disney World. The estate was even more beautiful than Dr. Clark's description. They stayed in the guest house and Dr. Clark used an upstairs suite in the main house. Their luggage was in their rooms by 3:00 Friday afternoon and everyone met in the great room adjoining the kitchen for what seemed like a celebration.

Tony and Johnny were like old soldiers enjoying a reunion. Elizabeth and Patti hit it off like sisters who were separated at birth. Dr. Clark sat in the big recliner enjoying the whole scene like the patriarch of the family. Of course, the center of attention was the bassinette in the middle of the room where baby Liz was reaching for the toy horses swinging around on a mobile above her head.

Patti lifted Liz out of the bassinette and held her as she and Elizabeth walked down the hall to the nursery. They talked about Elizabeth's surprise pregnancy and all that happened over the past year. Patti shared about hers and Johnny's new life at Palmetto Christian and the amazing turn of events in Boone. Liz's nanny arrived just in time to put her down for her afternoon nap. Elizabeth and Patti rejoined the men in the den.

Tony insisted Johnny and Patti take the obligatory walk to the barn and around the riding trail. Patti wasn't sure how far she could make it, but agreed she needed to stretch her legs. They would all meet for drinks and dinner on the porch at 6:30. Tony arranged for the two professional chefs who prepared the first dinner for Elizabeth to recreate another Italian feast.

Saturday morning, Tony and Elizabeth cooked omelets and they all sat around the kitchen counter drinking coffee before beginning their discussions at 9:00. Elizabeth took Liz back to the nursery. Her nanny agreed to spend the day and night to give Elizabeth more time with the group.

Dr. Clark positioned himself back in the large leather recliner in the great room adjoining the kitchen.

"I'd like to get us started this morning with a few thoughts. One of the most curious behaviors by human beings is the lack of seriousness about the afterlife. We all know we're going to die, but it seems most people never seriously consider their future destination.

"Most of us don't want to think about death because it's like opening the door to a dark and scary room. We don't want to turn on the light, so to speak—because we're afraid we'll find more questions than answers. The only potential answers are religious and therefore, not real.

"The problem with not contemplating the inevitability of death is people suppress fear and close parts of their minds. It is impossible to live a joyful life if you know in the dark recesses of your mind it's not going to end well—and we all know how it's going to end.

"I've reviewed my notes from over a year of work with Tony and Elizabeth, and just finished reading through the notes Johnny sent me earlier in the week from the first semester of his advanced Bible study class. It's remarkable to see the similarity of our theories and conclusions.

"The Bible, when considered as a whole, paints a clear picture of what people must know to be connected with their God and Savior, and be confident they have eternal life. It is more challenging—and not quite as clear—when we consider alternative interpretations of the Creation, the Flood, the war in heaven and the end times. What we believe about these things does not impact our salvation or relationship with God—unless confusion and lack of knowledge undermines our confidence in the inspiration and accuracy of the Bible.

"People can live joyfully with very simple faith. A belief in God and assurance Jesus will save them is all some people need. But unanswered questions and apparent contradictions between the Bible and credible science have led to a worldwide decline in confident believers and a corresponding increase in evil and wickedness in the world. This has weakened the body of Jesus, and as the church has become weaker, the body of Satan has become stronger. We may be approaching the final battle where God withdraws His hand completely and Satan's full force of evil is unleashed on the world.

"Our work is focused on developing a more credible understanding of the Bible, a clearer understanding of God's motives for creating the physical world, and a more rational explanation of how God saves His people from sin and death.

"We have a lot of additional work to prove beyond any doubt the Bible and science are in alignment. But we also need to point out how many times science has been wrong about many things. We may need to depart from some traditional orthodoxy, consider some alternative interpretations of Scripture and challenge some scientific findings, but we will have the research to show, for the most part, honest science actually proves the Bible is true.

"All of this needs to be accomplished before we can credibly use the Bible and science to determine the reasons God created the physical universe. What are God's motives? Why did God create this difficult passage for His children to the Promised Land?"

"Okay, that's enough from me. Tony, this is a good time for you to share your thoughts."

"Thanks, Dr. Clark, and welcome again to Johnny, Patti, and—in advance—welcome to your little baby. You haven't told us if it's a boy or girl."

Patti blushed and turned to Elizabeth. "I told Elizabeth last night. It's a boy!" Tony and Dr. Clark applauded. Dr. Clark got out of his chair and kissed Patti on the forehead. Then he shook Johnny's hand and returned to his chair.

Tony continued. "Johnny, I was particularly drawn to your notes about Julie's presentation in your class—her discussion about the apparent contradiction between God's sovereignty and Satan's rule over this world. I think Julie may have unlocked a great spiritual mystery. Her insights help explain why God's children must endure pain, suffering, and death in this physical world."

The discussions went on for hours with everyone feverishly making notes and looking for references in the Bible.

Johnny listened more than he spoke, but as the discussions were winding down, he was visibly invigorated. "It has been almost overwhelming to hear how closely your thoughts and theories track with the independent work of my students. I introduced some of these possibilities to them last year and we touched on them at the debate, but my students did their own research and came to many of the same conclusions. This gives me a lot of confidence we are on solid biblical ground and, hopefully, being led by the Holy Spirit. It's a little scary to think how much our work could change Christendom.

"For starters, we are saying God doesn't need our worship—we need to worship for our own good, for the good of those we love, for all God's children and to usher in the kingdom of God. We don't come together as congregations all around the world because God needs to know He is worthy. We worship God to empower Him to bless His people and restrain evil in this world.

"And the purpose of our prayers is not only to ask God for our personal needs and desires. Our prayers engage and empower the angels in the spiritual world who are in a continuous battle against Satan and his angels. Our prayers summon the power of God's people in the physical and spiritual worlds. Like Jesus tells us to pray, 'Your will be done on earth as it is in heaven.' We pray for God's will to be carried out. Why would Jesus tell us to pray this prayer if prayers weren't essential for God to accomplish His will on earth?

"This is an astonishing thought—God uses our worship, praise, prayers, and obedience to win the battle against Satan! Could this really be possible? Could God's power in this physical world depend on His children on earth? It makes sense because it was God's loyal angels in heaven—God's spiritual family who threw Satan and his angels to earth.

"If this is true, it creates a much higher priority for God's children to worship, pray, and live in a way that honor God. This means every time we come together as the body of believers in our churches and homes, we are joining the war in heaven."

Patti raised her hand and teased Johnny. "Dr. Wright, may I add a thought?"

"Well, certainly young lady." Johnny always enjoyed Patti's sense of humor.

"And just as important as formal worship and prayers—when we come together as believers with joy and gratitude, and support each other when we are suffering, laugh and sing together, live our lives together with love and goodwill toward others, and when our lives are a demonstration of the love of God—we prove Satan wrong and empower all the heavenly hosts to win the great spiritual war.

"Johnny and I experienced this with our youth group back in Boone and see it every day at Palmetto Christian. When people come together in Jesus, we unleash the power of God's Holy Spirit. We really are in a spiritual battle and we have many spiritual weapons to take into battle."

Patti continued, "Tony, I'd like to return to some of the verses you read in Ephesians 6 because they help define some of the important roles of the church. Believers are in a constant spiritual and physical battle and they must always be ready. Churches must teach the truth—the Bible—so believers can buckle the belt of truth around their waist. We must teach people about righteousness—which comes from knowing the Bible—so they can put the breastplate of righteousness over their hearts. We must preach the gospel in our churches so believers will have the readiness that comes with the gospel of peace. The gospel is only found in the Bible.

"My point is this: unless churches preach and teach the Bible as truth, they are wasting their time and likely doing harm rather than good to God's kingdom. The Bible calls God's children to faith and teaches believers how to engage in the battle against Satan and his minions."

"Patti, you've hit the nail on the head." Dr. Clark was beaming. "Once we understand followers of Jesus have the power and responsibility to restrain evil in the world, the credibility of the Bible and role of the organized church becomes much more important.

"It's getting late so let's spend some time before dinner trying to simplify and summarize our thinking."

The discussion continued for the rest of Saturday afternoon, through dinner Saturday night, and Sunday morning until Johnny, Patti, and Dr. Clark had to leave for the airport. They left Middleboro with a rough draft of a table of contents for their final document, and an outline of how they envisioned the second debate. The whole world would be surprised—perhaps in an uproar—by the presentations at that debate.

I have been crucified with Christ and I no longer live,
but Christ lives in me. The life I now live in the body,
I live by faith in the Son of God, who loved me and gave
himself for me.—Galatians 2:20

CHAPTER TWENTY-ONE

ELIMINATING ALL DOUBT

June 2018 – six months before the second debate
(Travelers Rest, SC)

"Patti, I'm not sure this orange stripe on the wall is appropriate for a baby's nursery." Johnny was looking through layouts of furniture locations and painting samples for their new house. Patti dropped a soft, stuffed tiger toy in Johnny's lap.

"I want Joshua to know he's a Clemson Tiger from the start. And I don't want you sneaking any Appalachian State paraphernalia into his room." Patti laughed and hugged Johnny from behind as he sat at his desk in the little house they enjoyed for almost a year. Their living conditions would soon change in a big way.

Johnny and Patti met James Rushing a few weeks after moving to Travelers Rest the previous September. Mr. Rushing, a golf course developer, was completing three new golf course communities within twenty miles of Palmetto Christian.

The project took almost ten years. He was from Chicago but wanted a place to live near his new courses while they were being developed. He bought and restored a large old home on a 300-acre estate less than a mile from the campus of Palmetto Christian.

Mr. Rushing's estate included a 10,000-square foot colonial mansion surrounded by giant oak trees, a pool with a waterfall, outdoor kitchen and fireplace, a large lake, and open pasture surrounded by white rail fence. He spent millions of dollars renovating and modernizing the home, landscaping and fencing the property, building a dock, and stocking the lake with bass and brim. But there was one out-of-character aspect in all the improvements with the old colonial style of the estate.

Mr. Rushing built a 20,000-square foot metal utility building with five large garage doors on the front corner of his property to keep some of the equipment he used to build golf courses and landscape the surrounding communities. The building was in a wooded area to the side of the property and had a separate drive way, so it didn't obscure the beauty of the large colonial home. But you could see it from the road and the unvarnished commercial white metal building certainly diminished the charm of the beautiful estate.

Mr. Rushing was divorced with three grown children and seven grandchildren. He was usually alone at his home in Travelers Rest, except when he had a group of out-of-town golfers visiting to try out his new courses. Johnny and Patti enjoyed many Sunday night dinners with Mr. Rushing at his beautiful home. He fell in love with the young couple and wanted to do all he could to encourage their ministry. Mr. Rushing was already a large contributor to Palmetto Christian and donated the chapel where they met for their Pub church.

"Johnny and Patti, I've bought several thousand acres on the coast in Oregon to build my last golf course—my dream course." Mr. Rushing was having his customary after-dinner port with Johnny and Patti on a Sunday night about a month after the January debate. "That project will take about six or seven years and I will need to buy a place there to supervise the work. My work here is essentially done, so I will be selling this property and moving to Oregon."

"Mr. Rushing, I hope you will always keep a part of your heart here at Palmetto Christian. You've done a lot to help Dr. Clark create a world-class institution. And your nearby developments have put this whole area on the map." Johnny was sipping his after dinner hot chocolate—a winter tradition for he and Patti—while looking around the beautiful dining room. "You've done an incredible job with this place." Johnny, ever visionary and opportunistic, was hoping and praying Mr. Rushing would consider making the estate available for the university to use as an activity center.

"I've considered donating this property to the university but have been very disappointed at the results of my gifts to several other universities. I know Palmetto Christian is different, but I don't know what will happen after Dr. Clark is gone. I'd like to give this place to you two, because I know you will use it for the glory of God as long as you live.

"The problem is, my accountants tell me, with all the loans I've taken out for my new property and development, I have to pay off all the current loans on this estate and all my developments in South Carolina. I'm a wealthy man on paper, but after making a very large commitment in Oregon, I'm cash poor. The financial partners of my golf course properties here in South Carolina have satisfied all my business loans, so the only debt left is on this house and estate. The mortgage on this place is about 500K. The appraised value is about six million and with all the new development in the area, I suspect it will be worth over ten million in five years. Do you think you could come up with five hundred thousand?"

Johnny looked at Patti. "Mr. Rushing, you've just given Patti and me the highest compliment we could ever receive. Thank you for your trust and faith in us. This property could be the heart and soul of Palmetto Christian and support the spread of the gospel for decades. We'd love to be God's stewards of this wonderful estate. We don't have any money now, but it is possible within a few months our financial situation could change. Will you give us a little time to pray and figure out how to make this work?"

"Take all the time you need. I will be packing up and heading for Oregon before the end of the summer, so let me know."

What seemed impossible in February became easy in less than two months. When Johnny returned from their week in Boone in March, he called Mr. Rushing to tell him they would have the money by July. The closing would be August 1, but the planning started immediately. Johnny and Patti calculated, between Johnny's share of the sale of his family's business and Patti's insurance settlement, they would have about $5 million after taxes in the bank by August 1.

They planned to donate 10 percent to Palmetto Christian, and $50,000 each to student ministries at Clemson and Appalachian State. They would put $2 million in a foundation to provide continuous support for youth ministries at Palmetto Christian, Clemson, Appalachian State, and several churches. They joked that would leave them almost $2 million "walking around money." They called themselves the Beverly Hillbillies after the "rags to riches" television series. Neither cared much about having a lot of money, but it was fun to have the means for the first time to support God's work financially.

They were also making big plans for their new home. Johnny and Patti began working with an architect, an interior designer, and a builder in June. They planned to move in September first, so their first priority was to make sure the house and nursery were ready for their new baby. The nursery would be in a large room with its own bathroom next to the master bedroom on the second floor. There was an upstairs kitchen and laundry room, so Patti would have everything she needed without having to go up and down the stairs.

The house had ten bedrooms, twelve bathrooms, and a garage apartment with a separate entrance. The upstairs was organized into three private suites, each with three bedrooms with their own bathrooms and a small sitting area with a television and kitchenette. The three suites were all connected by a large living area with a full kitchen and hidden laundry room. There was one additional bedroom at the top of the stairs which seemed to be set up for a live-in nanny or maid.

Patti was excited about having a place where her parents and her brother's family could visit. They talked about Tony, Elizabeth, and Liz visiting for long weekends. Missionaries and visiting professors could stay for month-long sabbaticals. The large estate would be difficult to maintain, but they had a plan for that, too. The garage apartment would be offered free to students who were willing to help maintain the house and grounds.

No major renovations were needed because Mr. Rushing did a thorough job modernizing almost everything. The walls between the downstairs kitchen, living, and dining rooms were removed to create a great room with a large rock fireplace. It was reminiscent of the great room in their first log home in Boone, only it was elegantly appointed from the triple-layered crown molding around the edges of the twelve-foot ceilings to the polished heart-of-pine wood floors. The room had large sliding glass doors opening to the pool, waterfall, and outdoor kitchen. The view captured a sloping green pasture, a ridge covered with trees and mountain tops as far as you could see.

Their big challenge was what to do with the 20,000-square foot industrial building on the front corner of their property about a quarter of a mile from the house. Mr. Rushing agreed to leave one tractor and a large mower, so the storage area behind one garage door on the left side of the building would be partitioned with a wall to create a space for lawn maintenance equipment. The remaining 16,000 square feet would be finished as a multi-purpose activity center.

The plans included insulating the entire building and installing heating and air conditioning. The concrete floors were covered with durable synthetic wood used for gymnasiums. The floors were painted to designate a half court for basketball and a volleyball court. Large roll-up nets were attached to the ceilings to section off the courts when they were being used. The whole room could be used as an auditorium or dining room with several closets full of folding chairs and tables. A stage was installed on the far-right wall for concerts and speakers.

The ugly commercial eyesore was transformed. The outside was covered with natural wood siding. The metal roof was extended and painted green to create a covered porch all around the building. The large garage doors were painted with a natural wood paint to match the siding. Wooden decks were built under the extended roof all around the building and twenty ceiling fans were installed to complete the casual country atmosphere. The whole building was landscaped with scrubs and trees.

Outdoor basketball and volleyball courts were constructed behind the building, and a 100-car parking lot was hidden in the trees behind the courts. When it was all finished, the unattractive industrial building was converted into a rustic country lodge. When the weather was pleasant, the large garage doors could be opened to create an indoor/outdoor space, perfect for large or small groups. The facility was less than a mile from the campus of Palmetto Christian University.

Johnny and Patti spent the summer planning and supervising the work on their new home. There were baby showers on campus and in Boone. Johnny preached a six-week series about prayer at Blue Ridge Baptist in Boone. His former church was still looking for a new pastor. These sermons gave him a chance to "test drive" some of the new ideas he was developing with his class, Dr. Clark and Tony. Johnny drove to Boone six straight weekends in June and July, preached on Sunday morning, led large youth rallies on Sunday night, and spent the night with his mother. Patti stayed at home because it was getting increasingly uncomfortable for her to ride in a car.

Patti made one trip to Clemson in July. It was only about an hour's drive and she wanted to spend some time with her former college volleyball coach. Patti was asked to serve the first ball at a regional volleyball tournament to be held at Palmetto Christian after Thanksgiving. Traditionally, the first ball was served underhanded by a former volleyball player dressed in street clothes. Middle schoolers are taught the simple underhanded serve when they first learn the game. But real volleyball players start their serve about ten feet behind the service line, run, leap as high as they can as they throw the ball up, and then hit the ball with their fist as they swing their arm as hard as they can over their heads.

Patti wanted to serve the first ball the way she served when she played at Clemson. But that was a tall order for someone who was hardly able to jog. And it was even harder to practice when she was seven months pregnant. Nevertheless, Patti spent a half day with her former coach and a trainer to get some advice from experts who helped hundreds return from injuries. They studied her X-Rays, manipulated her legs and hips, played videos from Patti's games in college, and typed up a regime of stretches and exercises. They also emailed her the videos of her playing in college and told her to burn those visuals into her mind. Recovery was 50 percent mental and 50 percent physical.

Back at home, Patti unrolled the poster of her smashing a ball over the net in one of her college games. It was the poster with "goal" taped to it she tacked on the wall in her office in Boone after her accident. She put it on the wall in their spare bedroom where they kept her treadmill and parallel bars. Patti knew she was dreaming another impossible dream but she prayed every day God would make her dream possible.

* * *

JOHNNY'S CLASS GOES TO DC

Johnny continued to communicate with his students over the summer. They kept an active email chain with updates almost every day. In July, the discussion turned to the new Bible museum recently opened in Washington, DC. All his students knew someone who visited the museum and all were over-whelmed by the experience.

One of Johnny's classmates from college was a tour guide at the museum. He agreed to give the class a special tour if they could come in late July. Johnny's students were busy with sum-mer jobs, but all of them were willing to ask for a couple of days off the last week in July. The only problem was; none of these students had the money to make the trip. Air travel along with three or four days in a hotel in DC in the summer could cost over $2,000 each.

Johnny's newfound wealth would be tied up for several months until the accountants and lawyers figured out how much taxes were owed. He racked his brain to think of some-one he knew in or around DC who could host six students for a long weekend. He had a small discretionary fund for books and supplies, but not enough to help defer the expenses for students. Then it hit him; Tony Guest. Tony's home in Mid-dleburg, Virginia, was only about an hour's drive from DC, and he might be willing to defray some of the travel expenses of the students. Johnny sent an email to Dr. Clark asking him to explore the idea with Tony. He had his answer within an hour. Tony would host everyone at his house and defer all travel expenses for the students.

All of this was perfect except for one thing: Johnny would have to tell his students the whole story about Tony, the first debate and their plans for the second debate. Johnny didn't know how they would respond when they found out he had been working with Tony and their class on the same project. He decided to tell them the truth before their fall class began. A trip to Tony's home might create the ideal setting to explain everything to his students and make them part of the team.

Once the students knew this would be a "free" trip, they were all on board within an hour. Dr. Clark also signed up for the trip. Tony agreed to send his jet to Greenville to pick up everyone who was in the area. He quickly found five passengers.

Johnny and Dr. Clark would drive to the airport together from the university. Ed lived in Greenville less than fifteen minutes from the airport. Lydia was working as a camp counselor near Asheville, North Carolina, about an hour's drive to the Greenville airport. Henry was working as an intern for a bank in Charlotte, just an hour and a half drive.

Julie was already in DC working as an intern for a congressman. Matt (Pennsylvania) and Rachel (New York) would take the train to DC. None of the students knew or seemed to care about the identity of their host and sponsor. The plan was to arrive in Middleburg by noon on Thursday, tour the Bible Museum on Friday, and spend Saturday discussing their project.

"I wish all my classes were like this one," Ed took his seat in Tony's eight-passenger jet at 8:30 a.m. Thursday morning. "Executive mahogany board rooms for our classes, private jet rides, and weekends in DC. I'm considering a career as a professional student."

"Whose jet is this anyway, Dr. J?" asked Henry.

"Oh, you'll meet him when we get to his house." Johnny tried not to reveal the exploding tension between the laughter and anxiety in his heart. This could be a shocking experience for everyone. Dr. Clark sparked a sly smile toward Johnny. They would both be glad when this secret conspiracy was exposed.

A van picked up the five jet passengers at the Middleburg airport about 10:00 a.m. Tony also arranged for a driver to pick up Matt, Rachel, and Julie at Union Station in DC. Everyone was at Tony's house before noon. Two airbeds were added in the guest house and the three girls were happy to have the private guest quarters to themselves. The three boys, along with Dr. Clark and Johnny, found plenty of room upstairs in the main house. They all met for lunch in the great room adjoining the kitchen, but they had yet to meet their host. Dr. Clark took a few minutes to prepare the students for the shock.

JOHNNY'S CLASS MEETS TONY

"Students, thank you for taking this time out of your busy summer schedules to visit what is already one of the most lauded museums in Washington. And I'm looking forward to spending the day on Saturday discussing your work in Dr. Wright's class. Our host for this weekend will be joining us because he is also very interested in what you're doing. In fact, he is working on the same project with me and Dr. Wright."

All the students looked at each other with puzzled expressions. The smiles on Dr. Clark's and Johnny's faces let them know they were unwitting participants in some big secret.

"What the heck is going on?" Ed didn't like secrets.

Dr. Clark used the next ten minutes to give them a quick summary of everything that happened over the previous two years.

"You are here because you are partners in an important project and we want to treat you as equal partners. Now I'd you to meet Dr. and Mrs. Tony Guest."

Tony and Elizabeth, dressed in jeans, walked hand-in-hand into the room. Lydia began the applause and she was quickly joined by everyone in the room. She was crying and laughing when Tony reached out his hand. Lydia grabbed him around the neck. She was deeply touched by his words in the debate. Most of the students welcomed Tony like a returning prodigal son.

They spent the next two hours asking Tony and Elizabeth questions. All but one of the students were incredulous at how many of their theories and conclusions were shared by Tony, Dr. Clark, and Johnny. But Rachel sat quietly through the discussion growing increasingly pale.

"Rachel, are you alright?" Johnny was worried she was sick. Everyone stopped talking as Rachel spoke.

"I'm sorry to be the skunk at the party, but I can't handle this. You don't want to hear the reason, but I need to leave."

"Of course we want to hear the reason—if you want to tell us." Johnny was now really worried.

"Dr. Guest, I'm grateful for your generosity and hospitality this weekend, but I have to admit I have spent the last six months hating you with all my heart." The room became deathly silent and a sense of darkness seemed to take the oxygen from the air.

"My brother, like me, is Jewish. He rejected Judaism growing up, dropped out of college, and has been in and out of drug rehab centers. But two years ago, my stepmother seemed to break through to his heart with the story of Jesus. He actually began to turn his life around—that is, until he read *God Fantasies*. He and a drug buddy rode a train from New York to Chicago to attend one of your speeches. He stood in line to get a signed copy of your book.

"He read your book on the train back to New York and by the time he got home, his new-found faith was gone. He laughed about a Christian bookstore selling your book on atheism at your event in Chicago. He said all Christians were hypocrites—including my stepmother. Everything went downhill from there. He got back on drugs, almost overdosed, ended up back in rehab, and then attempted suicide.

"I'm sorry, everyone, but I need to go home. Can I call a cab to take me back to the train in DC?"

Johnny walked across the room and reached for Rachel's hand. "We don't want you to leave, but I will call you a cab. Do you want to wait until the morning?"

"No, I would like to leave now—as soon as possible."

"I'm so sorry, Rachel," Tony spoke softly with his head down. "There's no need to call a cab. My driver lives right down the street. He'll be here in fifteen minutes."

Lydia and Julie accompanied Rachel back to the guest house and helped her pack.

Johnny met Rachel at the car. "Rachel, could I ride with you to the train. I don't think you should be alone."

"Thank you, Dr. Johnny, but this is one time I need to be alone." The driver put Rachel's bag in the trunk, opened the door, made sure Rachel was buckled in, and then closed the door slowly. Dr. Clark, Johnny, and all the other students stood in the courtyard as the car disappeared down the long driveway.

"Let's all pray for Rachel," Johnny spoke while everyone was still standing in the courtyard. "But let's remember our faith in Jesus is a story of redemption—and redemption applies to me, you, and Tony Guest. Is everyone else ready to continue our plans for the weekend?"

"Yes, sir," Ed spoke first and loudly. The other students quickly joined him. "Let's charge ahead." Julie raised her hand and waved it forward like a cavalry officer in front of the troops.

"Okay, forward march." Tony mimicked Julie and waved everyone to the side of the courtyard.

"Let's take a break before dinner. I have these three golf carts you can use to look around. There are maps of the property in each cart and coolers with soft drinks. I'll need you all back to help cook hamburgers and hot dogs on the grill tonight, so let's meet here at six thirty. Dr. J will supervise the cooking crew."

Johnny was terribly upset about Rachel but relieved his other students were willing to continue the weekend. In fact, they seem excited about the secretive conspiracy with Tony. Unlike Rachel, they didn't seem to view him as an enemy of God's kingdom. Instead of being alienated by Tony in the debate, he won their hearts with his brokenness. They were also ecstatic their work as a class was being confirmed by prominent biblical scholars. Most importantly to the students, they were being treated as equal partners in what had become for them a noble quest to discover some of the greatest truths for humanity.

The cookout was amazing and the evening discussion was all about the golf cart expedition around Tony's estate. All the students were full of questions for Tony. His honesty and humility won their hearts. A day that seemed headed toward disaster ended with great conversation and a joyful spirit. Everyone headed to bed at 10:00 because the van to the museum would pick them up at 7:00 the next morning.

"Tonight, we got a small taste of the damage I've done to the kingdom of God." Tony lay in bed next to Elizabeth with his hands over his face. "Rachel's brother is just one sample of how Satan has used me to destroy people."

Elizabeth tried to add some comfort. "Tony, did you notice the rest of the evening? Everyone else was gaining confidence and joy from your experience. Satan will try to poison it for you but don't get in the way of God making all this to turn out for good. For once in your life, sit back and let God work."

"Yes, ma'am." Tony turned out the light and went to sleep—much quicker than he expected.

* * *

The Bible Museum was even better than its billings. It is the third largest museum in DC and by all accounts, one of the most technologically advanced museums in the world. The students "flew" around DC on a virtual tour of the Capitol and monuments to see all the places Bible verses were inscribed by our nation's founders and leaders. Original copies of early Scriptures in the museum confirmed the accurate preservation of the original text to the Bibles used today.

Artifacts from the times and places described in the Bible confirmed the accuracy of events described in the Old and New Testaments. The students walked away from the tour with new confidence the Bible was written by authors inspired by God. One thing was certain; no other book ever written could fill a museum this size with evidence of its accuracy and impact on humanity.

Back at Tony's house, the students were treated to an Italian dinner Friday night prepared by Tony's caterers. He explained how Italian dinners recently became his tradition for big occasions; first with Elizabeth in Chicago when they met (he had to admit it was Elizabeth's Christian bookstore selling his books at the event attended by Rachel's brother), then when Elizabeth visited his house for the first time, then when Johnny,

Patti, and Dr. Clark visited, and now when Johnny's students are initiated as full partners in their quest to discover God's motives for creating the physical world. They spent Friday evening eating, reviewing their time at the Bible Museum, and outlining their discussion for Saturday.

Prior to their trip to DC, Johnny emailed each of his students a digital file of the proposed table of contents for their final document with summaries of the assumptions and theories gleaned from their class notes and Johnny's work with Dr. Clark and Tony. He handed out paper copies of the file Friday night.

"Let's use this table of contents as our discussion guide for tomorrow. Nothing is final at this point, but it reflects the parallel work from the first semester of our class and the work of Dr. Clark and Dr. Guest. Patti, Elizabeth, and I have also helped shaped some of the content. Breakfast will be at eight o'clock and we'll begin our discussion at nine. Any questions? If not, let's get some sleep." It was a long day and everyone was ready for bed.

Saturday's discussion moved quickly through the evidence of a creator God and the accuracy of the Bible. There was general agreement with several issues: the physical universe was likely millions of years old, the biblical account of creation likely occurred over six long periods of time, Adam and Eve were created much later—probably less than 15,000 years ago, and the Flood occurred less than 10,000 years ago and could be well-documented with credible science. They discussed how to align biblical and scientific evidence in their document in a simple and understandable way.

The afternoon discussion began to focus on God's motives. It was clear God, at some point, made the decision to add a physical dimension to the spiritual world. His ultimate purpose as expressed in the Bible was to unify elements from the physical and spiritual world into a new heaven on a new earth. This was likely motivated by several goals. First, combining spiritual and physical existence will offer a better quality of life for God and His creatures. Physical senses and emotions, when combined with the perfection, supernatural capabilities, and eternal life of spiritual bodies, will provide God's family—His body—with an existence more wonderful than we can image. This goal is an expression of God's perfect love.

The physical world also provided the necessary DNA for spiritual creatures to ultimately be born again as spiritual and physical beings. All spiritual beings must be joined with physical bodies before they can live in the new heaven on the new earth.

But the more important priority of creating the physical world was likely based on God's imperative of freedom. In the spiritual world, God's children have the freedom to choose evil over good—as we see with the war in heaven. But no one is free or wants to be separate from God in the eternal spiritual world. God fills the infinite spiritual world with His light.

The problem: God cannot coexist with evil, and Satan introduced evil into the spiritual world. The physical world was created to allow for the separation of good and evil. The creation account in the first chapter of Genesis is filled with the concept of separation, apparently, a concept that does not exist in the spiritual world.

Tony tried to summarize the discussion, "So, the physical world was created without evil, but God used it to separate evil from good. The physical world became the dominion of evil. Unfortunately, all of God's family—and everything in the spiritual world—must travel through this evil physical world to satisfy freedom and justice, and to acquire the physical DNA to live in the new heaven. Spiritual beings must leave the spiritual world because it is perishing. A biblical analogy is when the children of Israel, facing a famine, had to go down to Egypt to save themselves. They were saved from the famine in their homeland but became slaves to brutal task masters.

"God's people will be saved for eternity by the physical world because it is the only path to the new heaven, but while we're here, we inherit a sin nature. That means our physical blood is tainted with sin and we cannot enter the new heaven.

"Jesus is the only being who has ever existed with a sinless spiritual and physical blood type. His blood is spiritual and physical because He was conceived by His spiritual Father and His physical mother Mary. He is the only human since Adam who didn't inherit a sin nature because He didn't have a physical father.

"So, the blood of Jesus is necessary for eternal life. He figuratively sprinkles His blood onto all of His children just as the high priests in the Old Testament sprinkled the blood of animals around the temple. The blood of Jesus purifies us and only those with His blood can enter the new heaven. This means the physical world both saves and condemns. Physical blood and DNA are necessary to have eternal life in the new heaven, but our inherited sin in this physical world blocks us from entering the new heaven. All evil will be trapped in the physical world and be eternally separated from God and His body. That's why we call the physical world a filter for evil.

"If we must have the blood of Jesus to live forever, then how do we get it? That's another discussion, so I'll yield to whoever knows the answer."

Dr. Clark cleared his throat. "I'm not sure I know the answer, but I have some theories. Lots of people do lots of good things in the name of Jesus, but we know good works don't save people—good works don't give people the blood of Jesus.

"Let's assume for a minute when the blood of Jesus was spilled in this world, the price for the sins of all mankind was paid. All humanity, past, present, and future, was justified. This means everyone could be saved, but it doesn't mean they individually have the blood of Jesus. Another step is needed before people can be saved unto eternal life and enter the new heaven. Here are some alternative possibilities of how people might get the blood of Jesus. If Jesus' blood is the only way we get to heaven, we need to seriously consider how to get it. I've listed a few possible ways on the sheets I just gave you and you can add them to your binders.

- The blood of Jesus saves everyone whether they ask for it or not. This theory is very unlikely because the Bible is explicit that many people belong to Satan and will not be in the new heaven.

- God 'sprinkles' the blood of Jesus over all of His children whether they ask for it or not. This theory begs the question: Who are God's children and how were they selected? It seems to me, before the war in heaven, all spiritual beings were part of God's body or family. This suggests some of God's children decided to separate from God and some chose to stay. So, it's possible God's physical children chose to be His children in the spiritual world before they were born.

- Another theory is God created a special group of people in the spiritual world to be His children and He calls all of them to Himself when they are in the physical world. All who are called come to Jesus, receive His blood, and are forgiven their sin. In this scenario, God is in complete control, but people go through the motions of repenting and receiving Jesus.

- It is also possible, as the Bible seems to say, all people are free to seek Jesus and only those who receive Jesus in the physical world are saved by His blood. Those who don't receive Jesus in this life will spend eternity in Hell.

"Here's my best guess of how all of this works and I've provided some of Scripture references in the summary document Dr. J gave you last night. The stories and parables in the Bible suggest God chose a people who rejected Him. They were invited to the wedding and didn't come. But these chosen people were selected before they were in slavery in Egypt. I think Egypt represents the physical world. God's people were chosen before they left the Promised Land—which I think represents heaven. My guess is God's children were selected for salvation before we were born. God knew us before the creation of the world.

"Given God's character of love, freedom, justice, and mercy, it's hard for me to believe He created a whole class of people doomed from the start to be separated from Him and suffer eternal punishment. I know God is the potter and we are the clay and we have no standing to question His decisions. Nevertheless, I believe God loves all His creatures and He gave every creature the freedom to choose to stay or leave His body. Justice demands those who leave Him are by nature separated and sinful, but mercy requires God save all those who freely choose to be part of His body.

"I believe this choice was made in the spiritual world before we were born. I believe we are reconnected with God when we willfully accept Jesus and receive His blood in this life. I also believe all God's children will be saved by the blood of Jesus whether they accept it or not, but those who ignore so great a salvation will not know God in this life. And their rejection of Jesus in this life—whether they know it or not—means their lives support Satan in the great battle between good and evil. I think the Bible may be describing these people in 1 Cor 2:15 when it says they "will suffer loss but yet will be saved –even though only as one escaping through the flames."

"I'll offer one caveat to my theory. The Bible makes it clear the way we live and the decisions we make during our physical lives impacts the war in the spiritual world. The spiritual world is timeless and our decision to receive Jesus and accept His blood in this physical life may be the same decision we made to fight on God's side when we lived—or should I say as we now live—in the spiritual world. In other words, our decision in the spiritual world whether or not to stand with God in the war in heaven, may depend on our decision to accept Jesus in this physical life or vice versa. I would caution anyone who hears the gospel message and rejects it. That decision may seal your fate or provide a strong indication your fate has already been decided.

"That's enough from the old folks, what do you young people think about the salvation issue?"

Lydia raised her hand sheepishly. "It seems to me the simplest message is just to invite people to receive Jesus as their

Savior and Lord. That decision is the only aspect of the salvation issue people can control. All the other possibilities are out of our hands in this life."

"Exactly." Ed raised his hand and began talking at the same time. "All the different theories are interesting to ponder and discuss, but people just need to know God loves them and Jesus saves them. What am I missing?"

"What about the people who never hear the gospel?" Matt was playing the contrarian with the age-old question. "What about the millions of children who die before they are old enough to know anything? Do they all go to hell?"

"You know that's not what I'm saying, Matt." Lydia smiled as she jumped back into the fray. "We know only the blood of Jesus can save people. That's what we need to tell the world. It may be true His blood saves many who never know Him in this life, but we live in a country where the gospel is preached all around us. People should be warned that rejecting the love and forgiveness of Jesus is a strong indication they are not a child of God. We should encourage people to play it safe—cover their bases—and act on what they know."

"That's true." Matt was enjoying the give and take. "But many people reject the gospel message because they believe God is unfairly condemning children, poor illiterates, and people from other religions. The whole point of this project is to help people see God saves all He chooses, but we may have a role in our own salvation—either in the spiritual or physical worlds or both. We certainly have a role in accepting Jesus as Savior and Lord. So, like you said, we are encouraging people to respond to God's call—if they 'have ears to hear.'"

Julie added a caution, "What will evangelical leaders say if we even suggest the possibility that people may not need to accept Jesus as their personal Savior to be saved? I think it will bring charges of heresy against all of us."

Henry quietly listened as long as he could. "Our interpretations of Genesis and Revelation will be heresy to many in the church, and our efforts to ascribe motives to God will likely result in us being burned as witches. We shouldn't fool ourselves. Our theories will make a lot of people mad."

Johnny gave a "time out" sign with his hands. "The prophets made a lot of people mad, Jesus made a lot of people mad, and Martin Luther made a lot of people mad. We cannot challenge the status quo without making some people mad. But if we are careful, our work won't necessarily discredit traditional thinking. It will offer some alternatives for those who need to go beyond the basics to be assured their faith is consistent with science and logic."

Dr. Clark leaned forward in his chair. "Dr. J is right. We're not trying to develop a new theology. Basic evangelical teachings remains. But we're living in a culture where the predominate view from academia, the media, and science assumes there is no God—it is broadly accepted the physical world is the result of accidental origins and unplanned, random evolution. This is what they teach in our schools and universities. The Bible is not taught as truth, even in many churches. Biblical morality is considered prudish poppycock.

"Non-believers have been unleashed from any moral boundaries and many believers are confused, unsure, and cowed into submission. Believers have one set of beliefs on Sunday in church and a completely different set of beliefs for the rest of the week. There can be no real faith in this environment. Faith is being sure about what we believe. Faith is not just believing there is a God or Jesus was an actual person. It is being confident all the promises of God will come true. Faith is knowing God in a personal way and being sure of your eternal destination. Doubt undermines our faith as we read in James 1:6–8:

> *'But when you ask, you must believe and not doubt, because the one who doubts is like a wave of the sea, blown and tossed by the wind. That person should not expect to receive anything from the Lord. Such a person is double-minded and unstable in all they do.'*

"Doubt about God and the Bible makes us double-minded and unstable in all we do. That's a powerful warning.

"Our work will give believers all the certainty they need to live with a confident faith. Some believers are so filled with the Holy Spirit they don't need any outside assurance. They know God is real and Jesus will save them. They don't seem to have any doubts. These believers may not have any interest in our work. They may even find our ideas objectionable or worse.

"But I'm convinced the church of Jesus Christ is growing weaker and weaker—and the world is becoming increasingly wicked and sinful—because believers are cowering on the sidelines of the great battle between good and evil. Tony has rightly said too many believers have a Santa Claus God. Unfortunately, this is truer than any of us want to admit. And this situation produces a terrible result for the church. It means believers are not holding up the hands of God to restrain evil and defeat Satan.

"We must make our ideas understandable to anyone who is interested, so it's important for us to keep trying to focus and simplify our arguments. It may seem like we're just repeating the same theories and ideas, but repetition we will eventually make our message simpler.

"We have a solid scientific and statistical case for a creator God who sustains the physical world with meta-physical energy sources and dynamic forces holding the universe together. We can make a good statistical and evidentiary case the Bible is far superior to any other religious or historical document in its consistency and truth. Statistical probability strongly suggests supernatural guidance was required for the Bible to predict future events with such accuracy.

"We will establish a reasonable and logical argument, based on scientific evidence, that the physical world is co-existing with a meta-physical or spiritual dimension. We will also make a reasonable and logical argument that God's ultimate purpose is to unify spiritual and physical elements into a new and eternal dimension the Bible calls a new heaven on a new earth. The current physical and spiritual worlds will disappear. This will leave only two destinations for the souls of physical beings: the new heaven or a fiery void the Bible calls the Abyss.

"This brings us to an uncomfortable, but unavoidable truth; some of the people in this world will spend eternity in the new heaven and some will be trapped in the fiery Abyss. And, this also brings us to the unavoidable question; how do people qualify for the new heaven and how can people know they will be saved from the Abyss?

"The answer is not complicated for those who believe the Bible is true—that is, if people are willing to read and accept what the Bible really says. The Bible tells us all people are separated from God and blocked from the spiritual world because of our physical nature. There is a barrier between the spiritual and physical worlds. God exists in the spiritual world and humans live in a physical world separated from God. This separation creates a phenomenon the Bible calls sin.

"Nothing we do in this physical world causes our sin nature and nothing we do in this world can change our sin nature—except the blood of Jesus. People are not sinners because they do bad things. People do bad things because they are born sinners. Our physical nature is influenced, if not controlled, by satanic forces because we are separated from the righteousness of God.

"The Bible only gives us one way to cure our separation from God while we are alive in the physical world, and only one way to enter the new heaven when our physical lives are over. The blood of Jesus is the only cure for our sin and separation, and it is the only way we can enter the new heaven.

"This is not a complex spiritual mystery. Jesus is the only human in history who is both God and man. God was His father and Mary was His mother. He is the only human who has ever lived whose blood is both spiritual and physical. And Jesus was not born with a sin nature because His father was sinless. So, He was never separated from the righteousness of God. Jesus is the only one who could offer the perfect sacrifice for sin.

"The Bible describes God's children as part of the body of Jesus. Every part of a body is sustained by blood and only those who are part of a body have the blood in that body. Believers have received a spiritual transfusion of the only blood type that can save us. The death of Jesus and His shed blood redeems us—buys us back from Satan. His resurrection defeated death and qualified all who are part of His body to enter the new heaven.

"Think of Jesus as the High Priest who entered the Holy of Holies with the blood of a sacrifice to cover the sins of all the people. The people could not enter because they would die in the presence of a holy God. The Holy of Holies was separated from the people and the rest of the temple by a large, thick curtain. The High Priest could only enter after going through an elaborate purification process and could only stand in the presence of God with the blood of the sacrifice. The people were purified when the High Priest offered the blood, but the people were not involved with the transaction.

"When Jesus died on the cross, the great curtain separating the people from God was ripped open. This meant the blood of Jesus justified all the people and allowed them to enter the presence of God. The entire body of Jesus is redeemed—purchased—by His blood, whether they know it or not. But all people remain separated from God while in physical bodies until they willfully acknowledge their need of a savior and ask Jesus to save them. Jesus tore the curtain open—the door to the kingdom of God is open—but people must individually enter the Holy of Holies to receive God's Holy Spirit and become part of the body of Jesus.

"So, I think it is fair to say Jesus does everything for us except receive His gift of salvation. This is consistent with His character. He offers us perfect love, He satisfies justice by paying the price for sin, and he offers mercy to everyone. But Jesus will not violate our freedom by forcing us to come to Him. He opens the door and calls us to come in, but we are free to ignore His call and remain separated from His love in this life.

"I suspect there will be many of God's children in the new heaven who never knew or accepted Jesus in this life, but I would warn everyone not to count on it. Anyone who knows about Jesus and rejects Him is unlikely to be in the new heaven. God will not force anyone into His kingdom.

"That all sounds a bit convoluted but it can be said in one sentence: everyone is born into this world lost and separated from God, God came to earth as Jesus to rescue us, but we have to agree to be rescued if we want to know God while we live in this physical world. That's all you need to know. If people want to dig deeper, we will have plenty for them to read and consider. But let's get to the part when we ask, 'now what?'

"When we accept the sacrifice of Jesus for our sin and receive the Holy Spirit of God, we become a new creation. We are literally born again into the spiritual world. Being 'born again' is not about a physical rebirth. It is a spiritual rebirth. Our spirits are reborn and we rejoin the family of God. We become a 'new creation.'

"We will still sin against God, but we are no longer sinners. All of our sins—past, present, and future—are covered by the blood of Jesus.

"Think about this verse." Dr. Clark shuffled through a few pages in his Bible. "This is Galatians 2:19–20:

'For through the law I died to the law so that I might live for God. I have been crucified with Christ and I no longer live, but Christ lives in me. The life I now live in the body, I live by faith in the Son of God, who loved me and gave himself for me.'

"If you ever wonder why Christians must endure terrible suffering in this world, here's your answer. When we accept Jesus as Savior and become part of His body on this earth, we agree to be crucified with Him. We agree to let His Holy Spirit live in us and make us part of the physical body of Jesus. We become part of His body with His blood in our veins. All who give themselves to Jesus become part of His body in this world.

"Next question: What are the responsibilities of the body of Jesus in the world? I think the body of Jesus is here to demonstrate the love, freedom, justice, and mercy of God, and to hold up the hands of God against evil. The power of God flows through the body of Jesus in this physical world. We are the soldiers in the war between good and evil. When believers demonstrate the fruit of the Spirit, we advance good and defeat evil.

"I don't know about all of you, but when I began to think of myself as one of God's soldiers in the great battle against Satan, it totally changed how I think about my life. What if the outcome of this great battle depends on me? What if my prayers, praise, and obedience actually change what happens around me? What if evangelism means more than getting people saved? What if millions of God's people are standing on the sidelines and the purpose of preaching the gospel all around the world is to recruit soldiers to help us win the great war in heaven?"

Dr. Clark put his Bible on the coffee table next to his chair. "Now, I'd like to hear some of our young students say all this in a way the world might understand."

The afternoon was filled with discussion, arguments, many theories, and laughter. One phrase captured the sentiment of all the students, "Why don't churches have these kinds of discussions in their Sunday school classes? Pastors and teachers must think eliminating questions will eliminate doubts but that's completely backward. The kind of discussion we're having today eliminates all doubt."

So I say, walk by the Spirit, and you will not gratify the desires of the flesh. For the flesh desires what is contrary to the Spirit, and the Spirit what is contrary to the flesh. They are in conflict with each other, so that you are not to do whatever you want. —Galatians 5:16–17

CHAPTER TWENTY-TWO

THE BOOK OF LIFE

September 2018
(Travelers Rest, SC)

"Welcome home, Joshua!" Johnny's mother met her new grandson at the oversized front door of Johnny and Patti's new home. "Come to your Grandma." Patti carefully placed her baby in her mother-in-law's arms and they all walked into the great room to meet Patti's parents.

Johnny's mom and Patti's parents moved in two weeks before Joshua's birth to help get the house ready for the newest member of the family. They were overwhelmed by the size and old colonial décor of Johnny and Patti's new home. Patti's dad, an engineer by training, fixed everything in the house and even figured out how to operate the large mower Mr. Rushing left in the shed. The front lawn and back pasture were perfectly manicured when Joshua arrived home from the hospital.

Johnny's mother drove from Boone in a catering van formerly used by her family's business. It was filled with enough food to feed an army. All the food was needed. Between their families and the students returning to school, hundreds would stop by over the next week to meet Joshua and see the new home. It was a wonderful time of celebration—a time for Johnny and Patti, that seemed like redemption, restoration, and renewal.

Joshua immediately became the centerpiece of their lives. Patti worked from home through the fall semester. Johnny bought a road-capable golf cart to travel back and forth between campus and home. He came home for lunch and often worked from his home office in the afternoons when he didn't have a class.

They also found someone to be their part-time nanny. One of the students who moved into their garage apartment had a single mom, Joy, who wanted to live near her son. Living and working in the same house was a perfect solution. Joy moved into the room at the top of the stairs and immediately became a beloved part of the family. It was a perfect situation for everyone.

Patti exercised in their home gym every day to get back into shape. Her pregnancy and delivery actually turned out to be a boon to her recovery. X-rays after Joshua's birth revealed one of Patti's hips—the one dislocated in her accident and previously resistant to therapy—miraculously "popped" back into place during the strenuous delivery process. Within a month after her delivery, Patti could walk without a limp and jog without pain.

Johnny had his Advanced Bible Studies class on Tuesday and Thursday mornings and taught two freshman classes on Monday, Wednesday, and Friday. He was busy at home and at work, but his priority other than Patti and Joshua was preparing for the debate in January and completing the document now officially named *Satan's Dare*.

FINALIZING SATAN'S DARE

Johnny talked numerous times to Rachel after she left Tony's house. She finally agreed to rejoin the class in August. The six members of Johnny's Advanced Bible Studies class returned in late August and were now operating more like a board of directors than college students. They dressed like professionals, arrived early for class, carried briefcases full of books and research notes, and directed the class with little assistance from Johnny.

The class decided in October they had collected too much research, documentation, and reference material to include everything in the text of their final document. After spending the summer working with Johnny, Dr. Guest, and Dr. Clark to simplify their theories and conclusions, they didn't want to complicate the narrative of *Satan's Dare* with too much information. They decided to include an in-depth appendix along with a bibliography of books and references for readers who wanted to do more of their own research. The main document would be conceptual and "big picture" with just enough references to convince readers their findings were properly documented.

From mid-October through the end of the semester in December, the students made presentations in pairs to summarize the content and references for each section of the table of contents. The responsibility of writing everything down rotated between the students. The class presentations generally followed the syllabus from their first class in the Spring. The first section of the book was about 150 pages and followed the table of contents below. The second section was about 100 pages and dealt with issues of salvation and God's motives. There were over three hundred pages in the appendix.

The class repeated their conclusions numerous times trying to simply and make them more understandable. Their final draft presented three general conclusions in the first section backed up by enough evidence—they believed—to convince even their harshest critics. First, they proved it was statistically impossible for the physical world and all life forms to have been created by accidental origins and unplanned, random evolution. They didn't think any credible scientist could possibly refute their findings.

Second, they proved by deduction and default there is a creator God and a co-existing meta-physical dimension—a spiritual world. Third, they proved the Bible was the most enduring, credible, and accurate historical document in existence and the primary means used by God to communicate with His creation.

KEY ISSUES

The most difficult issue for the class was how a sovereign, all-powerful and loving God could allow all the pain, suffering, and death in the physical world. The only reasonable explanation seemed to be God's character has to allow the battle between good and evil to resolve itself on earth. Part of the body of God broke away from His family in the spiritual world and is continuously at war with those who chose to stay as part of God's body. The war results in much pain for all of God's creation. God uses pain and suffering to make us stronger and more like Jesus, but God doesn't cause pain, suffering, and death.

Satan uses many weapons to attack God's people: sickness, accidents, violent acts, immorality, and death. But Satan also uses our own physical nature against us. Even for those who have God's Holy Spirit, our physical natures are always at war with our spirits. This conflict is described in Galatians 5:16–26:

> So I say, walk by the Spirit, and you will not gratify the desires of the flesh. For the flesh desires what is contrary to the Spirit, and the Spirit what is contrary to the flesh. They are in conflict with each other, so that you are not to do whatever you want. But if you are led by the Spirit, you are not under the law.
>
> The acts of the flesh are obvious: sexual immorality, impurity and debauchery; idolatry and witchcraft; hatred, discord, jealousy, fits of rage, selfish ambition, dissensions, factions and envy; drunkenness, orgies, and the like. I warn you, as I did before, that those who live like this will not inherit the kingdom of God.

But the fruit of the Spirit is love, joy, peace, forbearance, kindness, goodness, faithfulness, gentleness and self-control. Against such things there is no law. Those who belong to Christ Jesus have crucified the flesh with its passions and desires. Since we live by the Spirit, let us keep in step with the Spirit. Let us not become conceited, provoking and envying each other.

The battle between the physical and spiritual natures of individuals is part of the larger war between good and evil in the physical world. For those who have not given themselves to Jesus and received God's Holy Spirit, they are separated from God and unknowingly work for Satan, even when they are practicing a religion or trying to do good deeds. Separation from God is sin, so everything people do while they are separated from God is sin.

Those who have accepted Jesus as Savior and Lord have joined the battle against evil and their weapons are the fruit of the Spirit. When they put on the armor of God and follow His commands, they defeat Satan. When they disobey God and practice the "acts of the flesh," they empower Satan to cause pain, suffering, and death on God's people. Matt was struggling with the whole idea. "I never considered the thought that my sinful behavior might give Satan the power to hurt someone in my family or one of my friends. It never occurred to me that one believer living in sin could be the reason another believer dies of cancer or loses a child. Could my disobedience cause someone to be murdered?"

Julie tried to help. "I think what we're saying is there is a cumulative impact of good and evil in this world. The physical world and our physical bodies are partially controlled by Satan, so the natural bent of this world is toward evil. This gives Satan power to harm us just like he did Job. God was in control of Job's life, but He reluctantly gave Satan the freedom to cause Job great harm in order to ultimately save Job and defeat Satan. When Job continued to praise God in his suffering, he proved

Satan wrong and justified God's favor. Job's faithfulness vindi-
cated God and empowered God to bless Job and many others.

"God is in control in heaven but—for the sake of freedom
and justice—He has yielded some of His control of the physical world to Satan and God's family on earth. The blood of
Jesus poured out on the physical world allows God's Holy
Spirit to overcome evil, but He limits Himself to the collective
power of His body.

"God's Holy Spirit and His physical body on earth are
continuously at war with Satan and his followers. We see this
played out in the Bible when Jesus was tempted by Satan for
forty days in the desert. Jesus suffered from starvation and
dehydration while Satan tempted Him with everything in the
physical world. When Jesus refused to yield, Satan was
defeated. The same is true for all of us who are part of the body
of Jesus in this world. When we obey God and resist evil, we
defeat Satan."

Johnny could tell the whole class was disturbed about the
idea of Satan having such power in the physical world and the
idea of God yielding to Satan in anything. "Let's think about
all this in the context of the Lord's Prayer from Matthew 6, the
only time Jesus told His disciples how to pray. Prayer is part of
the process of sanctification. It conforms us to Christ and aligns
us to His purposes. But it seems clear to me Jesus is also telling
us to use prayer to accomplish God's purposes in this world.
Let's look at the Lord's Prayer from that perspective:

'Our Father in heaven,'

"This tells us God the Father is in heaven. He exists as a spirit
in the spiritual world, but because of Jesus, His Holy Spirit is
now at work in the physical world.

'hallowed be your name,'

"This tells us God is holy and worthy of our praise.

'your kingdom come,'

"Jesus is telling us to pray for God's kingdom to come. He wants us to pray for the arrival of the new heaven on a new earth. Why would Jesus tell us to pray for God's kingdom to come if it is going to come anyway without our prayers?

> *'your will be done,*
> *on earth as it is in heaven.'*

"Jesus tells us to pray God's will is carried out on earth. Why would He tell us to pray this if God's will is going to be done without our prayers? He tells us God's will is being done in heaven and we should pray it will also be done on earth. This tells me God's will won't be done unless the body of God on earth prays.

> *'Give us today our daily bread.'*

"Jesus us tells us to pray for our daily needs and implicitly for the physical needs of all the body of Jesus.

> *'And forgive us our debts,*
> *as we also have forgiven our debtors.'*

"Here Jesus is telling us to pray God will forgive our sins and it suggests our forgiveness may be conditional on our forgiveness of others—or at least we should pray we are able to forgive others.

> *'And lead us not into temptation,*
> *but deliver us from the evil one.'*

"Jesus is telling us to pray God will not lead us into temptation. This suggests to me our prayers can help us and others avoid being tempted. It also tells us to pray God will protect us from Satan. Our prayers protect us and the entire body of Jesus from Satan. Why would Jesus tell us to pray this prayer if God was going to protect us regardless of our prayers?

"The unavoidable conclusion here is a lot of what happens in the world is dependent on the prayers, praise, and obedience of God's people. God has connected His sovereignty to us—His children! The urgency of our participation is undeniable.

"Okay, think about it another way. What was the real lesson of Job? It may be Job's faithfulness not only justified God's blessing of Job, it saved his friends. God forgave Job's friends after Job prayed for them. God gave Job more children and blessed them with beauty and wealth because of Job's prayers and faithfulness. Satan's evil was thwarted by the faithfulness of one believer. One faithful person in this world may bless millions and hold up God's hands of protection for His people. Imagine the power of the whole body of Jesus all around the world."

Another major concern of the class was the issue of salvation. How and when are people saved?

Lydia led the discussion. "Let's revisit the issue of salvation one more time before we finalize our ideas in the document. I think most of us agree, but let's make sure we agree because our conclusion about salvation will likely cause a lot of controversy.

"I think we have all generally agreed, as humans, we do not write our own names in God's Book of Life while on earth. Our decision to accept Jesus as Savior and Lord is a strong indication we were already a part of God's family. Our obedience to God, our love of others, and the demonstration of the fruits of the Spirit in our lives confirm we are part of God's family. These things tell us we have the blood of Jesus and will live for eternity with God. This confidence is our faith and our faith confirms our salvation.

"Most of us in this class believe our eternal life was determined before we were born—either by God's decision or our own choice to stay in the family of God when Satan rebelled. If we consider God's character of freedom and justice, it seems reasonable to assume He allowed the members of His body to make their own decision whether to remain in Him or to leave. That would mean we are chosen by God because we freely chose to be His when we had perfect knowledge of the choices between good and evil.

"If this is true, nothing we do in the physical world will change our eternal destination. But everything we do in this physical world impacts the war between good and evil and it impacts the lives of all God's people—past, present, and future. Our prayers impact a timeless spiritual world and that could change the outcome of physical battles against evil throughout time.

"We are all like Job, continuously being tested by Satan. When we resist Satan and praise God, we make this world a little better for ourselves and the whole family of God. Every believer makes a difference because every act of obedience to God empowers the angels in the spiritual world to win the war against Satan.

"Evangelism is important here on earth because it saves people from the power of sin during their physical lives, saves people from the misery of living their lives separated from God, and recruits people to help fight the war against evil. And when we lead people to Jesus in this life, it spares them—our brothers and sisters—the shame of entering eternity with nothing to show for their lives."

Johnny was silently cheering. "Lydia, you summarize the idea of salvation better than I've ever heard. God's family will all pass through this separated, sinful, physical world, but we always belong to the Father. Nothing can take us out of His hands. All of the examples and parables of salvation in the Bible—the prodigal son, the lost coins, the lost sheep—were all previous possessions lost and rescued.

"But let's make sure of one thing. Regardless what people believe about the days of Creation, the Flood, when salvation occurs, or who decides about our eternal destination and when, the bottom line of all of our work comes back to the most basic principle of Christianity. There is a God who loves everyone and He has given mankind only one way to be saved unto eternal life: Jesus Christ. We must have the blood of Jesus and be part of His body to enter the new heaven when our physical bodies die.

"The second part of our bottom line answers the question of why everyone has to go through the pain, suffering, and death of this physical life. Galatians 5:1 gives us at least part of the answer: 'It is for freedom that Christ has set us free.' God could have easily created slaves and robots to blindly follow and praise Him. But He created us to be His family, so He had to let His creation be free to stay or leave Him. Unfortunately, Satan and many angels decided to leave and go their own way—to separate from God's body.

"God's light fills the entire spiritual world, and there can be no darkness or evil. The physical world is the only way God can separate light from dark—good from evil. When God created the physical world, the first thing He did was separate light from darkness. The purpose of the physical world is to separate God from evil. Separation from God is the whole meaning of sin.

"Why does God's family have to go through the physical world? Two reasons. The first is to obtain physical bodies. The Bible tells us we have to be born physically and spiritually to enter the new heaven. That makes sense because the new heaven is both physical and spiritual. The second reason is *Satan's dare*. It's the story of Job. Satan demands justice. He challenges God to let His children be separated from Him, the knowledge of Him, and His protection. Satan accuses God of buying the loyalty of His children with blessings.

"This goes back to the idea we have discussed in class. This physical world is a bridge we must cross and Satan is the troll controlling the bridge. We've used this analogy several times, and it is a bit trite compared to reality, but I think it's important we put these extremely difficult concepts into terms anyone can understand. When God's children cry out to Him instead of yielding to Satan, God is faithful and just to restore us to His body, to give us His blood, and to tear down the wall separating us from His kingdom. One way or the other, God will get His people across this bridge.

"God is sovereign over everything that belongs to Him. He is sovereign over the spiritual world and the new heaven. But in this physical world—for the sake of freedom and justice—He answers *Satan's dare*. He allows His body—spiritual and physical—to fight the battle with Satan and his demons. And just as Jesus suffered and died in this battle, we should not be surprised when we suffer and die in this physical world.

"But let us live and die with the knowledge this life is but a brief and difficult crossing, our Lord and Savior will be with us every step of the way, all the angels of heaven are constantly fighting to protect us, our praises and prayers empower all God's army, and our God is in complete control of our eternal destination. Nothing can take us out of His hands."

Johnny held up a spiral-bound notebook with *Satan's Dare* on the front with large red type at the top of the cover, "Unedited Confidential Draft—not for distribution."

"Let's each ask someone to review a copy of this draft. I've got four professors who have agreed to discreetly review it and give me their comments. Dr. Guest and Dr. Clark will give it one more review as well. Please ask everyone who agrees to read it not to share it with anyone else. It's not quite ready for prime time. Try to get as much input as you can in the next few weeks and get your notes to me. I'll write a final draft and give it to our publisher for a professional edit before it's printed. We hope to have 1,000 initial copies ready for the debate.

"*Satan's Dare* won't put anyone's name in the Book of Life, but it will show people how to find out if their name is in it!"

Then Job replied to the Lord:
"I know that you can do all things;
no purpose of yours can be thwarted.
You asked, 'Who is this that obscures my plans
without knowledge?'
Surely I spoke of things I did not understand,
things too wonderful for me to know."—Job 42:1–3

CHAPTER TWENTY-THREE

THINGS TOO WONDERFUL TO KNOW

October 2018
(Craigsville, VA)

"Dr. Guest, I didn't want to see you. I can't forgive myself for what I did."

Tony Guest had a heavy and haunting burden he needed to release before the second debate. He had to forgive Don Johnson, the man who killed Pamela and Christine.

Don was serving two life sentences in Augusta Correctional Facility in Craigsville, Virginia, a maximum-security prison. It was about a two hour and fifteen-minute drive from Tony's home in Middleburg.

Don refused to see Tony for several months but one of Tony's old friends from Chuck Colson's Prison Fellowship finally convinced Don to meet. Tony's friend knew Don well. Don regularly attended a prayer group led by Prison

Fellowship. He told the prison chaplain he was too afraid and ashamed to see Tony.

Tony's friend at the prison reported Don had attended their morning prayer meetings without fail every day of the week for the past two years. He never spoke until the group leader asked for prayer requests. At the end of every meeting, Don stood, paused, and gave the same request, "Please pray with me that God will give Pastor Anthony Guest a wife and daughter." Then he sat, put his head in his hands, and cried.

Tony arrived at the prison on a clear, cool Saturday morning in October. Prison Fellowship arranged with the warden for Don and Tony to have a private meeting in one of the rooms normally used for spouses to meet prisoners. Despite Don's history of violence, the warden was convinced Tony would be in no danger alone with Don.

Don was in the room when Tony arrived. He was sitting in a folding chair looking at the floor. He didn't look up when Tony walked into the room. Tony put another folding chair in front of Don and sat down. Don wouldn't look up.

"Hello, Don." Tony was overcome with a painful mix of emotions. He was filled with anger, sadness, pity, compassion. His heart was in his throat and he could hardly talk.

Don didn't look up and spoke only in a whisper, "Dr. Guest, I didn't want to see you. I can't forgive myself for what I did."

"Don, you did a terrible thing. My wife and daughter were my whole world. They were wonderful gifts from God. I was trying to help you. You don't deserve to be forgiven."

"I know, I know, and I'm not asking you or God to forgive me. What I did is unforgiveable."

Tony spoke softly, "Don, Jesus told a story about you and me—two servants of God our master. Jesus said one servant owed his master a huge sum of money—much more than the servant could ever repay. The master had this servant dragged in front of his throne and demanded he repay his debts. The servant pleaded with the master not to put him in prison. He begged for more time to repay the money. The master was merciful and agreed to forgive the servant his entire debt. He was free from everything he owed.

"The first servant left the master rejoicing but on his way home, he met another servant who owed him a small debt. The second servant pleaded with the first to give him more time to repay his debt. Instead, the first servant had him thrown in jail. When the master heard what the first servant did, he had him thrown in prison until he could repay his entire debt.

"I am the first servant and my debt to God is so large I could never repay it. The same thing is true for every person who has ever lived. It doesn't matter that I've been a pastor and a good man. I was separated from God by a gulf I couldn't cross. God crossed that gulf and paid my debt Himself. He forgave me and removed all my sin. My slate is clean and the master loves me. However, if I accept His gift and then don't forgive you, I have betrayed the gift given me and wounded the heart of God.

"Don, we are both servants of the master. God has forgiven me a debt I could never pay myself. Without His forgiveness, I will never enter heaven. If I accept His forgiveness and then don't forgive you, I've empowered Satan to inflict pain and suffering on other members of God's family."

Don finally looked up into Tony's eyes. "Pastor, has God given you a family?"

"Yes, God has given me a beautiful wife and a precious daughter."

Don looked incredulous. He put his face in his hands and wept. Tony stood and put his hand on Don's head. Tears filled his eyes.

"Don, God has answered your prayers." Don was now wailing.

"Pastor Guest, how could God answer MY prayers? It makes no sense."

"No, it doesn't, Don. Because God is not like us."

Don looked up at Tony again. "Pastor, please make sure they never let me out of here. I thought Jesus changed me and

He really did. He turned my whole life around. But that morning at the hotel before you picked me up, I took one drink. I thought I was cured and one drink wouldn't be a problem. But as soon as I took one swallow it was like I opened the door again to Satan. It was like I gave Him complete control of me again. I lost all control of myself. I'll never trust myself again."

"Don, we can only have one master. We have to run from anything in this world that controls us. You have to stay away from drugs and alcohol. I am vulnerable to pride and anger. Satan has a lot of ways to become our master. Perhaps God has given you the walls of this prison to protect you from Satan."

"I can't do much here but pray for people like you on the outside. I don't know why God would ever listen to me, but I'm gonna' keep trying. I will pray every day for you, your wife, and your daughter."

"Don, I forgive you and God forgives you. And you have to forgive yourself. You are forgiven and your sins are as far from you as the east is from the west. Jesus died for what you did—for everything you have ever done. He paid the price. You will offend God if you tell Him Jesus is not sufficient to pay the price for your sin. Your job in this prison is to accept God's forgiveness and pray every day for God's kingdom to come on earth. Please pray for me, my wife Elizabeth, and our daughter Liz. Pray for the protection of all of God's people—every day."

Don looked up with a trembling smile. "That will give me a reason to keep living in this place. It will be an honor to pray for God's people. I am so grateful you came."

Tony gave Don a hug, shook his hand, and they walked out of the room together. They were met by the warden who came to meet Tony. "Don's a model prisoner, Dr. Guest. It was very kind of you to visit."

"Thank you for arranging our meeting." Tony was embarrassed because the warden, like almost everyone else in the world, knew he was an outspoken atheist. But, apparently, Don had not read his book or the news. He thought Tony was still a pastor.

Driving back to Middleburg, Tony tried to enjoy a few quiet moments of closure, but his mind and heart were embroiled in a fierce debate. It was completely illogical to forgive, pity, and love a man who could brutally murder women and children. But he genuinely felt pity and love for Don. And Tony believed the parable he told Don was true; unless he forgave Don, God could not give Tony the joy of being forgiven during his physical life.

Tony didn't believe forgiving Don was a matter of salvation, he believed it was a matter of victory and joy in this life. And he now believed the act of forgiving Don weakened Satan and protected other believers.

It was hard for Tony to process the thought of prayers from the man who killed his wife and daughter having a role in giving him Elizabeth and Liz. Could Don's faithful prayers and those of the other inmates have empowered angels and spiritual forces to bring Tony and Elizabeth together? Could Don's prayers have made it possible for them to have a child? Tony never prayed for a new wife and daughter. Don may have been the only one in the world who prayed that specific prayer.

As he turned into his driveway, Tony remembered the words Job spoke after God restored his fortunes: "Things too wonderful for me to know." Tony wouldn't have used the word "wonderful" to describe what he'd been through, but he was beginning to understand what Job was trying to say.

* * *

PATTI'S FIRST SERVE

Back across the mountain in South Carolina, Patti Wright was also trying to settle an important matter for herself: her "GOAL."

The regional tournament of Division I College women's volleyball was being held in late November at Palmetto Christian's new gymnasium. The gym could accommodate three courts, but for the opening game there was only one center court. And Travelers Rest, South Carolina had never seen so much excitement and energy.

All 5,000 seats were full with students and parents from twenty competing colleges. Hundreds of people stood along the walls and extra seats were set up around the center court on the gym floor. A local television station was broadcasting the tournament live. The event even inspired thousands of tailgaters all around the campus.

The first game was an exhibition competition between two of the nation's top college women's volleyball teams: Clemson and South Carolina. Patti used her relationship with coaches at Clemson to arrange the exhibition. And she was to serve the first ball for the Clemson team.

Most of the audience knew Patti's story and everyone was hoping she could just walk onto the court without falling. The two teams took their positions on the court and waited for Patti to join them. When the cheers for the introductions of both teams quieted, a voice over the loud speaker announced, "Please welcome former Clemson star, Palmetto Christian's own Patti Wright to open our tournament with the first serve."

Everyone in the gymnasium stood and cheered as Patti walked onto the court. She was dressed in her Clemson uniform, complete with her trademark orange scarf tied around her head. When she walked onto the court, the Clemson player in the server position handed her the ball and stepped aside.

Patti stood at the back line ready to deliver the traditional underhanded serve as expected for honorees serving the first ball. Everyone assumed Patti would send a soft serve over the net, a Carolina player would catch it and give it back to her as a souvenir.

Patti leaned forward and swung her arm but stopped without hitting the ball. She looked up at the audience, smiled, then turned and walked about ten feet behind the court. Tension filled the auditorium. Everyone was afraid she'd fail.

Holding the ball tight against her chest with her left hand, Patti ran toward the court, leapt high in the air, threw the ball above her head, and hit it as hard as she could with her right hand. The sound of her fist hitting the ball echoed around the quiet gym. The ball sped across the top of the net and landed in the back-left corner of the court. Ace!

The whole gym erupted with cheers and applause. The loud speaker played Tiger Rag, the well-known fight song for Clemson athletic teams. The large screen on the wall began playing clips of Patti slamming balls over the net and serving aces when she was in college.

Johnny arranged for Palmetto's audio/visual department to produce the video highlights. Patti was crying, laughing, and thanking the players on the court when she saw another group of girls running toward the court—all with Clemson volleyball uniforms. It was her former teammates! They lifted Patti onto their shoulders and paraded her around the gym floor.

When the parade passed Johnny standing next to Dr. Clark, Patti jumped down from her victory ride and grabbed Johnny around the neck. They went through the "valley of the shadow of death" together and were now back on top of a mountain. She was Johnny's strength and he was hers. And God used the love of many others to save them both from despair. It was all too wonderful for them to know.

Jesus said, "If you hold to my teaching, you are really my disciples. Then you will know the truth, and the truth will set you free."—John 8:31–32

CHAPTER TWENTY-FOUR

THE TRUTH WILL SET YOU FREE

January 2019 – the second debate
(Travelers Rest, SC)

Dr. Clark tapped the microphone several times to quiet the crowd. "Welcome back to Palmetto Christian University."

It was a cold, snowy Monday night, the third week of January. The auditorium was filled with students just returning from Christmas break. Parents and curious people from all around the country were squeezed into the balcony. The media platform in the back of the auditorium was overflowing with television cameras and reporters with their cell phones and note pads. The second debate between Johnny Wright and Tony Guest was ready to begin.

Johnny and Tony were in the "Green Room" behind the stage with their families: Patti, Joshua, Elizabeth, and Liz. The audience would soon meet them all.

The auditorium was full of chatter. People were pointing at the stage and asking each other questions. Why wasn't the stage set up for a debate? There was only one podium on the left side of the stage and three large chairs in the center.

"Everyone, please take your seats. My name is Dr. Howard Clark. I am the president of Palmetto Christian University and, on behalf of all our faculty, staff and students, we are honored to host the second debate between Dr. Anthony Guest and Dr. Johnny Wright. The topics they will discuss tonight address the most important questions facing mankind. Is there a God who created this world or did it all happen by accident? Can we know this God if He exists? Is there life after death or do we all just cease to exist? What must we do to receive eternal life if it is even possible? You will hear all this discussed tonight, but not in the context you expect.

"Many of you are familiar with the retail term 'bait and switch.' It describes a strategy when a store advertises something at a low price but when customers show up to buy it, the low-priced item is out-of-stock. Only higher priced alternatives are available. Well, my friends, I must confess I am guilty of 'bait and switch.' You have been invited here tonight to see two fierce competitors, who disagree about almost everything, slug it out in front of the whole world. Instead, you will hear the testimonies of two people who, after painful testing and years of research, have come to the same conclusions. I promise you will receive something of far greater value than you thought you came for."

Dr. Clark paused for a moment to give the audience time to digest his words. Heads turned and whispering quickly filled the auditorium. Reporters on the media platform were frantically feeding their blogposts. Dr. Clark gently tapped the microphone.

"Before I introduce Dr. Wright and Dr. Guest, please allow me to explain what I mean. When I'm finished, if you're not satisfied with my explanation, you can all have your money back."

The crowd erupted with laughter because no one paid anything to come.

"Almost two years ago, I received a phone call from a former student. It was Dr. Anthony Guest. You all know his story—at least part of it. Tony became one of the most famous pastors and effective evangelist in the world. Then tragic circumstances in his life sent him in a totally difference direction. He became the most famous and effective atheist in the world.

"Tony thought he was finished with God forever but God had different plans. For God, Tony was just another one of His lost sheep. So, while Tony was running in the opposite direction, God was pursuing him. God never gives up on His children. When Tony called me—and I'll let him tell you most of the story—he told me God sent someone into his life who made it impossible for him to continue to deny God's love.

"You can imagine Tony's consternation as he considered how to return to faith after making millions of dollars from his book on atheism. I devised a plan and I take all the blame. The first debate was designed to set the stage for the presentations tonight. The first debate was real. Many of you were here. I know it was extremely difficult for Tony to make the case for atheism and against the Bible, because he had returned to faith. Nevertheless, Tony made an excellent presentation about the apparent absurdities of some traditional biblical interpretations, but he could not deny the obvious facts presented by Johnny Wright. There has to be a creator God.

"Johnny Wright knew nothing about my plan. He did a masterful job destroying the traditional 'straw man' interpretations of the Bible used by atheists to discredit God's written Word. The first debate ended with a challenge from Tony Guest to Johnny Wright. He called the challenge 'Satan's dare.' Tony dared Johnny to do the research and to write down his arguments defending the accuracy of the Bible. Equally important, Tony challenged Johnny to discover and defend God's motive for creating a physical world filled with pain, suffering, and death."

Dr. Clark held up a copy of the final printed version of *Satan's Dare*.

"Tonight, you'll hear the results of this year-long effort to answer *Satan's dare*. This will not be the debate format you expected. The debate has taken place over the last year between Dr. Wright and six of our top Bible students, Dr. Guest, myself, and others you will hear more about in a few minutes. I've asked Johnny to start off tonight with his side of the story. When he is finished, Tony Guest will tell his story. Then the three of us will have a discussion panel to summarize our conclusions. Dr. Johnny Wright, please come and tell your story."

Johnny walked through the curtain on the left side of the stage. Dr. Clark shook Johnny's hand and gave him a bear hug before walking down the steps and taking his seat on the front row. Johnny looked very different than the year before. He was fit, trim, and standing erect. His hair was short and combed and he was wearing new kakis without the baggy pleats. His old Hush Puppy shoes were gone; replaced by dress casual shoes with heels. He looked taller. And he wore a new navy blazer. He stepped to the podium with a big smile. The audience was on their feet cheering and applauding. The ovation continued as students began to chant, "Johnny, Johnny, Johnny."

Johnny tapped the microphone several times, pointed at Dr. Clark, and smiled. "I've learned a lot from Dr. Clark." That restarted the applause. "But I'm innocent of his bait and switch!" Everyone enjoyed a laugh as Johnny tapped again on the microphone. The audience obeyed and quickly sat, anxious to hear more about the mysterious conspiracy.

"It's been a long year. It's been a long five years. Most of you know Patti's and my story. It's probably your story in different ways. The Bible warns us not to be surprised when trials and difficulties overwhelm us, but nevertheless, I was surprised and overwhelmed when it happened to me. It felt like God forsook me and it made me question if the God I thought I knew even existed.

"Before I overload you with research and conclusions, I'd like to frame our discussion with a few thoughts and questions. Have you ever taken a trip without making plans or reservations? Have you ever just left home for another city or country without knowing where you were going, how you were going to get there, and where you were going to stay when you got there? Maybe when we were young and stupid, but now I can't imagine going to an unknown place, far away in Europe or Asia without making plane and hotel reservations and, at least, having some plans about what I was going to do when I got there. Sounds silly, doesn't it?

"Almost every human being on earth knows, one day, their physical life will end. We are going to leave this place whether we like it or not and probably sooner than most of us think. It has always amazed me how many people avoid even thinking about their next destination. What's it like? What do I wear? How do I get a ticket? Obvious questions, but most people seem to live in denial.

"I think the real answer is most people are too afraid to even think about it. And, if you don't know how to get information or make your reservations, thinking about your trip makes the fear even worse. So, we live our lives avoiding the most important issues in life. Why are we here? What is my purpose in this life? Is there life after death? What do I need to do to have eternal life?

"Have you ever stood in a long line for hours only to be told you don't have the right paperwork to sign up for a class, register your new car or sign up for Medicare? Can you imagine arriving at the gates of heaven and being told, 'We'd love to have you, buddy, but you didn't attend Wednesday night dinners at the church, so you'll have to spend eternity in hell with your father-in-law.'" Johnny flashed a sly smile as the audience laughed and applauded.

"Now I'm being silly, but my point is this: we need to face our fears and ask questions about the reasons for this life and the path to eternity. This life is only a short journey through a foreign land. This is not our home or our destination. These bodies are temporary. They all get old and die. Tonight, we are going to ask the questions you may have been too afraid to ask and demonstrate there are answers you can be sure of.

"People here in America and around the world today are more confused than any previous generation. Most don't even realize how confused they are but I've been around enough to know they are—especially those I call 'shallow' believers. They want to believe in God but they are not sure what they really believe.

"There are good reasons most people don't know what they believe. We are all raised and live with wild contradictions. Psychologists call this cognitive dissonance; the reality we face every day is at odds with what we believe. Think about how most Christian parents raise their children in America today. We read them Bible stories and take them to church as young children. They learn God created the world and Jesus saves them. Then we send them to public schools when they are five or six where they are taught six hours a day for twelve years there is no God, no biblical truth, and they are the product of random evolution.

"I've heard many Christian parents insist the elementary school their child attends down the street does not teach there is no God. That may be technically true because God is never mentioned. History is taught without God. Science is taught without God. All 'truth' is taught without God. How could there be a real God if He is not relevant to anything taught in school?

"Let's not fool ourselves. Kids are smart. For most children raised in Christian homes, God is just another fairy tale they pretend is true until they are grown. And then we pay tens of thousands of dollars to send them to a university where most of the professors are aggressively anti-religious.

"Dr. Guest, who has done more research to prove and disprove the Bible than anyone on earth, will address the accuracy of the Bible and how it aligns with science. I will share some of our work distilling what the Bible actually says and means.

"If you have fixed ideas about the Bible, please don't be offended by this discussion. We have spent a lot of time identifying and studying alternative interpretations of the Scriptures within the framework of textual inerrancy. More simply stated, we believe every word of the Bible is true but we also believe there are possible alternatives to traditional interpretations that eliminate many of the apparent contradictions between science and the Bible. The key word here is 'possible.' We are not creating a new theology or religion. In fact, if you are a Christian, we are confident our work will confirm and buttress your faith.

"I said 'we' are confident and I want to be sure you know who 'we' are. Much of the research for *Satan's Dare* was done by six incredible students in my advanced Bible class. They're sitting on the front row tonight and I'd like them to stand when I introduce them. Lydia Johnson—Henry Harrison—Julie Black—Matt Hobson—Rachel Levin—and Ed Hart. These students represent different religious backgrounds and denominations but they all came together to discover the truth about God and the Bible. Most of the work behind *Satan's Dare* is their work. Please give them a round of applause."

The audience stood and applauded for more than a minute. Johnny held up his hands. "Thank you. Please be seated.

"Any discussion about religion or theology must begin with the knowledge there is a creator God. You don't need a Bible or science book to know there is a God. Common sense tells us everything we see around us—all nature and life forms—could not have happened without design or plan."

Johnny took a pencil out of his pocket and held it up. "What if I told you I found this pencil when I was digging in my backyard and theorized it was formed accidently by random acts of nature. The wood was carved by rocks rubbing sticks together over many years. Termites hollowed out the middle and molten lead worked its way through the wood. The wood was stained yellow by sulfur in the ground. The eraser was formed when animals ate the bark of a rubber tree and eventually attached it to the wood by molten metal spun around as it rotated between rocks.

"Okay, all of you are smiling and laughing because this is obviously a ridiculous theory. But this is a simple pencil! How many people today believe complex atomic structures with perpetually moving parts and incredible amounts of stored energy just happened by accident. It really is inexplicable. We teach our kids trillions of well-organized, complex atoms, and molecules just happened out of a big explosion in empty space billions of years ago. And we teach them life originated accidentally and all complex forms of life just randomly evolved from single cells over billions of years.

"Folks, how can anyone laugh at my theory about this pencil and then accept a completely implausible explanation of creation? The first law of thermodynamics states energy can neither be created nor destroyed. Yet the whole 'Big Bang' creation theory taught in our schools is based on the sudden creation of energy which was then transformed into complex, well-organized matter.

"It's easy to see how God could get angry when His people believe something so foolish. Like Paul says in Romans 1:18–21." The verse came up on the large screens on either side of the stage as Johnny recited.

> "'*The wrath of God is being revealed from heaven against all the godlessness and wickedness of people, who suppress the truth by their wickedness, since what may be known about God is plain to them, because God has made it plain to them. For since the creation of the world God's invisible qualities—his eternal power and divine nature—have been clearly seen, being understood from what has been made, so that people are without excuse. For although they knew God, they neither glorified him as God nor gave thanks to him, but their thinking became futile and their foolish hearts were darkened.*'"

Johnny held up a copy of *Satan's Dare*. "In the appendix of *Satan's Dare*, which will be on sale in the lobby after our event, there is a section with multiple references proving accidental origins and random evolution are statistically and physiologically impossible. The existence of God is undeniable. We can debate God's characteristics, motives, and plans but it is illogical to deny the existence of a creator God. I won't spend any more time on that fact tonight, but I wanted you to know any rational discussion about truth must begin with the assumption there is a creator God.

"Let's take a few logical steps from that assumption. God must have had a reason to create this world and the life in it. It would be logical for God to want His creatures to know why they were created and what He expected of them. So, it is reasonable to assume God would have devised a way to communicate with His creation.

"Creation tells us a lot about God—His power, His creativity, His attention to detail, His love of beauty, His love of variety, and His sense of humor. The Bible also tells us a lot about God and we have included an abundance of evidence in *Satan's Dare* supporting our conclusion the Bible was written over thousands of years by dozens of authors who were inspired and directed by God.

"In a few minutes, Dr. Guest will present how science and history confirm the Bible is not only historically accurate, but supernaturally inspired. So, my second assumption—our next logical building block—is God uses the Bible to communicate with His creation.

"The Bible is a historical account of creation, the travails of God's people, and God's life on earth in the form of Jesus Christ. The Bible describes coexisting spiritual and physical worlds. What happens in one world impacts what happens in the other. *Satan's Dare* details the underlying story of the Bible but I'll give you a quick summary.

"God created the physical world to separate good from evil and to provide a bridge to a new heaven that will unite the physical and spiritual worlds. God's ultimate purpose is to unite the spiritual and physical worlds into a perfect new heaven on a new earth where His people will live forever separated from all evil.

"The physical world was needed to separate good from evil because separation from God is not possible in a spiritual heaven. God's light fills heaven and there can be no darkness. So, when Satan and one-third of all the angels in heaven rebelled against God, they were thrown from heaven to earth—separated from God—where they continue to wage war against God and His family.

"God's family—His body—must pass through the physical world to obtain the physical characteristic needed to live in the new heaven: the spiritual and physical blood of God provided by the sacrifice of Jesus. All God's spiritual family must have a physical body and the blood of Jesus to live in the new heaven.

"When the physical bodies of God's family members die, they are resurrected with new physical and spiritual bodies like Jesus. They join all God's living creatures in an area of heaven where they wait for the rest of God's family to pass through the physical world. When all spiritual creatures have passed through the physical world, the current physical and spiritual worlds will pass away. Only those who have the blood of Jesus can enter the new heaven. Satan and his family will be eternally separated from the family of God.

"The Bible is clear: God's family was chosen before the physical world was created. Our research strongly suggests the members of God's family self-selected by choosing to be loyal to God when Satan and his angels rebelled. The Bible is also clear all God's family will be saved for eternity by the blood of Jesus.

"Here's the controversial part: we believe the act of praying to receive Jesus, obeying God, and the evidence of the fruits of the Spirit in our lives are all proofs we are part of God's family. These are not ways to earn eternal life. This is how we demonstrate we belong to God and how we confirm for ourselves we are His. If we believe in Jesus and follow Him, we know we have eternal life.

"We also believe there are many in God's family who will never hear about or know Jesus during their physical lives. But they will all be saved for eternity by the blood of Jesus. None will be lost. Jesus died for all of His body, He dies with all His body, and He raises all of His physical body from the dead and gives them new spiritual and physical bodies.

"With all this said, I will always make this plea to everyone I meet in this world: please ask God to forgive your sins and pray to receive Jesus. This is how we choose to fight on God's side against Satan. If you know about Jesus and don't receive Him, you are empowering Satan and evil in this world. And this brings me to my last point.

"The battle between God and Satan—good and evil—will continue in the spiritual and physical worlds until this world ends. God's people—His body—may determine who wins that battle. We know God and His family will ultimately win, but we also know the prayers, praise, obedience, and gratitude of God's people in this world is how we defeat Satan. Much of the pain and suffering we endure on this earth is the result of the ignorance and complacency of God's people. We are God's army on earth and we must put on the full armor of God and fight against evil.

"I'm sure I've confused you all but I'll stop here and ask Dr. Guest to come and share his story. When he's finished, Dr. Clark will lead a discussion with the three of us. If you'd like to text Dr. Clark your questions, his number is on the screens. Now, please welcome Dr. Anthony Guest to the stage."

Tony walked through the curtain and held it open for Johnny to retreat backstage. Tony stood behind the podium with a smile. He took a crinkled note out of his pocket and attempted to flatten it.

"I've been carrying this note with me every day since my little Christine gave it to me. I found it in my briefcase on a trip about a week before she died. She hid it in my case after I told her I always worried about her when I was traveling. The note—printed carefully with her mother's help I'm sure—says,

Don't worry about me, Dad. I'm in God's hands and so are you. Love you always, Christine.

"I carried it with me for a long time to remind me how God betrayed her. She trusted Him and He let her down. This note helped sustain my anger. Now I carry it to remind me God never left her for one minute of her life. God held her before she was born and He is holding her now. And He's holding me, too. Christine's note is true.

"Sometimes we mistake what happens to us in this world as indicators of whether God is with us. I sure made that mistake. I felt God's presence when He blessed me—when He blessed my ministry and when He blessed me with Pamela and Christine. But when all those blessings were taken away, I believed God forsook me. It seemed as though He gave Satan the power to destroy me and everything I loved.

"I knew the story of Job but I didn't know it personally. And I never liked the story even before it happened to me. Everything about the story of Job makes me angry. The story starts out just fine. Job is a righteous man who obeys God, so God blessed him with wealth, status, and lots of children. That's the way it should be, right? Good people get good things from God.

"But why does Satan have an audience with God? Satan admits to roaming all around the world—and we can assume he's causing misery and suffering. Why does God call Satan's attention to Job? Why does God allow Satan to destroy Job's family, wealth, and health? And why does God take the blame for what Satan did to Job?

"Job is no longer just a Bible story; it is exactly what happened to me. Satan challenged God to take away the blessings in my life, claiming I would deny Him and follow Satan if He did. And unlike Job, I did follow Satan. My anger gave Satan a foothold in my life and he used it to control me. I became an instrument of Satan, but God never let me go.

"I was never an atheist because I know too much and I'm too logical to deny the evidence of a creator God. But knowing there was a God made my anger even worse. I hated God with all my heart. I gave my whole life to serving God before my family was taken. But He played me. He set me up. Then He destroyed me in front of the whole world. So, I wanted to do everything I could to destroy Him and His work in this world. And, as you all know, I was largely successful in the lives of far too many people.

"You might think God would just laugh and crush me like a gnat under His thumb. I was His enemy. I was a prodigal son with no plans to return. I was a lost sheep who didn't want to be found. Why would God waste a single minute on someone who left Him and followed Satan at the first sign of trouble.

"I went from being like Job to being like Saul who persecuted Christians. Saul, who God renamed Paul, was traveling around—just like I was—trying to destroy the work of Jesus. But God used the same words to save me He used with Paul. A woman named Elizabeth confronted me with these words, 'Tony, Tony, why do you persecute Him. It is hard for you kick against the goads.'

"Elizabeth is now my wife and we have a beautiful daughter named Liz. You'll meet them tonight. They have torn the scales off my eyes and carved the stone out of my heart. They have shown me just how much God loves me. I could fight off the amorphous love of a spiritual God but when He channeled His love through the living body of Jesus, I melted like a candle in a kiln.

"What have I learned through this whole experience? It's actually simple. This physical world is the battleground between good and evil. The battle is both spiritual and physical. Spiritual forces are empowered or weakened by what happens in this world. During our physical lives, we live with the result of having the knowledge of good and evil. God is sovereign and omnipotent in heaven and He will be in the new heaven, so the souls within His family are safe for eternity.

"But, while God remains sovereign over all things in heaven and on earth, He constrains Himself by His own character in the physical world. Satan knows God's character and he uses it to bring suffering and pain into this world. *Satan's dare* is real. Satan means 'adversary' in Hebrew and he, along with all his demon angels, are constantly roaming the earth like vicious lions attacking God's people. But believers need not live in fear, because Jesus has defeated Satan, and no matter what happens to us in this world, God is always with us and our eternity is secure.

"Satan's demons possess humans, animals, and insects, and they stir up the forces of nature to inflict pain and death. They become more powerful when God's people follow Satan by doing evil but they are weakened when believers praise God, love others, and obey God's commands. All of us will physically suffer and die in this Great Tribulation on earth, but every member of God's family—every part of His body—will be saved because God gives us His one-of-a-kind, physical and spiritual blood. This is the blood of eternal life, the blood of Jesus, and the only passport into the new heaven.

"Many of you are here tonight hoping to receive some reassurance the Bible is true. After all, if it's not, none of what we believe as Jews or Christians is real. I have spent years proving the accuracy of the Bible and years trying to prove it is a fantasy. But here's the truth: there is no other source of truth in this world. Science is helpful, but it's flawed and evolving. And I can assure you, the more you study science, the more confidence you will have in the accuracy of the Bible. You'll find much of my research with Dr. Clark, Dr. Wright, and his students in this book we call *Satan's Dare*, but here's the short story.

"This physical world is filled with vast quantities of energy. The laws of physics—that is, the laws of the physical world—make it impossible for the energy in the physical world to have been created out of nothing. No 'Big Bang' could have created energy. Quite the opposite. A lot of energy would have been required to create a 'Big Bang.'

"Here's what we think happened. The Bible tells us God is light. Light is energy. When God said, 'Let there be light' in the physical world, He transferred energy from the spiritual world into the physical world. When light—that is energy—burst into the physical world, spiritual matter was also transferred into the physical world. Energy and matter traveled at the speed of light across the infinite physical universe forming suns and planets. Everything in this physical universe was created from and is still connected to coexisting spiritual substances.

"We also believe the physical world was programmed like a seed or embryo to develop and grow in a specific way. This is why scientists conclude natural evolution created more complex life forms, even though they cannot find any evidence of 'bridges' linking primitive and modern species. They can't find links between primitive and modern because they don't exist. Life didn't randomly evolve, it developed according to a preplanned program.

"Once we realize everything we see in this world was created out of things we can't see in the spiritual world—just as the Bible tells us—we can look at the creation story in Genesis in a totally different way. The order of creation in Genesis is the same order of creation theorized by many scientists. It could have easily happened in an instant because the physical world is a projection from things that already existed in the spiritual world. But an instant in the spiritual world might have been millions of years in the physical world.

"I believe, if we use time as we measure it in the physical world, God created the physical world billions of years ago as part of His plan to separate good from evil and as a bridge to take His family to a new heaven. Many thousands of years ago, spiritual creatures began to travel through the physical world and back to heaven. This included the first humans who were the physical image of angels—which translated from Hebrew means sons of God.

"Lucifer, one of the most glorious and powerful angels, apparently didn't like God's plan. He led a rebellion with one-third of the angels, but angels loyal to God defeated them and threw them out of heaven and down to earth. Heaven was purified from evil, but the earth became the dominion of Satan.

The path to the new heaven was then controlled by the forces of evil. All creation became dark and evil. The physical world was separated from God. Much of life on earth was wiped out and the surviving humans and animals were possessed and controlled by Satan.

"Thousands—perhaps millions of years later—God put a beautiful garden into this dark physical world. The Bible calls this garden the Garden of Eden. This happened long after the six days of creation and after Satan was thrown down to earth. God filled this garden with lush vegetation and modern species of animals. And from the water and dirt in this garden, God created the first modern human; a man named Adam which means 'the man.' From Adam's DNA, God created the first modern woman, Eve. The garden and the life in it probably developed over a long period of time but as we discussed, it could have been transferred in an instant from the spiritual world. There was no evil in the garden but there was a tree with fruit that could give Adam and Eve the knowledge of good and evil. Some propose this represented the first offer to man to replace their judgment for what's right and wrong for God's. The origin of what we call secular humanism today—man is God.

"Why did God give Adam and Eve the opportunity to have the knowledge of evil. Because 'freedom' is a core principle of God's character, and 'justice' requires that Satan have an equal opportunity to make his case to everyone who passes through this earth—even to Jesus, God in flesh—for forty days in the desert. And like all of us except for Jesus, Adam and Eve chose to have the knowledge of good and evil.

"God was not surprised by Adam and Eve's decision. The war between good and evil had to play out on earth. It is the only way to answer *Satan's dare*, to ultimately defeat Satan, and to permanently separate good from evil. God demonstrated in the Garden of Eden how His people could be freed from evil. He killed an animal—shed the blood of an innocent sacrifice— to make coverings for Adam and Eve. This foreshadowed how God would pay the price for sin for all mankind.

"The death of a living creature served as a substitute payment for Satan's requirement of death for those who are separated from God. The shedding of innocent blood covers the sin and heals the separation of those who accept the sacrifice as their substitute. Adam's son Abel followed the ritual of animal sacrifice, but his other son Cain did not. Evil took control of Cain who killed Abel.

"We see the ritual of substitutionary sacrifice continue with Job even before God established His laws and regulations through Moses. All of this set the stage for God to become human, physically die to permanently pay the price of sin, and share His blood with all who chose to be part of His body.

"For those of you who doubt the story of Adam and Eve is real, just keep following scientific research. One recent headline in the *Daily Mail News* in the United Kingdom reads, 'All humans are descended from just TWO people and a catastrophic event almost wiped out ALL species 100,000 years ago, scientists claim.' Mark Stoeckle at Rockefeller University and David Thaler at the University of Basel reached this striking conclusion. Here's the first paragraph from the article.

> *'Scientists surveyed the genetic "bar codes" of five million animals—including humans—from 100,000 different species and deduced that we sprang from a single pair of adults after a catastrophic event almost wiped out the human race. These bar codes, or snippets of DNA that reside outside the nuclei of living cells, suggest that it's not just people who came from a single pair of beings, but nine out of every 10 animal species, too.'*
> *(https://www.dailymail.co.uk/news/article-6424407/ Every-person-spawned-single-pair-adults-living-200-000-years-ago-scientists-claim.html)*

"This is a perfect fit with our analysis of the Bible. Long after the six days of creation, Satan and his angels were thrown out of heaven to earth creating a catastrophic event that destroyed most of life on earth. Adam and Eve, along with new species of modern animals, originated in the Garden of Eden. Most of life on earth today descended from the Garden of Eden, but many of us still have a small percent of DNA from primitive humans that descended from Cain intermarrying with women from tribes outside the garden.

"Another catastrophic event occurred thousands of years after Adam and Eve. This was the Great Flood that wiped out much of life on earth except for four pairs of humans, one pair of every animal on the ark, and those fish, reptiles, and insects that could survive in the water or on floating debris. Noah's sons and their wives apparently carried some of the DNA from Cain's descendants. That's how primitive DNA survived until today.

"The scientists still don't have it exactly right because most refuse to use the Bible as a resource. If they did, they would quickly find their data supports the theory a flood reshaped the entire globe less than 10,000 years ago and all humans today are descendants of Noah's family. There is much more about this, along with more scientific verification in *Satan's Dare*, but let me conclude with a few particularly relevant and worrisome thoughts about our world today.

"One of the most important findings of our research is we are all impacted by the collective good and evil in the world today. Job wasn't punished for his own sins and I wasn't either. Jesus has taken all my sins from me but He has taken my sins and all the sins of the world—all the evil—and put it on Himself, His body. God's people are the body of Jesus. We suffer and die as part of Jesus's body because of the evil in this world. So, whatever happens to the church as a whole is critically important to what happens to us as individuals in the physical world.

"But remember, the body of Jesus has been resurrected. We are sinless and destined for eternal life. Our spirits are alive in our physical bodies and our spirits are also alive in heaven right now. We have been raised to do good—to overcome evil. When we pray, praise God, love others, forgive, and have mercy on others, we defeat Satan and protect the body of Jesus from evil. But complacent and disobedient believers empower

Satan to attack and defeat the body of Jesus. We must invite and encourage all people to come to Jesus and follow Him. Those who belong to Jesus and hear His voice will respond.

"And we cannot forget we are always engaged in a war between good and evil. My greatest concern is for those who call themselves Christians today but are not even trying to follow Jesus by obeying His commands. They are on a dangerous path. I saw this firsthand as I traveled the world speaking against God and refuting the accuracy of the Bible. I met many people who called themselves Christians who denied the Bible was true. They rejected biblical morality. I have spoken to large churches—part of mainstream Christian denominations—whose leaders were anxious for me to disprove the inerrancy of the Scriptures because it freed them to teach their own progressive philosophies.

"The second conflict for what I call progressive Christians is unresolved answers to the problem of suffering and evil in the world. This is the whole reason for our research for *Satan's Dare*. Johnny and I were completely blindsided by evil and we began to question everything about our faith. This happens to every believer in different ways and if we sweep our unresolved questions and concerns under the rug—if we refuse to seek answers—Satan can use our ignorance to weaken or destroy our faith.

"The third conflict for progressive Christians is derived from the first two. This is when believers shun biblical morality and adapt their beliefs to a secular culture. Today, instead of shaping the morality of our culture, Christians are accepting and even teaching anti-biblical morality. This is particularly true as it relates to sexual morality.

"Progressive Christianity has spilled over into our politics and now anti-biblical laws and regulations are codifying a secular and atheistic culture. There is no fixed truth and everything is relative. Timeless principles, values, and natural laws are mocked by political leaders, the media, and even many in the church. This has unleashed the forces of evil in our country and our world. And, I'm afraid, this may be lowering God's hand and removing His protection from America.

"I will assure you all tonight, all the pain and suffering I've been through has given me more confidence in the Bible and a more genuine relationship with God. Even in my darkest hour, I could not deny His existence and, thankfully, He brought people into my life who forced me to get answers to my questions rather than continue to run from them. But despite learning a lot, I can only answer as Job did after God challenged him with His own questions. Job said 'it is all too wonderful for me know.' Or, perhaps, I will answer very simply like Paul, 'all I know is Jesus Christ and him crucified.'

"Through that intimate knowledge, I know His power can work through me to destroy the works of the enemy who has no other motive than to pour his evil on the world.

"I strenuously contend with all the energy Christ so power-fully works in me.

"The Bible is God's inspired and inerrant Word and while we may never understand it completely, the more you study the Scriptures and pray, the more convinced you will become it is completely accurate and the more the energy of Christ will flow through you. The truth is not afraid of questions, so ask questions—even seemingly stupid questions—keep digging and God will give you as much as you can understand. After all, what is life if not the pursuit of truth and what is truth if not the grasp of eternity?

"Now, I see Dr. Clark busily reading your questions on his tablet and I'm sure you're all ready for me to stop talking and for us to start answering those questions. But before we do, I'd like you to meet some of God's miracles, the answers to many prayers, and our confirmation that God will make all things work for good for those who love Him. Please welcome my wife, Elizabeth, and daughter, Liz. And welcome Johnny Wright back to the stage along with his wife, Patti, and their son, Joshua. Dr. Clark will also join us to lead our discussion."

Everyone in the auditorium was on their feet applauding and cheering as the two families stood on the stage. Even the reporters were cheering. People were hugging their friends, family members, and even strangers. There were many tears on and off the stage as Tony and Johnny hugged their children and wives.

But the most moving moment of all was when Rachel Levin got out of her seat, walked up the steps to the stage, and grabbed Tony around the neck. "Thank you, Dr. Guest." Unbeknownst to anyone but Rachel, Tony visited and spent a whole day with her brother at his rehab center.

"How is your brother?" Tony was beaming because Rachel's brother had already called him with his good news.

"Well, after your visit, he read your first book, left the rehab center, and got a job doing what he loves—developing computer apps for children's games. Ironically, he claims he would have never believed you if you hadn't first tried to refute Christianity. So, somehow, *God Fantasies* actually opened his heart. He began a discipleship program with my mom, started preaching to my dad, and you really won't believe this—he met a wonderful Christian girl. And—even more unbelievable—she works at a Christian bookstore. He met her trying to buy a birthday present for my mom. He knows he can't have the girl unless he has Jesus, so he is really serious about his faith. Thank you, Dr. Guest."

"When are you going to start calling me Tony?" They laughed together before Rachel returned to her seat. Tony had a wonderful thought as she walked away: Maybe, just maybe, God is going to use my failures to save many people.

Tony's warm thoughts suddenly vanished when deafening gun shots exploded from somewhere in the audience. Johnny spotted the shooter moving down an aisle toward the stage as he fired. To his horror, Johnny realized the shooter was firing at Patti who was holding their son, Joshua. Johnny lunged at Patti—pushing her and Joshua to the floor. He dived over them to shield them. One of the bullets hit Johnny in the shoulder. The shooter moved closer, but before he could get off another shot, several men from the audience, led by an off-duty sheriff's deputy, wrestled him to the floor.

The room was in chaos, punctuated by screams of profanity from the shooter. Almost everyone in the auditorium was on the floor, including everyone on stage. Johnny kneeled beside Patti as blood spread across his shirt.

"Patti, my God, are you okay? Was Joshua hit?"

"Johnny, I think we're fine," Patti answered. Joshua quickly got over the shock of the noise and the fall and started to cry, but he didn't seem to be hurt. "Johnny, oh no, you're bleeding!" Patti put her hand over the bloody hole in his shirt.

"I know. I'm sure it will hurt in a minute, but I can't feel anything now." He looked across the stage to see if anyone else was hurt. Everyone was getting back on their feet and seemed to be unharmed. Johnny felt dizzy and tired, then sleepy. He rolled over and passed out next to Patti.

Several doctors in the audience ran to the stage to assist Johnny. Medical bandages and supplies appeared from backstage. An EMS unit—always on site for large events at the university—was quickly called in from the parking lot. Johnny's wound was assessed by the medics as a clean "through and through." They quickly slowed the bleeding, loaded Johnny on a stretcher, and within minutes he was on the way to the hospital.

* * *

The next day Johnny was out of a brief precautionary stay in intensive care and sitting up in his bed in a private hospital room full of visitors—Patti, Dr. Clark, Tony, and Elizabeth. Sunlight filled the room and warmed everyone's spirits as Patti pulled opened the curtains covering a large window next to Johnny's bed.

"You're my hero," Patti teased.

"I'm not going to let Satan ever touch you again." Johnny was not teasing and he was almost too choked up to speak. "I only wish I had that kind of power."

"Together, I think we do." Dr. Clark was somber, too. "I believe the collective prayers of all of us—as we huddled on the floor—empowered God to stop Satan from handing us another tragedy. But it was a painful reminder that Satan will always be looking for an opportunity to hurt us and the people we love. I am hopeful we never see the day when God stops restraining Satan."

"Do we know anything about the shooter and why he was aiming at Patti?" Johnny looked at Dr. Clark.

"Yes, we do. He was a former student who was expelled last year for using drugs in his dorm room. He blamed Patti because of her student advisory role but it was my decision to send him home. And it was my mistake for ever admitting him in the first place. He had a record of trouble in high school, but his father is a prominent pastor and I thought I was doing him a favor. As it turned out, I almost got you killed.

"I also heard from the deputy who arrested him and found out he'd spent quite a bit of time at a local gun range honing his skill with a pistol. The deputy was amazed he missed Patti and Joshua. Even from the back of the venue, to miss that many times is implausible. But he got within thirty feet and still didn't hit them."

After some back and forth about the hand of Providence and how close Johnny came to losing his family, Johnny felt compelled to lighten the mood.

"Well, did we sell any books?"

"We didn't sell any, but they're all gone. I told everyone to take a book on their way out the door. It didn't seem right to ask them to pay for a book after we practically scared them to death," Dr. Clark replied.

Tony walked around the bed and put his hand on Johnny's unhurt shoulder. "We've got a lot to be thankful for. Working with all of you this last year has been wonderful. And I think we did some good work for the kingdom. I'd like to pray before we get out of here and let Johnny take his afternoon nap.

"Father, thank You for using Johnny to save Patti and Joshua, and thank You for keeping Johnny from a more serious injury. Thank You for spurring those men last night to get out of their seats and risk their lives to stop that young man from killing anyone. We are grateful for Your people—the body of Jesus—who are at work all over the world holding up Your hands, restraining Satan and proving him wrong. We accept *Satan's dare*—we will always praise You regardless what Satan and this world throws at us. Amen."

EPILOGUE

The publication of *Satan's Dare* changed the lives of everyone involved and charted a new course for Palmetto Christian University. The book was immediately controversial in all quarters. Fundamental, Bible-believing Christians were upset with the "possibility" non-Christians could be saved. Non-Christians were upset with the conclusion the blood of Jesus is the only means to eternal life. Progressive politicians scoffed at the suggestion they were secular and atheists. Scientists were embarrassed by the undeniable statistical refutation of random evolution. And atheists around the world felt betrayed by their hero, Tony Guest.

But controversy sells books. *Satan's Dare* stayed on the best-seller list for more than a year. Dr. Clark, Johnny, Patti, Tony, and Elizabeth hired a speaker's agency to set their speaking fees and coordinate their engagements around the world. The theories and possibilities presented in their book turned out to be only the beginning of new and different ways to look at the Bible and science. Hundreds of articles and books were written by other authors who agreed and disagreed with parts of *Satan's Dare*, added their own ideas, discovered new possibilities, all of which challenged the world to open their minds and study the Scriptures. The bottom line: *Satan's Dare* unleashed a world-wide revival of the Christian church and renewed passion for evangelism among believers.

The publication of *Satan's Dare* also brought harsh attacks on its authors and the university by the media and Washington politicians. These attacks set in motion a series of targeted

369

harassments, including IRS suits against the university's tax-exempt status, the loss of accreditation and student scholarship money from the state, lawsuits for hate speech and discrimination, and difficulty finding banks and contractors that would provide services to the university. The book seemed to unleash unprecedented attacks not only on the university, but on the Bible and Christianity worldwide. Satan was obviously still roaming the earth seeking to destroy God's people.

Yet Palmetto Christian University continued to grow. Donations poured in from around the world, and the waiting list for new students grew longer.

Johnny was offered the senior pastor's job at Blue Ridge Baptist Church in Boone, but he turned it down without a second thought. The church eventually closed and gave their building to a Christian school.

Johnny and Patti had a second child, a daughter who, at Johnny's insistence, was named Patrice. Johnny was made dean of Biblical Apologetics, a new department of undergraduate and graduate studies at Palmetto that attracted students and visiting fellows from around the world. Patti was appointed dean of students. The university doubled in size again and their endowment grew exponentially, led by a $10 million donation from Tony Guest.

Tony became a visiting lecturer for two years and then took a full-time professorship at Palmetto Christian. He and Elizabeth bought a 1,000-acre ranch near the university and moved from Virginia after Elizabeth discovered all the equestrian activities in South Carolina and nearby Tryon, North Carolina.

Dr. Clark wrote another book titled *Calling Satan's Bluff*. It told his story, along with the stories of Johnny, Tony, and several other prominent Christian leaders who were severely tested in their lives. His book became a best seller and was made into a movie with Dr. Clark starring as—Dr. Clark. The movie was followed by an online podcast series with Dr. Clark hosting interviews with believers who had Job-like experiences.

Dr. Clark retired as president of Palmetto five years after *Satan's Dare* was published. The new board of the university, with Dr. Clark's recommendation, made Dr. Anthony Guest their new president. The decision was controversial among many Southern Baptists—the sponsor of the university—but the right kind of controversy makes people think and, in this case, attracted attention, money, and students. It advances the pursuit of truth. And the truth will always set you free. "Praise God!"